HOUR
OF THE
RED GOD

HOUR OF THE RED GOD

RICHARD CROMPTON

SARAH CRICHTON BOOKS

FARRAR, STRAUS AND GIROUX   NEW YORK

Sarah Crichton Books
Farrar, Straus and Giroux
18 West 18th Street, New York 10011

Library of Congress Cataloging-in-Publication Data
Crompton, Richard, 1973–
    Hour of the Red God / Richard Crompton. — 1st ed.
        p.   cm.
    ISBN 978-0-374-17199-5 (hardcover : alk. paper)
    1. Maasai (African people)—Fiction.   2. Murder—Investigation—Fiction.
    3. Nairobi (Kenya)—Fiction.   4. Mystery fiction.   I. Title.

PR6103.R647 H66 2013
823'.92—dc23
                                                                2012034612

Designed by Abby Kagan

www.fsgbooks.com
www.twitter.com/fsgbooks • www.facebook.com/fsgbooks

1   3   5   7   9   10   8   6   4   2

FOR KATYA

PREFACE

This novel is set in the run-up to and the immediate aftermath of the Kenyan election of 27 December 2007.

Amid claims of vote rigging from both sides, the incumbent president, Mwai Kibaki, was sworn in on 30 December, immediately sparking protests and violence across the whole country.

Some of the worst violence was seen amid the slums of the capital, where long-standing ethnic tensions rose to the surface.

This book is a work of fiction. The time line is accurate, and most of the locations are real. But it is not intended to be a factual portrayal of events. Rather, it is an attempt to capture the spirit, energy, and courage of this remarkable city, Nairobi, that I call my home.

It is thought that between 800 and 1,500 Kenyans lost their lives in the post-electoral violence. Countless others lost their homes and livelihoods and experienced terror and deprivation. This book is a tribute to the memory of those who perished and to the resourcefulness of those who survived.

THE ORIGIN OF DEATH

In the beginning there was no death. This is the story of how death came into the world.

There was once a man known as Leeyio, who was the first man that Naiteru-kop brought to earth. Naiteru-kop then called Leeyio and said to him, "When a man dies and you dispose of the corpse, you must remember to say, 'Man die and come back again, moon die and remain away.'"

Many months passed before anyone died. When, in the end, a neighbor's child did die, Leeyio was summoned to dispose of the body. When he took the corpse outside, he made a mistake and said, "Moon die and come back again, man die and remain away." So after that, no man survived death.

A few more months elapsed, and Leeyio's own child died. So the father took the corpse outside and said, "Moon die and remain away, man die and come back again." On hearing this, Naiteru-kop said to Leeyio, "You are too late now, for, through your own mistake, death was born the day when your neighbor's child died." So that is how death came about, and that is why up to this day, when a man dies, he does not return, but when the moon dies, it always comes back again.

—Traditional Maasai story

HOUR
OF THE
RED GOD

The sun is at the vertical, and shade is as scarce as charity on Biashara Street. Where it exists—in shop fronts and alleyways, like cave mouths and canyons—life clings: eyes blink, and patiently they watch.

They see a man and a boy walking along the sidewalk, the boy turning every third or fourth step into a skip to match his companion's rangy stride.

The man, in concession, has stooped slightly to maintain a conversational height. Their posture suggests that if either reached out a hand, the other would grasp it, but for their own reasons, neither will offer. They are father and son.

—But where would you ride it? the father asks wearily. It's evidently a long-running conversation.

—Anywhere! says the boy. I could go to the shops for you.

—Adam, this is Nairobi. You go out on your own on a bike, you're going to get killed. Have you seen the drivers here?

—Then around the compound. Grandma's house. It's safe there. Michael's got a bike. And Imani, too, and she's only seven.

The tall man pauses in his stride, and the boy runs into the back of his legs. Something has disturbed the man: immediate, palpable, yet indefinable. The sense of trouble about to strike.

Just for once, thinks Mollel, just for *once*, I'd like to turn off this instinct. Be able to enjoy going shopping, enjoy spending time with my son. Be a member of the public instead of a policeman.

But he can't. He is what he is.

—That's the one I want! says Adam, pointing at the shopwindow.

Mollel is vaguely aware of a display of bicycles inside, but he is watching a reflection suspended in the glass: a group of teenage girls, all gossip and gum, mobile phones wafting like fans, handbags slung over shoulders like bandoliers, and from the shadows, other eyes—hungry now— emerging. Watching without watching, getting closer without moving in, the men nonchalant yet purposeful, disparate yet unified, circling their prey. Hunting dogs.

—Go inside the shop, Mollel tells Adam. Stay there till I come back for you.

—Can I choose a bike, Dad? Really?

—Just stay there, says Mollel, and he pushes the boy through the store's open door. He turns. It's happened already. The group of men are melting away, the girls still oblivious to what has just taken place. He clocks one of the guys walking swiftly from the scene, stuffing a gold vinyl clutch bag—*so not his style*—under his shirt.

Mollel takes off, matching the hunting dog's pace but keeping his distance, eager not to spook him. No point in letting him bolt into a backstreet now. Pace up a beat, narrow the gap. Quit Biashara Street. Cross Muindi Mbingu. Weave through traffic—ignore the car horns. Busier here.

The hunting dog is in his late teens or early twenties, judges Mollel. Athletic. His shirt has the sleeves cut off at the shoulders, not to expose his well-developed arms, but to ease its removal. The buttons at the front will be fake, Mollel knows, replaced with a strip of Velcro or snaps to confound any attempt to grab the bag snatcher's collar, leaving the pursuer holding nothing more than a raggedy shirt, like a slipped snake-skin.

While Mollel weighs his strategy—a dive to the legs rather than a clutch at the torso—he realizes that the thief is heading for the City Market. Got to close the gap now. Lose him in there, he's gone for good.

Taking up an entire city block, with more ways in and out than a hyrax burrow, on a day like this the market's dark interior is thronged with shoppers escaping the sun. Mollel considers yelling *Stop, mwizi!* or *Police!*—but calculates that this would lose him precious time. The thief leaps up the steps and deftly vaults a pile of fish guts, pauses a moment to look back—showing, Mollel thinks, signs of tiring—and dives into the dark interior. Mollel's gaunt frame is just a few seconds behind, his heart pounding as he gulps lungfuls of air even as his stomach rebels at the powerful reek of fish. He hasn't done this for a while. And he is enjoying it.

It takes his eyes a moment to adjust. At first, all he can see are tall windows high overhead, shafts of light like columns. Noise fills in what eyes cannot see: the hubbub of negotiation and exchange, the squawking of chickens, the multitudinous laughter and chatter and singing and hustle and bustle of life.

And among that hustle and bustle—a bustle, a hustle that should not be there. He sees it now as well as hears it, just a few stalls ahead. Figures tumbling, voices raised in protest. His quarry.

Through a gap in the crowd he sees the thief. He's scattering people and produce behind him in an attempt to obstruct his pursuer. No point going down that aisle. Mollel looks left and right, plumps for right, rounds a stall, and starts to run down a parallel row. Although he's keeping up with his prey, he's not going to catch him this way. Ahead, he sees sacks of millet stacked loosely against one of the stalls. It's his chance. He bounds up, one, two, and is atop the stall, balancing on the boards that bound the millet.

A howl of protest rises from the woman behind the stall as she swipes at his legs with her scoop. —Get down from there!

But he is already gone, leaping to the next stall, hoping the rickety wood will take his weight—it does—and run, leap, again—it does.

A better view from here, and a clearer run despite the efforts of stall-holders to push him, grab him, drag him to earth. He rises above the hands, above the stalls, intent only on the pursuit.

The fresh, clean smell of peppers and onions cuts through the dusty dryness of millet. Easier to negotiate. Mollel bounds across the stacked vegetables, skipping, skimming, recalling chasing goats across mountain scree when he was a child. Momentum is everything. Each footstep expects you to fall. Cheat it. Be gone.

Outraged yells fill his ears, but he feels that the great hall has fallen silent. There is no one in it but him and the fleeing man. Distance between them measured in heartbeats: arm's reach; finger's grasp.

And then the thief is out the door.

Mollel suddenly finds himself standing on the final stall, surrounded by furious faces. They barrack him and block him; hands reach for his ankles. He sees the back of the thief's head about to melt into the crowd outside the market. He sweeps his arm down, feels hair and hardness—coconuts—beneath his feet. Another goat-herding trick: if the animal is out of reach, throw something at it.

The coconut is out of his hand before he even thinks about it. It describes a shallow parabola over the heads of the stallholders, through the square, bright doorway. He even hears the crack, and he relaxes. He has time now to produce his card and clear the way to the doorway, where a circle has formed.

The crowd is now eager, anticipatory. The rear doorway of the City Market is inhabited by butchers' stalls, and the metallic smell of blood is in the air.

The people part before him, and Mollel steps into the ring. The thief is on his knees, dazed, gold handbag dropped to the ground, one hand rubbing the back of his head. The smashed coconut has already been snatched by a pair of children in front of the circle who suck on the sweet flesh and grin at Mollel. Free food and a floor show. What more could you want?

—You're coming with me, says Mollel. The thief does not respond. But he staggers groggily to his feet.

—I said, says Mollel, you're coming with me. He steps forward and takes the thief by his upper arm. It is wider than Mollel can grasp and as hard as rock. He hopes the guy's going to remain concussed long enough to drag him downtown. If only he had cuffs—

—and then the arm wheels away from his, Mollel just having time to step back to take a little force out of the blow that lands on the side of his head. No concussion—the faintness feigned—the thief now alert and springing on his heels. A lunge—missed—at Mollel. The crowd cheers. He is strong but top-heavy, this fighter, and the policeman judges that a swift shoulder ram would push him once more to the ground. Mollel seizes his chance, head down, body thrown at his opponent's chest, but he misjudges the timing, and the thief parries him easily. Mollel feels a sharp, agonizing pain in his head—everywhere—stabbing and yanking, the pain of capture, and of submission.

His opponent laughs, and a roar of approval comes from the crowd. No partisans, these. Mollel feels his head jerked from side to side, up and down. There is nothing he can do.

—I have you now, Maasai. The thief laughs.

He has put his thumbs through Mollel's earlobes.

The bane of his life, those earlobes. Long and looped, the flesh stretched since childhood to fall below his jawline, the *i-maroro* are a mark of pride and warriorhood within Maasai circles, but an object of ridicule and prejudice elsewhere. He knows many Maasai who have had the loops removed, but somehow the stumps sing of regret to him, and their ears seem just as conspicuous as his own.

One advantage, though: no one is going to grab them by the ears. The bystanders are convulsed in near-hysterical laughter; he can expect no help from that quarter. They have never seen a policeman led by his ears, like a bull with a ring through his nose. Even the thief, his face now leering at arm's length, seems hardly able to believe his luck.

—All right, so this is what we're going to do, Maasai, he says. We're going to walk together, slowly, out onto K Street. I'm not going to rip your pretty ears off. And you're not going to come after me. If you've got it, nod your head. Oh, I'm sorry, you can't, can you? Would you like me to nod it for you? Yeah, that's right!

Quite a comedian, this one, thinks Mollel as his head is tugged up and down. The thief enjoys the audience. He even swaggers somewhat as he holds the policeman captive—glancing at the crowd, relishing his moment of fame. Let him, thinks Mollel. Means he won't be ready for what I'm about to do.

What he does—brutally, swiftly—evinces a sympathetic groan from all the men in the watching crowd. They have no illusions about what a size-ten police-issue steel-capped boot can achieve when brought into such intimate contact with its target.

Almost tenderly, the thief lets go of Mollel's ears. His eyes look into the policeman's with a look of heartbreak and agony. This time, Mollel knows he'll have no problems bringing him in.

2 —If this was *China*, the Chinese woman sobs, we not mess around. We get this sorted out!

—Well, it's not China, says the desk sergeant. This is Kenya. Here, we do things *properly*. He licks the tip of his ballpoint and starts writing in a large ledger. —Work permit number?

—This not about me; this about my landlord! He take my money and change the locks! Who am I supposed to sleep with tonight, huh?

In the general merriment caused by this statement, Mollel catches the desk sergeant's eye over the heads of the throng. He is glad it is Keritch—no awkward questions. He just gets a quizzical look as the desk flap is lifted to allow him through. As Mollel leads his prisoner down the corridor to CID, he hears Keritch sighing once more: —Work permit number? And has *anyone* got a pen that works?

Central Police Post. It's a long time since he's been here. Nothing's changed. The smell is of sweat and fresh paint—it's easier to paint the walls every couple of years than to clean them daily. The single-story building was once a homestead and now sits dwarfed by the massive modern buildings around it. It's a sleepy, rustic image totally at odds with the constant activity within, presenting an aspiration of a Nairobi benignly overseen by one colonial-era bobby on a bicycle, which was probably the case when it was built. And it couldn't be further from the truth today.

▲ ▲ ▲

—Well, well. Maasai. Brought a gift for us, I see?

Mollel directs the prisoner into the CID office. Decrepit office furniture and overflowing filing cabinets are squeezed into what was obviously once a bedroom. Mwangi sits at his same old desk, feet up, reading the *Daily Nation*. Grizzled, cynical, slightly grayer of mustache.

Mollel approaches and flicks up the front page.

—What are you doing? Mwangi asks.

—Checking the date. It's the only way I can tell whether you've *moved* for two years.

—I wouldn't be so sure, says a younger man. Shirtsleeves, eating a *sambusa*, policeman's mustache on the way. —He has it delivered to his desk these days.

—Mollel, meet Kiunga. My new partner, says Mwangi. And believe it or not, Kiunga, this Maasai used to be my partner, too.

—I've heard about you, says Kiunga neutrally.

—*Everyone's* heard about him, says Mwangi. Question is, what is he doing back at Central? Last I heard, he'd been busted down to traffic duty in Loresho.

Kiunga laughs. —Is there any traffic in Loresho?

—There's a job to be done, replies Mollel. Overcrowded *matatus*, out-of-date car registrations. The occasional donkey-rage incident.

—And now you've brought us Oloo, says Mwangi, looking at the prisoner. The boss *will* be pleased.

—You know this guy?

—Oh, we know Oloo. Nice handbag, by the way, he says to the thief.

—What the hell is *he* doing here? thunders a voice from the back of the office. Mwangi casts Mollel a scathing glance and slowly lowers his feet to the ground. Oloo, the prisoner, visibly relaxes.

Otieno, the head of Central CID, has entered.

—I thought I told you I didn't want to see *him* in here again! he barks.

He is an imposing man, tall and massive, his round, blunt head retreating into his thick neck. His inky-dark skin is pocked, and the color bleeds into the whites of his eyes, which are stained like walnuts. Otieno, a Luo in a profession dominated by Kikuyus, has developed a hide as thick as the ox he resembles, and a reputation for being just as stubborn.

—It wasn't us, boss. Mwangi coughs. —It was our Maasai friend here.

Otieno turns to Mollel, seeing him for the first time. The wide face breaks into a dazzling grin—the last response Mollel had expected.

—There is an old Luo saying, says Otieno, slapping Mollel heartily on the back, that an unwelcome visitor brings good cheer. They mean, of course, when he leaves. But this time, this time, my unwelcome friend, you might just be able to help me out. Get rid of this nobody and I'll tell you all about it.

—I've got to charge him first, says Mollel. Robbery and resisting arrest.

Mwangi and Kiunga exchange a glance.

Otieno's grin disappears. He takes the gold handbag from Mollel and rifles through it.

—Mobile phone, purse, tampons, cigarettes . . . He holds up an ID card. —Amazing how careless some people can be with their valuables. Thank goodness there are good, honest citizens like Mr. Oloo here, prepared to hand in lost property.

Now it is Oloo's turn to grin. —My pleasure, he says smugly. Now, if you don't mind, officers, I think I'll be on my way.

—But, boss! protests Mollel.

—But nothing! Right now I'm running the best figures in Central Division since the nineties. Robbery is down eight percent. You think I'm going to let a little *mavwi* like this mess up my statistics? Ask your buddies here.

Mwangi and Kiunga look at Mollel with resignation.

—Yeah, butts in Oloo. That's right. So, about this lost property, then. Where do I get my reward?

Otieno laughs a hearty, jovial laugh. Then, still smiling, he raises his fist like a shovel and slams it into the thief's face.

—*There's* your reward.

Oloo is on the floor, blood gushing from his broken nose. Otieno turns to Mwangi and Kiunga.

—That was just to prove to you Kikuyus that there's no tribal favoritism going on. Mwangi, get him out of here. Kiunga, get the pool car. We're taking the Maasai on a little drive.

The police Land Rover weaves through the Nairobi traffic. Kiunga manages the jam with a young man's confidence, squeezing the vehicle into gaps with inches to spare, overtaking other cars on both sides, mounting the sidewalk when necessary.

—You never learned to drive, then, Mollel? Kiunga calls back as he pushes the car into a narrowing canyon formed by two Citi buses.

—No, replies Mollel. Did you?

Otieno, in the front passenger seat, gives a booming laugh. —That's why you ended up in traffic division. It was *someone's* idea of a joke.

Yes, and Mollel knows whose. Still, if Otieno wants him along for the ride today, he must have something interesting in store.

They pull off the Uhuru Highway and onto Kenyatta Avenue, past the Serena Hotel, where Otieno barks some directions and Kiunga pulls an illegal U-turn. They push through the opposing traffic, Kiunga pointing a warning at an irate *matatu* driver, Otieno retaining his bulky composure. Then, up a curb and off the road, between two concrete posts that Mollel thinks they couldn't possibly fit through—but they do—and into Uhuru Park.

Uhuru Park: Nairobi's playground. Named after freedom, but also granting it, a little freedom from the sprawl and the spread and the spleen of the city. Being Saturday, it is busy. People lying on the grass dotted in groups—families picnicking, lovers discreetly loving—or singly, people with nowhere else to go or a few hours to kill, sleeping on the ground. A larger group is standing in a circle, holding hands. They all wear the same red T-shirts: a prayer meeting. Vendors of sodas, nuts, and ice cream push their wagons lazily down the paths, only to dive out of the way as the Land Rover bears down on them.

They drive past the area known as Little Mombasa. In his forty-two years, Mollel has been to some extraordinary places, but he has never been to the Kenyan coast. He surmises, though, that the real Mombasa has a bit more going for it than a shallow boating lake and a paddling

pool. The place is popular enough, but today it seems to be losing customers to a new attraction over toward the rear of the park where the
ground slopes steeply away from the city and eventually becomes Upper
Hill.

The car draws to a halt by the mass of people, and the instant Kiunga
cuts the engine, Mollel knows what they're going to find. The only time
a group of Kenyans en masse is quiet like this is when there's a body.

They descend from the car and push their way through the strangely
reverent mob toward the mess of chain-link fence and barbed wire that
marks the boundary of the park. It seems far removed from the peaceful
green interior. As they draw to the front of the crowd, Mollel sees a
drainage culvert, some four feet deep, and a couple of uniformed city
cops keeping a desultory eye on the crowd, who are all looking into the
ditch.

Beyond them, standing in the concrete culvert but barely clearing
the top, is Dr. Achieng.

—Ah, Otieno. And you've brought your pet Maasai with you, I see.
Good thinking. Been a long time, Mollel.

—You not retired yet? Mollel asks the old man.

—Can't afford to. I thought *you'd* disappeared.

Otieno butts in: —From your description of the body, I thought it
would be useful to *re*-appear him. What have we got, a termite?

Termite: Nairobi police vernacular for a body washed out of the storm
drains after a heavy bout of rain, the way white ants are flushed from a
flooded nest.

—Could be. Rain was probably heavy enough last night to bring her
some distance. That could account for a lot of the impact wounds. Unless she was dead before she entered the drain.

Achieng beckons to Mollel. —Come, take a look. Tell me if our hunch
was right.

Mollel takes the pathologist's small hand and steps down into the
ditch. The steep concrete banks slope to a flat bottom about a meter wide,
along which runs a farther rill just a few inches deep, to keep water

flowing in dry times. There is barely a trickle now, despite the rains of some few hours earlier: such is Nairobi weather. Mollel places his feet on either side of the body, which lies on its side, partially in the central rill, its spine curved in an impossible contortion: a non-recovery position.

She is wearing a flimsy dress, torn and blackened with mud, but expensive-looking nonetheless. It has ridden up above her waist. There is no underwear. Smears of blood and mud snake back across her thighs.

—You'll see that she has many wounds on her body, most of them consistent with a beating, says Achieng. But there appears to be considerable bleeding from between the legs. Have to turn her over in a moment to see more.

Mollel follows the line of the body's curvature, one arm unseen below the corpse, the other tossed upward and above the head.

—Let me move this, says Achieng, lifting the arm. Are you ready to see the face?

Mollel nods. Achieng uses the arm to pull and pivot the corpse onto its back.

Mollel finds himself looking down at a young, oval face; the ashen grayness would have been a brilliant bluey black in life. High cheekbones, high forehead. Noble. On either cheek, a small, low *O* had been engraved a long time ago.

It is a familiar face. He does not recognize the person, but he knows the people: his own.

—Yes, she's Maasai, he says.

—Thought so. I'm not familiar with all tribal scars, but those looked typically Maasai to me. Can you tell which clan?

—Not really. It's a commonplace enough marking. Could be from the west, Sikirari, Matapato. But I'm confused about the ears.

—The ears? I didn't see anything remarkable.

—Exactly. They should be looped, like mine. Probably pierced at the top, too. But look at her lobes. There's only a small hole, for fashion jewelry. She's got the cheek scars that are given at childhood, but not the ear loops, which Maasai girls are given at puberty. So it could be that she left her village before that time.

—Could be.

—No ID, I suppose?

—What you see, says Achieng, is what you get. Now, I want to turn her, see if my suspicions are correct.

He beckons to a policeman nearby, who joins them in the culvert. Achieng takes the girl's shoulders and the policeman both ankles. Together, they roll the body over.

A dismayed gasp goes up from the watching crowd.

—Oh God, says Mollel.

He's seen plenty over the years. More dead bodies than he cares to think about. Blood, guts. But this is something else.

Achieng comes around to join him at the feet of the body.

—Vicious, he says. Looks like someone's taken a knife to her genitals. Brutally, too.

There is some commotion among the onlookers. Someone has fainted.

—Get those people out of here! shouts Otieno. Even he, under his dark complexion, looks shocked. —What do you think this is, a circus?

The uniformed policemen step forward and begin to disperse the crowd.

—Do you know anything about female circumcision, Mollel? asks Achieng quietly.

—I know it's not like this, Mollel replies.

—Maybe not as brutal. But among Maasai, it means removal of the clitoris, doesn't it?

Mollel nods. —*E-muruata.* I've never seen it done, myself. Men are strictly forbidden from the ceremony. But yes, teenage girls have their clitoris removed, by a female elder. It's illegal now. But it still happens, of course.

—You say it's usually done at puberty? Like the ear loops?

—Yes.

—Maybe she never had it done as a girl and someone was trying to put that right, mutters Otieno.

—I'll have to look more closely during the postmortem examination, says the doctor. But it looks like that's what happened here. Certainly, no care was taken for the health of the patient. I'm pretty sure this is what killed her.

—Right, says Otieno. If you're done, Doctor, let's get this body taken to the city mortuary. File it under "Unknown Maasai Prostitute."

—What makes you think she was a prostitute? asks Mollel angrily.

—Be realistic, Mollel, replies Otieno. They always are.

3 —I'll get you a temporary transfer back here to Central, Otieno says as the body is put into the back of the unmarked mortuary ambulance. A week or so should do it. Let's say ten days. I want this wrapped up quickly, Maasai. You can ask around. Talk to the hookers who work this patch. But also, follow this lead about it being a Maasai circumcision ceremony gone wrong.

—Gone wrong! I don't think we can put this down to accidental death. It's deliberate murder.

—Maybe. In the meantime, you can have Kiunga here to drive you around. Unless you want to borrow a bike.

A *bike* . . . the word nags at Mollel's memory. Something important to do with a bike.

Adam!

His chest constricts. He'd slipped so easily back into the role of policeman that he'd forgotten about being a father. He grabs Kiunga's arm.

—I need you right now, he says. We have to go to Biashara Street.

—That's why I love you, Maasai, calls Otieno as Mollel pulls Kiunga toward the Land Rover. The case has just begun, and you've got a lead already. See you back at the station.

▲ ▲ ▲

As they pull onto Biashara Street, Mollel feels his pulse quickening and panic rising. It is past one o'clock: on a Saturday, that means most stores are shutting up for lunch—many for the weekend. With the street emptied and the storefronts couched behind their blank steel shutters, Mollel has difficulty even locating the shop. When he does, he sees that the shutter is left open a few inches, darkness within. He orders Kiunga to stop the car, and he leaps out, rushes to the shutter, and bangs on it furiously.

—Go away! We're closed! says a voice from within.

—My boy. I left my boy here. About an hour ago. I was only going to be a few minutes . . .

—There's no boy here.

—Are you sure he's not behind a display or something? Even asleep? I told him not to leave until I came back.

—Look. The shutter comes up a few more inches, and the Indian storekeeper sticks his head out. —There is no boy here. There *was* a small lad here who said he was waiting for his father, but I kicked him out. What do you think I am, a child-minding service?

—Which way did he go? But the shutter thunders down and Mollel hears the clanking of a lock within. He slams his fist against the steel.

—Dad!

It is Adam, and Mollel's breath catches with relief. Despite the heat, he shivers. He suddenly realizes that he is drenched in sweat.

—I waited and waited, but you didn't come back!

—Good job he knows his grandmother's phone number, says Faith.

Adam has his hand firmly in Faith's. In the other hand he holds a rapidly melting ice cream.

Faith gives Mollel a look he's become familiar with over the years: a mixture of pity and contempt. Contempt seems to be winning out this time.

—The man in the shop wouldn't let me use his phone, continues Adam. But a lady in the shop next door did. Grandma came to collect me.

—Thanks, Faith, says Mollel sheepishly. It was police business.

—It's always police business, says Faith.

—Grandma says I can go home with her.

—I think that's for the best, says Faith. To Adam she says, —Give your father a hug.

The two of them look at each other awkwardly. It's not a natural gesture for either of them. Then Mollel bends to receive the hug, which makes him glow despite the cold ice cream on his neck.

—Thanks for the bike, Dad, whispers Adam in his ear. I know I wasn't supposed to find out about it until Christmas. But Grandma let slip.

Mollel stands. Faith casts him a challenging glance; he returns it, but softens. She is right. Better for the boy to have something to look forward to rather than dwell on being abandoned by his only parent. Mollel would never be able to say truthfully that he *liked* his mother-in-law. But she loves Adam, and for that reason alone he is silent when she says,

—You have got to remember where your priorities lie, Mollel.

Kiunga is shaking hands with Adam now. The boy has taken an instant liking to Mollel's colleague and is chatting freely about school.

—You've always had a powerful sense of justice, Faith continues. That's why Chiku loved you. I admired you for it myself. But there's a difference, Mollel, between justice and what's *right*.

She nods at Kiunga, who is showing Adam his police ID. —Does he know about what you did to your colleagues?

—Everyone in the department knows, says Mollel.

—And he still wants to work with you?

—I don't think he has much choice, Mollel answers.

—Loyalty works both ways, Mollel. He seems like a good man. You may need him to be on your side.

—And I should be more loyal to Adam, too, isn't that what you're saying?

—He is your son, Mollel, replies Faith, her voice tinged with sadness. I don't see how your loyalty to him could ever be put in second place.

—Sweet kid, says Kiunga after they've parted. And he's a red.

—A what?

—Supports Manchester United. Didn't you know?

—I don't really follow football. Have you got kids?

Kiunga laughs. —No way! The last thing I need is a dependent!

Dependent. Seems a curiously formal word to describe his son. But then, they have a curiously formal relationship.

When he was a child, back in the Kajiado foothills, his mother used to call him *ol-muraa.* Her little warrior. At fourteen, he became a *moran.* But she still called him *ol-muraa.*

You're not to call me little warrior anymore, Mother. I'm a real warrior now. And you'll address me with respect.

How she had laughed! And then chased him out of the *boma* with a ladle. The injustice of it burned him, as did the eyes of his younger brother, Lendeva.

Lendeva had never known their father. Mollel, who had lived in fear of his beatings, felt that the younger boy was lucky.

He'd attempted, in his way, to become the father his brother never had, but Lendeva did not let him. Assertions of authority were met with amused contempt, and before long, Mollel gave up. And now—he paused to work it out—it was nearly twenty years since he had seen his brother. Just like his father, Mollel had no idea whether Lendeva was living or dead.

His father. Lendeva. His mother. His wife. All gone.

No wonder, thinks Mollel, that he resists calling his son a dependent. If life had taught him one thing, it was that you could not be dependent upon anyone.

They're walking down Koinange Street—K Street—Nairobi's notorious red-light zone. Not that there are any red lights here—apart from the ones studiously ignored by motorists. It's discreet at this time of day. Respectable, even. City folk walk the sidewalks unmolested, and the few girls who choose to ply their trade by day have retreated to the shadows rather than prowling the curb.

Mollel walks directly up to three of them who are sheltering from the sun under the canopy of a Chinese restaurant.

—Excuse me, he begins. The girls cast him and Kiunga a scornful, contemptuous look—Mollel compares the look, mischievously, to that which Faith gave him a few minutes before—and they melt away, all three in different directions, not bothering to even reply.

—You're not in any trouble! calls Mollel, but they are gone.

Kiunga is laughing. —We might as well be in uniform, he says. Look, I know how to deal with these girls. Watch, and learn.

They set off but have gone only a couple of meters before Kiunga grabs his colleague's arm.

—Steady up. They're always going to know we're police, there's no way around that. They smell it or something. But there's no need to frighten them. Don't go storming up. Loosen. Relax your shoulders, walk with your palms out, like this. Yeah, I know it feels strange. But you're giving off a message: you have nothing to hide. Come on.

Sure enough, as they approach the next group of girls—Mollel hanging back, self-consciously aping Kiunga's ambling posture—they do not scatter, but regard the approaching policemen with a wry, skeptical attitude.

—Hello, ladies. Kiunga smiles. —Pleasant afternoon.

—What do you want? one of them shoots to him, warily but without apparent hostility.

—Just to make conversation. Why, are you afraid we'll drive away trade?

—Get on with it.

Mollel admires the way Kiunga talks to the prostitutes: professional yet affable. He asks them whether they've heard about the girl found in the park; whether they know of anyone missing from her regular beat; whether the description of a young Maasai hooker is familiar to them. The answers, all negative, strike Mollel as truthful and considered. These girls don't want a killer on the loose any more than the police do.

They move on. There's a girl on her own, not with any group. She's young, but her disheveled appearance is in contrast to most of the others working this street. And despite the heat, she is standing in the full sun, wearing black leggings and a black cutoff top. She sways slightly as she turns and beats the same tired loop on the sidewalk.

Mollel is ready to approach, but once more, Kiunga steadies him with a touch to the arm.

—Don't bother. You won't get anything out of her.

—Why not?

—Look at the eyes.

As they walk past, Mollel looks at the girl's face. Her eyes are deep set and sunken; they roll and slide under their lids.

—Hey boys, she slurs. And in Kiswahili: —*Mnataka ngono?*

The straightforward proposition is completely different from the nod-and-wink approach of the other girls, and Mollel understands why this one will provide them with nothing. She's a drug addict. Well, so are most of the others. But she's also high right now, probably the only way she can cope with doing what she does.

The pair of them walk on, pounding K Street for another hour or so, speaking to all the prostitutes they meet. Some gaze at them with the same blank, apathetic junkies' eyes. Others are more willing to speak, especially to Kiunga. But the answers are always the same.

No, we haven't heard anything.

No, I don't know who she is.

The city heat begins to take its toll, and Mollel suggests a change of scene. They have walked the length of K Street, anyway, and are back on Biashara Street, where the Land Rover is parked.

It's past four o'clock. Mollel sees that the bike shop has opened its shutters once more, obviously banking on getting some last-minute Christmas trade. Mollel enters; Kiunga follows him.

—Welcome, sir. Are you looking for anything in particular or just browsing?

—Remember the little boy who was here earlier?

—Oh, it's you, says the storekeeper, retreating behind the counter and switching instantly from obsequious to defensive. I told you before, other people's children are not my concern. I have got a business to run. And unless you want to buy something . . .

—Hold on, hold on, says Mollel. When he was here, did you notice him looking at any particular bike?

—Ah, I see. Well, now you come to mention it, I think it was this one that most occupied his attention, yes, yes, certainly.

The Indian storekeepers have a reputation for driving a hard bargain, and Mollel's heart sinks as he sees the man lead him toward what is obviously the most expensive child's bike in the shop. The man takes the handlebars and bounces the machine on its chunky tires.

—Fifteen speed, front and rear suspension, alloy frame. You really can't get any better than this.

—How much does it cost?

—Might as well ask, how much will you *save*? Think of the constant repairs you'd have to make on a cheaper model. All those punctures from inadequate tires, all the damage due to shoddy manufacture. Plus, think of the savings on fuel and *matatu* fares once the little man becomes independent.

—How much?

—Twenty. And that's the best price you'll find.

—Twenty thousand shillings? I can't afford that!

The storekeeper smiles. —It's a shame that sir was not present when the young man was looking at this model, he continues. The way his face lit up. It made it seem all the more tragic afterward, when he realized— when he realized his daddy wasn't coming back to get him.

Kiunga steps forward. His face is blank, his arms folded, chest out. Neutrality never looked more threatening.

—I don't think you understood my colleague. He didn't say he couldn't afford the *bike*. He said he couldn't afford the *price*.

—The price is nonnegotiable, sirs, the shopkeeper persists with a tremor in his voice. If you'd care to look at some of the cheaper ones— scarcely more than toys, really—but perhaps more fitting to your budget . . .

Kiunga places his hand on the bike's saddle. —I assume you have all the importation documents for this one? And the rest of your stock?

The storekeeper's mouth falls open, and Kiunga continues: —Because we can either have a very *long* conversation about that—and about your business permits and back taxes and social security contributions—or we can have a very *short* conversation about your police discount.

—Police discount? Why didn't you tell me that you were officers of the law? Did I say twenty thousand shillings? I meant fifteen. And did I mention that I'd throw in a crash helmet for free?

Bike in the back of the car, they drive out of the city center and back to Uhuru Park. Mollel wants to go over the
crime scene again before it gets too dark. The sun is
already low in the sky, and they have to pull down the
car's visors as they traverse the Kenyatta Avenue roundabout. The park
is less crowded now. People are making their way back to their homes.
With the heat less oppressive, those remaining in the park have a newfound vigor. Boys play football, children are flocked on the swings, lovers
amble hand in hand.

At the scene, the removal of the body has dispersed the curious onlookers. A solitary uniformed officer is sitting on the low wall by the
culvert, chatting on his mobile phone. He jumps to his feet and ends the
call as the other policemen pull up.

—Oh, it's you, he says to Kiunga. I thought it was the boss.

—I *am* your boss, Kiunga responds. Three months' seniority and an
extra five hundred shillings a week says so. You haven't met my new
partner yet, have you? Mollel, this is John Wainaina. A disgrace to the
service.

Wainaina grins broadly and shakes Mollel's hand. —Sorry you've
been lumbered with this piece of wood, he says, indicating Kiunga. We
were at school together. We always said he'd make detective—so long
as he's tracking down food, or pussy.

—He's a *noma*, says Kiunga. Mollel does not know much Sheng—the hybrid language of Swahili, English, and Kikuyu—but he infers that *noma* has a positive meaning. Someone who can be trusted.

The two *nomas* laugh heartily, and for a fleeting moment Mollel wonders why he'd never managed to make any friends on the force like this. Probably for the same reason that he'd never sit around chatting on the phone when there was a crime scene to be investigated.

—Everything under control here?

Wainaina stretches. —Seems to be.

Mollel has brought a flashlight from the car. He descends into the concrete ditch—empty now, but full of muddy footprints and smears where the body has been removed—and starts to track back along its length.

—Is this park part of your regular beat? he asks Wainaina.

—I suppose. I cover half of Central district one way or another.

—Do you come into the park at night?

—Not if I can help it. No reason to. It's officially closed, though, of course, there's no real way to stop people coming and going.

—And presumably they do? Mollel has reached the end of the ditch and is shining his flashlight up into the large concrete pipe that feeds it.

—There's always activity. Some people sleep in the bushes. Others come here for sex. The K Street hookers use it as a cheap alternative to hotel rooms.

—Right. So she could have been in the park with a client, killed some short distance from here, and thrown into the ditch?

—That'd be my take on it.

—I want you to come back later, round up some of the people who usually sleep or hang out near here at night. Find out if they saw anything.

Wainaina gives a loud sigh. Mollel pretends not to have heard it, and sticks his head into the pipe. It is wide enough to carry a person. With the flashlight, he can make out that it runs for a short distance more or less straight, then veers abruptly upward. The smell is awful; a greasy slime coats the base of the pipe. He pulls out and gulps fresh air.

—Has anyone been up here?

—You must be joking.

Mollel takes off his shirt and hands it to Kiunga. No point getting too filthy. Wainaina and Kiunga watch with amusement as Mollel, bare chested, pushes his way steadily into the mouth of the pipe.

The sounds of the city fade behind him as he gets farther in. The smell grows in intensity. There must have been an overflow from the sewage system in the heavy rains the previous night. He steps carefully on the surface below him, which is curved and slippery, a steadying arm pressed against the top of the pipe. He is bent nearly double but has no intention of getting onto his hands and knees if he can help it.

At the junction with the inclined section, he takes the flashlight and looks up. The pipe disappears into darkness, following a steady ascent of about fifteen degrees. There is no sign of any grille or mesh; a body could easily be carried down here by fast-flowing water. That could be one explanation for the corpse's battered state. He circles the light around, looking for a telltale fragment of fabric or a murder weapon. But there is nothing.

—Where does this lead?

He has backed out to find Wainaina and Kiunga waiting patiently for him. They look at his smeared body with disgust.

—There's a tap over there, Wainaina says, pointing to a gardener's standpipe nearby. Mollel goes over and starts washing.

In answer to his previous question, Kiunga says, —From the look of it, the drain goes straight up State House Avenue. Must bring water down from as far away as Kilimani and Lavington.

—Okay. Let's try to trace it. To Wainaina: —You stay here.

The pair of them walk around the chain-link fence that bounds the park and start trudging up Upper Hill. The road curves back around, and they are standing some ten meters above Wainaina down at the pipe outflow.

—Here, says Mollel, pointing at a manhole cover in the sidewalk. It is encrusted with mud and rust. He takes a penknife from his pocket and scrapes away enough to find an edge, which he prizes up. Looking in, he sees a short drop to a pipe running along the contour of the hill.

Mollel hears a shout. —I can see you!

He stands up and, looking back down the hill, sees Wainaina leaning into the mouth of the pipe. They are still close enough for him to have seen the light from the lifted cover.

—It's the same pipe, all right, says Kiunga.

—This cover hasn't been disturbed for years, says Mollel. Come on.

They continue up the hill, spotting the drain covers in the sidewalk or occasionally in the middle of the road, using them to track the course of the drainage pipe. All of them seem sealed by decades of neglect. But in a less salubrious part of town, they've been stolen for scrap metal long since.

They are on State House Avenue now, a quiet, leafy street that leads ultimately to the presidential palace.

—Please tell me, groans Kiunga, that we're not going to track this all the way back to State House. That would be one hassle I really don't need.

Mollel frowns. There should be another cover by now, yet he has scanned the road and the sidewalk for quite some distance and has failed to spot it. The others are spaced at pretty regular intervals. Why break the pattern?

—I think I found it, calls Kiunga. He is peering over a tall metal gate. —Isn't that it, there?

Mollel retraces his steps and joins Kiunga at the gate. —Hard to tell, with the leaves. Could be. What is this place?

Over the gate, they can see an old-fashioned colonial stone house. Two stories high, not very large, windows dark. It has decidedly seen better days. The front courtyard—once, presumably, a garden—has been graveled for parking but is covered with a layer of leaves from the massive eucalyptus trees that shower the area with dappled shade.

A freshly painted metal sign towers above them. They both step back to take a better look.

—Orpheus House, says Kiunga, reading the sign.

COMING SOON, it proclaims above a computer-generated image of a multistory building in creamy, fresh colors with white, curving roofs.

No sign of the dozens of stately trees that currently grace the site, though a foamy dot of green here and there on the picture's periphery suggests a sapling or two.

Mollel bangs on the gate. A small flock of mousebirds, disturbed by the noise, flee to the adjacent bushes. Otherwise, there is no sign that anyone has heard.

—Padlocked on the outside, says Kiunga, rattling the chain that secures the gate. —Which suggests to me that there's no one here.

Kiunga cups his hands to offer Mollel a boost. A quick look up and down the street—all is quiet—and Mollel is up and over, landing softly on the leaves on the other side.

—Keep a lookout.

—*Sawa sawa*, says Kiunga. Sure thing.

Despite Kiunga's confidence that the place is empty, Mollel can't shake the feeling that his movement toward the house is being observed. He scrutinizes the windows. They are barred, dark. Cataracted with dust. No sign of life.

The farther he gets from the gate, the more the sounds of the city melt into the background, muffled by the trees, whose steady, gentle swishing has completely overwhelmed the noise of the traffic. Mollel is amazed that a place like this still exists so close to the center of Nairobi, and he grieves a little for its imminent loss.

He walks around the house—gravel crackling under the leaves—and takes a look through a ground-floor window. Nothing. An empty room. He continues walking and looks through the next window: it is larger, but this time it is obscured by faded, heavy curtains on the other side. They're drawn tightly together. Not even a crack between them to get a clue about what lies within.

Moving on, Mollel sees that the plot extends far behind the house. Must be nearly two acres. Prime land. A small outbuilding lies at the far end, and this looks more promising. Mollel notices that a path seems to have been formed through the fallen leaves by the regular passage of feet. He approaches the brick outbuilding, a small house with two or three doors, each one a servant's quarter. One door is open, revealing a dark latrine. He smells charcoal burning, and as he rounds the building, he sees a glowing *jiko* with a fresh ear of maize roasting on top.

—Look out!

On hearing Kiunga's cry, Mollel spins around just in time to raise his arm against the metal bar that is brought down against him. He jumps back, ducking the second blow, seizing the moment when his assailant must raise the weapon again as his opportunity to grab it. He feels the cold metal in his palm and twists it, tugging it from the other man's grasp. He snatches it and now wields it high above his own head, ready to bring it down—

And nearly does so, onto Kiunga's head. Kiunga has come to Mollel's aid and has grasped the other man in both arms, holding him tight in a bear hug. The man is small and frail, and Kiunga towers over him.

—Watch it! says Kiunga. That's lethal. He could've put your skull in.

Mollel drops the iron bar with a clank. The old man looks up at him pitifully.

—Please, there is nothing to steal here. I'm just the day *askari*. The night guards will be here soon. And they've got dogs.

—Come off it, says Mollel. There's no sign of dogs here. They'd have padded a track around the perimeter. I'll bet there are no night guards, either. It's just you, isn't it? Why didn't you come to the gate when you heard us banging?

The old man points to his ear. —I'm very deaf, he says. Please, let me go. I'm not even a guard, properly. I used to be a caretaker here, and the owners let me stay on, to deter squatters. That's all.

—Don't worry, old man, says Kiunga, releasing him. We're not going to harm you. We're police officers.

The old man stumbles back, rubbing his arms. He doesn't appear overly reassured by that statement. Mollel shows him his card.

—What's your name?

—Githaka.

—Githaka, we want to take a look at the drain cover in the front yard. You don't have any objections, do you?

Githaka looks at them blankly. Mollel takes this as permission. The three of them walk around to the front of the house. Mollel and Kiunga kneel by the iron cover.

Mollel takes his knife and uses it to lift some of the leaves away. He points out the rim to Kiunga: at the edges, someone has scraped the rust and mud aside to lever it open. They've done it recently, too, and brushed the leaves back over to cover it up.

Kiunga lets out a low whistle.

—Get Wainaina on your phone, says Mollel. I want to try something out.

He lifts open the drain cover and sets it gently to one side. Taking his flashlight, he shines it around within. Nothing immediately apparent. He drops down and into the pipe. Crouching low, he sees it stretching before him up and down the hill—the same rank odor, the same blackness.

From above, Kiunga: —Wainaina's on the line.

—Tell him to get up in the pipe as far as he can without losing the signal. Let me know when he's there.

Kiunga chuckles. —He'll be happy!

Mollel hears Kiunga explaining the task to his friend, and then, in response to an apparent protest, forcefully ordering him. They wait.

—Okay, says Kiunga. He's there.

—Tell him to start shouting.

—Start shouting, says Kiunga into the telephone. I don't know what. Anything! Sing "God Bless Kenya" for all I care. Use your imagination.

In the semidarkness, Mollel strains to hear. He flicks off his flashlight, and somehow this heightens his hearing. Apart from the square of light above him and Kiunga's feet, he can hardly see a thing. He hears rustling nearby, scurrying. He tries not to think about rats.

And then he hears it, distant, echoing. A man's voice.

—Get me out of here, he says to Kiunga. I've heard enough.

Kiunga reaches down and hauls his colleague out.

—Could you hear him?

—I could hear something. Shouting. I think he was speaking Kikuyu. The only word I could make out was *Maasai*.

Kiunga laughs. He holds the phone up to his ear.

—He's still shouting. He's saying that there's a terrible smell of goat shit in this tunnel. It must be because there's a Maasai at the other end of it.

Mollel takes the phone. The shouting stops, and he hears the hoarse voice of Wainaina on the other end: —*Kiunga, can I stop now?*

—Not yet, Mollel tells him. Just keep shouting.

He hands the phone back to Kiunga and bends down to replace the drain cover. —Are you just going to keep him shouting down there? asks Kiunga.

—Why not? Mollel chuckles. —He can handle it. He's a *noma*.

5 They leave the old *askari* with a promise that they will return to look around inside the premises, and warn him not to tamper with the drain cover.

It is now dark. Time to go back to K Street.

In the car on the way there, Mollel goes over what they have learned about Orpheus House. Old Githaka told them that it had been empty for a few months. For about twenty years previously it was run as a women's shelter or refuge—a sort of safe house for those wanting to escape from prostitution. A year earlier, the charity had run into financial difficulties, and the house had been taken over by the church of George Nalo.

Nalo, Mollel has heard of. The pastor is something of a celebrity in town. Billboards proclaim his mission, and you can hardly avoid him on the television. He has a mega-church out in Embakasi and is renowned for his social projects.

According to Githaka, the site is sitting idle while the funds are finalized for redevelopment. Mollel wonders what a site like that would be worth. He really does not have a clue. Millions of dollars, probably, hundreds of millions of shillings.

—Can we stop for a bite to eat, boss?

As usual, Mollel has forgotten to eat, and the realization makes him feel a kind of queasy emptiness—not hunger. Time to take his pills, too.

They stop at Nelly's Country Inn on Koinange Street. The quaint name belies the bustling, functional interior: strip lights on the ceiling, worn linoleum on the floor, red plastic benches in the booths. The Country Inn is something of a Nairobi legend. It bears a sign above the counter that says ESTABLISHED 1970. NEVER CLOSED.

True enough. Mollel has been dropping in there for as long as he's been a policeman, even before, when he was a private *askari* on night shifts. There is something about their *chai masala*—spiced, milky tea— that no other café can replicate. Perhaps it is the patina of the ancient urn from which it is poured, surely a survivor, like the formidable ladies behind the counter, from the first day of business.

Kiunga grabs two high stools at a bar that faces the front window, an ideal, if somewhat conspicuous, location for scoping the street. —I'll have a plate of *sambusas*, says Kiunga to the waitress. Make it ten, mixed. And a *tangawizi* to drink. Mollel?

—*Chai masala* and a bowl of *matoke*.

—Is that all you're having? No meat? I thought Maasais ate only meat. Mollel shrugs. —It's all I feel like.

He does not mention that lately his medication has made him feel queasy after eating anything but the blandest food.

The clientele in Nelly's changes from hour to hour. During the day, it's almost respectable, making a good trade from office workers and shoppers looking for a snack. In the early evening, a student crowd tends to congregate, lining their stomachs with platters of greasy meat before an evening of beer. A group of high-spirited young men are spilling out from one of the booths now, making a lot of noise but not offending anyone. Later, the place will attract some of the street's more notorious residents: the call girls taking a break and having a gossip between clients. Somehow they know to stay away during the day, and Mollel wonders whether the management has warned them to steer clear or whether mingling with respectable folk makes the girls feel uncomfortable.

—That was excellent, says Kiunga, wiping the remains of his last *sambusa* around the plate to pick up the end of the *pili pili* sauce. He pops it into his mouth and swallows with pleasure.

—You've not touched yours.

—I'll make it last, says Mollel. I want to stay here while you go talk to some of the girls.

—Smart thinking. No need to crowd them. I'll be back in a bit.

When Kiunga has left, Mollel removes a packet of pills from his pocket and carefully counts out his three for this evening: one of each of three different kinds. He places all three on his tongue and washes them down with his lukewarm *chai*. Then, without relish, he starts spooning back his gray *matoke*.

For half an hour or so, he watches Kiunga approaching the girls on the street. At this time of the evening they tend to be alone rather than in groups. Soon Kiunga has moved out of sight. Mollel continues to watch the girls at work. They clearly have a relationship with the *askaris* who guard the shuttered-up shop fronts. Even in his own night-watchman days, fifteen years ago, Mollel recalls, these spots on Koinange Street were well prized among the guards. It may seem boring, dangerous, and cold to sit all night on a stool in front of a steel shutter, with little more than a truncheon and a transistor radio. But there is a lucrative sideline to be had. The *askaris* let the girls stash their belongings with them while they go off to stalk the sidewalks. Some turn up wearing long coats— presumably to avoid attention on the *matatu*—which they fold and leave beside an *askari*'s stool. It's discreet, but the *askaris* always charge something for this cloakroom service, often payment in kind. They offer other services, too. Protection. Pimping.

As for the johns, their uniformity is the only surprise: all middle-aged, in their forties, fifties, or sixties. Mostly paunchy. Mostly African, but a lot of Indians, too. They seem to share a relaxed, businesslike attitude regarding the whole transaction. They pull up in their cars looking for a face they know or a figure that takes their fancy. They chat awhile with the girl leaning into the passenger-side window. Then she gets in, and they go. Where? Mollel wonders.

As ever, it's the details that fascinate him. The Indian man who pulls up in an SUV, child seats in the back. The fat, bald African who seems to consider—then reject—at least ten girls before choosing two to disappear with. And the way in which the girls carry on their trade: the teamwork, the way they look out for one another, the surreptitious glances at licence plates and monitoring of suspicious activity, the scrutiny of the johns by the ones left behind.

Mollel is becoming convinced of a few basic truths. One, only junkies work alone. All the other girls maintain a network of friendships and alliances for their own convenience and protection. Two, if his victim had been working this street, she'd have been known about, at least by someone. And three, if she is known here, it is likely that these girls know her killer too.

Kiunga comes back into sight. He's had enough time to cover the length of K Street and is returning to speak to any girls he missed the first time around. At the same moment, Mollel notices another car pull up, a large silver Toyota Land Cruiser. Pretty new, slick without being ostentatious. He checks out the driver: a white man. No particular surprise there. Mollel can't see much of the face, as the man is wearing sunglasses, despite the darkness. A shock of white hair and flabby, pallid cheeks. The man is leaning over his steering wheel, scrutinizing the girls on the sidewalk. There's something different in his approach. He seems nervous, cagey. Not so brazen as the other johns. He hasn't stopped the car, but continues to crawl slowly along the edge of the road. As some of the girls approach his passenger-side window, he waves them away and keeps rolling. He's looking for a specific person. But he won't ask anyone where she is.

Mollel gets up and darts for the door. Kiunga is standing on the sidewalk on the other side of the street, about to be overtaken by the man in the silver car. Mollel calls to him, —Stop that car!

Kiunga looks over, then up at the car. He puts out his hand. The driver sees him, guns the accelerator. —Hey! Police! *Stop!* But Kiunga has to step away from the curb as the car speeds past him. Mollel runs across the street to join him, and together they watch the car hit the lights at the end of K Street, jump the red, squeal left onto University Way, and drive out of sight.

—I got the plate, says Kiunga. Shall we go after him?

—We'll never catch him. We'll have to follow it up later.

—I got a quick look at the driver. Looked like an old guy. A *mzungu*.

Mzungu: white man.

—I thought so, too, says Mollel. He takes out his notebook and gives it to Kiunga to write down the number, which Mollel tallies with his own reading.

—Now, if this were a movie, says Kiunga, I'd pick up my radio, put out an APB, get the driver's name off the central computer, have him hand-delivered to Central for questioning.

—Yep, says Mollel. But this is Nairobi. And we don't have a radio, can't put out an APB, and getting his name means waiting until Monday morning, going down to the motor vehicle licensing office, and hoping the clerk there will be in a good enough mood to fetch the card for you rather than making you go through the files yourself.

—Another job for Wainaina?

—We'll see. I want to go back to the park and see who he's rounded up.

—You're enjoying this, aren't you? asks Kiunga.

Mollel is surprised by the statement. —I'm just doing my job, he mutters. But even as he says it, he realizes how good it feels to be doing proper police work once more.

—Well, we're not ready to call it a day yet, says Kiunga. I got a lead from one of the girls. Looks like it's going to be a late night for us.

6 The lead is a rendezvous. According to Kiunga, one of the K Street girls had seemed edgy and upset. She had broken away from the others and briefly told him to meet her at midnight in a more private location.

—Are you sure you want me there? Mollel laughs.

—Are you kidding me? replies Kiunga. I don't need to pay for it. Besides, she knows I'm not a john. And the way I see it, there are two possible reasons she'd want to get me alone. And for either of them, I'd want company.

He's right. If she has information on the case, Mollel wants to hear it. And it's always possible that this is a trap, a scam to lure Kiunga into a secluded place and have him robbed—or worse.

They've rolled around to Uhuru Park once more, looking for Wainaina. The night is warm, but as they draw up near Little Mombasa, Wainaina is rubbing his hands exaggeratedly.

—If I'd known I was going to end up on the night shift, I'd have worn a coat, he says reproachfully. Oh, and thanks for leaving me hollering up that pipe. Must have been ten minutes before I realized you'd hung up the phone.

—I see you have someone for us, says Mollel. Beside Wainaina is a small, stooped figure wearing a floppy hat.

—Oh, yes. I got a terrific eyewitness. Saw everything.

As Mollel comes up to the two of them, he recognizes the small man. Kiunga knows him too.

—Superglue Sammy, says Kiunga. Great. Shall we take him down for an ID parade? Maybe look at some photos? Hell, why don't we buy him a box of crayons, he can draw us a sketch?

—You're both very funny, says Sammy, removing his hat and turning his sealed eyes toward them. But you don't need to see, to *see*.

Superglue Sammy is a well-known figure on the streets of Nairobi's downtown district. He is usually to be found outside one of the city's main banks or department stores, his brimmed hat in hand, eyes shut to the world.

Sammy is a young man, barely in his twenties—all those years spent on the streets. Mollel thinks he can recall seeing him there as a baby or a toddler, his mother holding him up into the faces of passersby, presenting his shuttered eyes as a plea for alms.

As the years passed, the mother-and-son begging team drew a measure of success, perhaps too much, because they attracted attention. First there was a group of doctors from the Nairobi Hospital who wanted to send the boy for specialist treatment—an offer that the mother always refused. Then there were rumors, and following the rumors, the journalists. One day the *Daily Nation* had a big splash on the mother who superglued her baby's eyes shut to increase his begging appeal. She denied it: the pots of discarded glue found all around her shack in Kibera were the result of her own addiction, she claimed. She was a loving mother who had nothing else in her life but her little boy, whom she looked after impeccably. Certainly his portion of the tiny shack was clean and comfortable. There were even some toys. Jealousy, she said, motivated the allegations.

The child—then a boy of six—was taken away. The good doctors found the skin of his eyelids fused to his corneas, some said because of the glue; others suggested a prenatal infection. Either way, there was nothing to be done. The closed lids at least had the benefit of concealing the useless jelly beneath.

So they sent him back to Kibera, but his mother was not there anymore. She'd become so lonely without Sammy that she'd downed a bottle of the illegal local spirits, *chang'aa*, poured all her glue into a plastic bag, and stuck her head into it.

After that, Sammy went back to doing the only thing he knew—and he has been on the streets ever since.

—So, Sammy, says Mollel. Tell us what you *heard* last night.

—Okay. Follow me.

Sammy leads them away from Little Mombasa, into the park, parallel to the large, wide-open space at the rear of the gardens. During the day this is a car park; at night it is empty. At the far side is the drainage ditch where the girl's body was discovered. Wainaina and Mollel both turn on their flashlights, which they use to pick their way down a narrow path, winding through shrubs and hedges alongside the open ground.

—What do you notice about this place? asks Sammy.

—I don't notice a damn thing, replies Wainaina, inadvertently flicking a branch back into Mollel's midriff. It's pitch-black!

—Exactly, says Sammy. And yet *I'm* leading *you*. See why I like to sleep here? It's safe, secluded, and I can hear anyone coming. *Karibu nyumbani.*

The phrase means *welcome home*, and Sammy has stopped before a large ornamental fan palm. He ducks behind it, and the three policemen follow. They find themselves in a small sheltered spot. The ground is dry, it is perfectly secluded, even comfortable. Mollel, certainly, has slept in much worse places. In a hollow by the palm's base is a blanket and a small stash: some clothing, a radio.

Kiunga peers through the leaves.

—There's a clear line of sight to where the body was found, he says. Clear line of hearing, I should say.

—Ringside seat. Sammy grins.

—What did you hear?

—Let's get out into the open. I don't want your dirty police boots ruining my fine carpet.

Together, they go by a different route through some more bushes and come out in the deserted car park.

—I stay there a couple of times a week, Sammy explains. Saves the *matatu* fare back to Kibera. Always Friday nights, as I need to be at my spot early on Saturdays, to get the shoppers, right? So I'm pretty familiar with the usual activity here. You get quite a few cars coming in, parking up. I hear the springs creaking, the moans. Even the money changing hands.

—No one here tonight, says Mollel.

—They're not going to bring their johns here now, are they? The place is cursed.

—What about last night?

—Last night. Now, *that* was out of the ordinary. Before I go on—he reaches out and touches Kiunga on the arm—could I trouble you for a cigarette?

—What the . . . Kiunga lifts his sleeve and sniffs it. —Is it that obvious I'm a smoker?

Mollel and Wainaina laugh. Kiunga grudgingly takes a packet of Sportsmans and some matches from his pocket and hands a cigarette to Sammy, offering the pack to the others too, but they refuse. He strikes a match, holds it up for Sammy to share the flame.

Their faces glow and flicker in the matchlight.

Sammy breathes the smoke deeply and exhales with satisfaction. —Where were we?

—Last night.

—Ah yes, last night. Well, last night was a strange one. About eleven, these buses started arriving. They woke me up. I counted them—four buses. They were here until three. I know that because I listened to the radio afterward, until it started raining.

—The K Street girls are doing them by the busload now? jokes Wainaina, but the others ignore him.

—When they unloaded, they sounded like school buses. You know, all the feet? But these weren't kids. By the sound of the boots, I thought at first they were policemen.

—What makes you think they weren't?

—I know they weren't. First, because you lot are here asking about them. I reckon you'd know about it if it was your own boys. Second—no offense—they were too disciplined to be policemen. The buses were full, I reckon, but they all got off and lined up in just a few minutes, no talking, no joking, just a load of whispered orders. I heard them spread out, sounded like they were in teams. As if they were checking the place out. Then I heard them marching about. Back and forth, and around.

He takes another long drag from his cigarette.

—Four buses? asks Kiunga skeptically. That's two hundred men at least. Our night patrols would have seen them.

—I thought there were no night patrols in the park, Mollel remarks.

—They'd have seen that sort of activity from the street! says Wainaina.

Mollel looks around. Easily visible above the trees are the lights from the office blocks of the city. Closest is Nyayo House, the home ministry headquarters, but there was no chance of any civil servant being at his desk at that time of night to look down into the park. At ground level, though, the highway is not visible, except for the occasional flash of light through the foliage.

It reminds him of a name—one of many—that the Maasai have for this city. Nakuso Intelon. It means *festooned trees*, and refers to the lights high on the skyline, visible from the plains for miles around.

—Nothing to see, continues Sammy. They were doing it in the dark.

—Oh, come on! protests Kiunga. We're supposed to believe that two hundred soldiers paraded around here for an hour in the middle of the night in pitch darkness and complete silence? And yet a *blind* man observed it all? Sammy, had you been at the *chang'aa* by any chance?

—I didn't say they were soldiers, says Sammy. But they did have weapons.

—Don't tell me—they started taking potshots?

Sammy sighs.

—Tell us, says Mollel.

—I heard them doing drills. You know, a whispered order, then lots of clanking of wood against wood.

—They were fighting themselves, in the middle of the night, in the dark! Brilliant! says Wainaina. Guys, can we go home now? It's so cold.

—How do you know they didn't have any lights? Mollel asks Sammy.

—The engines were silent. You don't leave the lights on for an hour without leaving the engine running. You get a flat battery on one of those old buses, you're going to need a tow truck.

—They might have had flashlights, says Kiunga.

—Possibly. But I don't think so. I heard a lot of whispering, a lot of orders given in low voices that I could not make out. But the only voice I heard out loud came from over here.

He beckons them to follow him to the edge of the open space. A shin-high hedge runs along the path at this point, the boundary between the gardens and the car park.

—I've walked into this myself a few times, admits Sammy. But then, as you keep reminding me, I am blind. You guys aren't going to walk into it with a flashlight, are you?

Mollel runs his flashlight along the low hedge. It's made from bougainvillea, with evenly spaced posts between which barbed wire has been stretched for the plants to grow over. No more than a foot from the ground, but he certainly wouldn't want to blunder into it in the dark.

—So at one point I heard the men marching this way. Then there's a yell of pain, and someone shouts *halt!* And then, some commotion. Now, even *policemen* aren't dumb enough to march into barbed wire if they have any way of seeing where they're going.

Mollel continues along the hedge, barbed wire glinting in his flashlight beam below the green-and-purple foliage of the bougainvillea. He stops. Suddenly the hedge is disrupted, footprints in the earth before it. Large ones—a lot of them. He pushes the leaves away to look at the wire. After some searching, he finds a section with a shred of cloth on one of the barbs. He takes it off and examines it under his flashlight. It is thick dark-green material, with a dark black patch.

—Blood, says Kiunga, echoing Mollel's thoughts.

Mollel shines the light on Sammy's trousers. They're gray. —Roll up your trouser legs, Sammy, he orders. The blind man does so: no sign of any injury.

—There were four buses, you say? Mollel asks Sammy. He walks away from the bushes and toward the center of the car park. The others follow him, Kiunga leading Sammy by the arm.

—Let me guess, Sammy, says Mollel—he is now some distance ahead of them—it sounded to you like they were parked about here. He walks farther. —And here. He walks farther still. —And here—and he's now got so distant that he has to shout —and here?

—Sounds about right, Sammy calls back.

Mollel casts his beam down on the ground. He's standing above a patch of oil. He strides seven even paces back toward the others, shines the beam down—a patch of oil. Seven more paces, a patch of oil. Seven more paces and he's back with them. He shines the beam once more down at their feet. A patch of oil.

—They even *parked* in formation, he says. Sammy's right. Whoever these guys are, their transport may be clapped out, but they are *disciplined*.

It is just turning midnight as Kiunga coaxes the Land Rover into Banda Street. Away from K Street—which never sleeps—the city center has an eerie feel at this time. Cats, never evident during the day, stalk the emptiness, turning their moonbeam eyes toward the oncoming car before scurrying into the darkness. Humans are still present, occasionally sleeping cocooned in doorways or, now and then, swaying intoxicated along the sidewalk.

—She said she'd meet us up here, says Kiunga, drawing the car to a halt and getting out. Mollel descends too, and Kiunga locks up.

—This is the time for night runners, he says.

He's whispering. The silence around them seems to demand it. Together, their footsteps echo along Banda Street. A flash of movement at the far end—gone before Mollel can make out what it is.

Mollel has never seen a night runner, but he's heard enough credible reports not to dismiss the idea as pure fantasy. Indeed, every so often one is caught and killed, usually in the villages. Of course, the night runner, once dead, returns to his or her form as a normal human, so there is no proving the stories of supernatural speed and strength. But what it does prove is that there are people who go about at night, usually naked. Whether truly possessed by a witch, merely mad, or simply up to no good, no one can say. What Mollel knows, though, is that there are enough malignant spirits of the criminal variety on the streets of Nairobi at this time of night to make the undercurrent of fear he's feeling right now a perfectly healthy and rational response.

They've stopped by the mosque—the largest one in the center of the city and even more of a focal point by night than it is in the day. A series of floodlights from within the main dome and minaret pick out the high arched windows lit in aqueous green. With no illumination, though, at ground level, the effect seems merely to increase the darkness in the street.

—Up here, says Kiunga, turning into a small alley that runs alongside the mosque, known, with typical Nairobi economy, as Mosque Alley.

—She asked to meet here?

—She said it was safe.

Safe for her, Mollel does not doubt. It is near enough to K Street for her to come on foot without crossing too much of town alone. And if she fears being seen talking to the police, it is certainly a good spot to avoid prying eyes.

That's if she's genuine. Mollel's fear, though, is a trap. And with the long, high wall of the mosque bounding one side of the alley and the facing wall equally blank and inaccessible, the two men would be easy prey if caught in the middle.

—She said midnight?

—It's only a few minutes past.

They get halfway down the alley and stop. On any day of the week this narrow lane is pretty busy. On a Friday afternoon it is thronged with the devout and the not so devout, the mosque-goers and the vendors of trinkets, Korans, and kufis. If you want to buy a plastic replica of the Ka'bah at Mecca, which tells the time and date and plays a series of tinny yet rousing recordings of Koranic verse, this is the place to come. If you want to buy a DVD entitled *Al-Qaeda's Greatest Hits* from certain shady, bearded youths—before they are chased off by the mosque elders—this is the place to come. If you are penniless, homeless, hopeless—Muslim or Kaffir—and want to tap some reliable Sabbatarian charity, this is the place to come. But only on Friday afternoons.

In these first few minutes of a Sunday morning, the alley is as silent as the grave. Perhaps it is the looming presence of the mosque itself that keeps away the street sleepers, the drug dealers, the junkies looking for a quiet place for a fix, or the hookers looking for a quiet place to take their clients for a knee trembler. Not even night runners would venture here. Or at least Mollel hopes they won't.

A distant, regular tapping echoes through the streets now. It becomes a clack-clack, a confident, purposeful stride. High heels, female footsteps. Mollel strains, listening, trying to discover an undercurrent to this high note: a hidden bass, a quiet drumming male footbeat accompanying the more evident feminine percussion. But he does not hear any footsteps other than hers. It sounds as if she is alone.

She rounds the corner at the head of the alleyway, and in the undersea green light reflected from the mosque, she is a silhouette.

She walks toward them, never breaking her stride, feet falling determinedly one in front of the other, tapered ankles crossing each other's path. Her long legs are bare, the skirt high, and her hips sway with the rhythm of her walk. Her shoulders are thrown back, and long, straight hair brushes her shoulders. Mollel is reminded of an impala, graceful, proud, powerful—and fragile.

She draws close and finally is illuminated in the half-light before them. Unsmiling, challenging, she scrutinizes the two men before her.

Mollel knows her.

And he does not know her.

And he *knows* her—or rather, he knows her face. It is the face of his mother and his sisters, the face of the girls of his village and of his youth.

It is the face of the dead girl.

It is a Maasai face. And now that the surprise has passed and he has more of a chance to make out the girl's features, he sees that beyond the high cheeks, the almond eyes, the typically Maasai straight nose, she is not a person he knows.

And yet, he knows her.

He might have anticipated this. The dead girl was Maasai, so she would naturally be friendly with another Maasai girl on the streets. They seem about the same age, too. Early twenties, he guesses. This girl is taller, and she does not have any tribal scarring on her cheeks. Her ears, too, are pierced only in the regular, non-Maasai way, to allow her to wear a pair of glinting earrings.

—So, she says. You're a Maasai too. I saw you watching from Nelly's window. You looked like someone I could trust.

—You can trust me, and my colleague here, says Mollel. Whatever you say to us is confidential. It does not get back to K Street. Or anywhere else.

—Do you think you might know the dead girl? asks Kiunga.

—I think so, she replies quietly. I think she may be my friend.

There is never a good time to visit the Nairobi city mortuary, but superstition and sentiment aside, the early hours of Sunday morning may be better than most. The visitor is spared the grieving families, women wailing and ululating; the hard-luck stories from smartly dressed, credible-looking beggars who need just a hundred bob to help repatriate their uncle's body to Garissa (tomorrow it will be their grandmother, to Kisumu); the vendors of trinkets and charms, candles and rosaries; the coffin makers, with their trays of small-scale replicas—or, hardly bigger, the real, ready-made baby and child coffins in which they do a good trade on the spot.

You are also spared the standing in queues; the standing in corridors; the standing around and about and wherever you can, squatting or sitting, and waiting and waiting and waiting; and returning once and again to the counter to try to get hold of someone—anyone—who will deal with your request.

So, for all practical reasons, the mortuary is best visited at night. Yet even Mollel—to whom this place is grimly familiar—needs to suppress a shiver as they crunch over the gravel toward the main entrance.

It's a while before anyone answers the door. When he comes, it's evident that the attendant has been sleeping. They watch him through the glass as he fumbles with the lock. His eyes are bleary and his cheeks creased. As he opens the door, the pungent, sour smell of home-brewed beer hits them. The attendant rubs his hand across his bristled, grizzled chin.

—Visiting hours are over.

Mollel shows him his card. —We've got an ID to do. Unknown female, found in Uhuru Park.

—Can't it wait until morning?

—It *is* morning, says Mollel. Point us in the right direction, and you can go back to sleep.

—Third along, says the attendant, indicating a door with a NO ENTRY sign before them.

—You sure about that? asks Kiunga. We don't want any surprises.

—I'm sure.

—Surprises? asks Mollel as he pushes open the heavy door. The immediate drop in temperature makes his skin prickle.

—I pulled back a sheet once, expecting to see a bank robber, found half a dozen babies, says Kiunga in a low voice. All the ones collected from the city that week. It was someone's idea of a joke.

Mollel looks over at the girl. She has come in too, but stays in the reception area, seemingly tuned out of their conversation.

—I'd better check it out first, before we show her.

He enters the morgue alone, finding a light switch and flicking it on. The fluorescent strips stutter and ping into life.

The room is the same as it was nine years ago, when he came to find his wife. Except then it was overflowing, with the living and the dead.

Days, he waited there. Nights, too. He used his policeman's privilege to bypass the formalities, the crowd of desperate relatives forced to wait outside. He was among the first to see each new corpse as it was brought in from the rubble.

He looked like one himself. The thick white concrete dust caked his clothes. His skin was a skin of ashes. Blood—some his own, most from others—streaked black against the white.

After a day or so, someone told him to go get cleaned up. They gave him some clothes.

He stood naked in the sluice room, rinsing the blood and dust from his body. That's where they cleaned the corpses, too. He had to dress hurriedly as another was brought in.

—It's not her, they said. We're still pulling out the ones from the upper stories. If she was on the third floor, there's no saying when they'll find her. There's no saying they'll find her at all.

▲ ▲ ▲

Now there is an orderly line of gurneys, about fifteen or so, with the first six covered. He goes to the third, takes the sheet in his hand, and gently, slowly, lifts it.

It is the Maasai girl. She's been laid out, stripped and washed, but the postmortem has not been performed yet. The body is battered. He sees that a gauze pad has been placed between the legs. He has no intention of removing it; he can wait for the results of the PM. Now his concern is with making her presentable. He walks down the line of trolleys and removes sheets from two of the empty ones. Then he folds the one draped across the dead girl so that it covers her up to her neck. He takes one sheet, folds it to a strip a few inches wide, and drapes it over her head like a nun's wimple, framing her face. She looks placid now. Then he takes the third sheet and softly covers her face once more.

There was no such ceremony when Chiku was brought in. It was the fourth day: Mollel had been sleeping crouched against a wall. He had been dreaming of his baby son.

Someone had roused him. *We think this might be her.*

He'd known the body would be in a bad way. By that stage, they were taking the corpses out of the embassy with diggers. But he wasn't prepared for what he saw.

That's why he wants no shocks this time. He says no prayer as he diligently shrouds the figure laid out before him. It is a purely practical measure. He is a detective, and he wants there to be no distraction when the living girl meets the dead.

He returns to the door and indicates to Kiunga that the body is ready for viewing.

The girl crosses the boundary. She walks to Mollel, who leads her to the table. He looks at her to ask, *Ready?* She nods.

The sheet is lifted. Kiunga's eyes inevitably drop to the body; Mollel's remain firmly on the girl. She winces in recognition.

—Yes, she says, almost inaudibly. Yes, it's Lucy.

—My name is Honey. Not my Maasai name, of course. That's En'cecoroi e-intoi Kipuri. It was Lucy who christened me Honey. She told me that if you washed your forehead when you took your new name, you washed away your past. That's what we were both trying to do. That's how we both ended up in Nairobi.

They're in the car, at the far end of the mortuary car park. Somehow it seems the best place to do this. Neither the harsh white interior nor the cold night air beyond is conducive to talk. The car, now, lights off, is intimate and secluded. The girl seems to feel close enough—and private enough—to open up.

—My Maa is pretty rusty, Mollel admits. *En'cecoroi*—that's a bird, isn't it?

—In English, it's called honeyguide. Lucy told me that.

Mollel recalls the bird: a drab little creature, but full of spirit. It does not fear humans, but leads them to bees' nests in the hope of picking off the larvae for its chicks once the man has taken the honey.

There was a story his mother used to tell. The story of the honeyguide—a tale that would have been as old as the Maasai people themselves. He could not remember the details, but he knew that it always made him sad.

Honey would know the tale. She would have been told it every year, upon the anniversary of her *en-teipa* ceremony, when a baby is taken by its mother, fresh from her confinement, to the dwelling place of an animal whose spirit they hope will inhabit the newborn.

Often it's a lion's den—deserted, of course—to imbue the child with courage. Or a buffalo's scratching tree, for strength. The choice of the modest little bird signified a hope that the little girl would, in her turn, become a caring mother. And a resourceful one.

Mollel can't help wondering what her parents would think of her now.

But it's more important to find out about the victim.

—Do you know Lucy's Maasai name?

—No. She was just Lucy. She said you need a street name that's easy enough for a drunk to remember. She was full of good advice like that, when I first started.

—So she's the one who got you into prostitution? asks Kiunga, leaning over from the driver's seat. Mollel, sitting next to her in the back, senses the girl bristling.

—She *helped* me, she says. Without her, I'd have starved.

—Do you know where she was from?

Honey shakes her head. —A village in the Loita Hills. She never told me its name.

—Well, this is helpful, Kiunga sighs.

Mollel has been impressed so far with his young partner, but— perhaps it's tiredness, perhaps it's something else—he seems edgy, irritable. He's certainly not helping the interview.

—Why don't you take a walk, Mollel suggests.

At least Kiunga's professional enough not to argue. He gets out and walks away from the car. They see a flash and glow as he lights a cigarette, cradles it, and it becomes nothing more than a red dot.

They sit in silence for a while. Then Mollel starts asking questions.

According to the stories, there are a few—a very select few—who see the world as it truly is: raveling slowly back toward creation. They are the lucky ones. For them, death is not an end; it is the beginning of life, when the scavengers, the hyenas, the birds, the worms come together to put flesh on the bones so that the morning wind can breathe animation into them. Life, for them, is a joyful process of ever-increasing strength and virility, until the final, happy years when one begins to shrink to perfection, safe in the arms of a mother.

Not for them this world of chaos and atrophy. No wonder some are envious, persecute them, call them idiots, cretins, *wazuzu*.

But Mollel remembers his mother telling him that these are the truly wise ones. That they have the ultimate gift of starting with knowledge and gradually unlearning it. What is left is truth.

So this is how he interviews. Starting in the here and now and steadily guiding the witness back. He finds the minutiae of recent memory un-helpful. He prefers the distillation granted by forgetting: what is left is truth.

Honey has not seen Lucy for three months. She's been keeping watch for her, hoping to see her, and hoping *not* to see her, because if she saw her, that meant Lucy was back on the streets.

She had told Honey that she'd met some people, some Christians. Lucy wasn't religious, but these people had not gone on too much about God and all that. They'd offered her somewhere to stay. They'd talked about training, even getting her school certificate. It was the chance of a new life, said Lucy. She'd be mad not to take it.

Honey wasn't interested, herself. She'd seen people like this before. Their idea of salvation more often than not meant dull drudgery. And for the first time in her life, she was doing well financially. Her plan in-volved saving enough to turn her back on the street on her own terms. But Lucy was different. She'd been having trouble lately with a certain client, and she wanted out.

Though they were flatmates—they shared a small one-room apart-ment in Kitengela—they did not see each other enough to share every intimacy. Both preferred not to discuss their clientele. It was one thing to do this job, quite another to talk about it. They overlapped rarely, Honey working nights and Lucy mostly days. But on one occasion, when they both found themselves at home and exhausted and had curled up to-gether on the narrow bed they usually shared in shifts, Lucy told Honey that she feared for her life.

She never told her the name. It was someone very powerful and in-fluential, though, and Lucy had made the mistake of demanding too much from him.

Not more money—he wouldn't have had a problem with that. No, she'd been seeing him for a while, and she had found him kind and charming, and very generous. Her mistake was thinking it was genuine. One evening, when she thought the time was right, she had told him that she wanted to quit the paid relationship, and she suggested a girl-friend arrangement instead.

Turned out he didn't like that one little bit. He already had plenty of girlfriends. Not to mention a wife. Why would he want to complicate matters?

He dropped her. When she tried to make contact again, to apolo-gize, she was warned off. But she was foolish. She didn't take the advice. She couldn't afford to lose such a regular client, one who treated her so well. He'd been so kind to her. Surely they could go back to the way things were?

He didn't see it that way. Nor did whoever he sent. Lucy had showed Honey the bruises on her wrist. The offer from the Christians had come at just the right time. She didn't need to be asked twice.

—Your friend's on his second cigarette, says Honey. He must be getting cold.

—He'll be okay, says Mollel. He's a tough guy. Tell me how you met Lucy.

—It was three years ago. I'd been told there was money to be made on K Street. I needed it. I hadn't eaten for days. But I didn't know what I was doing. Oh, I knew what to *do*—village life had prepared me for that. But I didn't know, for example, that you had to ask for the money up front. I learned that when I got thrown out of a moving car.

It was Lucy who picked me up.

She bought me egg and *chipsi*. And a soda, the first one I'd ever tasted. The bubbles made me laugh so hard they came out of my nose.

She was kind to me. She took me to her flat, cleaned me up, let me wear her clothes. She made me understand what this life meant: plenty of hassle, plenty of danger. But also money, freedom.

We worked together for a while. There's always demand for two girls. But that's really a beginner's game. You do it for the safety, to learn new tricks, but you can't charge double, so in the long run it works out better to operate alone.

—How long had Lucy been working the street before you met her?

—She told me she came to Nairobi a year or so before I did.

—Do you know what she was running away from?

Honey gives a hollow laugh. Then she is silent. In the darkness, Mollel tries to make out her face. Is she crying? Angry?

Eventually she says,—I know what I ran away from. I always assumed it was the same for her.

—What was that, Honey?

Instead of answering, Honey says,—I thought you'd understand, Mollel. Once, you were a Maasai. But the way you dress, the way you talk . . . you're a city man now. You've left it behind.

—Yes, I have.

—That's why you, of all people, should be *asipani*.

It takes him a moment to recall the meaning of the Maa word.

—I am trustworthy, he says.

—Prove it, she says. Promise me, whatever happens, you won't make me go back.

—No one can make you go back, Honey.

—I can't go back. I was betrothed the day I was born, and I knew I'd be put to the knife the first day I bled. But I escaped—and you know the punishment for that.

—And you think Lucy was running from the same thing?

—Whoever she was running from, says Honey, they caught up with her in the end.

Mollel shaves by touch, a relic of his village days, when he learned to shave his head years before the razor ever touched his face. This being Sunday, he takes the blade to his scalp once more. He does not need the mirror before him to know that he is going gray. The stubble falling in the sink tells him that story. He does not need to look to know that he is getting thinner. He knows it every time he puts on his clothes.

His wife used to say to him, *If you get any thinner, you're going to disappear.* He feels as if he's been getting thinner for the last nine years, but he is still around.

He bends and washes cold water over his smooth head. It runs clear. No blood. He can hardly remember the last time he nicked himself.

He recalls the day he became an elder. He'd already moved from the village, then, but this was before he'd rejected that life completely. He had been working in the city as a guard, his dreadlocks as fearsome as any uniform. They were long, impeccably plaited, and stained red with henna. During the day, when the guards were off duty, the Maasai used to work on each other's locks, singing faintly and dreaming themselves out of the city.

The dreadlocks were Mollel's mark of being a *moran*—a warrior. Then, when he was in his mid-twenties, word reached him that the village elders had decided he was to join their number. He felt grief—grief for his locks, grief for his youth. He felt resentment, too: many *morans* continued into their thirties. They were, in many ways, more powerful than the elders. They could have jobs, they could live in the city. He did not want to move back to the village, to marry, to have children to herd the goats the way he had done. Besides, there was a girl who lived in the compound he guarded in the city, a pretty Kikuyu girl with an open smile, training to be a secretary, who always took the time to talk to a Maasai when he came off duty.

Still, he went.

It was the mother's duty to shave her son's locks. They woke before dawn, his nose full of the strange, familiar smell of smoke and dung and animals. He was led to the *boma*, the women ululating, the other *morans* chanting the deep, breathy, rhythmic song that rang in the ears. There he saw his mother. She had laid out a freshly tanned calfskin, specially prepared. He knelt before her, bowed his head in submission for a final time. She took a gourd filled with milk and spirits and poured it gently over his head. The milk ran down his cheeks. She commenced the cutting, tugging each lock as she applied the blade, taking it back to the skin. When she had a clear patch, she'd start to shave, and Mollel remembered the taste of milk changing to a taste of blood as she cut into his scalp: it was a sign of honor to bleed without flinching, and because his mother knew that this was expected, she had cut him gently where a small vein ran high on his temple, so that he bled profusely but without pain.

When he rose and washed his head, he looked down at the small, bloody pile of locks in the center of the calfskin. He rubbed his hand over his scalp, which had not been bare since boyhood, and felt the breeze on his skin. It was as though his past had been cleansed from him and his future was his to determine. He knew then that he would not become an elder. He felt free.

This Sunday morning, Mollel finishes shaving. He takes his pills. Then he goes to his cupboard and takes out a suit: black. He pulls the plastic wrapper from it and sniffs for mustiness. It has been a long time in there, but the suit smells okay. He puts on one of his usual work shirts, a white one, and slips into the suit. The trousers are loose. He has to double up the waist an inch or two and tighten his belt. The jacket feels all right, so long as he wears it open. He takes a pair of shiny shoes from a box at the base of the cupboard, taps them instinctively to remove any scorpion that might have nested there, and puts them on his feet. Then he rises, finds his only tie—gray—hidden at the back of the sock drawer. He hangs it around his neck but does not tie it. Only then does he step into the hallway to look at himself in the tall mirror there.

And he smiles. He always feels slightly comical dressed like this. An impostor. He is much more comfortable in the slacks and shirt he wears most days, or even his police uniform. They are work clothes. No attempt to better himself. Yet this suit—even if the style is somewhat out of fashion these days—is a good suit. He wife chose it. It makes him look—her word—*distinguished.*

Not bad for a Kajiado goatherd, she would say on occasions like this. *Not bad at all.*

Kiunga raises his eyebrows when Mollel answers the door. —God, boss, you make me look shabby.

—You look fine, says Mollel. Kiunga is wearing jeans, a shirt, and a lightweight jacket, all made from the same denim material. The shirt is untucked and the trousers hang low on the hips—but deliberately, unlike Mollel's. Kiunga's ensemble has printed letters all over it, brand names, and despite the affected casualness, all the items are crisply pressed. Mollel even gets a whiff of cologne. The young man has gone to even more trouble than he has.

—What time does the service begin? Mollel asks.

—Nine. We have to hit the road. Traffic shouldn't be too bad, but— where do you want this? Don't want you to get oil on your good suit.

Kiunga has brought the bike up with him.

—Leave it in the hallway. Adam's staying with his grandmother for a few days. That reminds me— Mollel takes the tie from around his neck.

—Knot this for me, would you? He normally ties my ties for me.

▲ ▲ ▲

Calling George Nalo Ministries a church is a bit like calling the Maasai Mara a petting zoo. The *campus*—as the sign terms it—is sited just off the main Embakasi road, down a specially laid section of gleaming, fresh tarmac with sidewalks and neatly clipped lawns and bushes alongside, smoother and cleaner than any stretch of public road in the whole city. Approaching from this driveway, one sees a tower emerging from above the trees. It is modern and elegant: a twenty-first-century mission campanile.

Kiunga is directed by a warden in an official vest to an overflow car park, which leaves them some distance to walk. This suits Mollel. He wants to get a sense of the place. They park and join the ever-increasing throng flocking to the sound of the bells.

Mollel is glad that he'd dug out his suit. There's quite a range of finery on display: here, a father and three young boys clad in identical designer outfits descending from a gold Range Rover; there, a family knocking the dust from their shoes, repairs visible on some of their clothing, but all neatly and respectfully presented nonetheless, the little girl in pale yellow and gold chiffon with a broad satin sash and lace around the hem, suitable for a fairy princess going to a ball.

Mollel notices that there are a lot of younger adults present. This church appears to be particularly popular among that generation. The girls are smartly dressed, modest without being conservative—a few knee-length skirts, plenty of patent leather high heels. The men are in sharp suits or, like Kiunga, the strange, hybrid baggy-chic, American-style, all immaculately pressed.

They round a bend in the path, and Mollel sees the church, a wide, low structure with a pair of massive doors standing open at the front. It makes him think of one of the aircraft hangars at Wilson Aerodrome, and indeed, as he approaches, he realizes that the building is much larger than he first thought; it looks low only because it is so wide. Drawing near to the doorway, which must stand four meters high, he feels as though he is being sucked into the mouth of a giant whale.

▲ ▲ ▲

—Hi! says a young man, taking Mollel's hand and shaking it vigorously. I don't think I've seen you here before. Is this your first time?

Mollel looks at the space before him, which is slowly filling up. Inside, the building reminds him less of an aircraft hangar and more of Nyayo Stadium.

—First time here, he confirms. How can you tell? You must have hundreds of people coming here.

—Thousands! The young man laughs. He is dressed all in black, black jacket, shirt, and tie. Mollel sees twenty or so others identically dressed, greeting everyone as they come in. This usher, though, has one differentiating feature: the thick dreadlocks, pulled back and tied behind his head. For the second time that day, Mollel is reminded of his own youth. Such dreadlocks are not a common sight these days, being mostly a preserve of Maasai and of reggae fans. And there is one other group that favors the style: the criminal sect, the dreaded Kikuyu gang–cum–mystery cult whose very name inspires a unique terror in Nairobi. The Mungiki.

He looks around for Kiunga, who has effortlessly maneuvered himself to be greeted by an attractive young woman.

—We have seats for six thousand here, the usher continues, and on a Sunday there are two thousand more standing. Plus the people who come during the week. But you know, you get to spot the people who stand out. Like you, for example, with the ears.

Mollel impulsively raises his right hand to his earlobe.

—We've got a few Maasai, not many, continues the young man. My name is Benjamin, by the way. You are?

—Mollel.

—As it's your first time, *Ole* Mollel, can I suggest that you and your friend sit near the front, on the bank of seats over there? You'll get a good view and be able to follow the service more easily.

Mollel thanks him. He is impressed that the youngster has addressed him with a Maasai honorific. The greeters are obviously well trained. But despite his use of the Maa word, that young man is no Maasai himself. His accent sounds Kikuyu. Which would tie in with the dreadlocks—unless they really are just a fashion statement.

Kiunga gives a low whistle as they make their way to their seats.

—Did you see the sweetie I was talking to? he asks. Wow. I gotta change churches. Where do you usually go?

—I don't, replies Mollel. Adam's grandmother takes him to the Catholic cathedral. Me, I've not been inside one of these for ten years.

They make their way through toward the front of the enormous hall and along a bank of plastic seats, smiles of other congregants greeting them. The place is filling up. To one side of the large stage before them, a band is setting up. The guitarist picks out some notes on his electric guitar; the drummer checks his kit. In front of the stage, a man carrying a TV camera on his shoulder is chatting to a young woman with an earpiece and a microphone. Looking around, Mollel sees another couple of TV cameras alongside the stage and another high up behind him.

—They record this? he asks Kiunga.

—It's broadcast live. You haven't seen it?

—I don't have a TV, confesses Mollel.

—How do you watch football games? Do you go to a bar?

—I don't drink. And you know I don't like football. Adam watches it at his grandmother's.

—Man! says Kiunga, shaking his head. You're going to need to buy that kid more than a bike.

Before Mollel can ask what he means, a man takes to the stage. He picks up a microphone from a stand, taps it, prepares to speak. The hall is still filling up, but the background buzz drops slightly.

—Is this Nalo? asks Mollel.

—No. This must be one of the junior pastors. He's kind of a warm-up man.

—*Are you here to praise JEE-SUS?* comes the call from the stage.

Around them, the churchgoers say yes.

The pastor cups his ear. —*I said are you here to puh-raise Juh-EEEE-SUS?*

—Yes!

—*I can't hear you, Nairobi. I am saying: Are. You. Here. To puh-RAISE the LORD?*

This time, even Kiunga shouts: —Yes!

—Amen!

Whooping and clapping fill the hall. The place is now nearly full. The band members have taken their positions and are providing an accompaniment to the preacher, punctuating his pauses with drumrolls, his questions with cymbal clashes, his exclamation marks with short bursts of rhythm.

—Praise the Lord. It is so good to see you all again, brothers and sisters, on this day. And what a blessed day it is. For this is the last Sunday of Advent, the last Sabbath day before we celebrate the birth of our Lord.

—Amen!

Mollel is familiar with the story. As someone who had actually been born in a stable—or something very similar—he has always felt a certain affinity. But he can't help feeling that as far as miraculous babies are concerned, he prefers the Maasai story of Ntemelua, who was born with full faculties of speech. Ntemelua's mother and father were so frightened of their prodigy—and tired of his nagging—that they sneaked away one night, leaving him in the custody of a cow, a donkey, and a goat. When some *morans* tried to steal the animals, little Ntemelua hid himself up the cow's arse.

Now *that* is a trick Mollel would like to read about in the Gospels.

—I have to say I'm pleased to see so many brothers here today, the preacher continues. Particularly when there are so many important football matches being played.

Gentle laughter ripples through the audience. Kiunga groans. —Don't remind me! he says in Mollel's ear.

—Yes, right now, Manchester United are playing Everton. Who wants to know the score? asks the preacher.

A few hands go up. Kiunga puts his fingers in his ears. —Don't say it, don't say it, he mutters.

—Don't worry, I won't ruin the suspense, booms the preacher. You can catch the highlights when you get home. You know, it's funny. When I'm watching a big match live, my hands get clammy, my heart starts racing . . .

He mimes leaning forward, watching a game. The audience laughs in recognition.

—I hate preachers like this, whispers Kiunga to Mollel. They want to be stand-up comedians.

—I feel that, even though I'm thousands of miles away, I can still affect the outcome. I *will* my team to score. I *will* the ball to go into the goal. It's never the same, watching a recording. And you know, that's a little bit what prayer is like.

—Here comes the scripture, murmurs Kiunga.

—James four, verse two, says the preacher, and there is a ruffle of Bible pages around the room. You desire what you do not have, so you kill. You covet, but you cannot get what you want, so you quarrel and fight. You do not have, because you do not ask God.

He pauses, letting the words sink in.

—Now, I'm not saying you can pray for your team to win a football match. It doesn't work like that. However much you'd like it to!

Some more polite laughter from the listeners.

—But you can change things in your own life if you allow God to guide you. The only thing you can't change is what's already happened.

Mollel thinks of Chiku. She had had faith. She always tried to convince him, too. Whenever she spoke about Jesus, her face lit up and her eyes shone with happiness. It was one of the things that had first attracted him to her. It did him no harm to attend services and pray to the man nailed to a cross. If doing so made Chiku happy, it made him happy. But he could never understand her strange father-son God. Even though he'd long ceased to believe in his own people's mythology, he still felt it simply made much more sense.

There was Naiteru-kop, who created the world: an act that was as neutral as the animals and plants with which he furnished it.

Then there was Enkai Narok, the Black God. He was the god of love, of family, of goodness. You thanked Enkai Narok when a child was born and appealed to his protection for the spirit of a loved one when they died. At times, in the Christian Church, he recognized Enkai Narok.

When all around him closed their eyes in prayer, he felt that Enkai Narok inhabited even this place.

But there was also Enkai Nanyokie. The Red God. Enkai Nanyokie was vengeful and capricious, full of jealousy and wrath. Mollel recognized Enkai Nanyokie, too, in parts of what he heard in church. But he could never reconcile this god with the loving one. That the Christians thought the red and black gods the same entity required an intellectual leap of acrobatic proportions that Mollel had never been able to master.

The Christians called him the Old Testament God; said he was a thing of the past. And yet it was this god, this Enkai Nanyokie, who manifested himself every day. You only had to walk the streets of Nairobi to see his works. You didn't even need to go looking. If you waited long enough, the Red God would come to you. He had come to Mollel when he took Chiku away, so violently, just at the moment of his greatest happiness. And thus Mollel knew that if any god existed, his color was red.

He has stopped listening to the man and has allowed his eyes to wander to the area at one side of the stage. The young woman wearing a headset is talking into her microphone; an expectant buzz of activity surrounds the dark curtain there. The warm-up preacher is doing his best to keep the audience's attention, but it is clear that their excitement is not for his theatrics, but for the main act.

—*Amen! Thank you! Hallelujah!* finishes the preacher, and the congregation joins in, leaping to their feet. Mollel and Kiunga stand too. The band strikes up a new tune, and from the PA system, a voice starts to boom.

—Ladies and gentlemen. Brothers and sisters. From Nairobi, Kenya, direct to viewers all around the world. This is George Nalo Ministries. The word of God from the heart of Africa. Now, will you please welcome the cofounder and director of George Nalo Ministries, Dr. Wanjiku Nalo.

The curtain opens, and a large middle-aged lady walks out. She is tall and well built, with a pleasant, youthful face despite her gray hair. Her determination and dynamism are palpable even at a distance. She waves to the audience, picks out a few individuals for a special smile of acknowledgment, then takes a seat beside the large gold lectern at center stage.

—And now, here he is. Please give the most blessed Nairobi welcome to our founder, our shepherd, our guide. The one. The only. Reverend. George. Nalo!

The audience erupts, and the band bursts into a frantic, uplifting, crashing melody. Suddenly Mollel becomes aware of a previously unseen choir, at least two hundred strong, in spotless crimson gowns, at the far side of the hall. It is immaculate stagecraft. Everyone seems to know what happens next, for as the choir begins its hymn, the congregation all around them joins in with perfect unity. It is not a hymn that Mollel knows, but despite himself, he claps along to the rhythm. It is infectious. Even Kiunga's face has broken into a big, somewhat foolish grin. Just as the hymn reaches its chorus, a huge, suited man glides out from behind the curtain. He waves casually in acknowledgment of the frisson his presence causes, and he walks slowly across to the podium. He passes his wife, touching her briefly on the shoulder, and gathers some notes at the lectern. He also produces a large white handkerchief from his pocket and waits for the hymn to end.

—Hallelujah, he says.

He has a voice like a hundredweight of sharp sand. Deep, sonorous. And yet with a dry treble note. Almost like several voices. And he begins quietly, taking the microphone but holding it nonchalantly away from his face. The effect is to silence the audience, focusing them on his words.

His quietness implies power withheld.

—Exodus, chapter eighteen, verse twenty-one, he says, and Mollel sees many of those around him reach for their Bibles and flick through to the appropriate page.

—When Moses founded Israel, Nalo continues drily, he knew that the country needed temporal law as well as spiritual. He was told: look for able men from all the people, men who fear God, who are trustworthy and hate a bribe—here he turns his gaze directly to the audience for the first time, glaring outward—place such men over the people as chiefs, and let them judge the people at all times.

—Now. We may not call them chiefs anymore. We may call them politicians. But the commandment remains. Men who fear God. Men who are trustworthy. Men who hate a bribe. Does that sound like any politician you know?

A ripple of laughter reverberates around the hall.

—Those are the criteria. That is how we should select our chiefs, come the twenty-seventh day of this month. Men who fear God. Men who are trustworthy. Men who hate a bribe. And, in deference to my dear wife, I should point out that this applies to women, too.

Another polite laugh. Nalo takes his handkerchief and mops his massy brow. The act is a kind of punctuation point.

—And yet, he says. And yet I still have dear members of my flock—he waves his hand to encompass all those before him—my children, who come to me and say, Pastor, who should I vote for? Perhaps, even now, you are hoping to hear me say a name, a party, or to drop a hint, a color—orange, perhaps, or blue, or red . . . but my answer will always be the same. Who *should* you vote for?

—Those who fear God. Those who are trustworthy. Those who hate a bribe.

—Perhaps it is no wonder, when we look upon our politicians and find them so failing in every regard, that we turn to tribalism instead. If they are all corrupt, the logic goes, then we may as well vote for our kinsman. When he comes to disperse those government jobs, those constituency funds, those education grants, he'll remember his own. It may not be perfect, but life is not perfect. What more can we do?

—Fear God. Be trustworthy. Hate a bribe.

—Look around this great hall. Look around you.

The people in front of Mollel turn and look back at him and Kiunga. He takes their lead and looks back up the row of seats. It's a dizzying experience. Everyone in the room is looking around them, and then Mollel sees a flash of white hair, of pink skin high up at the back of the hall.

—Turn to those around you and shake their hands. Go on.

Kiunga puts his hand out to Mollel, and Mollel shakes it distractedly. He is straining to see the white man. He feels a tap on his elbow, and the middle-aged lady in the seat beside him proffers her hand. He can't refuse it, so he shakes her hand and then others, the hands of the couple in the row in front and the family behind, even the little girl in her father's lap.

—Praise the Lord. Hallelujah.

The audience falls quiet again, a few keen stragglers still reaching for a final handshake. Mollel bobs his head to try to see the *mzungu* again, but can't make him out.

—We greet each other in the name of the Lord because we have come together in defiance of ethnic division. When you shook your neighbors' hands just then, did you think, I am shaking hands with a Kikuyu, with a Luo, with a Kamba, with a Kisii? Did a Luhya shake hands with a Kalenjin, a Maasai with an Embu? I don't know. Because from down here, I could not tell the difference. I just saw God-fearing, trustworthy Kenyans sharing in the love of the Lord. Amen.

—*Amen.*

Mollel leans over to Kiunga and whispers, —I'll see you at the main entrance at the end of the service. Then, delicately, trying not to attract attention, he stands and picks his way past the lady next to him and to the end of the row. Once there, he goes up the steps, scanning each row as he does so. He reaches the top without seeing the *mzungu* again. At the back, there is a set of double doors and a stairwell. He slips through and follows the stairs back down to ground level. He finds himself in some sort of service corridor, windowless and bare, with ducting and pipes running along the ceiling. He hears a sudden commotion and barely has time to leap aside before dozens of choristers race past him, pulling off their crimson gowns, revealing pure white ones underneath. Following them is the woman with the headset.—*Choir two almost in position,* she shouts into her microphone. *Where on earth are those dancers?*

Mollel follows the choir along the corridor, which is curved. He passes a door and looks through the small window set into it. He's looking back up at the stage.

—Hey! What are you doing here? The voice is aggressive.

Mollel spins around. It is the young man who greeted him at the entrance, Benjamin. He stands with his arms crossed. Unsmiling. He's not wearing the black jacket he wore earlier, just a T-shirt. Now Mollel can see the strength in his arms.

—This is not a public area.

—I was looking for someone, says Mollel. A *mzungu*. He must have just passed this way.

—You're a week too late, says the young man. Last Sunday we had two hundred *wazungu,* visitors from one of our sister churches in North Carolina. But this week . . . no. Now, please . . .

—Are you sure? White hair. Old guy.

—Sir, says Benjamin in a quiet, threatening tone, you can go inside and worship the Lord or step outside and enjoy his creation. But you can't stay here.

Mollel shows his police identity card.

—Now, let me ask again, says Mollel. Have you seen a white man here today, at all? An elderly man with white hair? Do you know anyone who fits that description? The usher shakes his head, reluctantly compliant now that he's seen the ID.

—Right. I need to speak with Reverend Nalo when he comes off-stage.

—You'd better come to the greenroom, says Benjamin.

It doesn't look very green to Mollel. In fact, the only green things in the wood-paneled room are the bottles of mineral water on the sideboard, glistening attractively with beads of condensation. Mollel ponders, waiting, then thinks, What the hell, and pours himself a glassful.

He's been left alone here, but he's able to follow the show's progress thanks to a huge TV screen on one wall. Nalo in full flow, the sandy tones filled out into a deep-throated, gravelly roar. Every time he shouts the name Jesus, he brings the microphone right next to his mouth. The TV is on mute. Mollel hears him, with a few seconds' delay, through the wall.

Along the bottom of the TV screen, a scrolling text bar urges donations and offers a telephone number and Web address.

The water is cool and delicious. Mollel finishes his glass and replaces it alongside the others. He continues to inspect the room. There is no window. On the wall opposite the TV hangs a large oil painting of an eagle in full flight, a snake grasped between its talons. The inscription on a brass plaque below reads TO OUR FRIENDS IN GEORGE NALO MINISTRIES. FROM THE UNITED TABERNACLE OF CHRIST, TASHKENT, UZBEKISTAN.

Elsewhere the walls are dotted with pictures of George and Wanjiku Nalo. The Nalos shaking hands with former president Moi, President

Kibaki. President Museveni of Uganda. Bill Clinton. George W. Bush. A lot of presidents.

Nalo has finished invoking Jesus and is now visible on the screen, laying his hands upon congregants who have been brought to the stage. His mouth hangs open, his eyes are rolled back orgiastically. As he touches the temple of each person presented to him, he shakes, and they fall back, caught in the arms of their supporters. With each new case, Nalo seems to weaken, his physicality shrinking, as though it is *his* strength that is being transferred. Through the wall, Mollel hears a massed wailing, howling.

Catholic church was never like *this*.

The noise level rises abruptly, and on the TV screen Mollel sees Nalo preparing to leave the stage. At the same instant—there must be a few seconds' delay on the broadcast—the door of the greenroom bursts open and Nalo pushes in. He's even bigger than he seemed from a distance, though he is hunched and leaning wearily on the arm of the woman with the headset. She leads him to a leather sofa, where he collapses. Then she darts to the sideboard and pours cold water into Mollel's used glass and gives it to Nalo, who downs it in one gulp. She produces a towel from a drawer, and he wipes his face and neck, pulling open his collar.

Mollel makes to speak, but the woman holds up a warning finger. She leans over Nalo, removes a small black device from his pocket, and flicks a switch on it.

—The mic was live, she explains. You can talk now.

Nalo slumps back. His eyes seem shut, but he says, —Who are you?

—I'm Sergeant Mollel. Nairobi Central CID.

—Thanks, Esther. You can leave us.

—Back on in five, the woman reminds him as she leaves the room.

—That was quite a sermon, says Mollel when the door is closed.

—Glad you enjoyed it, Sergeant.

—You're not endorsing a candidate? According to the papers, most of the major preachers have come out in favor of one party or another.

Nalo raises a weary finger skyward. —*His* is the only endorsement that matters.

—The papers say you may be a candidate yourself in five years. I suppose in that case, it's best to be neutral now.

—Neutral. Fearing God. Trustworthy. And hates a bribe. That's me, Sergeant. Does it describe you, too?

—Most of it.

—Only it seems to me that whenever I have the pleasure of meeting one of our public custodians, there's usually a certain *tithe* to be extracted. What is it this time? Our singing has broken city noise regulations? You've found a fire door somewhere obstructed by a fallen leaf? Or perhaps the grass outside was growing a little too quickly, and you want to book it for speeding? Whatever it is, please talk to one of our church wardens. I never handle cash.

—Surely, replies Mollel, a bribe is equally hateful whether you're giving or receiving?

—There is a difference between bribery and extortion. If I pay a policeman to let me off a legitimate offense, that's a bribe. If he's fabricated the fine, that's extortion, backed up by the threat of force. Look around you. Look at what I've created. Do you think I could have made an organization like this without attracting the worst sort of attention? Wherever there's an eagle, there are vultures. Let me tell you something. Back in the days when we were still running from a tin shack in Kibera, we were building a following. We'd started to put up awnings outside to give shade to all the people who could not fit in for the services. When we passed around the collection pots in those days, we didn't see notes, checks. We saw fifty-cent, one-bob coins. We saw homemade trinkets and bags of millet. One day I saw a child's doll—a little girl had given her favorite toy. These people had nothing, Sergeant, nothing. And yet they gave. And it added up.

—Well, you can imagine what sort of effect that had in Kibera. Pretty soon we had the gangs come around. The Mungiki. Wanted to tithe our tithes. I said fine. You can have your payment. You know what would have happened if I'd said no?

—I can imagine.

—So I gave it to them. But, I said, on the condition that you come to service. That way you can see what's going into the pot and know I'm not cheating you. So they started coming to service. And you know what? Some of them stayed. They stopped taking their commission and started helping out.

The door to the stage opens and Benjamin enters, followed by Wanjiku Nalo.

—In fact, continued Nalo, here is one of those young men now.

Benjamin glares at Mollel.

—I wondered if you were ex-Mungiki, Mollel says. The dreadlocks.

—Once, I believed that the only way to leave the Mungiki was with a police bullet in the head. Reverend Nalo gave me an alternative.

—Thank you, Benjamin, says Wanjiku Nalo. Tell Sophie we'll be right out.

Benjamin leaves, and Wanjiku takes a seat on the sofa next to her husband. —What's all this about? she asks.

—I was just wondering the same thing, says Nalo.

—I need to ask you some questions about Orpheus House, says Mollel. He has not been offered a seat and is still standing.

—On a Sunday? says Wanjiku. Officer, this is the busiest day of our week. Can't you come by the office tomorrow?

—This is a murder inquiry.

That silences them.

—A young woman was found murdered in Uhuru Park on Saturday morning. We have reason to believe that her body may have been dumped in the storm drain at Orpheus House.

—How awful, says Wanjiku. But Officer, the place is shut up. Awaiting renovation. If someone's illegally accessed the site, we can't be held responsible.

—There's a second line of inquiry, replies Mollel. The victim had recently come under the protection of a religious group, one that helps prostitutes get off the streets. That would be your organization, wouldn't it?

—It could be, admits Wanjiku. There are a few charities doing similar work. Orpheus House is probably the best known. Can you tell us the poor girl's name?

—We only know her as Lucy, says Mollel. A Maasai.

George Nalo glances at his wife. He pulls the towel from around his neck and wipes his corpulent face with it.

—Lucy, says Wanjiku quietly. Yes. She was one of our clients. So she's dead?

—You don't seem shocked at the idea.

—It's very sad. But no, I am not shocked. Officer, you know the sort of life these girls lead. That's what we're trying to save them from. If they insist upon returning to the streets, there's very little we can do for them.

—And that's what Lucy did? She returned to the streets?

—I suppose she must have. She just vanished one night. Upped and left. A while ago. Just before we shut down the old building.

The greenroom door opens again and the woman with the headset looks in. She holds a fresh shirt, tie, and jacket on a hanger. —Reverend, you're on in two!

Nalo rises to his feet and takes the clothing.

—This is where I must bid you adieu, Officer, he says, pulling off his shirt. I hope you find whoever did this vile act. We'll pray for Lucy.

—I may need to speak to you again, says Mollel. And I need access to the building on Upper Hill—

—There's no point bothering my husband with this, interjects Wanjiku. He's just the spiritual guide. I'm the medical director of that project. I deal with the day-to-day side of things.

Nalo has hastily pulled on his new shirt and jacket. He stands still while Wanjiku ties his tie. She kisses him on the lips—tall as he is, she is almost the same height—and Nalo bursts through the door and heads back onto the stage, a wave of euphoric cheering greeting his return.

Then she turns to Mollel. —I have a meeting of the women's caucus after the service, but I can take you to the project quickly. We should be able to find Lucy's records. But I warn you: as far as patient confidentiality is concerned, I believe it applies just as much after death. You can have her contact information, but not her medical notes. If you want them, you'll need a court order. And for that matter, the Upper Hill house is half demolished inside, and dangerous. The only way you're getting in there is with a hard hat and a warrant.

As Mollel follows her out the door into the service corridor, he glances back at Benjamin the usher.

—The Lord watches over his errant lambs, he says to Mollel. May you not stray too far from the path.

Mollel wonders whether that is a blessing or a threat.

—This, says Wanjiku as they walk into a small building not far from the church, is Orpheus House. At least its present incarnation.

Mollel looks around the schoolroom. For there's no disguising what it is: posters of cartoonish biblical scenes adorn the walls, and the desks and chairs stacked up against the whiteboard are almost laughably child-size. The rest of the room is partitioned, sectioned off by green medical screens.

—We're conducting Sunday school in the open air until the new building is ready. Right now we don't have any residential clients. We're just offering a medical and counseling service.

Mollel thinks about the old abandoned house on Upper Hill, the childish surroundings of this converted schoolroom, and the bright white architect's vision of the future Orpheus House. He remembers a snatch of catechism from his time with Chiku at the Catholic church: the Father, the Son, and the Holy Ghost. He's never understood the concept—frankly, he doubts anyone really does—but perhaps this has something to do with it: the way the old becomes renewed in pursuit of the ideal.

—Was Lucy a residential client? asks Mollel.

—Yes. Our last one, at the old place.

—How many others were there?

—Three or four at a time. They stayed between one week and six months. We've had dozens of women pass through.

—And your success rate?

—Pretty high. I can put you in touch with dozens of women who are now leading fulfilling lives in our community. You might even have seen some of them in church just now. Of course, there are always those, like Lucy, who fall by the wayside.

—How long was she with you?

—From memory, it was just a few weeks. But I'll have to find the records. Excuse me.

Wanjiku opens the door to a closet. The door jangles. On its inner surface it is covered with cup hooks, on each hook a set of keys. A scrawl of marker pen above each hook seems to indicate the purpose of each set.

The floor and shelves of the closet are piled high with cardboard filing boxes, lids barely shut, overflowing with ledgers, files, and stacks of paper.

—We haven't had a chance to sort out the paperwork yet. I think Lucy's records should be in this box.

Wanjiku reaches up to the topmost box. Despite the fact that she's probably an inch or two taller than he is—and, he guesses, just as strong—Mollel chivalrously steps forward. Wanjiku steps aside so that Mollel can get into the closet doorway. He takes the box. It's heavy—he turns on his axis and looks for somewhere to put it down.

—Here, she says, pushing aside one of the medical screens.

He sees an examination table with steel stirrups spread wide; a trolley piled high with kidney dishes, clamps, swabs. He drops the box with a thump onto the table.

—I'm a gynecologist, says Wanjiku, sensing his surprise at the sudden appearance of this incongruous apparatus. The most important thing we can do for these women, even if we can't persuade them to give up the business, is to take care of their health. We give them a checkup, a blood test. Talk to them about STDs.

She lifts the lid off the box and starts to sift through its contents.

—Ever see any cases of female circumcision? Mollel asks.

She turns to him with a flash of anger. —Female genital mutilation, you mean! Don't soften it by suggesting it's merely ceremonial. Or some kind of cosmetic procedure. A clitoris is not a foreskin, you know. How'd you like to have the whole top of your penis cut off?

—I wouldn't! Mollel says defensively. And honestly.

—Statistically, it's on the decrease. The message seems to be getting through, especially among you Maasai. But it's still common practice in many tribes. The worst cases I've seen are from some of the northern nomads. They don't stop at a clitorectomy, you know. They can remove the whole labia. And there's nothing subtle about the way they do it.

With the image of Lucy's corpse in his mind, Mollel begins to feel queasy.

Wanjiku takes a set of stapled notes from the box. She glares at him with a fierce passion.

—You know *why* they do it, don't you?

She's drawn level with him, and Mollel is conscious of her physical presence: if a man squared up to him like this, he would be preparing for a fight. But this is a woman. A gray-haired doctor. A pastor's wife.

He is utterly unnerved.

He answers, weakly,—Tradition?

—Tradition be damned! They do it for *power*. These pathetic men. *Old* men. You know full well, a Maasai can't wed until he's an elder. That's well into his thirties. Then, when he's rich, he can take another wife. He's getting on by then. A third, if he's successful enough. Probably in his sixties by now. These girls, they're child brides. But they grow up. The old man can't even satisfy one of them, let alone three. And all those young, virile, unmarried *morans* in the village. What to do? You cut off female sexuality at its source.

Mollel does not answer.

He knows it is true. It is all part of why he left. It is why Honey and Lucy and countless others left, and are leaving, and will leave.

But it's hard for him to hear these words in the mouth of a Kikuyu.

To a Maasai, a Kikuyu is the ultimate sellout.

The two tribes once considered themselves cousins. The white man might class one Bantu, the other Nilotic—but the Kikuyu and the Maasai have always overlapped when it comes to territory, not to mention costume, mythology, and vocabulary.

Sometimes they fought—minor skirmishes to full-scale wars—but it was a rivalry based on respect. Time was, the only outsider it was acceptable for a Maasai to marry was a Kikuyu, and vice versa.

When the Kikuyu rose up against the white man, it seemed to be a replay of the Maasai wars against the invaders of the previous century. But then they won, and they renamed the country after their holy Kikuyu mountain. By this time, you never saw a Kikuyu in traditional dress. They seemed to prefer the ridiculous trousers and neckties of the foreigners.

Even though he married one—even though his son is half Kikuyu— even though he himself has long since rejected such tradition, it pains Mollel to hear a Kikuyu criticize the Maasai way of life. The Maasai might as well be invisible when it comes to government posts, civil servants, or—as Mollel well knows—the police. They may not be the great industrialists, the celebrities, the movers and shakers, but when the tourist board wants to attract visitors, who do they put on the billboards? If ever a picturesque African is needed for a pop video or fashion shoot, whose image do they use?

Tradition, unfortunately, cuts both ways.

Wanjiku Nalo is glaring at him as though he, personally, is responsible for centuries of gender oppression. She rips the cover sheet from the stack of notes.

—This is all I can give you without a court order. Full name, age, the dates of her stay.

—That's enough to be going on with. One more thing. When Lucy came to you, had she been—was she already—mutilated?

—Medical confidentiality, Sergeant.

—And you're still insisting on a warrant before you let me into the old Orpheus House?

—We've gutted the place. It's not safe. I'm not prepared to take liability.

—Fine, concedes Mollel. Well, there's little chance of getting court time for a warrant until after Christmas. We'll just have to leave it until then, if it proves necessary at all. Thank you for your time, Doctor. I'd better find my colleague. I'm sure he's wondering where I've got to.

On the way out, Mollel feels the keys in his pocket. The ones he palmed when going to get the file box. The ones that had been hanging inside the closet door on the hook marked ORPHEUS HOUSE.

There was a time—not so long ago—when Nairobi stopped on a Sunday. Apart from churches, the only places that opened their doors were some of the Muslim businesses in areas such as Eastleigh. Now, Sunday is pretty much like a weekday, especially as far as the Mombasa Road traffic is concerned.

Mollel rolls down the window of the Land Rover and sighs. They are stuck by Nyayo Stadium, the low roadside trees providing some relief from the overhead sun but also creating a fresh danger: marabou storks. They love this stretch of highway and have colonized the trees here, feasting on the pickings dropped by the numerous hawkers who ply their trade through the stationary traffic. Four feet tall, with long, sharp beaks, they are totally fearless of humans, and they teeter among the crowds of waiting *matatu* passengers, pouncing on tidbits. When threatened, they spread their dirty gray wings and flap lazily into the trees above, whence their frequent and hefty bowel movements turn them into a menace for pedestrians and cars alike.

There is something about the marabou stork—*en-tialoo* in Mollel's language—that reminds him of an ancient Maasai: skinny legs propping up a hunched body wrapped in a shabby *shuka*; scrawny neck emerging to a bald, mottled head. Even its movements are those of an old, dying man.

He realizes that he's not thinking about marabou storks anymore. He's recalling the time—one long, dry season—when he had been moving the family herd from the dry Kajiado plains up into the lush pastures of the highlands. The sky was darkening, and he had promised his mother and Lendeva that he would return to their temporary *boma* in time to protect the animals from the creatures of the night.

But the dogs would not return at his call, and investigating, he found them, whining anxiously, at the feet of an old man huddled in his *shuka,* sitting against a rock and watching the sun descend in the sky.

The old man's hollow cheeks were covered with gray stubble, and his eyes were pale blue and cataract-ridden. He seemed impossibly frail and featherlight to the young Mollel, as though the slightest breath of wind would simply pick him up and carry him away.

He had come there to die.

It was the Maasai way, to die alone like this, and Mollel had wondered whether he might deftly retrace his steps and escape without disturbing the man. But he beckoned, and Mollel came closer. Neither spoke, but the old man raised a bony finger to the sheep and goats, and Mollel knew he must attend to them. He gathered them into a thicket and tied the largest ones there, and the youngsters huddled around for warmth. Then he cut a few thorn branches, placed them all around, and tied some of the goat's bells to them, as warning, should a lion or leopard attempt to get close. Then he returned to the old man's side.

He was dead. But he had wanted Mollel beside him so that the boy could guide his spirit into the night. So Mollel sat beside the stranger's corpse, guarding it and his flock until the first rays of gold gave shadows to the trees of the landscape before them.

Long ago, Mollel had begun to conflate the memory of the old man with his few memories of his father. His father had been a vigorous man the last time Mollel saw him. But had he lived, he would now be old and frail. If his time had already come, Mollel hoped that he had someone to sit vigil beside him.

He is shaken from his dreamlike state by the beeping of Kiunga's phone. Kiunga laughs. He had noticed that Mollel was dropping off.

—These police Land Rovers don't have AC. Makes it hard to stay awake in traffic jams.

—It's not that, says Mollel. I was just thinking.

—I do my best thinking in traffic, says Kiunga. Which I suppose, given that I live in Nairobi, ought to make me some kind of genius.

He slips the car into neutral and puts on the hand brake so that he can rise up in his seat and reach into his trouser pocket for his mobile phone. He slides back into place and looks at the phone's screen. Then he tut-tut-tuts.

—What is it?

—Take a look.

He hands Mollel the phone. Mollel looks at the message on the screen.

—My Kikuyu is too rusty. I can't read it.

—You're better off. It's another one of those hate messages doing the rounds. Says the Luos are massing. If their man loses the election, they're going to take Nairobi and kill any Kikuyu who stands in their way.

—Who's it from?

—I don't know. The number doesn't show. They have a way of bypassing the sender ID.

Some cars move up ahead, and Kiunga starts the engine. He edges the Land Rover forward less than a car's length and then stops, inches from the bumper of the vehicle in front. He kills the engine once more.

—You been getting a lot of these messages? asks Mollel.

—That's the second today. Scroll through, you'll see more.

Mollel looks through the message folder on Kiunga's phone. He opens one from someone called Mandy. He reads it aloud, trying to decipher the text shorthand.

—See you L-eight-R big boy I M gonna . . .

—Give it here! says Kiunga, snatching the phone back. Not that one! That's personal.

—Sorry, says Mollel. How come you've got all these messages and I haven't?

—The ladies just find me irresistible, I guess.

—I meant the anonymous ones.

—You have an account or use phone cards?

—An account.

—Me too. I reckon whoever's sending these has someone at the phone company checking off the names. Kiunga, Ngugi, Mungai, Mwangi, Wachira, Wambui. Not hard to tell the Kikuyus. It's even easier to spot the names of Luo subscribers. Otieno, Oketch, Odhiambo. You know Orengo, the desk sergeant? He's been getting messages in Jaluo saying that the Kikuyus are the ones who are going to attack first.

Although all the major political parties denied it, this election was firmly dividing along ethnic lines. President Kibaki's Party of National Unity was dominated by the Kikuyu. Raila Odinga's opposition, the Orange Democratic Movement, had the western Luo tribe at its core. Others among Kenya's forty or so tribal groups tended to gravitate to one or the other.

—*Esaa Enkai Nanyokie*, mutters Mollel, and despite the heat, he shudders.

—What's that? asks Kiunga.

—Something I just recalled, replies Mollel. In my language, it means Hour of the Red God. The Maasai believe it's a time when madness descends. When people turn against each other and when anger is the only human instinct.

—Sounds about right, says Kiunga. I know you Maasai think there are only two tribes in Kenya, yourselves and everyone else, but the way this election's shaping up, things are going to get nasty. And it looks like I'm not the only one who thinks so.

Kiunga gestures out the window. —All this jam. It's people queuing for Nakumatt. Look.

Mollel looks out his window and notices for the first time that the traffic jam they're stuck in is caused by cars backed up to get into the car park of the large supermarket whose entrance lies ahead. Now that he's seen this, something else clicks too: the people passing by the car on both sides are not the usual traffic hawkers selling newspapers, trinkets, and fruit. They're ordinary people, carrying loads of shopping, laden with cardboard cartons and plastic bags. Bags of grain like maize, flour, and millet; bottles of water; canned goods. A lady strides purposefully past with a baby strapped to her back in a *khanga*; a similar shawl across her breast bulges with tin cans.

—Tell me this is just normal Christmas shopping, says Mollel.

Kiunga laughs. —Haven't you been stocking up, Mollel? You must be the only person in Nairobi who thinks this election is going to pass off with no trouble.

Mollel feels a hit of dismay. He has not stocked up. His meager provisions would barely feed himself and Adam for a day. It's lucky the boy is with Faith.

He has been so caught up in this murder case that he has completely underestimated the looming situation. The threat of political violence has been a remote one for him, until now.

—The General Service Unit! he croaks.

—What about them?

—It must have been the GSU that Superglue Sammy heard in Uhuru Park. If there's going to be trouble, they'd need to set up some sort of command post in the center of the city. That's the ideal location. It's the closest open space to both Parliament and the Central Business District.

—Why the secrecy, then? asks Kiunga.

—The GSU only take commands from State House, says Mollel. If word spread that they're already preparing a command post—

Kiunga finishes his thought. —It would be taken as a sign that the government is planning to steal this election.

—Would they kill someone to cover it up? asks Mollel.

—Who knows what those bastards are capable of? What I do know is that if Lucy got in their way . . .

He leaves this thought unfinished. He does not need to elaborate. Everyone knows that no woman is safe when the GSU are around.

The common perception of the General Service Unit is that they make the Mungiki look like girl scouts. Rumor has it that they are the direct descendants of the paid death squads the British used against the Mau Mau: when the former freedom fighters took over, they inherited the whole apparatus and, rather than disband them, employed them against their rivals.

In Moi's day, the GSU became a byword for repression, and the very presence of their dark green uniforms and crimson berets was enough to quell dissent. Those who were not intimidated tended to end up in the basement of the Interior Ministry building, where construction workers in the late nineties found an abandoned complex of hidden torture chambers.

Even though Moi has long since entered enforced retirement, the GSU retains its fearful reputation.

—Maybe they killed Lucy because she was a witness, says Mollel. She might have taken a client to Uhuru Park and stumbled across their maneuvers. But what happened to the client? And why mutilate her like that?

—Perhaps the client's body has yet to turn up, says Kiunga darkly. And as for the mutilation . . . some of those guys regard rape as an occupational benefit. Who knows how far they'd go when they're let off the leash?

—We need to warn Sammy. If they've eliminated one witness . . .

It's not easy to get off the static dual highway, and it's another twenty minutes before they get to a stretch where the median strip is clear enough of trees, rocks, and fencing for the Land Rover to get across. Although the traffic is still heavy in this direction, it is moving, and they reach Uhuru Park in another half hour.

The car parked, they head immediately back to Sammy's palm among the bushes, but there is no sign of him. They cruise the streets for a couple of hours, checking all of Superglue Sammy's regular haunts, speaking to some of the other beggars who are known to hang out with him.

He seems to have vanished off the face of the earth.

They're heading south again. They've left the snarl-up of city traffic behind them and are back on Mombasa Road, but long past the stadium. They have taken a detour through the district known as South C, and now the traffic is more free-flowing. They pass the new office blocks being built on either side of the highway. Construction work is taking place wherever Mollel looks. This part of town is barely recognizable from even a few months before. It seems at times as though the whole city is in a state of flux.

The road itself does not escape the constant churn of development. At Athi River they are forced to take a diversion where a new stretch of highway is being built, and they quit the tarmac and rumble and judder along a rutted, dusty track.

Progress sometimes means taking a step back.

The traffic is still heavy, and numerous *matatus* and even long-distance buses take advantage of the informal setup to deviate from the track and plow across the open country on both sides, swerving around any obstacles, creating new paths and clouds of dust as they do so. It's a free-for-all, and Mollel is glad of the Land Rover's ground clearance when they are forced to swerve off the track by an intercity bus bearing down on them, lights flashing and horn blaring out a ghastly tune. So what if they have right-of-way? Their two tons can't argue with his fifteen.

The road reconvenes at the cement works, and there's a bottleneck as all the vehicles jockey to regain the tarmac. Mollel rolls up his window to block the choking dust that floods in any time they slow down. The only way to avoid it is to drive faster than it can blow in. Here, it has an acrid, alkaline taste from the spill-off from the factory and the waste ash that falls from the trucks bringing it to make cinder blocks. It is said that Athi River dwellers dare not go outside with their hair wet for fear of their locks setting hard.

Mollel recalls his own circumcision ceremony—he and his brother, Lendeva, both in their early teens, grinning at each other with their faces whitened with ash—and he puts the thought from his mind.

They cross the bridge over the river, low at this time of year, despite the rains. If the girl's body had not been stopped in the park, this is where she would have washed up—or, ultimately, six hundred kilometers away in the Indian Ocean. This river also serves as sewer to most of Nairobi's informal settlements—in other words, the city's slums. Mollel notices a tanker truck parked down at the water's edge, a man holding a thick suction pipe in the six inches or so of river. The sign on the tanker's side reads CLEAN DRINKING WATER.

They roll into Kitengela, the last significant township this side of Nairobi, before the city gives way to the Kajiado plain. It's a busy, thriving area. Church is out, and Sunday night is a time for socializing, for seeing friends, and for being seen in one's finery. The *nyama choma* joints along the roadside are doing a brisk business, and the smell of roast meat makes Kiunga cast a longing glance at Mollel.

—I haven't eaten since lunchtime, boss, he pleads.

—It's only six!

—Exactly. I usually have something midafternoon. Just to keep me going.

—We're nearly there. Mollel takes out his notepad and looks at the address Honey wrote for them the previous night. "Paradise Towers, Prison Road, Kitengela. Next to the Happy Days Abattoir." Take this right.

▲ ▲ ▲

They turn down Prison Road. Paradise Towers is a four-story apartment block—four and a half, to be accurate, as the fifth level is a concrete floor with reinforced piles sticking out of it, the owners presumably awaiting a time when they can afford to build further. The ground floor is occupied by the usual array of enterprises—a mobile phone shop, a barber, a *nyama choma* joint.

—Remember, she asked us to park away from the building, says Mollel.

—*Sawa sawa.* Kiunga drives past a few buildings and stops the car outside a corrugated iron shack with a sign advertising VIDEO GAMES 10/- PER GO. As they get out, Mollel sees a group within, young men and boys clustered around a TV screen. A car-racing game is being played, and the whole group leans from left to right as the player takes the corners of the racetrack.

A couple of youths are hanging around at the door. —You two, says Kiunga. Watch this car. Anything happens to it, you're paying for the damage.

—And if nothing happens? asks one of the boys.

—Ten bob.

They grin. —Each?

—*If* nothing happens.

—Don't worry, Officer. We'll take good care of your wheels.

The two detectives walk to Paradise Towers. There's enough foot traffic for them to discreetly melt away from the police Land Rover. At the center of the facade, between a shop front and a noisy bar, there's a staircase, where they pause.

—Listen, Kiunga, says Mollel. With Sammy gone, Honey is our only witness. I don't want you to upset her.

—Upset her? Kiunga gives him a quizzical look.

—You know what I mean. Last time you were pretty hard on her.

—She's a *poko*, Mollel. Prostitutes like her are used to worse than us.

—Maybe. But that's not the way I want to play it.

A frown crosses Kiunga's brow, but he seems to assent to his superior officer, and they make their way up to the fourth floor. Once there, the landing takes the form of a balcony that runs the length of the front of the building. There are no numbers on the doors. By the close spacing, Mollel reckons they're just single rooms. His suspicion is confirmed when he walks past an open door and catches a glimpse of a family living in a space not much bigger than one of the holding cells at Central. Next, they pass a communal bathroom with the door open, a woman inside washing what seems like a schoolful of children.

They come to the end of the balcony. —She said it was this one, says Mollel. He raps on the door with his knuckles. He wonders whether anyone inside could hear it above the sounds of traffic and screaming kids and passersby and music from the bar below. But after only a moment he hears the scrape of a latch being pulled back, and the door opens.

A woman answers, and Kiunga says, —Sorry. We were looking for someone else.

Mollel looks at her closely: smooth, shaved head; average height; Maasai features. It is Honey.

She laughs. —Come in, she says.

Kiunga still looks nonplussed as they enter the cramped, bare space. He breathes an *oh* of realization when he sees the long, glossy wig carefully placed upon a stand.

—The four-inch heels make a difference, too, she says with a smile. Sorry to disappoint you, boys. Not quite so attractive in the real world, eh?

Mollel surprises himself when he says, —You look lovely. Then, in his embarrassment, he looks at Kiunga, who raises an eyebrow at him.

Honey laughs again. —Kind of you to say so, Sergeant. But fellow Maasai aren't really my target market. You know? Now, I would offer you a seat, but . . .

She waves a hand around the small room. It is bare except for a foam mattress on the floor, covered by a *shuka*; a cooking ring attached directly to a gas cylinder and a few utensils in a pot next to it; a dressing table; and a row of clothes on hangers, dangling from a cane suspended from two pieces of string tied to two nails tacked to the ceiling. Another *shuka* covers the small window on the far wall.

—You both lived here? asks Kiunga.

—We shared, yes, says Honey. This is just somewhere to sleep. We both managed pretty well. This is not somewhere to bring clients, if that's what you're thinking.

—No, I'm sure it's not to their taste, says Kiunga, a note of sarcasm creeping into his voice. I expect you take them to the international hotels—the Balmoral, the Splendid. Perhaps you slip the night manager a hundred bob to let you ply the bars. Or is the lunchtime trade more your thing? Bribing the housekeepers to give you an hour in a vacant room before the paying guest checks in?

Honey flashes Mollel a distressed look. —I thought we were going to be all right about—about what I do?

—What you do, says Kiunga flatly, is what got your friend killed.

—That's one theory, says Mollel, flashing his colleague a glance of warning.

Honey turns to Mollel, eyes glistening. —Can I speak to you alone, please? she asks in Maa.

Just as the night before, Mollel is stumped for a reply, so long has it been since he's conversed in his own language. Finally he says to Kiunga in English, —Why don't you go get some food?

—With pleasure, says Kiunga. Then, to Honey: —We're only try-ing to help, you know.

She acknowledges him with a nod.

—Get you something? he asks Mollel.

—No, thanks. I'll see you downstairs.

—Give me a shout if you need anything, says Kiunga, and he meets Mollel's eye. Mollel just wants to be rid of him and is cross that Kiunga has disregarded his advice. But Kiuga's look says *be careful.* Then he leaves.

—He's a good guy, really, says Mollel.

—I'm sure he is, says Honey. But you know, I can hear it in his voice. The contempt. The disgust. To him I'm just another K Street *poko.* Lucy's the same. Dead or alive, the job is all we are. That's why I came to you. I thought perhaps you'd have more sympathy for a poor little Maasai girl who went and got herself killed. That you'd see the person, not just the profession.

—I do.

—Yet you think it was the job that got her killed?

—We just go on the evidence. It is what it is. The location, what she was wearing, the time of night. We think she may have gone there with a client. Perhaps he did it, perhaps she disturbed someone, saw something. If we could just find the client . . .

Honey throws her hands up in exasperation. Mollel continues: —Statistically, prostitute murders . . .

—Statistics! she wails. I'll show you statistics!

She flies to the door and to the balcony rail outside. For an instant Mollel believes she is about to throw herself over. But she stops there, hands gripping the rail tightly, knuckles pale, elbows locked.

—Come! she shouts. Look for yourself!

Mollel joins her at the rail.

The sun is setting. The skyscrapers of the city center are just visible as inky purple silhouettes on the horizon against the crimson sky. The foreground is a panorama of houses and water towers, a landscape of corrugated iron, concrete, and thatched *makuti* roofs. Every square inch seems populated. Television aerials sprout like seedlings, satellite dishes like fungi. Mobile phone masts and mosque minarets break the monotony, pushing up as if attempting to escape the humanity below. And where the sky darkens, away from the city, the cement works stand illuminated in halogen and phosphorus, steaming and suppurating dust—a white, powdery moon city in contrast with sun-soaked, blood-soaked Nairobi to the northwest.

The noise is constant: mechanical crashing from the cement works, the rumble of traffic on the highway, music, prayer, shouts, screams, laughter, life. Mollel can hear hundreds of human voices, but apart from the woman at his side, he cannot see a single human being until he looks down. Then the street opens up before him with all its pulsing vitality. People course its length, moving like ants in a trail, each picking his own way but each a constituent part of the two-way flow. Mollel spots Kiunga leaning on the counter of a *nyama choma* joint across the street; he's chewing on a chicken leg and chatting up the serving girl. Farther down the street is their car, the two boys from the video shack lounging proprietarily against a wheel arch. Families, spruce in their Sunday best, little girls in puffy satin dresses and boys in replica lounge suits; a sausage vendor pushing his brazier; hawkers selling fruit and mosquito bats and magazines; *matatu* touts drumming up trade; goats and chickens nonchalantly grazing on trash whenever a spot of clear ground appears.

—You know, says Honey, this city didn't even exist a hundred years ago. It was our land then. *N'garan'airobi*. The place of cold springs. All these people—these Kikuyus, Luos, Merus, Embus, Kalenjin, Luhyas, and whatever else—they're here because the white man came here one day and said, *This is a nice, cool, fertile part of the country. I'll build my city here.* Look down at that street. How many people do you reckon there are there?

—Five, six hundred? guesses Mollel.

—And that's one little side street. There are twenty, thirty streets like it in Kitengela. And Kitengela's just one district. There's Mlolongo, Athi, South B, South C, Embakasi, Donholm, Pipeline, Industrial Area. They all have streets like this, full of people. And we're only talking about the districts in this part of town. What's that, a quarter, an *eighth* of the city?

He shrugs. The scale of the place seems unknowable. Dizzying.

—There are all the rich areas, Karen, Hardy, Lavington, Westlands. The Indian districts. Then Somali-town—Eastleigh. And I've not even started on Mathare, Kibera, Kawangware, Dagoretti—if you think it's crowded here, those areas make this place look like the Mara.

Mollel feels a slight tightening in his chest, a shallowness of breath. It's a physical memory of his first arrival in the city, a boy who'd grown up in a village of two dozen, whose only experience of crowds had been a herd of goats or market day with two or three hundred people milling about. He'd found Nairobi overwhelming, terrifying, exciting, invigorating: he'd hated it and loved it and realized, with joy and fear, that *this* was the wilderness he'd been hoping to lose himself in.

—It's not our place anymore, he says.

—No, she replies. Nairobi does not belong to the Maasai. It belongs to those people down there. People from all over Kenya. All over the world. Ten million of them. There's your statistic. Ten million people in this city. What's one *poko* less?

—That's not the way I feel, says Mollel.

—Really? And yet that's the way you're conducting this investigation. She was killed because she was a prostitute.

—It's the way the evidence points, protests Mollel.

The sky is dark. A lightbulb flickers to life on the balcony. Honey turns to Mollel.

—What about Orpheus House? she demands. I told you, the last time I saw her, she was staying there. You admitted that the drain leads to the spot where she was found.

—It's a stretch, he says. If she wasn't dumped in the park, there are dozens of places farther up the drain where the body could have been washed from.

Honey is silent a moment. Then she says, —So you don't believe me, that she'd quit the streets. You still think it's the fact that she was working as a prostitute that caused her death?

Mollel's answer is silence.

—What if I told you she could not have been working? What if I could prove that she had not been working for months?

—That might change things, says Mollel.

Honey fixes him with her dark eyes. —Last time I saw her, she says, Lucy was pregnant. She was going to have a baby. And it would have been born anytime now.

Mollel reels. For a moment he doubts his ears. He casts his mind back to the body. There had been no sign of pregnancy. He hardly dares contemplate what that means. But he must.

—Why didn't you tell me this before?

—I'm only just beginning to trust you. There's a chance—a slim chance—that this baby might still be alive. Lucy might have delivered it before she was murdered. In which case, that baby's in danger.

—From who?

—Don't you see? The father. Lucy's powerful, important client. He eliminated her. And to keep his secret, he'll probably want to eliminate the baby, too. From what she told me, he has contacts all the way through the police department. That's why I needed to know I could trust you.

—You're going to have to trust me now, says Mollel. You're going to have to tell me everything.

—But you won't tell anyone about the baby? Even— She nods down to the street, where Kiunga is still eating.

—No.

—Then there is more I need to tell you. The last time I saw Lucy was not three months ago. It was last week. I was missing her. I wanted to track her down. I knew the place they'd taken her to, that old house on Upper Hill. I banged on the gate, but the whole place looked closed up. Then, as I was about to leave, I saw her. At the window by the front door. Just for a second. Then the old man came, the guard, and chased me away. If you want to find out what happened to Lucy, that's where you need to go. Orpheus House.

13 Mollel asks Kiunga to drop him in town, tells him he wants to walk home.

—At this time of night? Kiunga says. Are you crazy, boss?

Mollel shakes the flashlight he's taken from the car. The batteries are dead. He passes it back to Kiunga, who drops it into the glove box and fumbles in his pocket. —Here. Take this. Good job I'm trying to cut down, anyway.

He throws Mollel his cigarette lighter. —Not as good as a flashlight, but it might be some use to you.

—Thanks.

Mollel watches the Land Rover disappear, Kiunga off to his cozy bed. Then he swiftly changes direction and heads for Upper Hill.

Outside Orpheus House, he looks over the gate for any sign of the old man, Githaka. But the place is deserted.

In the light of a distant streetlamp he looks through the keys he swiped from Wanjiku Nalo's closet, selects one, and tries it in the padlock on the gate. It clicks open. Gingerly, he opens it just wide enough to slip through. Inside, he crouches and feels around in the leaf litter until he finds what he needs: a stick, just large enough to keep the gate shut while he is within.

▲ ▲ ▲

Every footstep seems to crackle with explosive potential in that silent darkness. But he creeps over the gravel, past the storm drain cover, into the greater, looming mass that is all he can distinguish of the house.

Here, he dares not flick the lighter into life, so he gropes his way forward until he feels the cold stone wall. Then, by memory, he works his way toward the door, which is concealed behind a heavy iron grille. Instinct tells him there should be another padlock there. There is. His fingertips find it eventually, and he fumbles with the keys, trying them at random until one slides into the barrel.

Then, one more door, for this a large iron latchkey whose keyhole is mercifully easy to locate.

And now he stands within Orpheus House. Getting in has not been difficult.

Mollel does not believe in ghosts. But he believes that evil endures. And inside this empty house, he can feel it. It has a dry, dusty, empty smell. The only light is a murky grayness that leaches in through the barred window next to the front door.

That must be the window at which Honey had seen Lucy. Mollel shivers and reminds himself once again that he does not believe in ghosts. All the same, he is sorely tempted to spark up Kiunga's lighter for a moment, just to get a sense of the space around him.

He does not do it. He recalls from his daytime visit that the window to this room has no curtain. Can't risk Githaka or anyone else seeing a light within.

It's only natural to be afraid, he tells himself. If I'm caught here trespassing, entering without a warrant, I'll be kicked off the force.

Yes, he decides. *That's* why I'm afraid. Perfectly natural caution.

He almost convinces himself, too, when he hears a scratching noise travel along the ceiling above him, right across the room and beyond. It's all he can do to prevent himself from using the lighter, if only for the comfort the flame would bring. But he does not, and by the time the sound has gone, he is sure it was just a mouse.

He edges forward, heading toward the outline of a door. The next room he enters gives out onto the back of the property, where there are fewer trees to cover the sky. In the dribble of extra light he can make out slightly more of what is around him.

This is a kitchen. The countertops and cupboards are still in place, though there are gaps where the oven and fridge would have been. The cupboard doors hang open. There's nothing significant here.

Back into the main corridor and to the next door along. This opens onto a small room that seems to have once been a bedroom. He feels the softness of carpet underfoot, rather than the peeling linoleum of the previous rooms. No furniture, but the dark shape of a crucifix is just discernible above where the bed must have stood.

He finds another couple of rooms that are much the same. He is beginning to wonder whether this is worth the risk, whether it wasn't merely Honey's overactive imagination that has sent him here, when he tries the door at the end of the corridor.

It is locked.

He produces the bunch of keys from his pocket and feels his way through them. There is one left that he thinks he hasn't used. He hopes it works.

He finds the keyhole. Inserts the key. It turns.

This room is different from the others. It's pitch-black, for a start. No hope of seeing anything in here. But he senses that it's bigger, too, and something in the echo of his footstep makes him think that there must be furniture or other objects in here.

He recalls how he tried to look into this window from the outside when he came in the daytime. It had been obscured by heavy curtains, not even a gap between them.

Which means he can try a light.

He closes the door quietly behind him, produces Kiunga's lighter from his pocket, and sparks the flame alive.

The sudden light dazzles him at first despite the blueness of the flame. He extinguishes it. In that first moment, though, he's taken in a chilling sight: an examination table, just like the one in the Sunday school, steel stirrups pointed high in the air and spread wide. But this bench has something on it.

He lights the flame once more.

A crumpled, dark towel. One corner of it seems to have been bleached white.

He looks closer and revises his opinion. It's a white towel, entirely stained a deep, dark brown except for one corner. It appears dried, hard, encrusted.

Blood.

The blood smears show up glossy on the black plastic of the table cover. They show up black on the linoleum floor, leading to a sink at one side of the room, where steel dishes and implements lie carelessly discarded and spattered, as is the sink itself, with blood.

A sudden burning pain causes him to drop the lighter. It clatters away from him on the floor in the darkness. He kneels and pats the floor around him. After a few frantic moments he finds it, stands, and presses the lighter's button once more.

He holds the flickering light and turns around the room with mounting horror. In one corner, a crumpled pile of green surgical scrubs. Stained with blood. More blood on the floor. Here, a footprint in blood. A latex glove, fingers sucked in, palm covered in blood. A black garbage bag, swabs and gauze overflowing from the top. Covered in blood.

Everything is covered in blood.

Mollel's dreams are fractured and tainted with blood. When he wakes, he picks up his phone to look at the time. It's 9:40 a.m. Four missed calls. Honey.

—Mollel. Finally. I've been calling you.

—I was sleeping.

—Are you okay? You sound terrible.

—I'm fine. And then he remembers.

Orpheus House. The blood. The operating table. Something happened in that place. Something more than a simple murder.

—I think you're right. I think we're looking for a baby.

—And I know where to start, she says. Have you got any smart clothes?

—I have the suit I was wearing last night.

—That'll have to do. Can you meet me in town?

—Sure. I'll call Kiunga.

—No, says Honey. Not him. It has to be just you and me.

He meets her at the bus stop near the Ambassador Hotel. It's a busy interchange, serving all the *matatus* that run to the eastern half of the city, not to mention the numerous up-country buses. The touts accost him, as they do anyone standing still, assuming that he's looking for a cheap fare. *Beba, beba,* is the incessant cry: *All aboard.* Nearly full minivans blare their air horns in competition; passengers push for the final places rather than wait for another vehicle to fill. They throw their bags to the *kondos*—the conductors—to be lashed to the roof with lengths of inner-tube rubber. Others juggle their possessions in tied-up bundles, along with trussed chickens and swaddled children. Whatever rides on your lap is free.

Many are returning home for Christmas. Still others, Mollel gathers from snatches of conversation all around him, are leaving the city for the election. Not with the intent of exercising their democratic right at home, but of keeping away from trouble.

The touts are aware of this new imperative and are taking advantage. —Come on, *brazza*, one hisses at him, spitting a wad of *miraa* into the gutter. You can hold out all you like, but you won't get a better price. Everyone's leaving town. You wanna be left behind?

—I'm waiting for someone, replies Mollel. And I'm not your brother.

—Maybe I've seen them, says the tout, ever eager for a tip. Whatta they look like?

Mollel ignores him. What would he say? Tall, high heels, long hair, short dress? He can imagine the response. *You're on the wrong street, brazza.*

Or would he say shaved head, average height, young Maasai woman? *Make your mind up, brazza!*

Someone touches his arm. He turns to see a smartly dressed businesswoman with a leather document folder under her arm. Her hair is shoulder length and as conservative as her suit. She smiles at him broadly.

—Honey!

She reaches up and gives him a peck on the cheek.

—It's all about looking the part, she says in response to his surprise. Don't you have a tie, Mollel?

He pulls his tie out of his pocket and shows it to her sheepishly. Her bottom lip plumps with amused disdain. —That's the only one you've got? Come on, Mollel. Let's get you a new one.

—Now I see what you were waiting for, *brazza*, says the tout, leering. I've been waiting for a girl like that all my life.

▲ ▲ ▲

They stop at a street stand that sells ties, socks, and prophetic literature. The ties are rolled up neatly and arranged according to color; the effect is of a rainbow of exotic fruit. Mollel's hand gravitates toward the browns and grays.

Honey reaches out and stops him.

—What is it about Nairobi men, she asks, that makes you all so afraid of color? Everything's got to be drab. The West Africans aren't like that. You ever seen a Ghanaian or Nigerian here on business? They're finer and more colorful than the women. But here we seem to think we have to be like Europeans, all in black. It's you Maasai men I feel most sorry for. You're the finest of all, back in our homeland. Dyed dreadlocks. Necklaces and bangles. Red *shukas* you can see from miles away.

—In the bush, you want to be seen, says Mollel. In the city it's more important to fit in. Especially in this profession.

—You can compromise, though, can't you? she says. She picks a deep-red tie. Flame-tree red. Maasai red. —Here. Try this.

She hands it to him. It's silky. Sheened. Its contours glimmer as she glides it over Mollel's hands.

—Good choice, sister, says the stallholder.

—Put it on, she says.

Mollel threads the tie under his collar, then stops, awkwardly.

—I don't know . . . he says hesitantly.

—Oh, it suits you, she says. Don't you think?

The stallholder nods eagerly.

—I mean . . . He lowers his voice. He's ashamed to admit it. —I mean, I don't know how to . . .

—Oh, you mean you can't tie it without a mirror? replies Honey with a wink. Don't worry. Let me do it for you.

She reaches up and knots the tie deftly, the silken material rustling against itself as she weaves it. The tie drops against his shirt, and she slides the knot up against his neck.

—There, she says. Very handsome. And not at all like a . . .

She mouths the word *policeman*.

—How much? asks Mollel.

—Three hundred, says the stallholder.

Honey reaches into her document folder and produces some notes. Mollel begins to protest.

—Don't even think about it, she insists. I chose it, I pay for it. You have to let me buy it for you, Mollel.

They take a taxi for the trip out of the city center to Karen. Mollel doesn't know this part of town well; it is named for a white woman who lived here years earlier. It seems as though ever since, the whites— the *wazungu*—have wanted to create a suburb in the image of their own. Signs with crests and golden letters proclaim preparatory schools and country clubs while high, immaculately clipped hedges and ornate wrought-iron gates hint at luxurious domesticity beyond.

And then, next to a sign for a shelter run by the Kenyan Society for the Prevention of Cruelty to Animals, is a smaller, hand-painted placard: DIVINE MERCY ORPHANAGE. A PROJECT OF GEORGE NALO MINISTRIES. BY APPOINTMENT ONLY.

—I phoned ahead, says Honey.

The orphanage is off the main road and down a dirt track, causing the taxi driver, in his low-slung saloon, to slow to a crawl and curse under his breath. But it's not far, and he visibly perks up when Honey says to him, —We won't be lòng.

Being paid to wait is every Nairobi taxi driver's dream.

—We don't normally see people at such short notice, says the matron. But as it's so nearly Christmas . . .

She leaves the point unfinished, as though understood. Mollel and Honey nod.

—Do you have any children? the matron asks.

—I have a son, says Mollel. Nine years old.

The matron looks questioningly at him, then at Honey.

Honey quickly adds, —My husband's first wife died shortly after his son was born. We've been trying for several years. But the doctors say I can't.

Mollel looks at Honey, startled. She takes his hand in both of hers; he sees on her left ring finger a wedding band.

—I'm sorry, says the matron. But perhaps it is God's will that your misfortune will provide happiness for one of our children.

—I do hope so, says Honey.

—Will you excuse me a moment? asks Mollel.

—Of course.

Mollel gets up and walks to the open door. He steps outside. In the shade of a jacaranda tree a group of children are playing with plastic cartons, happily scooping and piling mounds of dust. Others are chatting to the young woman who tends to them, while a couple of older boys mock-fight with twigs.

A girl approaches. She is about six years old, and she twirls one foot beneath her in a mixture of boldness and bashfulness.

—*Jambo*, she greets him.

—*Jambo*, he replies. What's your name?

She runs away, giggling. Honey comes out and joins him.

—I told her that you get upset when you think about your first wife, she says.

—My *only* wife, he corrects her.

He recalls the look Kiunga gave him in Honey's flat: *Be careful*. He's angry at the thought that Honey might be manipulating him. And he's angry about the ring.

—I'm sorry, Mollel. But we have to pose as a couple. It's the only way we'll get information about what happens to the children who come through here.

—Where did you get the wedding ring? It sits loose on your finger. Stole it from one of your clients, I suppose.

Honey pulls him around to face her. She looks into his eyes imploringly.

—Don't be like that, she says. Please. Don't let her get suspicious. I don't think she's noticed anything yet. We can get away with a little bit of tension between us. We are supposed to be married, after all. Remember, we're trying to find a baby.

—A baby? The matron has appeared at the doorway. —You're interested in a baby?

Honey links her arm with Mollel's. —Oh! You overheard us. Well, it's a point of difference between us. My husband thinks an older child would be better. But I can't help wanting a baby, you see.

The matron nods her head. —Everyone wants a baby, she agrees. But we try to encourage people to consider the older children. That's one of the reasons we put a premium on fees for adopting newborns.

Mollel feels Honey's arm tighten in his. —And how much are they, these fees? she asks.

—We consider a hundred thousand to be a suitable donation. The matron smiles.

—A hundred thousand! Honey laughs. Then her voice drops a tone. Bitterness tinges her words. —So that's the price of a child.

Honey's abrupt change of manner causes the matron to look at her warily. This time it is Mollel who hastily tries to put the conversation back on track.

—I suppose you don't have any newborns up for adoption at the moment? he asks.

—None at all. Our last was several months ago. And there's a considerable waiting list, as you might imagine. Now, perhaps you would like to talk to some of the older children? Get to know them a little? Some of them are very charming, I can assure you.

The little girl looks over at them and waves shyly at Mollel. He waves back.

—That's Felicity, says the matron. An adorable child. And we could let you have her in time for the new year, should all the arrangements work out.

—All the arrangements? asks Honey, now barely bothering to disguise her contempt. You mean, your *donation*? I presume she would cost less, being so much older?

—Well, yes, concedes the matron uncertainly. We'd be keen to get her into a good home. Perhaps . . . She turns to Mollel. —Perhaps you need to talk about this. As a *couple*.

—Perhaps we do, agrees Mollel.

—Tell me, says Honey. What'll happen to that girl? Felicity? If she doesn't find someone to take her in?

The matron looks at them both. Her eyes are wary now. —We do our best for all our children, she says. But you never know. It's tough being an orphan. Who knows where she might end up? Some of them, you know—she lowers her voice—get hooked into prostitution.

—Some people might prefer that to being bought and sold like slaves, says Honey, her voice full of challenge. After all, if you're going to be pimped out to the highest bidder, you might as well take a fair cut.

The matron stiffens. —I think you'd better come back when our director is here, she says. Dr. Nalo. She's the best one to deal with those kinds of questions.

—What's the matter? spits Honey. Her voice wavers with emotion. —We're not good enough parents for you? I bet if we were a pair of rich *wazungu* looking for a little black baby, with a big, fat check in our hands, you'd find one soon enough, wouldn't you?

—I think you'd better leave, says the matron.

As they walk to their taxi, Mollel casts a look back. Felicity is standing under the jacaranda tree, watching them leave. Her hand is raised.

He imagines it is still raised a long time after they have gone.

In the back of the cab, Honey buries her head in Mollel's shoulder. —I'm sorry, she says. Just the thought of those children in there. Lost. Without their mothers to look after them.

—Some of them will find homes, he says.

—Some of them *had* homes, she replies. While you were outside, that woman told me more about where the children come from. It's called an orphanage, but a lot of those children have parents, you know. Parents who can't afford them or can't cope, or who have been told by the church that they're unworthy. *Unworthy*, Mollel. Like Lucy. Or me.

She sits up and looks out the window. —Did you hear her, Mollel? *Everyone wants a baby*. A hundred thousand shillings. I'd heard that was the going rate. It's not just older children they steal, you know. She'd never admit it, but I've heard the rumors. Some of these places take babies away from mothers in the delivery room. They lie to them. Tell them they had a stillborn. Everyone wants a newborn. Do you know what a fresh, healthy baby can fetch on the open market? No. Lucy's baby's alive out there, somewhere. We've got to find it.

—Even if it is alive, concedes Mollel, we don't know whether Lucy's baby ever came through here. The matron denied having had a newborn recently.

—No, says Honey. But we can find out. The other thing I learned is that every adoption has to be registered. If Lucy's child was sold, there'll be a record of it with the government.

—They took her baby away, Mollel, she says with something like a sob, and he folds his arm around her. Can you even imagine that, Mollel? Can you even imagine what that's like?

—Where the hell have you been, boss? I've been trying to get hold of you.

—I got your messages. I was following another lead.

—I thought you might have got mugged or killed or something after I left you last night.

—No. But I want to revisit Orpheus House. And I want to pull in any favors we've got, to try to get a forensic team down there.

—You're a bit behind the game, I'm afraid, boss. Where are you? I'll pick you up.

When they get to Orpheus House, one of the big, ancient city fire trucks is standing in the driveway. A crew of men are dousing the smoldering rafters, which are exposed like ribs. A rainbow plays in the spray as the afternoon sun pushes through the leaves, creating shafts in the lingering smoke.

—If it wasn't already scheduled for demolition, I'd call it an insurance job, one of the firemen is saying. The old man claims he saw no sign of any intruders, so I guess we'll just have to put it down to ghosts.

They laugh. Mollel and Kiunga walk past them to where Wanjiku Nalo is standing, talking to the caretaker.

—Ah, Sergeant Mollel, she says as she looks up and sees him. Githaka was just telling me that we've had a vermin problem here for some time.

I suppose one of them must have chewed through an electric cable. Nasty little creatures. You know, it was only last night that I noticed I'd somehow foolishly mislaid my keys for this place. But I guess I won't be needing them now.

She casts him a triumphant smile.

Mollel turns his back and walks away.

He rounds the back of the house, where the damage is even worse. The makeshift operating theater had obviously been the seat of the fire. The glass in the large window has caved in, revealing the bare black walls. The roof is open to the sky, and water drips down from the burned rafters. The floor is covered with roof tiles and the remains of the ceiling; the twisted stirrups gleam in the middle of the room.

There is an old tree stump farther down the plot, and Mollel sits on it, his head in his hands.

—What's up, boss? asks Kiunga. If you don't mind me saying so, you seem a little—strange.

Mollel is scouring his memory. Could he have been seen last night? Had he left the door open on his way out? He can't even remember leaving. Whatever the reason, his most valuable evidence has been lost forever.

For a moment he even doubts whether he saw what he saw. But no. How else would he have known about the examination table, its remains still barely visible under the rubble of the collapsed roof?

He gets like this when he misses his medication. He left the flat without taking his pills this morning. Well, he's skipped a dose before. He took it last night—didn't he?

But when he tries to recall whether he did take his pills last night, he can't remember that, either.

—Boss, we're partners, aren't we?

—What? Sure.

—If there was anything you weren't telling me, you'd tell me, wouldn't you? If you know what I mean.

—Yes, Kiunga.

—I got some good leads this morning, the young man continues. Want to hear about them?

—Go on, says Mollel without enthusiasm.

—Well, I got hold of someone at the motor vehicle department. That silver Land Cruiser we saw on K Street, with the cagey *mzungu* behind the wheel? It's registered in the name of Equator Investments.

Mollel is hardly listening. Alternative lines of inquiry seem pointless. He's more concerned now with how he can make a case against Wanjiku Nalo with no evidence. And no motive. He scours his mind for a possible reason for the doctor to have done what she did to Lucy. But he comes up blank.

—Well, Equator Investments sounded familiar to me. And then I remembered: here. This place.

Kiunga's words are starting to break through to Mollel.

—What about this place?

—It's on the sign, out front. Orpheus House. A project of George Nalo Ministries, with the support of international donors and Equator Investments. So I called a contact down at City Hall. She confirmed it. This land is owned by Equator Investments.

—Who are Equator Investments?

Kiunga laughs. —Boss, don't you read the papers? Equator Investments *is* David Kingori. The most powerful, influential businessman in Nairobi. He's the one—

But Mollel has leaped to his feet.

Powerful, influential. Those were the words Honey had used about Lucy's client. The one she was scared of.

There might be life in this case yet.

Mollel strides excitedly through the business district. Equator House is just a short way from Upper Hill and Uhuru Park. Kiunga trots behind him, trying to keep up and filling Mollel in with background on Kingori as they go.

The businessman has been the subject of half a dozen official investigations, at least, that Kiunga knows about, everything from insider trading to gunrunning. Yet the accusations always evaporate, key witnesses always retract their statements, evidence seems to miraculously disappear, and Kingori always emerges more bullish and brash than ever.

—It's a good job we decided to walk, says Kiunga. The traffic here's completely backed up. I wonder what's going on.

A young man pushes past them. Something registers about him: his green T-shirt. Not in itself unusual. But Mollel notices for the first time that several people around them are wearing the same shirt. They are all headed the same way. It's a political rally, by the looks of things, one of the smaller opposition parties.

—Better go the other way, says Kiunga.

But Mollel continues on his path. More green T-shirts join them to the left and right. He gets a kick out of watching their numbers grow. Soon, as they are making their way down Kenyatta Avenue, he and Kiunga become a minority. They are flanked by green. Banners are unfurled, and Mollel sees shopkeepers pulling down their shutters with a clatter.

—*What do we want?* calls out a shrill woman's voice way ahead of them.

—*Justice!* comes the reply from all around them.

—*When do we want it?*

—*Now!*

A startled-looking businessman is stopped in the middle of the sidewalk as he attempts to go against the green tide. As Mollel and Kiunga pass him, he says to them, —What should I do?

—Go home, says Kiunga.

—But I need to go that way, protests the businessman, pointing in the direction of the flow.

—Then ask her for a shirt, says Kiunga. A girl passes them, handing out green T-shirts from a large plastic bag. —Thank you, sweetie. Kiunga takes two, offers one to Mollel, who shakes his head, then throws one to the businessman.

—Congratulations! he shouts. You've just joined the opposition!

Kiunga stuffs the remaining T-shirt into his trouser pocket. —That'll be good for the gym, he says with a grin. A few paces later the two policemen draw to a stop. They have arrived.

▲ ▲ ▲

Equator House. It sits anonymously in Nairobi's high-rise center, but when it was built during the heady optimism of a newly independent nation, its fourteen stories earned it the title of *skyscraper*. Over the years, it has seen numerous name changes as corporate clients have come and gone, none of them seeming to have made a profit on the site. Rumor had it that the building used to be secretly owned by Moi, the former president slashing or hiking the rent as he saw fit, according to favors deserving reward or slights requiring punishment. But today the building belongs to Equator Investments, whose proprietor, David Kingori, also happens to be the sole residential occupant. On a Friday or Saturday night it is not unusual for the deserted streets to ring with the noise of a party drifting down from the penthouse above.

Mollel and Kiunga walk into the building's shadow, push open the doors, and plunge into the air-conditioned lobby. They both blink as their eyes become accustomed to the darkness. Everything is steel, marble, and smoked glass. Even the chants of the demonstrators on the street outside disappear as the doors swing smoothly shut. A receptionist sits behind a desk, absorbed in her mobile phone. She raises her eyes to the visitors, but not her head.

Mollel shows his badge.

—What do you know about the company cars?

—Nothing to do with me. You want to see the head of security?

—Is Mr. Kingori in?

—You have an appointment? she asks with a skeptical click of her gum. Kiunga slides over.

—Hi, he says, with a grin. So, they've got you working Christmas Eve? Must be kinda boring.

The girl raises her eyebrows as if to say *No shit.*

—Us too. No letup for the brave guardians of law and order.

Despite herself, she giggles. How does he do it? wonders Mollel.

—Look, my friend here is a bit embarrassed, continues Kiunga. The fact is, we're on an important investigation—nothing to do with this place. We're watching the place across the road.

—Across the road? Her curiosity is piqued. —The dry cleaners?

—Yeah, we think they might be money laundering.

The girl laughs, catches Kiunga's eye, looks back down.

—Anyway, my friend needs to use the bathroom. You know these Maasai, they think they can just *kojoe* anywhere, but I told him, You've got to go somewhere *respectable* . . .

She giggles again and puts down her phone.

—I'll just be a minute, says Mollel, squeezing his knees together and making an agonized face.

—Go on, she says, hitting a buzzer beneath the desk. Next to her, the waist-high entry gate clicks. —It's on the right.

—Thanks, says Mollel, but the girl is already back to chatting with Kiunga. He pushes the gate and goes through. There is a pair of doors marked with toilet signs, and two lifts, but Mollel heads immediately to an unmarked door, which he delicately pushes open with his fingertips. It swings open just wide enough to slip through. He's in a stairwell. The steps lead up and down; down feels cooler, with a slight edge of exhaust fumes. The car park. He creeps down the stairs and through another swing door.

Most of the spaces are vacant, but he's drawn to a row with several cars parked in it. A large notice on the wall proclaims PARKING FOR EQUATOR INVESTMENTS ONLY.

One vehicle attracts his attention immediately. It was designed to do so: bright yellow, overspilling the parking lines painted on the floor. It's chunky and square. To Mollel, it looks more like one of Adam's toys than a real car. The chrome grille gleams, and the windows are so black it's a wonder that anyone can see out.

But it is not the flashy Hummer that interests him. A couple of cars down is a silver Land Cruiser—the license plate matches the one he saw on K Street.

Glancing around for a guard, Mollel crosses the car park and goes to examine the Land Cruiser. He walks around it. Looks inside. No litter on the floor or personal possessions in the back, no sign of any personality or ownership. It is probably a pool car. He continues around and, reaching the front once more, notices a dent and a scrape on the front fender. He runs his finger along it, feeling minute, gritty particles. The damage is not from another car. More likely a wall or a concrete post.

There is the sound of footsteps and talking, and Mollel ducks down. He recognizes the booming, self-important voice from radio news reports. David Kingori. Like his car, he exists to be the center of attention, even when there's nobody around. He's complaining loudly about something or other on his mobile phone. Mollel squeezes himself down behind the Land Cruiser. Kingori passes within inches of his face, but does not look down. He blips the Hummer and climbs inside. The car roars into life, and Mollel is choked by a cloud of fumes. As soon as the Hummer turns the corner and mounts the ramp, Mollel darts back to the stairwell and runs to reception. Kiunga and the girl are chatting away.

—All done? says Kiunga.

—Let's go, says Mollel, dashing to the entrance.

—So, you'll call me? asks the receptionist.

Kiunga turns back with a grin and makes a telephone sign with his fingers.

On the street, the green crowd is still massing, heading toward Parliament. The yellow Hummer is up ahead, slowly parting its way through the throng. Mollel and Kiunga pace behind it, keeping a distance but watching intently, stalking.

—Can I give you some advice, boss? asks Kiunga chattily. If it's not too personal. When you're dealing with women, you can't come out with what you want straightaway. It's too direct. You got to sweet-talk them a bit, make them laugh, flatter them. Get them to open up. Then, maybe, you get what you want.

He hands Mollel a piece of paper. On it is written the name Estelle and a mobile phone number.

Not that side, says Kiunga. Mollel turns it over.

—James Lethebridge, he reads.

—These *wazungu* have some crazy names, huh?

—This is our Land Cruiser driver? Mollel slaps Kiunga on the back. In his way, the young man is proving a pretty good hunter.

Kiunga continues. —He's not a member of the staff, apparently, but the girl sees him coming into the building every now and then. He comes, collects a pool car or drops it off. That's the name he puts in the signing-in book. She says he's old—sixties probably—white hair, bit of a gut, and skin like an undercooked chapati—you know, all pale, speckled, and doughy.

Kiunga trails off as he notices that Mollel has stopped. The Hummer has drawn to a halt and the crowd has begun to cluster around it. The horn is blasting impatiently. Mollel and Kiunga draw closer.

The driver's-side window of the Hummer glides down, and Kingori's head emerges. He waves his arm furiously. —You should watch where you're going!

A howl of protest rises up from around the car. —You watch where *you're* going! Another voice: —Learn how to drive, you stupid bastard!

As Mollel and Kiunga push their way around to the front of the car, they hear cries of pain. A young man is kneeling down, clutching his foot, while his friends hold his shoulders in concern.

Another blast of the horn. —Get out of the way!

Someone thumps the hood of the Hummer angrily. —You've run over his foot!

—I'll run you all down, you dogs, if you don't let me through!

Mollel and Kiunga exchange glances. The good-humored mood of the crowd has turned. Things are in danger of getting ugly. Someone mutters, —Do you know who that is? David Kingori. And another, angrily: —Government puppet!

The driver's window draws silkily to a close and the engine revs loudly, but the crowd presses closer. The huge car begins, gently at first, to rock from side to side on its chassis. A placard—nothing more than a piece of cardboard tacked to a light wooden stick—bounces against the Hummer's windscreen. Mollel knows that a bottle or stone could be next.

He has seen enough. He pushes himself forward to the side of the car and jumps onto the running board. He pulls himself up to full height, head and shoulders above the melee. Cheers go up at first, turning to jeers as he holds his police badge aloft, waving it in a slow, wide arm's-length arc for all to see.

—Step away from the vehicle! he shouts. Despite the ill humor, the rocking of the car ceases. He scans the faces, gauging the mood. There is anger in the eyes, but it's an instant, hot anger, easily dissipated, unlike the cold, calculated fury he fears. This is not a crowd in search of trouble—at least not today.

—Typical police! shouts one protester. Protect their own! The cry is greeted with calls of agreement.

—Now listen to me! shouts Mollel. There's been a small accident here, and a man's been hurt. We're going to deal with this properly. Now, step back from the car.

There are some muted grumbles, and mutters about police bias, but the people at the front shuffle back slightly. Kiunga helps the injured man hobble to his feet. Mollel presses his badge against the driver's window and the window whirrs down a reluctant inch. Mollel leans in and speaks through the crack.

—Now, sir, he says softly, what you're going to do is, you're going to lean back and unlock the rear door here. Don't use the central locking, just this door by me. I'm going to get in with two other people. Don't do anything else until I say so, *sawa?*

The window snaps shut again, and Mollel wonders for a moment whether Kingori is ignoring him. Then he hears the click of the rear passenger door being unlocked. He edges toward it along the running board.

—Now, we're going to take this man to hospital, he shouts, for the benefit of the crowd. He beckons to Kiunga, who has put the limping figure's arm around his shoulder, and the two of them come forward.

—Then, continues Mollel, we're going to the police station, and we're going to talk about compensation and charges against the driver. Okay?

—Yeah! call out a few members of the crowd. Charge him!

Mollel heaves open the Hummer's rear door, Kiunga bundles the protester in and follows suit, and then Mollel himself dives inside the darkened car and pulls it shut behind him, snapping the lock down.

—Right, carefully, slowly: drive!

Kingori edges the Hummer forward, the crowd shuffling out of the way, letting it pass, scowling at their own reflections in the blacked-out windows. There is a halfhearted thud of a fist, but nothing more sinister. The people melt back, and with a clear road ahead, Kingori guns the accelerator, speeding them away from the scene.

▲ ▲ ▲

—Oh, it hurts, it hurts! You broke my foot!

—Let me take your shoe off, says Kiunga, but the young man keeps brushing him away.

—Oh, you're going to pay for this, he groans at Kingori. I'm going to sue you!

—Let me see, says Kiunga, finally succeeding in getting hold of the man's training shoe and pulling it off. Why you—let me get this sock off. Your foot would be swollen like a melon if this car went over it. There's nothing wrong with you at all!

—There is, there is! He broke my foot! I need an X-ray! I need compensation!

—Pull over here, orders Mollel. As the car comes to a halt, he leans across and opens the door next to the young man.

—Get out.

—What? This isn't the hospital!

—Get out, or we'll push you out.

Reproachfully, the man gets out, feigning a whimper as he puts his shoeless foot onto the sidewalk.

—Here, says Kiunga. Take your shoe.

—You take it! says the young man, standing upright. He makes to fling it into the car, but Kiunga pulls the door shut just in time and the shoe bounces pathetically off the window. Kingori accelerates, and they leave the man behind them. Kiunga looks out the back window.

—He's walking away normally. He chuckles. —What an operator!

From the driver's seat, Kingori roars with laughter. —Brilliant! Officers, thank you so much. Please allow me to show my appreciation.

Still driving, he fumbles in his pocket for a money clip and rips out a couple of thousand-shilling bills. —Now, is there anywhere I can drop you?

—Central Police Post, says Mollel.

—It's a bit out of my way. I have an important meeting in Westlands. Perhaps I could stop at a *matatu* stand?

—Central Police Post will be fine, says Mollel evenly. —While we're there, we can discuss a few matters. Like attempting to bribe a police officer.

16

—I want a lawyer!

Mollel and Kiunga are standing outside the filing room, which gets used for interviews at Central Police Post. They can hear a fist pounding on a desk inside. Then a chair falls over, and the fist pounds on the door.

—Get me a lawyer! Now!

—This is decent *chai*, says Mollel, sipping from his mug.

—Mmm, we all chip in and get the good highland stuff, says Kiunga.

—You use masala?

—That's my special technique. Mix the spices in with the sugar.

—It's lovely.

—Thank you.

They drain their mugs, and each lets out a satisfied sigh.

—Shall we go in? asks Mollel.

—Delighted, says Kiunga.

Inside the room, Kingori is pacing furiously. He rushes to the door as it opens, but Mollel holds up a hand of warning.

—Take a seat, please, sir.

—I don't want a seat. I've been sitting here for forty-five minutes!

—Please be seated.

Kingori picks the chair off the floor and sits, crossing his arms. Mollel and Kiunga also sit.

—I demand to see a lawyer immediately.

—Did you say you've been here forty-five minutes, sir? asks Mollel innocently.

—At least!

—Well that must make it—what time is it, Kiunga?

Kiunga looks at his watch. —Just past five.

—Just past five? And the duty lawyer finishes at five, doesn't he, Kiunga?

—Saw him leaving myself.

—Oh dear, says Mollel.

—Give me my phone! barks Kingori. I'll have my lawyer here in a shot.

—That's your right, sir. Mollel takes Kingori's mobile phone—gold plated—from his pocket and makes as if to hand it to him, then pauses. —Of course, that would add a certain formality to the proceedings. We'd need to charge you.

Kiunga nods. —Most definitely.

—And then you and your lawyer could discuss your case with the magistrate—oh, but I'm forgetting. It's Christmas Eve, isn't it? They'll have gone home now, too. When will they sit again, Kiunga?

—Well, there's Christmas Day tomorrow, a public holiday on the twenty-sixth, then another holiday for the election, so it won't be until Friday, I'm afraid.

—Four days? Mollel tuts. —And I hear the cells are fit to burst. But I'm sure we can squeeze you in somewhere, sir, if that's what you want.

He holds out the phone. Kingori takes it and lays it on the desk.

—So, two thousand wasn't enough for you? You should have just said. I can buy and sell a couple of farmers like you a million times. What shall we say, ten thousand? Each? I can give it to you right now. Call it a Christmas bonus.

—It's not about money, says Kiunga.

—Tell us about James Lethebridge, says Mollel.

A slow grin speads over Kingori's face, and he leans back in his chair. His attitude says, *now we're getting somewhere.*

—Jimmy's in trouble, is he?

—So you know him?

—I know him. First, you're saying it wrong. It's not Leather-bridge, it's *Leethie*-bridge. Like the river.

—What's the nature of your relationship with Mr. *Leethie*-bridge?

Kingori laughs again.

—He's my fag. Oh, don't look so shocked, gentlemen. I'm aware of the contemporary understanding of the term. But in a British public school, the word is slang for *factotum.* Your do-everything person. Fetching, carrying, odd jobs. We were at school together long before you were born. Long before this nation was born.

Mollel looks at him with surprise. From his brief glimpse of Lethebridge in the car—and the description provided by the receptionist—he's confident that the man must be in his late sixties or seventies. That certainly tallies with being at school before Independence. But if Kingori is the same age, he's remarkably well preserved. A full head of hair, hardly a wrinkle, dazzling teeth. All too perfect. Mollel wonders if anything about this guy would stand up to close scrutiny.

—So he is your employee? asks Kiunga.

—I keep him in work. Little tasks here and there. He wouldn't be able to do anything else.

—Would one of these little tasks be procuring prostitutes from K Street?

Kingori's smile disappears.

—I wouldn't know anything about that.

—He was seen curb-crawling the other night.

—That's his concern.

—In a company car?

—Not my Hummer, I hope.

—A silver Toyota Land Cruiser.

—A lot of people use that car.

—Do you employ many *wazungu*, Mr. Kingori?

—He's the only one. So he's been a naughty boy. I wouldn't have thought he had it in him, myself. But what has this got to do with me?

—What it has to do with you is that a K Street hooker was found dead last Saturday morning. And she'd told her friend that she was scared of someone. Someone powerful. Now, from what I've heard, that doesn't match the description of Mr. Lethebridge. But it could, pretty accurately, describe you. So how about it? Your movements, please, on Friday night.

—This is ridiculous! You've got nothing on me!

—We can always resume this conversation after a visit to the cells, if you prefer.

Kingori scowls. —For what it's worth, from early morning until about seven in the evening I was at State House, with the President, among about fifty others. We were discussing election strategy. Any number of people can place me there. In fact, I think it was even reported in *The Standard*. Is the head of state a good enough alibi for you?

—And afterward?

—Well, I take it you'll be speaking to James. We were together all evening at my flat. Demolishing some rather fine single malt and reminiscing about school.

Mollel takes an envelope out of the desk drawer and pushes it across to Kingori.

—Take a look.

It is a photo of Lucy, postmortem. Somewhere under the Botox, Kingori's face flickers. With pity? Recognition? Guilt?

—This is the girl?

—Her name was Lucy e-intoi Sambu.

—A Maasai? Like you? I'm sorry she is dead. But I have never seen her before in my life. James will tell you all that.

Now it is Kiunga's turn to push something across the table: a notepad and pen.

—James Lethebridge's contact details, please. Address, phone number.

Kingori scrawls an address in Lavington, then picks up his phone, finds a number, and copies it down.

—What do you know of George and Wanjiku Nalo? asks Mollel, taking the pad.

—The preacher? I know he's living proof that Bible school can be more profitable than an M.B.A.

—Meaning?

—Meaning, he is a sharp one. And his wife is even sharper.

—It sounds like you're speaking from experience.

—We've done business.

—What kind of business?

—Real estate. They're kind of tenants of mine.

—*Kind of* tenants?

Kingori shrugs. —They run a project out of some property I own. I'm allowing them to redevelop it rent-free.

—Seems pretty generous, says Kiunga pointedly. If that was my land, I'd put a bunch of apartment blocks on it.

—What can I say? That's the sort of guy I am.

After a moment's skeptical silence Kingori adds, —Okay, it's not pure philanthropy. Look, the Americans have a lot of money that their president says has to go to faith-based initiatives. Our government wants a prestige development in a visible location. Nalo makes all the right noises, I have the land. It's small beer for me. I let them use the property, I get help with some planning issues I have elsewhere.

—Have you been to Orpheus House?

Kingori laughs. —If I visited every property I owned, I'd never have time to get anything done.

—Has James Lethebridge?

—I don't know. Ask him.

Mollel replies, —We will. We're going to have him brought in right now.

—So be it. If you don't need me anymore, I shall—

—No, says Mollel. You're going to stay here while we speak to Mr. Lethebridge. You're not going to have any chance to compare alibis.

—Now, look here! Kingori slams the table. —I've been damn patient with you two and your stupid games. But be warned. If you don't let me go right now, it'll be more than your careers on the line. Do you understand?

The door opens, and the massive presence of Otieno bursts into the room. Instinctively, Mollel and Kiunga stand. Kingori remains seated.

—David, says Otieno cordially.

—Otieno. They shake hands. —Your clowns here have been treating me to a rather boring performance.

—Don't worry. I'll deal with them.

—I want them off the force.

—Oh, I have a far worse punishment in mind than that. I see your car's outside; please allow me to escort you there.

As Kingori passes, he turns to Mollel and hisses, —If I see you again, Maasai— He leaves the threat hanging in the air, shakes his head, and walks out.

17 —This case, says Otieno, is officially closed.

The two policemen stand before him like schoolboys in the principal's office. Mollel wishes he could take a seat. He is suddenly feeling an overwhelming sense of weariness.

—You can't do that! protests Kiunga.

—I can see you've learned some bad habits from our Maasai friend here. Tell me, Kiunga, did you happen to notice the sign on my door as you came in? It says Superintendent. You know what that means? Super—that means above. And intendent—well, let's just say, that means you. Above. You. Which means that in my station, I can do what the hell I like.

—You can't shut down this case. We're getting somewhere. We just need a few more days.

—We don't *have* a few more days, Kiunga. Have you been paying attention to what's going on in this city? I need every available man for election duty—doing our job—trying to keep a lid on this cauldron.

—*That's* why you wanted me transferred here, Mollel says, suddenly understanding. It wasn't to solve the girl's death. It was just to boost your numbers during the election. Help keep the peace. Help you look good. You always intended to drop the case, once you had an excuse.

He feels the blood thumping in his head. Uninvited, he takes a chair from in front of Otieno's desk and crashes down into it. Kiunga remains standing.

—How's this for an excuse? replies Otieno. A complaint from a member of the public. A *highly influential* member of the public. False arrest, intimidation . . .

—We never arrested him, Kiunga says.

The argument rings back and forth above him. He needs to get home. He needs to take his pills. But above all, what he needs is to solve this case.

Otieno's voice pounds remorselessly on. The words mean nothing now. Just that sanctimonious, booming, bull-like bellow. Why can't he just stop talking, thinks Mollel. For just one second? Why can't he just shut the hell up and *listen?*

The room falls silent.

They're both looking at him. Mollel realizes that he has spoken aloud.

He has the heady, blissful sensation of freedom. The same feeling he had when he decided to abandon his village, to turn his back on his tribe.

He does not care about the consequences. Instead, while Kiunga and Otieno listen to him in amazement, he tells them the truth.

He speaks with the bright, intense lucidity of anger. He tells them about stealing the keys, about his discovery of the operating theater at Orpheus House. He tells them about his conviction that Wanjiku Nalo delivered a baby to Lucy. That somehow the delivery was botched. Lucy either died during the procedure or bled to death shortly afterward. Wanjiku, helped by someone, dumped the body in the storm drain, having deliberately mutilated the body's genitals to try to disguise the fact that Lucy had recently given birth. She knew about female genital mutilation, and probably hoped that if the body was discovered, Maasai circumcision rites would get the blame.

Kiunga has slumped into the room's remaining chair. Otieno has tipped his own chair back, hands behind his head, big sweat patches under his arms. His expression has become totally neutral.

▲ ▲ ▲

Mollel tells them about David Kingori. About the fact that he believes Kingori to be the father of the missing baby. That he was probably in league with Wanjiku Nalo, probably even ordered her to preside over the secretive birth—as the price he would exact for allowing the Nalos to build their new project on his site.

Mollel finishes his story. No one speaks. He feels the dramatic, shocked silence of the forest in the moments after a tree has fallen. And then his confidence drains. His anger evaporates. He senses, from the way Kiunga refuses to meet his eye, that he has humiliated himself.

He's also betrayed his promise to Honey.

—Well, Maasai, Otieno says, I guess I have to thank you.

—For what?

—For giving me everything I need to have you thrown out of the police force and into prison. To Kiunga, he adds, —Did you know anything about all this?

—No.

—Haven't you been listening to me? pleads Mollel. We're talking murder here. Including murder, or abduction, of a child. Not to mention arson, conspiracy . . .

—No, says Otieno slowly, deliberately. What you've told me, if I'm even to believe your ridiculous hypothesis, is accidental death.

—What about the child?

Otieno sighs. —Can't you see, Mollel, that this is not our problem? If the baby is alive, that means it's being cared for. And no doubt, much better than any cheap hooker could have cared for it. If it's dead, it's dead. We'd have no way of proving murder. We don't even have a body. All we have is unsubstantiated allegations against Nairobi's most powerful businessman, its most successful pastor, and its most respected gynecologist.

—What about justice? croaks Mollel.

Otieno gives a sad smile. —Mollel, you're in the wrong country. The wrong continent. Don't you know there's something more valuable than justice here?

—What?

—Peace.

Mollel leans forward. His eyes are fixed, glazed. He seems to be repeating a personal mantra.

—Justice is a luxury. Peace is a necessity. You want justice, move to
some first-world state with sophisticated crime labs and DNA tests and
judges who can't be bought off. That's the only way you'd get to bring a
case against people like this. Better still, become a judge yourself. They're
the ones who are supposed to look after justice. We're only supposed to
keep the peace.

Kiunga is saying nothing. Mollel feels drained.

—I feel sorry for you, says Otieno. You were a hero, once. No one
can forget what you did when the bomb went off. You won a lot of ad-
mirers that day, Mollel, including me.

—But this rage of yours. You don't think about the consequences of
your actions. Like when you were stationed here, before. You got so en-
raged about some petty little minor corruption that you went running to
the newspapers . . . I had to get rid of some good officers because of that.
And for what? Just doing what everyone else does, trying to get by.

—I ought to get rid of you. I've got every reason to. But I can't lose another officer right now. Besides, the press would crucify me. They'd see it
as a sign that we were persecuting a whistle-blower. Did you know, Mollel,
that the commissioner himself has taken a personal interest in your career?

Mollel shakes his head.

—Oh yes. You're to be kept well away from anywhere you can cause
trouble. I wish I'd taken his advice.

Mollel is silent as he gradually deals with the realization that he is
not going to lose his job.

—Just to make it perfectly clear. You forget about this case. It's
done. Closed. There's nothing we can do about it. I'm sorry, but that's
the way it is. Understood?

They both reply, —Yes, sir.

—Okay. It's late. Two days remaining until the election. Tomorrow
will be the quiet before the storm. You've got the day off. Go spend
Christmas with your families. Look to the living, not the dead.

18 —Come on, says Kiunga. Let's go for a drink.

—I don't drink, says Mollel.

—Then you can damn well sit next to me while I do, replies Kiunga. And I'm warning you, I intend to get completely *kutindi*.

They head off on foot across town. Mollel is expecting to be dragged to the Flamingo, the bar favored by Nairobi's law enforcement community, where at any given time of day or night you're likely to find as many on-duty officers as off.

But they go straight past it and head toward River Road. This part of the city is busy. Anyone still here has obviously decided to stay in town and make the most of the Christmas holiday. The bars are full, and many have decided to entice customers by setting up their *nyama choma* barbecues on the sidewalk. The smell makes Mollel's stomach protest in a queasy mixture of hunger and agony.

—Here we are, says Kiunga. I thought I'd make you feel at home.

They are outside a bar with a large window giving straight onto the street. One can't see inside, though: the window is a closed display, a sort of cupboard, with a whole flayed goat hanging inside and various cuts of meat beside it. Despite the flies, it is obviously appetizing enough to draw a regular flow of customers. Mollel and Kiunga have to wait at the door, where a man is giving detailed instructions to a member of the staff about which exact cut he wants taken from the goat. When they get inside, it takes a moment for Mollel's eyes to adjust to the darkness.

—Mama Naitiku's, says Mollel. It's a long time since I've been here.

Its official name is the Hoteli Narok, but no one knows it as that. It is the first port of call for most Maasai in Nairobi, and a home away from home for many who have migrated permanently to the city. For some, it has become a byword for the city itself: *going to Mama Naitiku's* is a familiar phrase in many villages, somehow more congenial, less daunting, less final than saying *going to Nairobi*.

Groups of red-shawled Maasai men look up at them with suspicion. Kiunga strides purposefully to the bar. Mollel follows him.

—I'll have a Tusker. Cold. And my friend here . . .

—A Fanta, says Mollel.

The barman is a Maasai youth, his hair braided, *shuka* knotted over one shoulder. His bracelets jangle as he reaches down to a beer crate at his feet and pulls out a bottle.

—Cold enough for you? he asks Kiunga, challengingly.

—It'll do.

The barman pops the cap and slides the beer over. He does the same with a bottle of fluorescent soda for Mollel.

Kiunga pays. —Is Mama here? he asks.

—Where else would she be?

—Tell her we want to talk to her.

The two of them go over to a table and sit down. —Why are we here, Kiunga? Mollel asks.

Kiunga takes a long drink from the neck of his bottle and smacks his lips.

—We've looked into the fact that Lucy was a *poko*, he says. We've dug into Orpheus House. The Nalos. But the one thing we haven't dealt with yet is the biggest fact of all. She was a Maasai.

—I don't think it's relevant, says Mollel.

—Of course not. You're a Maasai yourself. But I think it is. So humor me awhile, Mollel.

He looks up. An old woman is shuffling toward them, shaved head bent, long *shuka* brushing the floor. She wears a white beaded necklace, like a dinner plate around her neck, and it looks as though the weight—although it can't weigh anything at all—is dragging her down.

She pulls up a chair and sits beside them.

—What can I do for you, officers?

Hardly surprising that she recognizes them as police. What's more surprising to Mollel is how little she's changed. She looked ancient even back when he first met her.

—Do you remember me, Mama? he asks.

She looks up at him through eyes that are watery but alert. He sees her processing the information: looped ears, Maasai face, but Nairobi suit. He fingers Honey's tie nervously. The old woman reminds him of his own mother, and he can't help projecting a sense of disapproval, disappointment, into her expression.

—I see a lot of people, she says.

—I came here on my first night in Nairobi, Mollel says. I was with my brother, Lendeva. We were too poor to afford any meat, so you gave us both a bowl of *ugali*. We'd never seen *ugali* before. We didn't even know it was food. We sat out there, on the sidewalk, wondering what to do with it. When you came out to see how we were getting on, we'd made shapes out of it. Lendeva made a cow. I made a donkey.

Mama Naitiku smiles. She has fewer teeth, but the smile is the same.

—Are you a Leliani?

—That's right. Mollel.

—You were just boys.

—It was twenty years ago. You let us sleep on the floor, out back, while we looked for work.

—And you found it. With the police.

—That was much later.

—I do remember you, she says. And your brother. He was the bold one, as I recall. Dressed so fine in all the warrior garb, with not a shilling in the world. He had great plans. I thought you would follow him everywhere. And what has become of him now? Is he a policeman, too?

Mollel shakes his head. —I don't know where he is, he replies.

Kiunga shoots him a questioning glance. But already Mollel has been thinking more about his brother in the last few days than he has for years. He does not want to continue the conversation.

—That's what happens when we turn our back on the village life, says the old woman sadly.

—We need your help, says Kiunga. He brings out the photograph of Lucy that he had been using on K Street. —Do you know anything about this girl?

Mama Naitiku takes the photograph and looks at it. She turns to Mollel.

—*Shore lai kishoriki enapiak*, she says to him in Maa.

He remembers the expression. *Old friends bring evil.*

—Do you know her?

—Is she dead? Mama Naitiku asks.

—Yes.

She shudders. —I knew her. She arrived, like you, penniless. A year or so ago. She was fleeing her village. I didn't ask why. I see so many girls like that. I assumed it was an arranged marriage that she didn't want to go through with.

—Did anyone come looking for her? asks Kiunga. Anyone try to take her back to her village?

She shakes her head. —Not that I know of.

—This is pretty unpleasant, says Kiunga. But please think about it. When we found this girl's body, she had been mutilated. Her genitals were slashed. Is there anything you know of—any ritual, any ceremony— that might involve that sort of thing?

—There's the circumcision ceremony, of course, she says. But that's done on much younger girls. I've heard of people dying from it. But much later, because of infection. No, done properly, there's no danger at all. It's not how you describe this poor girl's wounds. Not slashing. It has to be done precisely. Delicately.

She pauses a moment. Discretion and professional pride seem to battle for an instant in her breast before she says, —I should know. I do it myself.

—It's illegal! says Mollel.

The old woman's posture changes. She draws herself up. —You've chosen the new laws, she says. I choose the old ones.

Kiunga shifts uneasily. Some of the men at the tables around them have begun to watch them with hostility. He picks up his bottle and drains it. —I think we should be going, he says. Mollel?

—Just a moment, says Mama Naitiku. What about the other girl? Have you spoken to her?

—The other girl? asks Mollel.

—Yes. I haven't seen this girl, the dead one, for over a year. But last time she was here, she left with another Maasai girl. Well dressed. Pretty obvious where her money came from. I chased her out. I don't allow that sort in my bar. But this poor girl followed her. If you ask me, that's the reason she ended up killed. Not because she was a Maasai.

Outside on the street, Kiunga says, —Okay, Mollel. It looks like you were right. But we had to look into the Maasai angle.

But Mollel is silent.

—What is it, boss? Is it what she said about the circumcisions? Look, we all know it still goes on. There's nothing we can do about it.

—It's not that, says Mollel. It's about what Honey said. About how she met Lucy. She told us that Lucy approached her when she had just started working the streets. That Lucy was the one who showed her the ropes, taught her how to do it properly. That doesn't fit with what Mama Naitiku says.

—If you ask me, boss, replies Kiunga, you ought to be careful about getting too close to Honey. She's a *poko*, remember? And sleeping with men is only part of what they do for a living. The rest of it is lying. And to a good *poko*, that's second nature.

—What's your problem? asks Mollel, stopping on the sidewalk. Can't you see this attitude is what stops people like Honey from coming to the police in the first place? We're all outsiders in one way or another, Kiunga. Why can't you see her as another human being? Besides, *you're* hardly one to lecture others on morality.

Kiunga turns and squares up to him. For a moment Mollel thinks he's going to get hit. Then Kiunga gives a grim smile.

—I love sex, he says. I've never disguised it. But I love *love*, too. And all the girls I go with, whether it leads to anything or not, I love them. At least while we're doing it. I'm sorry, but once money comes into it, I don't want to know.

—You're a hypocrite, says Mollel.

—No. Like the old woman says, I choose the rules I live by. They may not be yours, Mollel, but at least I'm consistent. Now, if you'll excuse me, I'm going to find a *cold* beer. And I don't think they serve Fanta where I'm headed. Good night, Mollel.

19 He took his medication before he went to sleep, and perhaps because of it, Mollel was untroubled by dreams of blood—or of anything. But he still feels an uncharacteristic jumpiness when the doorbell to his flat rings.

—Hi, says Kiunga. Happy Christmas. Can I come in?

They stand in Mollel's bare galley kitchen, drinking instant coffee with no milk.

—I'm sorry for what I said last night, says Kiunga. Blame it on tiredness. Frustration. On your Red God.

Mollel gives a short laugh. —I guess he visited us both yesterday. Don't worry. People have said a lot worse to me.

After a while, Kiunga continues: —You know, you're the first partner I ever had who actually believes in proper detective work. Down at the station, there's old Mwangi, who doesn't give a shit. And Otieno, with his politics and his pragmatism. Then you come along, and you're standing up for justice. You remind me of why I wanted to become a policeman in the first place. And you know, don't you, that just because I'm suspicious of *pokos* doesn't mean I don't want justice for Lucy.

—I know that.

—Okay, says Kiunga. So I dropped by James Lethebridge's place on the way here. His *askari* told me he's gone up-country. Doesn't know where. But if you ask me, he wasn't telling the truth.

—No, agrees Mollel. So you've decided to stick with the case?

Kiunga shrugs. —It's Christmas Day. My family's all up-country. Why the hell not? I've got nothing better to do.

Mollel smiles. Then he says, —You know what the consequences might be, don't you?

—Of course.

—Even after what Otieno said? You realize you could lose your job. I'm quite happy to go it alone. It seems like I've got some degree of protection. You haven't.

—You didn't know that when you admitted breaking in to Orpheus House.

He takes a sip of his coffee. Then he says, —Listen, Mollel, if you want people to stop following your example, you need to take a page from Mwangi's book. Don't give a shit. For God's sake, he's never going to get people fired up about things like *justice*.

Kiunga grins. Mollel grins back.

—We've got a day to try to make headway in this case before we both get dragged into election duty, says Mollel. Talking of which, where has he put you for the big day?

—*Kosovo.*

Mollel chuckles. —Mathare?

The slum got the nickname at the height of the Kosovo war, when images of shelled-out buildings were on the TV screens and Mathare residents recognized the similarity.

—Where will you be? Kiunga asks.

—Kibera. Otieno's really got it in for us, hasn't he?

—Do you reckon he's on the take? asks Kiunga, his smile fading.

—I don't know.

—He certainly shut down the case pretty rapidly once Kingori came on the scene. And they obviously know each other.

—If you're suggesting that Kingori might have bribed him, I don't think that's Otieno's style. For all his arrogance, I think he's more concerned about his career than his wallet. Who knows what pressure might have been brought in that department.

—Talking about little gifts, says Kiunga, don't we have a Christmas present to deliver?

Districts mean a lot in Nairobi. Take, for example, Lavington, one of the most desirable neighborhoods in the city. Most people would agree that Lavington ends at the James Gichuru Road. West of there, it's Kawangware.

Most people would agree, but not Faith. It's well known, she insists, that Lavington extends at least one block west of James Gichuru. And that's where her house is. Any attempt to persuade her otherwise is met with a stern look and the response, —I've lived here twenty years and it's always been Lavington.

However, James Gichuru Road is more than a psychological barrier. As soon as you cross it, a change as sudden as the Great Rift's rain shadow comes over the environment. The genteel colonial bungalows with their clipped lawns and jacaranda confetti are replaced with cinderblock walls and hastily erected apartment buildings. Street hawkers, who seemingly feel discomforted across the road, sell their maize and secondhand clothing openly, and in recent years this also appears to have become the destination of choice to buy knockoff DVDs. Even the *matatus* respect the apparent frontier, coasting peacefully along Gitanga Road as far as James Gichuru, then pushing their way across their rivals' paths, jockeying for space alongside—and on—what passes for sidewalk, blasting their horns at any pedestrians who fail to fly into the bushes at their approach.

—I thought Faith lived in Lavington, says Kiunga as Mollel gives him directions to her house.

—If she mentions it, just accept that her house *is* in Lavington. It's a little piece of Lavington in the middle of Kawangware. Think of it as an embassy.

Today this part of Lavington-cum-Kawangware is quieter than usual. Mollel directs Kiunga to pull off the main road, and they go a short way down a dirt track. It's a few weeks since Mollel has been to Faith's house, and the first thing he notices is a frothy metallic swirl gleaming along the top of the wall. For a moment he thinks it's a Christmas decoration. Then he realizes it is razor wire.

Next he notices the youths loitering outside the gate. Actually, *youths* is an inaccurate description. They have the shiftless, cagey manner of truant schoolboys, simultaneously nervous and challenging. But these five men are no adolescents.

Even so, they instinctively palm their cigarettes when the police Land Rover approaches. Kiunga's defense instincts have clicked in, just as Mollel's have. Instead of driving to the gate, he pulls up opposite the house and stops the engine.

—Ho, says one of the men. Looks like the old Kikuyu woman has visitors for Christmas lunch.

Mollel and Kiunga get out.

—*Habari, vijana,* Kiunga says. What's up, boys?

—Nothing.

They mutter some words that Mollel recognizes as belonging to the Luo language, and they laugh. Then Kiunga addresses them in the same tongue. They look at him in shock.

—Yes, I speak Jaluo, says Kiunga, switching now to English. My first posting, straight after basic training, was to Kisumu. So I've heard every slang term for Kikuyu and policeman that you could possibly come up with. Now, what's all this tribalist nonsense?

—It's not us, says the man at the front of the group. Ask those thieving Kikuyus! He waves his hand at Faith's gate, and Mollel sees a glint of glass bottle.

—Us Luos always get a bad deal, complains another. These Kikuyus come here, pushing up the rent.

—She's probably been here longer than you! protests Kiunga.

—Doesn't give her the right to tell us where we can and can't go. This is a public highway, isn't it?

—So she's complained about you hanging out here?

There is muttered assent.

—I don't blame her! says Kiunga. Look at you!

The men shuffle and eye one another. Kiunga laughs. Slowly, grudgingly, they smile too.

—You want to talk about grievances? continues Kiunga. He's on a roll. He points to Mollel. —Look at this guy. A Maasai. His lot were fighting off the *wazungu* with bows and arrows while you were still dragging *dagaa* out of the lake!

They give a reluctant laugh.

—Come on, says Kiunga. It's Christmas. I know the old woman can be a bit of a *jike*, but give her a break, huh? Can't you find somewhere else to drink your *chang'aa*?

—Suppose so.

—And we're all Kenyans, aren't we? Let's hear no more of this tribalist crap.

The men swagger away. The policemen watch them until they have cleared the corner.

—You handled that well, says Mollel.

—You've got to deal with it with humor, says Kiunga, otherwise you'll end up with a *panga* in your head. Christ, I can't stand all this tribalism. You know, I spent the happiest five years of my life in Kisumu. I like Luos. I love Lake Victoria. Imagine, a Kikuyu whose favorite food is fish. And Luo girls . . .

The blissful, distant look on his face completes the sentence.

—And I do believe, says Mollel, that you called my mother-in-law a bitch.

—Sorry about that.

—I didn't say you were wrong.

Faith's first words, once they've brought the car inside the compound: —You saw those no-good *wamera* outside, then?

Mollel glares at her. —I hope you don't use language like that in front of Adam.

—What's wrong with that? They're Luos, aren't they? So they must be uncircumcised. It's simply a statement of fact.

—I don't want him picking up tribalist terms.

Faith scoffs. —You think he doesn't hear them every time he goes through the gate? He used to play on the street there, until it got too much. They're trying to drive us out, me and the other Kikuyus. They want to make this a Luo-only zone.

—That's what they said about the Kikuyus.

—Well, it will have to be one or the other, says Faith. She looks at Kiunga. —I suppose I'm going to have to set an extra place for lunch?

—Happy Christmas, Faith, says Kiunga. Don't worry about me. I've just come to help drop off Adam's present.

—Actually, says Mollel, getting the bicycle out of the back of the Land Rover, I won't be staying for lunch either.

—It's Christmas Day, says Faith. I've killed a chicken.

—I know. There's nothing I can do about it. It's work. I'll be here for supper.

—Well, you can tell him yourself. I'm not going to break it to him. He's around the back.

Behind the house, in the laundry area, Adam is kicking a football against the wall. Mollel feels a pang of dismay at the small square of sky above; the whole space seems so curtailed. At the same age, he'd easily cover five, sometimes ten miles a day. Forest, ravine, mountain, plain.

And then he thinks of the smart shoes on Adam's feet, his clean clothes, his school, his opportunities.

The boy is well-off, he decides.

—Hi, Adam.

—Dad! He rushes up and hugs him. —Happy Christmas!

—Happy Christmas. What's this, a new football?

Adam looks embarrassed. —Yes. Grandma bought it for me.

Mollel picks up the football. He turns it in his hands. It's light, springy. It's orange in color. A fun gift for a boy.

—Sorry, he says. I should have bought you a football before now. I never thought of it, not having had one myself as a child.

—Oh, no worries, Dad.

The football in his hand, Mollel has an idea forming in his mind.

—Can I borrow this for a while?

—I suppose so, says Adam.

—Don't worry. I've got something else for you instead. Come and see what your dad has bought you for Christmas.

They stay an hour or so, Adam wobbling up and down the road, Kiunga holding on to his saddle, the new bike getting smiles from passing neighbors and envious glances from their children. With the Luo boys gone, the atmosphere in the street is relaxed, friendly. Even the roar of traffic from the nearby main road fades into the background, and the place feels like a village.

—Look, Dad! I'm doing it on my own!

He pulls away from Kiunga, who stops running and puts his hands on his knees, laughing. Adam speeds toward the main road.

—Okay, Adam, stop now!

—I can't! Panic in his voice.

—Stop him! cries Faith. But Mollel, who has never ridden a bike, is unable to think what to do. He feels the rush of air past him as Kiunga sprints after Adam. He watches as Kiunga catches up with the bike, grabs the boy's shoulders, and pulls, bringing the bike crashing to the ground just a few feet short of the main road as a truck roars past.

He doesn't run to his father. It's Kiunga's shoulder the boy chooses to bury his tearful face into.

20 —I wish it was Christmas every day, says Kiunga. Then, getting no response from Mollel, he continues: —Not that I'm a big fan of festivities. I just like the lack of traffic. It would take us, what, an hour to get here normally? And we've just done it in ten minutes.

They pull up at the entrance to Uhuru Park. Kiunga squeezes through the concrete posts. There are a couple of other cars in the car park, but no other signs of life.

—Stop here, says Mollel.

Kiunga parks, and they get out. Mollel approaches the posts. He examines one, then the other. At the right-hand one, he crouches, rubs it with his fingers.

—What is it? asks Kiunga, bending over for a better look.

—See here? This post's been hit. Not hard. Just enough to chip the concrete, probably dent the fender of the car. And leave a few flecks of paint behind.

He holds up his fingernail.

—Silver paint, he says. The Land Cruiser owned by Equator Investments has a scrape on the fender.

—Could be a coincidence, says Kiunga.

—Could be. Or it could be that James Lethebridge, or someone else driving that car, was here before Lucy's body was discovered.

—It doesn't really fit in with your theory, though, does it? I mean, according to you, Lucy was dumped up the hill, at Orpheus House. They didn't know she was going to wash out down here.

—True, says Mollel. And he tries to convince himself that there are plenty of silver cars in Nairobi, plenty of places where that Land Cruiser could have picked up a scrape. This is all a distraction. It's Wanjiku Nalo he's after, and he has a baby to find, alive or dead.

And then he thinks, If the facts don't fit the theory, maybe the theory's wrong.

But no. He's convinced of Wanjiku Nalo's guilt. And he's come here today to try to prove it.

—Get me the football from the car, would you?

At the place where Lucy's body was found, all that remains is a lot of smeared mud and footprints. A steady stream of water runs down the central rill of the drainage ditch. Mollel takes the orange plastic football from Kiunga and drops it down, like flowers into a grave.

The ball bounces off the concrete and rolls into the water. The current bears it swiftly away, and they watch it skitter and bob until it disappears from sight, into the gloomy round mouth of a pipe.

—Do you ever wish you'd gone to university, Mollel?

—Never thought about it.

—All those student girls, says Kiunga wistfully.

They've left the park and are now crossing the main quadrangle of the adjacent Nairobi University. Casting their glances down, they try to divine the course of the underground pipe into which the ball vanished. After their investigations upstream, spotting manhole covers has become second nature to them.

Usually, the neatly clipped grass here is dotted with youngsters reading, chatting, or flirting. If it wasn't for their smart appearance and studious air, you might mistake them for pleasure seekers overflowing from the park. But today the place is empty.

The two men cross the lawn and turn a corner around a building called Faculty of Science. The genteel facade gives way to a standard industrial-type building. A row of Dumpsters overflow with yellow plastic bags, and a smell best described as biological fills the air.

—This is the place they do all the *experiments*, says Kiunga in a low voice. You know, all the human heads on rat bodies, and the like.

As if on cue, a rat scurries from under one of the Dumpsters, runs along the narrow alleyway, and disappears into a low sewer grate built at the bottom of a high wall some distance up ahead.

—That's where we're going, says Mollel.

—Oh, Jesus.

The iron grate looks solidly cemented in place, but with a swift jerk up and out, Mollel lifts it and places it to one side.

—I chased a *chokora* down here once, he explains. He went around the corner. I thought it was a dead end, so I stopped running. By the time I got here, he was gone. Took me ages to figure out how he got away.

—These street boys have secret escape routes everywhere.

—Look at the wall above the grate. See it?

—Just looks like scratches to me.

—That's what I thought, too. But see, they're not just random. Three lines, in a row. Once I'd spotted it, I started seeing this mark all over town. Under bridges, beside manhole covers, on loose planks in fences. It means *place of safety*.

—Doesn't look very safe to me.

—We should be okay, as long as you watch your step.

Mollel lowers himself through the grate and drops a few feet into ankle-deep water.

—Hold on, says Kiunga. I'll take off my shoes.

—You'll want to keep them on, replies Mollel from below.

Kiunga groans. —I only bought these a week ago.

—They'll wash.

He drops down, and Mollel steadies him as he lands.

—Dark, isn't it?

—Yeah, well, I suppose they haven't got around to putting street-lights down here yet. Oh, what a smell!

—Come on, says Mollel.

21 —Fresh batteries, says Kiunga, producing his flashlight from his pocket and turning it on. He passes it to Mollel, who has gone ahead.

They pick their way through the muddy water. Even at this low level, there is a discernible push against their ankles.

—According to my reckoning, says Mollel, this is a direct continuation of the drainage ditch in Uhuru Park and, above that, Orpheus House.

—And a whole lot of other places, besides.

—Sure. But right now it's downstream that interests us. Wherever that ball ends up, we should find anything that was dumped at the same time as Lucy's body.

Like a baby, he thinks.

Kiunga lets out a cry of disgust. Mollel follows the beam of his flashlight down to their feet, where excrement and wads of paper wash around them.

—It's only *mavwi*, says Mollel.

—Human *mavwi!* Forget about washing these shoes. I'm going to burn them!

The drain narrows, and they walk single file, Kiunga holding on to Mollel's belt. The sound of running water mingles with the occasional rumble of a heavy vehicle overhead. At fairly regular intervals they pass under a grate, and a shaft of sunlight falls through the crack above.

—Look, says Mollel, pointing. Two large concrete pipes join the drain. Mollel shines his beam at the wall.

—There are your three lines, scratched next to one of the pipes, says Kiunga. And on the other one—a cross. What do you suppose that means?

—I don't know. But these are both inlets. We're headed down-stream, remember.

They trudge on. Mollel senses a void ahead of them before it is even discernible by sight. There is a change in the sound of the water, splash-ing and echoing, and the dense, confined odor of the tunnel is replaced by an earthier, more open smell. Mollel puts his foot forward and feels nothing beneath it. Just in time, he extends a hand and finds an iron bar set in the wall. The flashlight, however, falls into the darkness with a splash, and he sees its suffused beam for a second as it sinks greenly into deep water below.

—I'm okay, he gasps.

—Oh, I'm so glad, mutters Kiunga sarcastically. He has grasped Mollel tightly around the waist. —Now, are you going to go down and get the light?

But it's already died. Gradually, they become aware of gray daylight up ahead, just enough to see by.

Mollel extends his hand along the rail, and his foot finds a narrow ledge running perpendicular to the tunnel exit. It's some inches above the water level, and dry. He steps onto it and edges along, entering a new space where there is just enough light for them to see around them.

He lets out a low whistle.

The void, though not large, feels massive after the confines of the tunnel. It's at least twenty meters long and ten across. The ledge on which they are standing is less than half a meter wide, and the center of the room is a large cistern that acts as a sediment trap. At the far end is another grille, and beyond it, a wide corrugated tube, along which the reflection of gloomy daylight is just visible.

—I know where this is! says Kiunga. That tube comes out in the river just below the Globe Roundabout. You can see it from the *matatu* stop.

At their feet, the water froths into black depths, but as it gets to the grille, it is clogged with floating material, most of which is indistinguishable.

—Well, this is where your orange football should've ended up, says Kiunga.

They look around the walls of the chamber. Aside from the tunnel they came from, there are four other inlets of varying sizes. Mollel wants to get a closer look at the flotsam caught in the grille, so he edges along the ledge. His foot touches something soft, and he instinctively recoils.

—Watch it! shouts Kiunga. You nearly landed us in it!

—Look at this.

They both peer down at their feet. There, on the ledge, is what can only be described as a bed.

One of the most disgusting and precarious beds Mollel has ever seen, one that makes Superglue Sammy's hideout in the bushes look like the Nairobi Hilton, but a bed, nonetheless.

A strip of unfolded cardboard carton is topped with a pile of filthy blankets. A crumpled porn magazine completes the scene.

—And our friend Kingori thinks he's the only one with a luxury pad in the center of town! says Kiunga.

A distant sound of cheering rises from beyond the grille. Mollel has no option but to walk over the bed; he shudders as he treads gingerly across it, reaching the other side near the grille. From there, bending down, he can just make out the end of the corrugated pipe, but the small circle of light is too dazzling, in contrast to the darkness, for him to see anything further. He seizes the grille and tries to raise it, but it does not shift.

He stands up and peers back.

—Look, that's the tunnel we came in from, he says.

Above the tunnel, just discernible, are three scratched lines. Above the next inlet, a cross. The next one, another cross. The same for the next two. Then, the final inlet pipe—barely wider than the ledge they are standing on and at shoulder height—with three lines above it.

—And there's our way out.

Nairobi's *matatus* still run on Christmas Day, though there are fewer of them, and those that are running hike up the fare. That's why there are only a handful of people waiting at the stand to witness a manhole cover pop open and Mollel emerge, coughing.

He bends down and extends his hand to Kiunga, who squelches to a low fence where some of the waiting passengers sit. He examines his clothes with dismay.

The people near him get up and move away.

—What? protests Kiunga. You're too good to sit next to an officer of the law?

He takes off one of his shoes and drains it on the ground. He groans.

Meanwhile, Mollel crosses the road and heads for the center of the Globe Roundabout. It is a large open patch, supposedly earmarked for development for as long as anyone can remember, but mostly used as an impromptu *matatu* depot. Today it's uncannily quiet, apart from the sound Mollel and Kiunga had heard echoing up through the tunnel. A group of about twenty skinny, raggedy street boys—*chokora*—have taken the opportunity to grab some space for themselves, and they whoop and cheer, delirious with the opportunity to play.

Although all the *chokora* playing here probably live and work the streets within a short radius of this spot, none of them has ever played in the public park just three blocks away. Once, street boys infested the park as they do the sewers. But they were an inconvenience, so everyone was happy when they stopped seeing them in Uhuru Park, and few people asked questions. Perhaps it's only among the *chokora* that memory persists of the cleanup—the GSU, the raid, the beatings—and the faces and street names of the boys who were never seen again.

Mollel approaches them with caution, knowing that the sight of a policeman is usually enough to send them scattering. But today they hardly pay him any attention. It could be because of his unusual appearance—battered and stained, trousers soaked from the knee down—or it could be because they are too absorbed in their own game, gleefully kicking around a football.

A plastic orange football.

—What do you want, old man? The game's full!

—I just want a word with you.

—You stink of *mavwi*. Get lost.

—I want to buy that ball off you.

That gets their interest.

—You know, I think you guys have talent. I really do. With a proper football and a bit of practice, you might make it on the team for Mathare United.

One of the older boys, almost the same height as Mollel but as skinny as a Samburu goat, approaches him warily.

—You've made a mistake, old man. We're not the kind of boys you're looking for. You want them, you need to go to Mombasa.

They laugh raucously.

—Panya will let you touch him for fifty bob!

—I will not!

—Make it a hundred, then!

That gets an even bigger laugh.

—No, no, says Mollel. That's not what it's about. Come, with the money I'll give you, you could buy a decent leather ball. Much better than that cheap plastic one.

He notices that one of the smaller boys, the one they called Panya, has picked up the orange ball and is hugging it to his chest. He is frowning, annoyed at Mollel's dismissal of his prize possession. How old is he? It's hard to tell. He's no bigger than Adam, who, at nine, is already up to Mollel's chest. But Adam is well nourished and healthy. Even Panya's childish features are no indication of age in a street boy. The only thing to go on is the eyes: how wary are they, how cautious? From the way he hangs back now, glancing about him, Mollel reckons that despite his baby face, Panya is about fifteen.

—Hey, he says to Panya. Tell you what, I'll give you five hundred shillings.

Panya shakes his head.

—Six hundred. Think about it.

—Go on, Panya, urge the others. We need a *real* ball to play with.

The boy comes closer, eyes on Mollel, but ever grasping the ball to his chest.

—You can even keep that one, says Mollel. I'll give you the money anyway. All I want is some information . . .

As soon as he utters the word *information*, a cry goes up: —*Polisi!*

The boys scatter, but Mollel lunges out and grabs Panya by the arm.

—I knew you were no good, the boy hisses, writhing and twisting in Mollel's grip. Damn *polisi* and your *information!*

Kiunga hobbles up. —Sorry, Mollel. I tried to put my shoes back on, and I just . . . *couldn't*. Did I miss anything important?

—I got the one that matters. His name is Panya.

—Oho. So you're the little rat whose nest we found in the sewers?

Panya makes to bite Mollel's arm, but Kiunga grabs his head. For a moment the three of them struggle, and Mollel is struck by the sad thought that two grown men can attempt to subdue a small boy in the middle of the day, in full view of passengers waiting for their bus, and no one—*no one*—does anything.

Welcome to Nairobi.

—Had enough? asks Kiunga once they've got Panya back under control. The boy spits at him.

—Spit all you like, says Kiunga. I'm going to wash myself in bleach when I get home anyway.

—Relax, urges Mollel. We don't want to hurt you, and you're not in trouble. *Sawa?*

He lets go, and the boy snatches his wrist back and rubs it.

—I'm serious about the money. You can have it if you tell us where you got that ball.

—I didn't steal it!

—I know. You found it, right?

Panya nods.

—In the drain? Where you sleep?

—Yeah. It got washed down there. About half an hour ago. I reckoned some kid had lost it in the park. That's where most of the drains come in from. I only took it so the others would let me hang out with them. They don't, usually.

—How long have you been living there?

—Few weeks.

—Have you ever found anything else down there? Anything unusual?

The boy mutters something.

—What's that? What are you saying?

Kiunga shakes him. He mutters again. Mollel still doesn't catch what he says.

—The dirty magazine, explains Kiunga.

—We don't care about that. Anything else?

He shakes his head.

—How about—don't be alarmed—a body? A *baby's* body?

The boy's eyes widen, and instinctively he steps back. —No! Oh, no! Nothing like that!

Mollel tries to suppress his disappointment. He reminds himself that no body at least means that the baby might still be alive. But he can't help wishing for the breakthrough that would help him make this case.

—Any clothing? continues Kiunga. Women's clothes? Shoes?

Panya is starting to edge away from them. Kiunga puts his hand on his neck.

—What is it, Panya?

The boy puts his arm behind his back, as if struggling to free himself. But when he whips his hand back, something glints from his fist.

Kiunga releases him and steps away. The boy holds the knife forward. His hand is shaking. The blade is small, only two inches long. But it is cruel.

—What's that, Panya? Is that what you found?

—Stay back! You'd better leave me alone!

With a swift, fluid movement, Kiunga swirls his arm toward Panya's and grabs his wrist. At the same time, he clasps his other hand around the boy's fist and prizes the knife from between his fingers.

—Not very clever, Panya, he says. He releases him, and the boy slumps to the ground.

Kiunga passes the knife to Mollel. It is leaf-shaped, razor sharp, cut from flat metal plate. The handle—no longer than the blade itself—is wrapped in a strip of greasy, worn leather.

Panya mutters, —I saw it, shining. Down at the bottom of the water. Thought it might be a ten-bob coin. I jumped in, picked it out. I thought it might be useful. You never know when you might need something like that. I didn't mean to do anything wrong.

—You've told us enough, says Mollel. Here. He takes a thousand-shilling note from his wallet. —It's yours. Don't go spending it on *chang'aa*, or glue, or whatever.

—I won't.

Panya takes the money, then scurries after the orange ball, which is still on the ground. He lets out a childish laugh, as though he cannot believe his luck. As he runs away, Mollel shouts to him, —Happy Christmas!

—What's Christmas? the boy shouts back.

The *pilao*, at lunchtime, must have been delicious—
steaming, fluffy white rice, a few grains every handful
dyed a festive red or green. Chicken flesh falling off the
bone. Now the rice is sticky and hard, blackened where it
has caught the pan. The chicken is greasy and cold.

Mollel pushes it around his plate.

—No appetite? says Faith.

He shakes his head.

—I'm glad you came home before he went to bed. He was wondering if you'd make it at all.

—It took longer than I thought. Then I had to go back to the flat to
change.

He wrinkles his nose. He can still smell the sewer inside his nostrils,
like the smell of carrion.

—I want to talk to you, Mollel.

—Is it about the football? He pushes his plate away. —I'm sorry
about that. I know you'd just bought it. Tell me where you got it, and as
soon as the shops are open again, I'll get a replacement.

—It's not about the football. Though how you could take away the
boy's present on Christmas Day . . . some Christmas he's had!

Mollel has learned over the years to let his mother-in-law's chastise-
ments wash over him. But tonight he feels a pang of remorse. True,

Christmas meant nothing to him. But he recalled the boy's excitement at seeing him turn up, and the disappointment in his eyes when he left. It was like the moment when the bike got out of control. Mollel just didn't know what to do. When it came to his son, he never seemed to know what to do.

He looks over at the frail woman sitting opposite him. She isn't even old, but something about her manner always makes her seem so. For a moment he feels an urge to reach his hand over the table to hers; it's a fleeting thought, rejected. In all the years he's known her, there has never been any physical contact between them apart from a brush of his lips against her cheek on his wedding day. And he felt her shudder that time, however much she attempted to suppress it.

She is looking down, composing herself. Her lips move, as though recalling rehearsed lines. And now he feels unnerved, on guard. He senses an imminent attack, but the quarter is unfamiliar. He'd rather take on the Mungiki than this small woman.

—I want to talk about Chiku's father.

That was certainly unexpected.

—Did she ever tell you about him? Faith continues.

—Of course. Many times. She worshipped him.

—Yes. What did she tell you?

Mollel puffs out his cheeks. —Well, that he was a Mau Mau hero. Fought the English. Turned down a cabinet post from Kenyatta. She always said there could have been a Harry Ngugi Street in town if he'd wanted it.

—All true.

—And then he saw the way the wind was blowing. Corruption, dictatorship. Tribal politics. It wasn't what he fought for. After Tom Mboya was killed, he became disillusioned. He dropped out of politics, became a teacher. Died of a broken heart.

Faith sighs. —That is not so true.

Mollel looks at her with surprise. —She lied?

—No, she didn't, says Faith. I did.

—Frankly, our family had done well out of the English. My father had risen to foreman at the plantation. That meant we got our own front door, some space to raise some chickens, a vegetable patch. And I got sent to school.

Then, a new teacher came. And the word was, he'd been Mau Mau. I was afraid. Convinced he'd come and slit our throats in the night.

And yet I couldn't take my eyes off him. I remember the day I had the revelation. I was shocked. I felt like I'd left my own body and had shot up to the ceiling and bobbed there like a cork. I knew then that it wasn't terror I felt. He was simply the most beautiful man I'd ever seen in my life.

You must realize, even though this was some years after Uhuru, we knew very little about how it had all come about. We had only one history book at school, and that was all English kings. What we heard about Mau Mau was mostly horror stories from the newspapers. It was in Kenyatta's interest to keep those stories going. He'd turned against Mau Mau by that time: too much of a threat to his interests.

So when this teacher sat there telling us his tales, we were spellbound. He spoke so softly, sometimes we had to strain to hear him. But we never interrupted. It was as though he were speaking to himself as much as to us. His arrest, his escape. How he'd broken into the camp and led his whole village to freedom.

Massacres. Administration Police, mostly Luos and Luhyas, killing twenty, fifty prisoners at a time. The truck would stop in the middle of the night and the back would drop down . . .

Secret meetings. In the forest. In hotels. Kampala, Khartoum, Cairo. Suitcases full of dollars, trucks full of guns. It made me tingle, hearing about our nation being formed, being just inches away from someone who formed it.

He was a gentleman. He didn't propose until I'd graduated from school. I was hoping my father would be outraged, but he took the news well. He always loved the elites, and Harry Ngugi was the new elite.

Except that he was already a long way from the elite. He knew how to handle a rifle, but not a committee. He was disgusted when he saw Kenyatta shaking hands with the English. He became an embarrassment. He drank.

He kept holding out for a better offer, even as the offers got worse and worse. Schools minister. Ambassador to Hungary. A professorship. A lecturing post. Headmaster. Schoolmaster. He took that one. Back to teaching, the job he'd qualified for ten years before. A small village school near Kiambu . . .

Chiku came along. She adored her father from the first day. The first minute. They put her on my chest and she just scowled. Then he held her, whispered to her, and she opened her eyes. She just knew him. She just looked at him, drinking him in. As if saying, *So this is what you look like.*

I'd never before seen two people fall in love with each other at the same time. I've never seen it since.

He lost his job. Used to go to Nairobi or Thika, looking for old friends to borrow money from. They were fond of him. Many had links with struggles elsewhere. He was offered work in Tanzania.

—Training rebels, Mollel says. Chiku told me about it. Fighters from the south. Rhodesia. She said he taught the leaders of the continent.

—After he'd been gone a month, Faith continues, I got word from the camp. They were still waiting for him to start. He'd never turned up. He rolled home half a year later, broke. Camp not paying on time, he said. Chinese money not coming through. I never told him I knew the truth.

Chiku was ten. She organized a *harambee* to welcome her father home. A ten-year-old. The whole village came. Everyone put something in the hat—ten bob, a hundred bob. Money to liberate our African brothers.

He couldn't even find the vein when he slaughtered the goat. He virtually hacked its head off. I had to step in, hold it down. He said it was emotion. But he was drunk.

We didn't see him again for over a year. As far as Chiku knew, as far as anyone in the village knew, he was fighting in some foreign country, leading the resistance. But I heard reports. Someone told me they'd seen him in Tigoni with a woman and kids. It wasn't even an hour away. I went. It was true.

I told him, if you want to write Chiku a letter, you'd better do it now. His hand was shaking. He dated it "Somewhere outside Windhoek," a month before. It was a nice touch: he was an accomplished liar.

—I think I still have that letter among her things, says Mollel.

—I told her, *Your daddy died fighting for what he believed in. Your daddy was a hero.*

▲ ▲ ▲

Mollel takes a drink of his water. His curiosity has not eliminated his sense of foreboding.

—And you never told her the truth?

—That her father was a polygamist, an alcoholic? That he abandoned her?

—Yes.

She shakes her head. —Her imaginary father was better than the real one.

—Why are you telling me this now, Faith?

—I want custody of Adam, she says. I want you to sign him over to me.

—It's not like it will make much difference, she says in response to Mollel's silence. He spends so much of his time here, anyway. You can still see him, of course. But look, he idolizes you. Let him continue. Just—at a distance.

—I'm a policeman, Faith. I'm not like Harry.

—You are. You just don't know it.

—How?

—I called the station today. You're not supposed to be on duty. You should have been here with your son.

—I'm on a case!

—There will always be an excuse! When Chiku was killed, you got a payout you could have retired on. You had a safe nine-to-five post in the traffic division. But you got yourself switched back to CID. It's not about the money. You could raise chickens and grow beans for all I care. But you'd be there for your son.

—You don't understand.

—No. And neither will your son.

—It's not going to happen, Faith. I'm grateful for your looking after him, but that's as far as it goes.

—That's not what my lawyer says.

—Lawyer?

—I'm sorry, Mollel, she says. Adam can have everything he needs here. A stable home, school, attention. I'm not going to lose another child.

Look to the living, not the dead.

He'd woken before dawn with Otieno's words in his head. He was supposed to be attending a preelection briefing in Kibera, but he had time to do some more digging first.

Honey had said that the orphanage had to lodge its adoptions with the government, so he had come to the city records office.

If the baby was living, whoever had taken it would want to legitimize it as soon as possible. They would not want questions asked about why the birth was not registered sooner.

A pile of documents lands with a thud on the desk before him, raising a cloud of dust.

—Birth records, last four weeks, says the clerk.

—I asked for the last three months! protests Mollel.

—Just start on those, says the clerk. Can't you see I'm the only one here? It is a holiday, you know.

Mollel props himself against the counter and begins to browse through the folder. It's fairly bulky, but does not contain as many entries as he thought, as most are duplicates: a white sheet, filled in by the parent, and a pink one, by the attending physician. There are probably three or four hundred births recorded here.

—Is this a usual amount for a month?

—About usual, calls the clerk from the back of the office. Of course, more will come in over the next few weeks. We won't close December's file until January fifteenth.

—What happens to births recorded late?

—There's a fine for that. They go into a separate file that gets consolidated at the end of the year.

—So this year's won't have been consolidated yet?

—I suppose you'll be wanting that one too, the clerk sighs.

There's nothing in the December file that stands out. Most of the entries are from the main hospital, Kenyatta. Several from the other big ones, the Nairobi, the Aga Khan, the Coptic. The rest are from smaller clinics. All of the information between the two sheets, white and pink, seems to match.

Mollel turns to the next bundle.

—When I started here, says the clerk, climbing a stepladder, they told me that this would all be on computer within twelve months.

—When did you start here?

—Nineteen ninety-two.

The November file is fuller, but equally unrevealing. As more files arrive, the story is the same. Nothing from Wanjiku Nalo. Nothing from Orpheus House.

—Thanks, he says to the clerk after working his way back to January.

—Did you find what you were looking for?

—I found nothing, replies Mollel.

—Oh, great! moans the clerk in dismay. I suppose you want 2006 now.

But Mollel is already out the door. Nothing is as good as something for him. It means that if there ever was a baby, it was delivered illegally. *Look to the living, not the dead.*

—Let's go pick her up, says Kiunga over the phone.

—Not yet.

—Why not? We can use Honey's testimony and the disparity in the birth records to squeeze her. Might be able to get a confession from her that way.

—We still don't have enough.

—The word of a *poko,* you mean, says Kiunga. No, we can't give Otieno any excuse to let Wanjiku off the hook.

—How's Kosovo? Mollel asks, changing the subject.

—Exquisite. Kiunga laughs. —But I hear Kibera's even nicer this time of year. I'm almost envious of you.

Despite his levity, Mollel can hear the exasperation in Kiunga's voice. He'd rather be on the case than guarding a slum polling station. Mollel will be in the same boat in the morning, but he hardly dares consider how much worse Kibera will be.

As if reading his thoughts, Kiunga says, —If I were you, I'd chill out tonight. Try to get some rest. Do you get your briefing this afternoon?

—I'm going there now. Mollel hangs up.

But he's not going there directly. He wants to see someone first.

He's at Honey's apartment block in Kitengela. A gaggle of children are playing around the entrance, and they stop and gawp at him as he approaches. He thinks it strange; usually he manages to be more or less anonymous. He brushes past them. A fat woman mopping the stairs glares angrily and splashes his feet with black water.

By the time he reaches Honey's landing, Mollel knows that something is wrong. A group of women are there, falling silent as the new arrival rounds the corner from the staircase. There are too many people here. Their eyes fall upon Mollel with cold hatred.

A low, contemptuous hiss accompanies him as he makes his way to Honey's door. It stands open. The lock hangs uselessly from the splintered jamb.

—Dirty bastard, hisses a bystander. Another: —We got *children* here. Do your filthy business elsewhere.

He's accustomed to abuse as a police officer. But this is different. He pushes his way past them, and they shrink from him as though he is infectious. On her mattress, face in her hands, sits Honey. All around her, Mollel sees her little nest destroyed: bed tipped over, cupboard facedown, drawers ransacked. On the far wall, across the window, blotting out the view of the plains, red paint: POKO.

—Whore! they yell from behind him. You're not wanted here!

—And *you* should be ashamed of yourself, someone else hisses in Mollel's ear. A jab in the ribs rams the point home.

He goes forward, and Honey flies into his arms, sobbing. He slips his hand protectively around her shoulder and takes her to the doorway.

As they step out onto the landing, Honey screams. Her hair is pulled from her head and waved triumphantly by one of the women before widening, arcing over the railing, floating like a crow to the street below.

Nails flash—Honey's hands are to her eyes—the women descend. Mollel pushes between them, parting them, pulling them apart like the thorn gates of a *boma*, touching Honey, pulling her—taking her, sheltering her, crouched over her—to the staircase.

—And don't come back! rings out behind them.

The fat old woman mopping the steps is still there. Mollel now understands the dirty look she gave him as he went up. He grasps her T-shirt and pins her to the wall.

—Who did this?

—Don't hurt me! the old woman cries.

He pulls back his arm, his hand open.

—Mollel! yells Honey.

He lowers his hand. —Who did it?

—I don't know.

—You know! You must have been mopping the same stair for hours. Worth the wait, was it? To see the expression on her face?

—I can't tell you.

—You'll tell me, says Mollel, or I'll take you in. I'll chuck you in prison and lose the paperwork. I'll see you inside for the rest of your life. You got a family?

—Mollel! Honey cries again. You're going too far!

The woman is shaking, blubbering. She says something he can't make out. Snot pours from her nose.

—Muh-muh-muh, she mutters.

—For God's sake, Mollel! Honey claws at his arm. —Leave her! Don't be like this! Don't be like *them*!

—Mungiki, sobs the woman. It was Mungiki. Mungiki did this!

24 They manage to find a cab, eventually. On the way, Honey explains what happened. She'd gone out to get some groceries. She came back to find her apartment already trashed. She hadn't been there long when Mollel came in.

It is past seven by the time the taxi drops them at Mollel's apartment block, and dark. Honey puts a hand on his arm to steady herself as her heels crunch over the gravel driveway.

—Thank you for this. I really don't have anywhere else to go. I'll call my landlord in the morning. See about getting a new lock put on. More security.

—No, says Mollel. You think your neighbors would have you back now that they've found out—what you do? Besides, you can't risk the Mungiki returning and finding you home.

But he does not believe it was Mungiki. The old woman said it was a couple of men with dreadlocks. And he knows at least one who fits that description.

—Look, he says, reaching into his jacket pocket. It's there: small and hard and cold. He takes it out and gives it to Honey.

—Lucy's knife, she gasps. Where did you find it?

—In the sewer. Don't worry about that. The thing is, you might as well have it, for the time being. It has no purpose as evidence, being in the water for so long. And I don't have anything else to give you.

—Thank you, Mollel, says Honey, a catch in her voice. You don't know how much this means to me. It takes a murder to get anyone's interest around here, and even then, it's only you who seems to care, Mollel.

—Just be careful, he says. It's for self-defense. Let's hope you don't need to use it.

She clasps her hands in his as she takes the knife. —You can trust me, Mollel.

He hesitates.

—What is it? she asks, sensing his doubt.

—It's just something someone said. Honey . . . were you telling me the truth about how you and Lucy met?

Honey drops her eyes. —Mostly, she concedes. But you're right. It wasn't her who helped me get into the game. It was the other way around. Oh, Mollel—she clutches his hands tightly—you've got to understand. If she hadn't been on the streets, she wouldn't be dead. I blame myself. I didn't want you to blame me too. I needed you on my side if you were to take me seriously. It's hard to tell someone the whole truth. And believe me, you wouldn't like it if I was completely open. But I promise, I won't lie to you again.

—I believe you, says Mollel. And he opens her hands and relinquishes the knife.

When they reach the top of the stairs to the first floor, Mollel sees that the door to his apartment is open.

—Stay here.

He puts out the landing light, the better to see within, and so as not to present a silhouette.

Slowly he edges to the door: no sign of forced entry.

Lights are on inside. He hears movement.

He has no weapon now that he has given away the knife, not that it would have been much good in this situation, so, entering, he picks up an umbrella from beside the door. It's better than nothing.

The noise of drawers opening comes from Adam's room. He edges along the hallway, umbrella raised. As he passes the entrance to the sitting room—

—Dad!

—Adam!

—Is it raining? Grandma said we had to come and get some clothes for me. I told her I didn't mind wearing the same clothes.

—No, but I mind, says Faith, coming out of the boy's room with a pile of folded clothing in her hands. I'll not have the women at church thinking my grandson is a street boy. I let myself in, she says to Mollel. I didn't know when you'd be back.

—Can't I stay here, now you're home, Dad? Adam has flung his arms around Mollel's waist.

—Best not. I've got to leave early for election duty tomorrow, and God knows what time I'll be back. The next few days are going to be very difficult, Adam. Best you stay with your grandmother.

There is a cough, and the three of them turn.

—Oh, says Faith. I didn't realize you had company.

—This is— Honey, this is my son, Adam, and his grandmother, Faith. This is Honey. Her name is Honey.

—Hi! says Honey to Adam, approaching him and placing her palm on the top of his head, crowning him. It's a curiously Maasai gesture. Instinctively, Adam smiles.

—Well, really! says Faith. We must be going. Come along, Adam. Let's leave your father and his—friend.

—Faith!

—No, no. I can see you've got your priorities. Work, indeed! And as she passes: —We'll see what the lawyer has to say about *this*!

—Grandma!

—Not now, Adam.

—But Grandma! The lady—she's crying!

There is a creature—in Maa, called *en-kelesure*, in English, pangolin—a hard, scaly eater of ants. It has powerful arms and long, sharp claws, and, when cornered, it will rise on its hind legs and display. Jab it with your stick or spear and it rolls into a ball. Hard. Impenetrable. Boys love to taunt such a creature when they catch one. And when they do, it always ends the same way: on the fire, blackened in the embers, the scales roasting with the smell of burned hair, sweet flesh picked straight from the shell.

Irritable, defensive, but soft inside. Sometimes Faith reminds Mollel of a pangolin.

The three adults are around the kitchen table, nursing *chai*.

—I never would have thought it of the Nalos. They seem like such good Christians. I mean, I know they're not Catholic, but—

—We can't prove *anything* yet, says Mollel, his sense of procedure demanding the caveat.

—Oh, come on! After all this poor girl has told us?

Faith through and through. Half an hour earlier, she could barely look at Honey. Now she's *this poor girl.*

—Mollel's right. If they killed my friend and sold her baby, who knows what else they've done. We have to make a strong case against them. We have to find out if there are other children—and where they are.

—Lord above, says Faith. What has this country come to? Selling our children!

—The buyers are guilty too, says Mollel. He pushes away his *chai*.

The gesture is noticed by Faith, who says to Honey, —It's late. My dear, you are coming home with me.

—What? says Honey. No, I couldn't impose.

—It is no imposition. You don't even have any clothes with you, do you? You can borrow some of mine. And tomorrow, with the election, there's no point going out anyway. What would you do, stay here on your own all day? No, it's much better you come with me.

—You're very kind.

—I think you're owed a bit of Christian charity, don't you, dear?

Faith calls to the sitting room. —Adam, we're leaving soon. Before we go, Honey would like to see your video game. Can you show her?

—Sure.

As Honey walks in, the little boy excitedly begins to explain his game to her and passes her one of the controllers. He clearly relishes having someone to play with: Mollel has never done so. It's the sort of thing Chiku would have done.

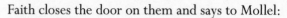
Faith closes the door on them and says to Mollel:

—Did Chiku ever tell you about Koki?

—No. Don't think so. Who's Koki?

Faith gets up and looks out the darkened window.

—It was rainy season. Chiku noticed a tiny puppy. Pure white. There were lots of stray dogs living near our house, but none of them seemed to be its mother. She pestered and pestered me about that dog. *Mama, who's going to look after it? Mama, it will die.*

—So I took in the dog. Washed it, fed it. Got it treated for rabies, everything. I have to say, it was a cute little thing. And it adored Chiku. She called it Koki.

—But?

—But? It was wild. Even though it was so tiny, those days on the streets had left their mark. When it grew up, it never lost its jealousy, its temper. And if you ever came between Koki and Chiku . . .

She rolls up her sleeve and runs her finger along a small crescent scar on her arm.

—You can bring who you like into your house, she said quietly. But if it affects the safety of those already there—

—She was only going to stay the night, Faith. I would've slept on the sofa.

—Well, now she can go into my spare room. Where I can keep an eye on her.

—Believe it or not, I'm grateful. I'm not really set up for guests.

—Just be warned. If necessary, I will do anything, *anything*, to protect my grandson.

—Even if that means taking him away from me?

The door opens. They both look up at the same time. Honey is in the doorway.

—Adam wants to know if he can bring his video game with him.

—Sure, says Mollel. Honey turns and goes back to the sitting room. Faith scoops her car keys from the table and rises.

—Aren't you going to ask me what happened to Koki? she says.

—I don't want to know, answers Mollel.

25 Kibera. Mollel has heard that a million people live here, two million. No one knows. Least of all the government. They don't even officially acknowledge that the settlement exists.

The slum is so close to the city center that the towers of the business district are glimpsed now and then from between the tin roofs. It seems like a different world. But the shit and trash underfoot—under everything—ends up flowing into the same river as the water from the tunnels Mollel crawled through two days earlier.

He arrives at the edge of the slum half an hour before his shift is due to start. Trying to make up for missing the briefing yesterday, he's also concerned about getting lost. He has been into Kibera only twice before, and it would take many more than two visits to learn his way around.

As it is, he need not have worried. From the Langata Road, there are only a handful of access points, and each one is steeled with lines of GSU. He even gets a salute, and stumbles over returning it—a strange feeling, being back in uniform.

—I need to report to Champions Primary School.

—If you wait a few minutes, we've got a group going in.

—Any trouble?

The GSU man's only response is a hearty chuckle.

Kibera might be an informal settlement, but Kiberans vote. The local MP is the leader of the opposition—the slum his Luo power base in the capital. The threat—real or imagined—of an uprising from this massed humanity has often won him a place at the bargaining table.

The government has long practiced a policy of containment in all the country's major slums. Why else are police dormitories and army camps always found adjacent to such areas? But this time they're leaving nothing to chance. The GSU, in their green uniforms and crimson helmets, flow around the exterior like a troop of forest ants. Mollel spies a water-cannon truck and dozens of Administration Police Land Rovers, their green bodies and crimson roofs mirroring the uniforms of their occupants.

—We have a group reporting to Champions Primary? calls one of the uniformed men.

Mollel steps forward, as do a half dozen other regular police officers and a couple of nervous-looking officials, their breath steaming in the chilly morning air.

—Right. This polling station is in part of Kibera known as Half London.

There's a humorless laugh from some of the other officers. Half London is a common name for any district that is fancy, lively, or exclusive. Nairobi's slum dwellers have a good line in irony. Sometimes they can be almost literal, too: Mollel wonders how Kiunga is getting on in Mathare slum's Kosovo.

—The ballots and boxes are already on-site, continues the GSU officer, as are plenty of your colleagues. There's quite a queue already, waiting to get in, but no reports of any problems so far. Now, there is no vehicular access to this site. We have to walk in—and out. That's why we're going in groups. Do not step away from the group. Do not depart from our route. Do not enter any residence or building other than the polling station. Do not accept or buy any food or drink from locals. There are refreshments on-site, securely prepared. Watch your step— the ground is treacherous even when dry. Take a tip: don't try to jump over things. The locals have a saying: the only thing worse than stepping in it is landing in it. And last, look out for flying toilets.

—Flying toilets? asks one of the election officials.

—Plastic bags, says the GSU man with a smile. Flung over the roof-tops. I'll leave you to imagine the contents.

A whistle blows, and they move off.

The crimson helmets part, and the group of officials enters the slum.

The first sight is a kiosk, a small hut selling Coca-Cola, *chai* and *mandazi*, clumps of *sukuma*, and strips of chewing gum. It is doing a good trade even at this early hour. Despite the public holiday for the election, there are still a large number of people bottled up on the Kibera side of the cordon, huddled against the cold, attempting to leave for work in the city. Many wear the clothing of domestic servants—blue overalls and gum boots for gardeners, green or pink pinafores on the maids. One man, incongruous in suit and tie, sees the oncoming party and shakes his fist.

—They're not letting us out! he cries. No one said they could arrest all of Kibera! What is this, intimidation? Well, it won't work!

—Shut up, growls the GSU man leading the way. You'll get out in due course. Then, in an aside to Mollel, he adds,—That one'll be going nowhere today if he carries on like that.

The street narrows swiftly, and Mollel finds himself straddling a trickle of water. The compacted trash underfoot has some give in it, spongy, the one-story houses around them are made from sticks and rusting iron sheets, ragged curtains in doorways, everywhere the smell of food, of smoke, the sound of babies crying and music playing and laughter. Chickens and children compete for space around the legs of women standing around the doorways. The place feels alive, organic. Mollel has a vision of himself and his colleagues as antibodies, invaders in a larger organism. That makes Nairobi the body—so which organ is Kibera? Dark, dense, condensing. Kibera is the liver.

—Look up there, says one of the policemen. Mollel sees a group of five or six men standing on a tin-roofed shack atop a small rise, silhouetted against the dawning light. He clearly sees their long, matted dreadlocks.

—Mungiki, says the policeman.

As they see the oncoming party, one of the dreadlocked men produces a blue flag, which carries the ruling party's emblem, and waves it. They jeer and whoop as Mollel and the others pass.

—Is he mad? They'll get ripped to shreds! It was only a few days ago that some kid got lynched for wearing a pro-government T-shirt here. He didn't even know what the logo meant.

—But the GSU weren't here a few days ago, says Mollel.

—What's that supposed to mean? demands the GSU man.

—Everyone knows there are no Mungiki in Kibera. If they're here, they must have got through your lines somehow. Word has it that they're working for their Kikuyu brothers in the government. Trying to stir up trouble. I'll bet that just on the other side of that rooftop is a GSU snatch squad, ready to take anyone who rises to the bait.

—You be careful what accusations you make, brother, says the GSU man.

As if on cue, a rain of missiles—empty bottles, stones, and detritus—flies over their heads, sending the dreadlocked men hopping off the rooftop like vultures. Mollel and the others duck their heads and wait until the volley dies down. A sound of hooting and cheering greets the disappearance from the rooftop.

—I hope for their sake there are none of your men on the other side of that house, says Mollel. I saw quite a few flying toilets among that lot.

The polling station is little more than a cement-block shell with a tin roof. The windows and the doors are mere openings in the walls, and a black-painted wall serves as a blackboard. There is no school furniture, books, or anything else: probably easier than having them stolen, supposes Mollel. Out back, though, there is the staple of the Kenyan workplace, a charcoal stove and a pair of sturdy women stirring a massive *sufuria* of *chai*. The rest of the party head toward them eagerly. In the otherwise empty room, a set of cardboard polling booths have been erected, and some officials sit at a trestle table with papers, ink, and stamps.

There is a sizable queue outside. Some of those waiting shuffle their feet, and as Mollel passes, he is asked the time anxiously. He feels that the inquirer is almost disappointed when he hears it is not yet seven. He is sure that there are many present who would like nothing more than the chance to make accusations of irregularities.

Farther down the line, he sees a familiar face. He is standing with one hand on the wall, the other hand holding a cane with a small plastic cup taped to the bottom.

—Where have you been, Sammy?

—Oh, hello, Sergeant. How are things? Guess I never expected to run into you here. How do you like Half London?

—Never mind that. You disappeared. I've been looking for you.

—Well, now you've found me. Eh, sounds like something's happening. You wouldn't want me to miss my chance of exercising my democratic right, would you, Sergeant?

Seven o'clock has arrived. The guards have started letting people into the school hall.

—I need to talk to you.

—Not here, hisses Sammy through a grin. He's right: far too many curious eyes.

—Well, where? When?

—A few days' time. When the elections are over and I can get back to the city center. I'll see you then.

Mollel puts his arm around the blind man's shoulder and digs his fingers in. —If you think I'm going to let you vanish again—

Sammy grimaces, then attempts to disguise it with a smile. —As a registered blind person, you know, I am allowed someone to assist me with my vote, he says through gritted teeth. I usually rely on the officials. But perhaps you'd care to be my helper?

It is a good idea. After they've presented his ID and done some paperwork, Mollel escorts Sammy to a cardboard booth on the far side of the hall. He waits a moment for the booths on either side to be free; then he stands facing outward while Sammy goes into the box. Mollel shakes his head at the official who guides voters to the booths, a signal not to send anyone else to their section.

—What's it all about, Sammy?

—Nothing, Sergeant, nothing. I told you everything I could that night.

—So why did you go? I thought someone had got to you.

—No, no, nothing like that. I just wanted a change of scene, you know. It was getting kind of crowded around the park.

—And gave up your pitch in town too? We looked for you for hours. Come off it!

—I swear to God!

—Look. We're already taking too long about this. If you like, we can walk out of here arm in arm, and I can announce to the world that you're kindly helping the police with our inquiries. How would that go down?

—Don't do that, for God's sake.

—Right. So let's talk.

—You never told me it was the GSU in the park that night, Sammy says. If they wanted to keep it secret, I didn't want to hang around waiting for them to hear from one of your guys that I was a witness.

—How did you find out it was GSU?

—Come on, Mollel, says Sammy. If it was police, you'd have known about it. Who does that leave? And if *you* worked out that it was them, why shouldn't I?

—And that's it?

—Not quite, says Sammy. He shuffles uneasily. —There is something else. Something I didn't tell you. I was going to tell you soon, honest. But I thought that if I held out a little longer, there might be . . .

He rubs his thumb and forefinger together.

—Oh, there'll be a reward all right, Sammy. The reward is, I don't shout from the rooftops of Kibera that you're nothing more than a police informant.

—Okay, okay. The blind man frowns. —It was probably nothing, anyway. But just before those buses turned up, I heard a row. A woman screaming. And another woman's voice. I couldn't hear what she was saying or who she was arguing with.

—And the woman shouting was different from the one screaming? Are you sure?

Sammy nods. —I have a good ear, he says.

—Could you identify the shouting voice if you heard it again?

—I'm sure I could.

—And this was *before* the buses came into the park, you say?

—Right before. It was them coming in that shut her up. But look, there's nothing else. That's all I know. Honest.

—It had better be, Sammy, says Mollel.

As they leave the polling station, Sammy holds up his ink-blotted pinkie for all to see.

—Thanks for your assistance, Officer!

—Will you be all right from here? I can't really leave the polling station.

—Oh, yes. I know every inch of this place. Good thing about a slum: no cars to worry about. And if you put out your hand—he stretches his arm and places his fingers against a corrugated sheet—there's always a familiar wall within reach.

Mollel watches the blind man go, cane tapping, the fingers of his free hand dancing over iron, cardboard, sticks, and plastic sheeting. So Sammy heard two women at the park that night. The screams must have come from Lucy. If the woman shouting was Wanjiku—and if Sammy could ID her—it might be enough to pin the murder on her. If a court was not convinced by the testimony of a prostitute, perhaps they'd take the word of a blind beggar.

He becomes aware of someone else watching, too, and looking down the line of waiting voters, he sees the black-clad figure of Benjamin, Nalo's supposedly ex-Mungiki right-hand man. Benjamin gives him a smile and a sharp nod, then turns and walks away.

26 Three in the afternoon, and the time for Mollel and his shift colleagues to be relieved has come and gone.

—I don't mind how long they take, says one of the younger policemen, barely out of training. Just think of that lovely overtime!

Neither Mollel nor anyone else has a mind to tell him that this will fall under *special provisions*—the catchall clause that superiors always invoke to avoid paying out overtime.

—I don't like it, says another policeman.

—It's all gone peacefully so far.

It has. As the day warmed up, so did the attendance, and the police were required to start double queuing, snaking the line back and forth. Queuing is not a habit that comes naturally to the *matatu*-faring Nairobian, but this time the practice was adopted with grace and even good humor. Mollel was struck by how the dominant mood of the morning was enthusiasm, even optimism. This was opposition heartland, and the absence of any pro-government voice on this territory created a sense of inevitability, invincibility.

Kibera felt it was going to be heard.

Around lunchtime the relaxed atmosphere had been shattered by a disturbance. A middle-aged man, reeking of sour *chang'aa*, had staggered to the front of the queue and demanded to be allowed to vote.

Those at the head of the line, who had been waiting patiently for over an hour, objected. The young policeman intervened. He pushed the man away from the line, and *chang'aa* and gravity did the rest. He went flying into the mud. Most of the people who saw it laughed and thought nothing more of it.

But soon the drunk returned with a handful of his buddies. He began to harangue the officials. He'd been prevented from voting, he said. It was because he was Luo, he insisted. The polls were rigged. There was no way this Kikuyu government was going to allow the other tribes to speak.

This time, the people in the queue did not laugh. They were no longer the same people who had seen the drunk try to break into the line. His accusations were met with dark murmuring and hostile glances at the officials.

It was Benjamin who defused the situation. He had been hanging around all day, talking to people in the line and passersby, always just out of Mollel's earshot. As ex-Mungiki, he was certainly a Kikuyu, and in that sense was either brave or foolhardy to be in a place like this on a day like this one. But Nalo's church drew a considerable constituency from Kibera; it was evident from the way many people greeted him that they knew Benjamin from there. Mollel wondered whether they would be so forgiving if they knew about his past, and then reflected, probably, yes. He had learned many times, from his own experience, that the capacity for forgiveness is greater among the poor than the rich.

Benjamin had approached the man, and Mollel saw the drunk's anger dissipate as Benjamin first listened to his protest, then spoke with him quietly for a while.

Benjamin then came to Mollel, who was supervising the head of the voting queue. It was the first time they had spoken since meeting at Nalo's church on Sunday.

—I need you to do something, said Benjamin.

—*You* need *me* to do something? How about you tell me what you're even doing here today?

—I'm an official observer. Call it part of my pastoral duties. Ministering to our flock. And heading off trouble before it begins.

—Trouble, like a trashed apartment in Kitengela?

—You want to talk to me, fine. Let's do that. But let's do this first. There's a lot more at stake here than you realize.

Mollel, against his will, found himself beginning to trust the man. There was something about his intensity that suggested he was genuine.

—What do you want?

—I want you to let our friend here—he pointed at the drunk—in at the front of the line. He's to go into the voting hall, wait a few minutes, then walk out with his finger inked.

—What about voting?

Benjamin shook his head.

—Then why— Suddenly Mollel laughed. —I get it. That was what your little chat was about. He's not even registered, is he?

Benjamin smiled. —He didn't know he had to be.

—All that fuss about being denied his vote, and he wasn't eligible anyway!

—True. But the thing is, he's got a big mouth and a lot of drinking buddies.

—So you want to give him a face-saver. Better he boasts about skipping the queues than mouths off about being turned away.

—Exactly.

Mollel found himself feeling unexpected respect for Nalo's young man.

That was a couple of hours ago. Mollel had done as Benjamin requested, and the situation had calmed. For the moment.

One of Mollel's colleagues takes over from him at the main entrance to the polling station, and Mollel seizes the opportunity to walk around. The line is longer than ever, but—blame the afternoon heat or something else—the atmosphere is different.

There is a tension in the air. People lower their voices to talk to one another. Laughter and chatter have been replaced by quick, concerned glances. And another thing: seems like everyone who has a phone is using it, looking at screens, tapping out replies.

—Something's wrong, he says, as much to himself as to anyone else, but a voice replies, —Yes.

It is Benjamin. —Seems like word is reaching here of what's been going on at Old Kibera.

Old Kibera is one of the other polling stations in the district, half a mile or so away as the crow flies, but considerably farther through the narrow, mazelike passages. In the age of the mobile phone, however, even the crow seems sluggish compared with the spread of news by text message.

—What's happened?

—People being turned away all day, by all accounts. Irregularities on the register. A big blank page where most of the letter O's should be.

Old Kibera ward is more mixed than this one. If the vote is going to be gerrymandered, it would make more sense to do it there. But surely no one would be as blatant as to strike out all the names that begin with O—disenfranchising nearly all the Luos at one stroke?

—I'm just telling you what is being said, says Benjamin. The latest is, Raila himself turned up, half an hour ago, to cast his vote. He wasn't allowed in.

Raila Odinga. Leader of the opposition. True or not, if that story was doing the rounds—

—This place is going to explode, says Benjamin, finishing Mollel's thought for him.

The sound, when it comes, makes everyone stop. For a moment they hope it is something innocuous—gravel raining down on tin roofs, perhaps, or construction work somewhere. But even those unfamiliar with it—and in Kibera there are few—quickly recognize it as gunfire.

—It's some way off yet, Mollel says.

The two tea ladies, four policemen, four officials, and one GSU officer are gathered at the entrance to the polling station. Voting is continuing, though the queue has dissipated.

Somehow, Benjamin has been accepted into their group. Mollel is glad of his presence. He does not altogether trust the ex-Mungiki man yet, but he recognizes his usefulness.

—That pop-pop-pop, that's automatic fire. Probably intimidating fire, says Mollel. He's not the ranking officer here—technically, that's the GSU man—but his calm assurance has naturally gravitated all eyes toward him.

—Who's shooting? Us or them?

—I'm guessing, them. Our guys would be firing off single rounds.

The two armed policemen tote their AKs nervously. They have only a handful of rounds between them. If a situation arises, they're going to have to make each bullet count.

—There's every chance the trouble won't reach us, says Benjamin. It's been calm here all day.

—Equally, there's every chance it will, says Mollel. If so, all we can do is hole up and wait for relief. This building is the closest thing to shelter we have. We'll have to make a call on closing the poll.

—As election officer, I insist that the ballots be preserved.

Mollel suppresses a smile. The small man's terrified face is at odds with his words. But Mollel is pleased to see someone taking his job seriously.

—We'll do our best, he promises. Now, this building is constructed from concrete blocks. I'm afraid that's poor defense against AK-47 rounds. Our best hope is to stay in the building, and stay low. Avoid presenting a target.

—You sound like a soldier. The young policeman laughs nervously. No one else smiles.

—You two, Mollel continues, turning to the tea ladies, who are quivering, holding hands. Are you from here? Local?

They shake their heads, yes.

—You're going to need some kind of white flag. Can you make one?

They look around them. —We have tea towels. We can find a stick.

—Okay. That's for when assistance comes. As soon as you see the crimson helmets, you start waving that flag and you keep waving. Understood?

They nod, but it's clear they've not fully understood the implications of what Mollel is saying. Probably none of them have, except Benjamin: his fixed jaw says it all. The policemen's uniforms, the officials' suits, even Benjamin's smart suit—by enabling them to be quickly recognized, their clothes should afford them some measure of protection in any GSU counterassault. But the two women, wearing common Kenyan *khangas* and T-shirts, will have no such status. They might be seen as a threat by some trigger-happy cop. Or, in the confusion, they might end up getting the standard GSU treatment for any woman they find in their path. And that, Mollel reminds himself, is still a possible scenario for what happened to Lucy.

On reflection, he's not sure a white flag is going to be enough.

—You stay with these two, he says to the young policeman. The man nods.

—Now, we've got four hours until the polls close, he continues. Then we're out of here. So let's do all we can to ensure that happens.

As they all return to their posts, Benjamin sidles up to Mollel.

—What's the betting that these ballot boxes won't make it as far as the count?

It's the first time the thought has occurred to Mollel. He's been wary of vote stuffing, of irregularities at the count, but he never considered that the whole ballot box might go astray. Of course, nearly every one of those papers inside the boxes must be an opposition vote. And they rely on the security services to get them out. Surely—*surely*—they would not be so brazen?

And the only outside observer here is Benjamin.

They have been in close proximity to each other all day, but this is the first opportunity Mollel has to speak to him properly.

—Whose side are you on? he asks frankly.

—Weren't you listening to the sermon on Sunday? We don't take sides.

—Oh, sure. Nalo's a business partner of David Kingori, who's hand in glove with the government. Don't tell me your church is a disinterested onlooker. And as for the Mungiki—word is, they're taking their orders directly from State House these days.

—I wouldn't know.

—Because your Mungiki days are far behind you, right? Then who ordered your Mungiki brothers to destroy an innocent girl's apartment?

Benjamin sighs. —That should not have happened.

—So you admit it?

—I admit nothing. But say—just say—someone's going around making serious allegations. You'd want to find out more about them.

—You mean, the Nalos wanted to find out what she had on them?

—Put it this way, says Benjamin. Intimidation is not my style.

—So you were looking for evidence. You thought she might have something that could prove the case against them.

—If there was any so-called evidence, it would be fabricated. The allegations are false.

—Either way. You say your guys didn't trash Honey's place. What did they do, leave the door open?

Benjamin remains silent.

—And the neighbors did the rest, continues Mollel. They'd probably been waiting for a chance for some time.

—I think we're understanding each other, says Benjamin.

—It doesn't let you off the hook. If I manage to pin it on you, I'll get you for obstructing an official investigation.

—There is no official investigation, says Benjamin. The way I hear it, you continue like this, you'll be off the force.

—The way you hear it?

Suddenly it becomes clear to Mollel. Benjamin's presence here today is no coincidence.

—You knew I'd been stationed here. I thought you said intimidation is not your style.

—This is not intimidation, says Benjamin. We had to find out if you were pursuing these false allegations. The fact that you know about the break-in at the girl's flat tells me you are. In fact, I would not be surprised if you knew, very well, where she is right now. And that's information I'm sure your superior would be very keen to hear.

But Mollel is no longer listening. He's tuned in to something else—a sound of cries and panic underscored by a distant, yet distinct smell.

—You smell that?

—Just burning charcoal.

—No. It's too pungent.

They rush outside, greeted on the doorstep by the sight of the young policeman dealing with a group of wild-eyed youths.

—I'm telling you, we don't have a fire extinguisher, the policeman is saying.

Mollel looks up. Black smoke is pounding into the air, the occasional flame leaping into the sky.

—What's burning?

—One house, says one of the youths. But it will spread.

—Where can we get water here?

—Down at the stream. It's nearly dry.

—Put a call in to the command post, Mollel orders the GSU man. Tell them to raise the fire brigade.

—There's no way they'd get a fire truck in here!

—No, but with some extinguishers and a bucket chain from the stream, we should be able to get this under control.

He and Benjamin run with the youth to the scene of the fire. It's about three rows back from the polling station. A woman stands in the alley, a few pitiful possessions around her, a baby clutched tightly to her chest. She is crying.

—Anyone inside?

—No.

—All the neighbors out?

Mollel can see that the inhabitants of the neighboring shacks are leaving little to chance, throwing mattresses, furniture, and foodstuff out of their doorways. This has the undesirable effect of further obstructing the alleyway, which is already crowded with onlookers.

—It was Mungiki! cries one bystander. Mollel wheels around and grabs him by the shirt.

—Did you see them?

—No, but others did! They set the fire, then ran off over the rooftops!

—She was cooking indoors, shouted a woman. She always does it! We told her it was dangerous, but would she listen?

—It was Mungiki, I tell you!

Mollel delivers the man a powerful slap with his open hand, and the man slumps to the ground. —Shut up! You think we need panic now, on top of everything else?

—I think you may be too late, says Benjamin.

They look up to see a gang of young men rounding the corner of the alley. They are carrying *pangas* and sticks.

—Ha! So the *polisi* are here! shouts the leader. Not in time to stop their friends the Mungiki from burning Kibera to the ground!

Mollel looks behind him desperately. The crowd is thick in that direction, too. They gasp as the second building begins to burn. Benjamin has started frantically punching on his mobile phone, but the leader of the gang steps forward and knocks it from his hand with a stick.

—I'm trying to get help to put this fire out, he cries.

—Get help for *this*! shouts the youth, and brings the stick down toward Benjamin's head. Benjamin parries it with his forearm, and Mollel hears the cracking of bone.

—Ask *her*! Mollel is amazed to hear his voice reaching a scream. —Ask *her*! It's her house! She can tell you how the fire started!

He points to the woman with the baby, but she is still crying, and she raises her face to him dumbly, tears and mucus running down her chin.

By now, flames are leaping from the top of three shacks in this alleyway, and Mollel is sure that those behind must also be ablaze. The fire is out of control. Benjamin, cradling his shattered arm, is slumped to his knees, Mollel supporting him. They are less than twenty meters from the polling station and his armed colleagues. He considers shouting for them, but even if they could hear his cries, they would not come for him. They would not be foolish enough to abandon their post. He wildly scans the faces around him, looking for someone who might speak up for them, might offer them some mercy. But he finds none. The faces stare back blankly at two men who are about to die.

—Enough!

The voice is familiar, but wholly unexpected. Mollel has only heard him speaking softly, meekly. But now, all eyes turn to the blind man. Superglue Sammy holds his cane aloft like a sword. His face is full of rage, and spit flies from his lips as he shouts, —These are not our enemy! *They're trying to help!*

—They're in league with the Mungiki! And the government!

—This Maasai? I've known him fifteen years. Do you know who he

is? He's the one who pulled a hundred people out of the American embassy the day it was bombed!

A strange hush comes over the mob. Mollel's story—if not the man
himself—is widely known, even in the depths of Kibera.

—Yes, he's the one. He's the one who kept going back, kept bringing
out survivors even though his own wife was among the dead. And how
did the government reward him?

Sammy has tapped his way around to Mollel and Benjamin. —You
know what they did. They *demoted* him, sent him away for daring to
speak the truth about what goes on in the police department! He's no
government stooge! He's on our side!

Mollel looks up. The youths are lowering their weapons, but the fire
is breathing down his neck. He can feel his skin singeing.

—If he is who you say he is, Sammy—

—He is!

—Come on, boys, the leader says grudgingly. It's getting hot around
here.

The gang members turn to leave.

—No, wait!

It is Benjamin.

—Don't go. We need you—and your *pangas*.

—He's right, says Mollel. There's no chance of putting out this fire
now. We've got to create a firebreak.

Energized, he reels off commands. Take down any structure within
three meters of the fire. Pull out everything inside, take it away from
the flames. What little water they have—stinking, brown, in pans and
sufurias—should not be wasted on the flames, but instead used to douse
the roofs and walls of the shacks on the other side of the firebreak.
Meanwhile, anyone left without a task should be on hand with a blanket
or a broom, to tamp sparks.

It's remarkable—even in this confusion Mollel notices it—how bid-
dable the gang has become. Their rage has evaporated, and they take
their orders with relish. With a newly instilled sense of purpose, they
dash off to their duties.

Benjamin groans. —We should not hang around.

Mollel agrees. The two of them stagger back to the polling station. The door is closed. They hammer on it and call, and one of the armed policemen raises his muzzle over the sill of the unglazed window.

—It's you! he says. We thought you were dead.

—Just let us in!

They go in. —They're not letting the fire brigade through, says the GSU man once they're inside. To his credit, he seems embarrassed by the decision. But Mollel ignores him. He runs over to one of the officials' desks, pulls it to a window, and jumps up. From there, he can reach to the outside, where he is able to pull himself up onto the flat concrete roof.

—Wait for me!

Mollel lowers his hand, and Benjamin offers him his good arm, wincing as Mollel pulls him up.

The roof of the school is concrete and baking in the sun, and the heat from the nearby blaze stings the skin on their cheeks and eyes. Mercifully, the thick smoke is trailing almost straight up on this windless day, affording them a clear view of nearly all of Kibera.

For a moment they turn from the fire and take in the panorama before them.

The black smoke carves a deep groove in the blue sky, serving to highlight the crystalline clearness of the view. On the horizon is the city, the skyscrapers looking close enough to touch. Then the lush green of trees abruptly cuts along a geometric boundary, stopping against red—the earth-red, rust-red, iron-red roofs of the slum, rolling like furrowed fields, a corrugated carpet, down the valley and flipping up the other side. In the fold sits a fine mist, like morning haze.

—Tear gas, says Mollel.

—That's Old Kibera, confirms Benjamin, his words accompanied by a renewed pop-pop-popping, and they hear a whiz of bullets over their heads.

They both drop.

—So much for not presenting a target. Benjamin laughs.

They crawl to the edge and look over. Below them, they can see the gang clearing the firebreak. Five of them have taken the tin roof off one shack and are now pushing and rolling the thin wooden structure below, while an elderly woman—the occupant, no doubt—looks on, sobbing. With a crash and a cloud of dust, the walls collapse.

—Look, says Benjamin.

Children are scampering into the flattened shack, weaving through the legs of the demolition team, picking up whatever they can find, all accompanied by the screams of the owner. The young men hardly heed the kids as they begin hurling everything they can lay their hands on out of the fire's path. They're just in time, too; flames are already beginning to encroach across the gap. The children dance away, laughing. The peril is nothing to them.

Meanwhile, Mollel sees that several other shacks have come down. The gang is working well. A rough square is being formed around the blaze, and the roofs and walls disappear all around while water hisses from buckets onto the sunbaked roofs of the houses beyond.

—They're doing a good job, says Benjamin.

—Let's hope so, Mollel replies. They don't have much time.

Suddenly Mollel sees something that makes him lurch with desperate fear. Emerging from the smoke in one of the newly created clearings, stumbling over debris: —Sammy!

The blind man has his hand out, flapping futilely for a wall, searching in vain for a navigation point.

Mollel leaps to his feet. Benjamin stands too. Together, they shout out desperately, trying to raise the attention of some of the gang below. But their cries are lost in the tumult of destruction.

—He doesn't know where he is!

—Oh God, oh God, cries Benjamin.

Sammy turns, trying to judge by sound a safe passage. He puts his hand up to gauge the heat—and makes a decision which way to go.

The wrong decision.

—No, Sammy! No!

A flaming shack collapses a few feet before him; debris scatters at his feet. He stumbles, drops his cane. He wheels around helplessly.

He trips, sinks to his knees. The fire is almost upon him. He puts his hands up to his sightless eyes, skin crackling and peeling in the heat.

—I'm going, yells Mollel.

—No!

But Mollel is already over the ledge. As he leaps, he hears the whiz-zing of bullets. He is not even aware of landing. He runs to the fire. He runs so slowly he seems to cover no ground at all. And yet within an instant he is among the choking smoke.

He hears Benjamin's voice, though he can't make out what he's shout-ing. He looks back at the school roof. Through the smoke, he can just see him standing on the edge, indifferent to bullets. He is pointing franti-cally ahead of Mollel.

He takes a breath.

He plunges into blackness.

THE HONEYGUIDE

27 Once there was a girl who was sent by her mother to collect berries. Before she even started to pick the berries, she was approached by a little bird. The bird told her, "These berries are sweet, but I know of something sweeter still. It is my secret. I would like to share it with you, but because I do not wish others to know of it, you must close your eyes. Follow the sound of my voice."

The girl closed her eyes and followed the sound of the little bird's voice. The bird guided her well, patiently sitting on branches while the girl rounded thickets and crossed streams.

The bird guided her this way for some distance, and she felt the coolness of night approach. But she thought that her mother would be pleased with her for finding the sweetness, so she kept her eyes closed tightly and followed the song of the little bird.

Finally she heard a loud buzzing, which began to fill her ears with noise and her heart with dread. She opened her eyes and said, "This is a place of danger. You have tricked me."

"There is no danger," protested the little bird. "Simply do as I say, and we shall both get what we desire."

So the little bird told the girl to gather a pile of stones. She did so. Then the bird told her to build a fire directly beneath where the bee's nest hung, high on the branches of the whistling thorn tree. Fearfully, she gathered kindling, but the bees were too busy returning home for nightfall to molest her.

She found a discarded weaverbird's nest and struck sparks into it from her little knife. Then she placed it among the kindling and lay on the earth, blowing into the pile of sticks until flames lapped their edges. Still the bees took no notice of her. Then the little bird told her, "Gather the moss from the stones by the stream and lay it upon the fire." She did as she was bidden.

Immediately, thick gray smoke began to rise. The moment it curled up to the branches, the bees retreated inside, and the little bird shrieked excitedly, "Now! Throw the stones at the nest!"

The girl was afraid, for she knew the insects would attack her. And she was angry, for she knew she had been tricked. But she knew that she could not find her way home without the little bird to guide her. And still she craved the sweetness that the bird had promised.

So she threw the stones, and the third one struck the nest and it tumbled. It tumbled onto the fire, thick with smoke, and the bees poured out, and she began to run, but even as they alighted upon her, they crawled distractedly and did not sting, and she brushed them easily to the ground.

All around they crawled, confused and harmless. Amid the smoke, the little bird hopped and flapped gleefully, ripping away at the broken nest with her beak. As she widened the hole, rich, dark honey oozed from within. The girl approached and dipped a finger in, raising it to her mouth. She had never tasted such sweetness. Greedily she took more and sucked it, rolling it around her mouth, letting it slip warmly down her throat.

Though she could gorge like this for hours, time was against her. Soon it would be too dark to see. She had a calabash, and she tipped its water onto the soil and began to gather the honey within. As she did so, she looked down at the little bird beside her. It was not honey the bird sought: the girl saw that deeper still, the nest writhed with life. Tiny gray grubs teemed and pulsed blindly as the bird repeatedly plunged her beak into the mass, each time withdrawing it to pull her head back and pour more of the larvae down her throat. She gave a small cackle of joy before returning to the nest.'

Repulsed, the girl drew away. Her calabash fell onto the smoldering fire. She pushed her way through the smoke, crunching over bodies of stupefied bees and stumbling blindly into the thornbushes all around.

28 He is woken by the storm, a proper Nairobi storm. The sort that comes in like a drunken husband, makes a lot of noise, wakes the kids, and throws the place around a bit, if only for form's sake.

This time the fury is real. The thunderclap sounds as if it is directly overhead, the sky being ripped apart from the heavens all the way to the ground. Now the atmosphere vibrates and crackles with tension. The rain has yet to come. It is awaiting its cue, holding back until the wind has played its part.

In his groggy state, Mollel can make out that he's lying on a cot in a tent of some kind. A fresh squall causes the fabric to bulge and rise, giving him the queasy sensation of being in a falling elevator. There is commotion beyond as voices fight to be heard against the storm. They're attempting to lash down the tent before it capsizes. The steel poles groan and creak with the strain. Mollel attempts to rise, but weakness overcomes him. His head falls back onto the cot.

As his eyes slide, he takes in the scene around him. There's a strip light hanging from the tent's central pole by a short chain. It sways to and fro, casting fluorescent shadows over the faces of the people rushing about. The tent's roof, a large expanse of white plasticized canvas, falls away from the ridgepole. Its height and shallow pitch suggest to Mollel that this is a large tent, of the type people might hire for a wedding or *harambee*.

With effort, he manages to raise himself onto his elbows. He's aware of a bulkiness around his hands, and looking down, he sees that they're wrapped in thick mitts of gauze bandage. But he feels no pain.

He looks to his right and sees a young man sleeping, or unconscious, in the cot next to him. He has a heavy bandage over his shaved head, an ominous dark patch insinuating through the weave. Two men rush up and grasp handles at the head and foot of the cot. With a groan, they lift the young man.

A dazzling pinpoint of red light bursts into Mollel's face.

—Ah, you're awake, says a voice from somewhere behind the light. Good. Do you think you can walk?

—I don't know.

—Let's try. We've got to get everyone out of here. Take this jacket. Your uniform's in shreds. We're going to get pretty wet outside, but it's better than having the tent collapse on us.

Mollel takes the man's arm as he pulls himself to his feet. Then he squeezes his bandaged hands through the sleeves of the dark green jacket. He recognizes the camouflage pattern and the insignia.

GSU.

—Bloody paranoia, the man mutters, as much to himself as to Mollel. Everyone knows you can't start treating patients while the field hospital is being put up around you. But no, they said. They've recced the site, but we'd have to wait until voting was over to put up the tents. Well, this is what you get for it!

A stark white flash picks out the tent's canvas and is followed, in less than a heartbeat, by a stomach-churning clash of thunder.

The man—he's a medic, Mollel has decided—has put his arm around Mollel's waist, and the two of them stagger unsteadily toward the exit. They push through a heavy canvas flap, and Mollel's breath is taken away by a sudden blast of stinging rain.

—Can you make it on your own now? yells the medic. I've got to get the other patients out. Mollel nods. —*Sawa sawa*, the medic shouts. Head for those buses over there.

Mollel raises a bandaged hand. Now that the rain has started, it is remorseless, it runs down his face, distorting the blinding light of arc lamps and vehicle headlights. Men in uniform run around him on all sides. Many of them carry the same red-filtered flashlight as the medic used. Mollel bows his head and pushes toward the vehicles. His bare feet stumble on the rough gravel. The gravel kicks up a memory within him: in this dizzying, disorienting place he has an indefinable sense of location. But before he can pin it down, he feels a shove between the shoulders. A violent gust of wind sends him spinning, nearly toppling him from his feet.

The shouts and cries all around him intensify. Mollel has turned around, away from the lights, squinting into the wind and rain. Before him appears the ghostly white shape of the tent, illuminated in the arc lamps, rising lazily from the ground, a dozen or more GSU men struggling to hold it as it tips forward, crashes, crunches, and rolls to rest like a downed bird, flapping with futility against the side of a military truck.

The gust drops as suddenly as it arose, and the men scurry to detach the canvas from the frame before it picks up again. No longer blinded by the rain, Mollel sees other tents—still standing, these—trucks coming and going. Another roars past him now, and he catches a glimpse of rows of grim-looking GSU men in their green fatigues and crimson helmets serried in the back before they disappear in a cloud of diesel smoke. There is some sort of communications truck, bristling with aerials, and the buses: four big, old military buses, their windows steamed, parked in a neat row on the gravel ground.

—I know this place, Mollel says aloud, barely hearing his own words.

Everything beyond the lights is black. But back where the tent had been, he sees the raised ridge of a concrete drainage ditch. He lunges forward, almost breaking into a run despite his weakness and his bare feet. He goes past the cursing GSU men, over the flapping, exposed groundsheet, the neat hospital cots now exposed and overturned, to where the water gushes and bubbles in the ditch below, the torrent bursting forth from the pipe that leads all the way to Upper Hill, running swiftly and blackly at his feet.

He is in Uhuru Park.

He is at the spot where Lucy's body had been found.

29 —Mollel? Are you Mollel?

He gasps with pain. He raises his hands. They feel as if they're on fire.

He sits up stiffly. The whole bus smells of sweat and old blankets. He uses his two bandaged hands to pull the damp blanket off himself. He's still wearing the GSU jacket.

Daylight. The sun is pouring through the windows of the bus. Beyond, the fresh green foliage of Uhuru Park, plumped by the rain, seems to burst with color and life under the brilliant clarity of a blue Nairobi morning sky.

—I'm Mollel.

—Someone's here looking for you. How are the hands this morning?

He recognizes the voice as that of the medic who helped him from the tent the previous night.

—Sore.

—We'll get you something for that. Your friend is outside.

The medic helps Mollel to his feet, and they pick their way out of the bus, stepping over the limbs and boots of GSU men sleeping or lolling in the seats on either side of the aisle.

Despite the pain in his hands and the stiffness of his body, Mollel can't help smiling when he sees Kiunga's broad grin. Kiunga offers his hand and assists Mollel down the last step.

—You would not believe the *shida* I've had trying to find you, he says. They told me the GSU had rescued you from a fire in Kibera, but no one would let me know where they'd taken you. I've been to all the hospitals in the city. Then, on the way back from Kenyatta, I drove past Uhuru Park. Saw the whole place cordoned off, crawling with GSU. I spent more than an hour trying to persuade them to let me in. Quite a change, huh, from a few days ago?

The medic—whom Mollel sees now properly for the first time, an anxious-looking man in a GSU uniform, wearing a white armband with a red cross on it—hands Mollel a couple of pills and a paper cup of water.

—Are you on any other medication? he asks.

—No, says Mollel. Kiunga casts him a doubtful look, but Mollel ignores him.

As he lifts the cup to his lips, Mollel becomes aware for the first time of a thirst almost as intense as his pain, and he drinks greedily after downing the pills.

—Those are all you'll get from me, says the medic. You were only brought here by mistake in the first place. You'll have to make your own way to the police infirmary.

—What is this place? asks Mollel.

—Forward command post, replies the medic. The GSU HQ in Ruaraka is too far away from town to be effective. So we've set up here. It's the closest open space to Parliament and the Central Business District.

—You told me last night, says Mollel, that they didn't want to set up this command post until the voting was over. That means they were expecting trouble? Anticipating accusations that the vote had been rigged?

—I don't know anything about that, says the medic, shifting on his feet. You guys really need to get out of here now.

—Not until we've spoken to your OIC, says Kiunga.

—Be my guest. You'll find him in the communications truck.

He disappears into the activity all around them.

—I noticed last night that a lot of these GSU men have been issued flashlights that have red filters over the lens, says Mollel.

—Army trick, replies Kiunga. Scatters the light, makes the beams less likely to be seen.

—And less effective, says Mollel. Remember the shred of fabric we found where someone had blundered into the barbed wire? The red filters covered the light well enough to ensure that the passing police patrol didn't see the GSU last Friday night. But that's probably also why they didn't spot Lucy's body.

—Now we know why they were here, says Kiunga. They were doing a recce for this camp. They had to do it under cover of darkness. The last thing the government wanted was to give the impression that they were preempting the protests. So it seems our little blind friend was right all along, eh, boss?

Mollel feels a wave of pain and dismay.

—Sammy!

—What, boss?

—Superglue Sammy. He was there, in Kibera. It was him I was trying to save. What happened to him?

Kiunga casts his eyes down.

—There was no one else brought out of the fire, boss. Only you.

In daylight, it's easy to find Sammy's den once more, now that they know where it is. Mollel is just a few feet away from Kiunga—all he needs to do is hop over the low barbed-wire fence and duck between a fan palm and an ornamental papyrus—but it feels strangely sheltered, cocooned from the hubbub in the park beyond.

Sammy's blanket lies on the floor, and beside it, his treasured battery radio. Mollel picks it up. Awkwardly, with his bandaged hands, he manages to turn it on.

. . . *with the worst violence reported in the Lang'ata district of the capital. Meanwhile, the count continues at the Kenyatta International Conference Centre. The media have been ejected from the scene, but shortly before the ban, one official observer, the businessman David Kingori, categorically denied accusations of vote rigging.*

Mollel hears the familiar, condescending tones of David Kingori. Irresponsible forces, he is saying, were attempting to influence the outcome of the ballot before all the results were even counted. The reporter asks him about discrepancies in the count: pro-government wins that appeared to be higher even than the number of registered voters. Mollel can hear the smile in Kingori's voice as he replies: *That's a matter for the electoral commissioner. All I can tell you is that I've been here at the count since the first boxes came in, and I've not seen anything suspicious.*

Mollel turns off the radio angrily. He thinks of Sammy, optimistically queuing up to cast his vote in Kibera, and he nearly slams the radio into the bushes in disgust. But instead he folds the aerial and puts it into the gym bag Kiunga had given him. His colleague had raided his own wardrobe to bring Mollel a change of clothes, and Mollel is glad to see that although they are somewhat big for him, they're sober and discreet, a white shirt and trousers, socks and shoes. And a belt, which will be needed if he's going to be able to wear Kiunga's trousers without having them fall down. He leaves the surgical gown and GSU jacket on the ground.

When he emerges from the bushes, Kiunga says, —I was beginning to wonder if you were ever going to come out.

Mollel holds the belt between his bandaged hands.

—I need you to do this up for me.

With an embarrassed glance over his shoulder, Kiunga stands close to Mollel and hastily wraps the belt through the loops and pulls it tight. He stands back.

—Sorry about Sammy, boss, he says. But you know, you mustn't feel guilty. You can't save everybody. There aren't many people who would have even tried.

Mollel feels the young man's admiration like a burden. He feels the urge to confess: *I didn't go in there to try to save Sammy's life. I was trying to save a witness. I was doing it for the case.*

You can't save everybody.

If only he knew, thought Mollel. If only they all knew that back then, in the rubble of the American embassy, he wasn't trying to save everybody. He was only trying to save one person. He kept pulling the others out because they were getting in the way.

—You all right, boss?

—Sure. Come on, we have to speak to the guy in charge of this place.

—But you're looking pretty bad. Do you want to see the doctor again?

—I feel fine.

—Boss, I'm worried about you. When the doctor gave you those pills, you said you weren't on any other medication. Well, I know you are. You've tried to hide it, but I've noticed all the same. If you're feeling ill, boss, we can always go to the police infirmary, try to get what you need there.

—I feel fine, snaps Mollel. And we've got work to do. Unless you think the case doesn't matter anymore? Perhaps you think we should give up on it, just like everyone else?

—No, boss, says Kiunga.

—We need to speak to whoever's in charge, says Mollel.

At the top of a set of aluminum steps, the rear door of the communications truck stands open. At the bottom of the steps, a GSU sergeant is picking his teeth.

—We're police, adds Kiunga, showing his badge.

—I don't care, replies the GSU man. *Nenda huko.*

Which is about as close as you can get in Swahili to *fuck off.*

—Okay, *rafiki*, keep cool, says Kiunga. We're on a murder investigation.

—It doesn't matter. The only people who get in here are GSU and the President himself.

—I bet you boys are quite fond of this place by now, aren't you? It was you having a little midnight picnic party last Friday, wasn't it?

—What do you know about that?

—So it was you?

—You shut your mouth, *mtundu.*

—We need to speak to your boss, Mollel says. It won't take a minute.

—Lieutenant Kodhek hasn't got a minute, Maasai. In case you hadn't noticed, this country's heading for civil war. And what are you laughing at?

—Ashiruma Kodhek? asks Kiunga with a grin. Shitkicker Kodhek? They made him lieutenant, did they?

—Has been for some time now, says the GSU man grudgingly.

—Tell him Collins Kiunga's here. We were at Embakasi together. Go on!

Somehow the injunction works, and the sergeant flicks his toothpick, gets up, and lumbers into the back of the truck.

After a short while, a GSU officer comes over. Like the others, he's tall, over six feet, and wears the paramilitary dark green. Instead of a helmet, though, he wears a crimson beret. At the sight of Kiunga, he grimaces. He does not even bother to look at Mollel. The guard looms threateningly at his shoulder.

—So you're lieutenant now, Shitkicker? says Kiunga.

—And you're still a constable? No surprise there.

—*Detective* constable.

—Great. So you get the same pay, but have to work in your own clothes. Well done.

—I wondered if this might be your regiment, says Kiunga. I notice your boys have all removed their unit insignia. Makes it kind of difficult working out who's who.

—What do you want, Kiunga?

—Well, much as I'd love to stand around and reminisce, says Kiunga, we've got a murder investigation to conduct. The body was found just inside the park, here. We think the victim was killed, or dumped here, around the time your colleagues were conducting their little hush-hush nighttime recce of the site. We'd like to ask a few questions, if you don't mind.

—I do mind. And what's this you've been saying about the other night?

—Just that we know you were here. We have witnesses. And it would be helpful to know whether you or any of your men saw anything that might help us with our investigation.

—We were not here. This is the first time that any GSU have been near this park. Isn't that right, Mwathi?

—That's right, Lieut, says the sergeant. Besides, they can't have a witness, 'cause no one saw us.

Kodhek rolls his eyes, and Kiunga and Mollel try to hide their smiles.

—Look, says Mollel. A girl was killed on Friday night. Her body was found there, in the drainage ditch. We're not accusing you lot of anything. We just want to verify a few things.

—Come back when the trouble's over.

—Oh yeah? When's that going to be? Do you know something we don't? Like the fact that there was always going to be trouble in the first place?

Kodhek stares at him mutely. Kiunga decides on a change of tack, and adopts a friendly tone.

—Come on, Shitkicker, pleads Kiunga. How's that sweet little sister of yours? She must be about twenty, right?

—You leave my sister out of this, warns Kodhek. The guard at his side bristles, ready for the order to attack.

—I'm just saying, says Kiunga. I'm just saying, this girl. The one we found in the ditch. She was about twenty. Just like your sister.

—That girl, spits Kodhek, was nothing like my sister.

Then, realizing he's said too much, he barks, —Mwathi! Get rid of these two. If they're not off this site in two minutes, chuck them in the happy wagon.

He turns on his heel and storms back into the truck, slamming the door behind him.

—You heard him. Get moving.

Mwathi has a pickax handle in his hand, and he swings it menacingly. He gestures to the park exit, which is guarded by a line of languid troops, many of them holding or leaning on the same standard-issue club.

—This way.

He leads them around the back of a canvas-covered truck and looks over his shoulder. Kiunga readies his stance for a fight. But Mwathi puts down his club and leans it against the wheel of the truck.

—It's all right, I just want to talk to you. That girl was twenty years old, you say? I got a daughter that age myself.

Kiunga grins. —You don't look old enough.

—Save the flattery. We got to make this quick. If the lieut finds out I've been talking to you . . .

—*Sawa sawa*, says Mollel. What have you got to tell us?

—You were right, says Mwathi. We were here that night. I don't know if the bosses had prior warning of trouble or not. All we were told was that we had to prepare in secret, otherwise it wouldn't look good. We got here around eleven.

Just as Sammy said, thinks Mollel.

—Anyway, just as we come in—four buses, lights off—we see a couple come out of the bushes, there.

—By the ditch? asks Mollel.

—Yes.

—Did you see them yourself? Can you describe them?

—Like I say, it was dark. But we knew what they'd been up to. The boys in the bus had a good laugh. They were pretty mismatched. She towered over him. We couldn't make out much of her in the darkness. But him, though! That was the funny thing. White hair, white skin. Showed up, even in the darkness. A *mzungu*. The two of them were pretty startled, I reckon, 'cause they ran off to their car. A nice four-by-four, silver or white, I think. Drove off as fast as they could.

—Did they hit one of the posts as they left? asks Mollel.

—Not that I noticed.

They're interrupted by the arrival of twenty or so GSU, fully rigged up in riot gear. They storm past Mwathi and the two policemen and start plunging into the back of the truck.

—Where are you off to? shouts Mwathi.

—The KICC, one shouts back. They need reinforcements at the count.

—Any chance of a lift? yells Mollel.

The truck roars into life.

—The lieut told me to get you out of here. He didn't say how!

Mwathi gives Mollel and Kiunga a leg up to the back of the truck. They squeeze onto the bench, attracting quizzical looks from the riot troops.

The truck is already moving as Mwathi pushes up the tailgate and Kiunga locks it into place. Mwathi gives the two policemen a wave as the truck sweeps through the cordon and out of the park.

Kiunga leans over and says in Mollel's ear, —You know, sometimes you could mistake a GSU man for a human being.

Mollel looks at the blank, visored faces all around him.

—Only sometimes, he says.

30 The truck is too loud for conversation, but even if it hadn't been, the scene outside would have quelled any words.

Even the GSU men seem shocked by the city.

The truck bowls down Kenyatta Avenue, the traffic lights even more inconsequential than usual.

Outside the truck, there is not a single human being in sight.

The shops are shut, shuttered. As they speed past Simmers, even that legendary Nairobi sleazepot is closed. No Lingala music drifts from behind the tables, which are tipped and hastily placed across the doorway as a makeshift barrier. A yellow dog trots down the sidewalk, her triangular teats flapping, ribs bare. She glances at a couple of white-shouldered crows going through a garbage bag, decides they would put up a better fight than she could, and slinks away. In the slipstream of the truck, pieces of paper and plastic whirl and eddy, then join the downdraft from the avenue's skyscrapers, floating upward to where gray eagles, exuberant as the new masters of the city, gyre and scream.

The eye rises: above the steel-shuttered storefronts, signage proclaims barbershops, beauty salons, gymnasiums, even a marriage bureau—the first to third floors seem the preserve of the body and heart. Higher, more hand-painted signs: business colleges, stockbrokers, import-export agents. The upper floors are home to the speculative and aspirational. Perhaps they're the only ones who can manage the stairs.

These buildings speak of a different era, optimistic but shortsighted. The growth of this city was never anticipated. Six, seven stories were thought to be enough. Never intended for multiple tenants, the buildings bear the scar of each subsequent resident: windows boarded up like broken teeth, air-conditioning units hanging from them like cigarettes from a lip. Their roofs are ridged in slate or terra-cotta tiles, patched here and there with sheets of galvanized steel. So much for what Nairobi might have been.

But beyond, the glinting skyscrapers of the new Nairobi look down impassively. The twin towers of the Nation Centre; the blue mirror-glass of the Standard Building, reflecting its taller, stockier cousin, Lonrho House, across the street. The glass elevators of the ICEA Building hang static from the sides. There are no passengers today.

And over and above them all, the first sign of humanity Mollel has seen since leaving Uhuru Park. On the lip of the helipad atop the KICC tower, a plump military helicopter wobbles into the air and wallows a moment before pointing its head down purposefully and speeding away.

The Kenyatta International Conference Centre, its tower the most distinctive, if no longer the highest, in the whole city, crowned with its dinner plate of a helipad. It's like the chimney of a termite mound, an expression of the energy and ambition of what lies beneath. The conference center itself is a city within a city, a statement of Nairobi's intent to proclaim itself a world destination. A pin stuck in the map.

The truck dives off Kenyatta Avenue the wrong way up a one-way street and into the administrative district: City Hall, Parliament. Life is back on the streets, even if the majority of it is crimson helmeted. As they approach the gates of the KICC, the truck slows, and halts for a moment while the GSU officers attempt to make way for it. A woman is there with a sheaf of papers.

—I'm an electoral official, she is shouting. You cannot deny me access to the count!

In her fury, she spills the papers and they scatter in the wind. The

GSU men laugh. Nearby, a TV reporter is trying to shoot a piece to camera.

—Some moments ago, he shouts into his microphone, all media outlets and observers were ejected from the KICC. Despite early exit polls predicting a landslide victory for the opposition, recent official results have shown the government edging ahead. It's unclear . . .

A GSU officer, baton in hand, interposes himself between the reporter and the cameraman and thrusts his free hand into the lens. As the scene descends into a scuffle, the truck's engine roars to life again.

—We're going in, says Mollel.

WELCOME TO THE KENYATTA INTERNATIONAL CONFERENCE CENTRE, proclaim the red letters on the massive LED screen. Below it, a barricade of GSU men, elbows interlocked, three deep and at least thirty wide, stand at the base of the stairs to the main entrance. The truck Mollel and Kiunga arrived in has driven off, having disgorged its occupants. Somehow, because they leaped out first, their presence is not questioned, and as their traveling companions race up the steps to join the picket, Mollel and Kiunga do the same. In the shuffling to accommodate the newcomers, the two policemen manage to slip through, and they find themselves at the glass doors of the main entrance. The doors are locked.

Kiunga pounds on the glass and cups his hands to look inside. The face of one of the KICC's private security guards appears. Little more than a teenager, he looks terrified. Kiunga slams his police ID against the window.

—Let us in, he shouts.

The youth withdraws. Then there is the sound of a chain slipping, and the door opens a crack.

—We're only supposed to let in army and GSU, he says.

—We're police, says Kiunga. We're all supposed to be on the same side.

—Until a couple of hours ago, says the youth, I didn't even know there *were* sides.

He opens the door wide enough for them to come in, then hurriedly closes it and replaces the chain.

Inside, twenty or more private security guards stand awkwardly. The arrival of the GSU has left them feeling usurped, redundant. Toy soldiers.

—We're looking for David Kingori, says Mollel. Anyone seen him?

The guards avoid eye contact and resist answering. They are used to obeying authority. Now they are unsure who the authority is. Eventually one says, —I think I saw him in the Plenary Hall.

—Which way is that? asks Mollel.

Relieved to have a question they can answer, the guards point in unison to a staircase.

—Thank you, says Kiunga with a sarcastic bow. You've really earned your overtime today, boys.

On the staircase, Kiunga says, —How did you know Kingori was here, boss?

Mollel thinks of the little battery radio he found in the park, the news report he heard on it.

—Sammy told me, he says.

Kiunga looks confused for an instant but lets it pass.

—Our GSU witness has Lethebridge and Lucy walking *away* from where the body was found, he says.

—It might not have been Lucy, replies Mollel. He said it was a tall woman, remember? Lucy was not so tall. But Wanjiku Nalo is.

Kiunga puffs out his cheeks. —Seems a vague sort of identification.

It is. If only Sammy could have identified her voice, but that is no longer a possibility.

—But we have Lethebridge there, continues Mollel. He does nothing without Kingori's say-so. If we can get Kingori to connect Lucy with Wanjiku and Nalo, we'll have enough for an arrest.

—Yes, replies Kiunga, but *who*?

—Come on.

▲ ▲ ▲

At the top of the staircase is a wide landing. The entrance to the Plenary Hall is crowded, and there are more scuffles. Incongruously, the benches along the walls of this space are full of people either sleeping or sitting with their heads in their hands, as if in a waiting room. They seem either inured to the kerfuffle or studiously ignoring it.

—Let me in, booms a familiar voice. Don't you know who I am?

Mollel pulls Kiunga back behind a pillar. Otieno is arguing with a pair of plainclothes detectives in smart suits and sunglasses. One of them has his hand on Otieno's chest, and possibly for the first time ever, Otieno seems dwarfed by another man.

—I'm Otieno, head of Central CID, he shouts. *I'm part of this.*

—Go and catch some criminals, old man, scoffs one of the plainclothes officers. Better still, go home. Plenty of crooks in Luo land. Leave the politics to the big boys.

—You've not heard the last of this, thunders Otieno. He turns on his heel, and Mollel and Kiunga duck back behind the pillar as he storms past them.

—That was close, says Kiunga. But if he can't get in, we haven't got a chance.

—But we don't need to get in, says Mollel. We just need to find Kingori. He points up to where the double-height foyer overlooks the upper windows of the Plenary Hall. There is a walkway there.

From where they stand, the true expanse of the Plenary Hall can be appreciated. George Nalo's church could be dropped inside and still leave room for parking. But every inch of the space is packed. And despite the chaos outside, the activity has a diligent, harmonious quality to it, emphasized by the almost complete lack of sound getting through the glass. Steel boxes of ballots are brought in and upturned beside large trestle tables. Several figures around each table descend immediately on the papers and start stacking and sorting them methodically, mechanistically. Other figures are seated, inputting data on machines.

—There are hundreds of people there, says Kiunga. How are we going to spot Kingori?

—You start that side, says Mollel. I'll start this.

Kiunga runs to the far end of the walkway, jumping over the feet of a sleeping figure slumped against the wall halfway along. Mollel starts looking at the people below him. Foreshortening and the distance make it hard to discern individual features. He spends more than a minute scrutinizing the back of a coiffured head that resembles Kingori's, only for the figure to turn and reveal that it is a woman. With all the movement in the hall, it is a futile task.

Besides, this is not Kingori's scene. He's a commander, not a foot soldier. Mollel bangs the pane in frustration.

—Have you worked it out yet? someone says.

—What?

—Have you worked out how they're doing it?

It's the slumped figure on the floor, who Mollel had assumed was asleep. His suit is crumpled, his tie pulled to one side. His cheeks are grizzled with stubble and his eyes are ringed with exhaustion, but also something else: defeat.

—How they're doing what?

—Rigging the election, of course. That's what you're looking for, isn't it?

—And you'd know all about it? asks Kiunga, who has returned to join them.

—Of course. I'm with the electoral commission. Or was. I suppose I've resigned. Just like all the others downstairs. We walked out. Let me show you.

He begins to heave himself to his feet. Mollel and Kiunga help him up, and the three of them cross to the glass.

—You see the results coming in, in locked boxes. They're being brought in by truck from all over the city. They come in the service entrance under police guard, accompanied by the election officer and observers from the polling station. Then they're brought up here in the elevator. The boxes are opened, supervised by a scrutineer. The sorters—those are the ones at the end of each table—put them into piles for each candidate. The counters tally the result for each, discarding or returning any blanks or spoiled papers. Then the clerk enters the results on the machine. A printout is made and attached to the file box you see there.

Then the papers are put in, the box is sealed, and they move on to the next one.

—Who are the people walking around?

—Some are my lot, the ones who can't, or won't, see what's really happening. Others are independent observers, but only a chosen few. The really independent ones have all been kicked out.

—I still don't see it, says Kiunga. Is it the clerks? Are they putting false numbers in the machines?

The man laughs. —That would be picked up on a recount. Those boxes become evidence in any legal challenge.

—The sorters?

—You can look all day, says the man, and you won't find anything wrong in that room. It's all being done by the book.

—The ballot boxes, says Mollel quietly. They're being switched before they get here.

—That's right, says the man. Not all of them. Just a certain number from certain polling stations. Enough to tip the balance. We began to figure it out when the results made no sense. We were comparing an electoral roll from districts full of Luos and Luhyas with results of ninety, ninety-five percent government. I mean, I know it's a secret ballot, but that's like chickens voting for a jackal.

—But where's the switch being done? asks Kiunga. You said the boxes arrive here under guard, and with observers.

—The elevator, gasps Mollel. The boxes go in the elevator. They'd take up all the floor space. The observers won't be able to fit in. It's only a couple of floors. They wait for the next one, or walk. And that's where the switch is made.

He thinks about the helicopters coming and going above them. The ones bringing in the ballots from distant rural polling stations. What if they are not only bringing—but taking away?

And suddenly Mollel knows where he will find David Kingori.

—It's thirty stories, boss. You don't look fit to reach the mezzanine.

—Twenty-seven. We're already three levels up.

—Can we at least try to talk our way onto the elevator?

—You saw the guards. They'll never let us on.

—Let me go alone, then. I'll take the stairs, arrest Kingori, bring him back down. You have a rest. You look like you need one.

—We can't arrest him. I need to talk to him. In person.

—If he's even there.

—He's there.

A commander, not a foot soldier.

—Seriously, boss. Look at yourself. You'll never make it. The climb will kill you.

Mollel has to admit that Kiunga may have a point. In his colleague's clothes, he looks even more gaunt than usual. And his bandaged hands are causing him pain again.

But he hasn't come this far to give up the hunt now. He leans over the banister and looks up at the levels disappearing above him.

—I'm not going to die today, he says.

—With respect, boss, says Kiunga, you don't know shit about dying.

The statement stops Mollel in his stride. He turns and looks at Kiunga, a couple of steps below him.

—What did you say?

—I said, you don't know shit about dying.

—Oh, really?

Kiunga's eyes remain steady against Mollel's glare. —If you did, he says coolly, you wouldn't push yourself like this.

—I've been surrounded by death, says Mollel, since I was a baby. I found my grandfather's corpse up on the mountain when I was herding sheep. I was five years old. Thirty years later I pulled my wife's body out of the American embassy. You might remember that day. I certainly do.

—I didn't say you don't know *death*, Mollel. I said you don't know *dying*.

—We don't have time for this.

Mollel starts up the stairs. He is halfway up the first flight before he pauses. His bandaged right hand is sliding on the banister, and in frustration, he bites at the gauze, loosens the end, and pulls the bandage off. He grimaces as the last layer peels away from his burned skin, and he spits the bandage to the ground. Then, the skin on his knuckles splitting as he does so, he uses his free right hand to liberate the left.

The pain blazes through him, but he manages to brush away Kiunga's concerned touch on his sleeve. The cold of the metal banister is like balm when he grabs it but like fire when he hauls himself forward. Still, his grip is good. Blindly, he takes one step, two; then he reaches forward again. He grunts as his raw palm makes contact for a second time. He steels himself, squeezes, and pulls. Two steps, three. And he's reached the landing.

—Twenty-six floors to go, he gasps.

After that, it is all he can do to count off the stories. Kiunga, though, keeps talking. It is as though he does not care whether Mollel is hearing him or not. It is enough that his voice reverberates in this spiral.

—Death comes, says Kiunga. But dying takes effort.

Barely have his words ceased ringing from the walls before he calls, —I had a lot of people dying around me at that time. I know, you've known death too. But do you know dying?

Mollel is silent.

—If you live, you're dying. But that means you're still living. You know who told me that? A girlfriend. She was so beautiful, Mollel. The most beautiful woman you've ever seen. And I mean it. You know, you could just see her and you'd forget to take your next breath, man. Your heart would forget to beat. But by the time she died—

Keep trudging, Mollel tells himself. Keep lifting one foot, placing it in front of the other.

Twenty-five floors to go.

—It was her husband who'd given it to her. The irony was, we were always so careful. Condoms every time. Extra strong. And I hate condoms, man. But I did it because I loved her. I really loved that girl.

—God knows where he'd picked it up. She said he was always a flop in bed, so maybe he was an *mbasha*. Who knows. Who cares. The thing was, he knew about it. He'd known about it a long time. He'd been on the ARVs for years. But *he* didn't use a condom, because, hey, he didn't want his wife to suspect anything. And she—well, she didn't suspect, did she? Didn't suspect a thing until it was too late.

Twenty-four.

—It was too late to manage the HIV. The doctors said that the best they could do was give her time to get her affairs in order. That's how they put it. If she was admitted to the hospital immediately, there were things they could do—drips, transfusions, things—to mitigate the worst effects. Buy her a few extra weeks, months. It was going to be costly. But he had a good job, didn't he? Nice benefits, company car, and a first-rate health insurance package.

—She went home, packed a bag. Never confronted her husband about the HIV. They both knew he was the one who gave it to her. But she figured he had his own price to pay. She didn't possess one trace of cruelty or malice, that girl. She told him she was going to the hospital and he wouldn't see her again. And she left.

Twenty-three.

—She called me. She told me. She had to. You never knew, however careful we'd been. It was all right, by the way. I was all clear. But you know, I was pretty fucked up by the whole thing. I couldn't bring myself to go see her straightaway. I needed to get my own head around it. What the hell, I wasn't as good as she was. I didn't deserve her. And when she needed me most, I wasn't there for her.

—After I got my results, I went out. Got trashed. Got myself beaten up—I mean, really. Somehow I found myself in a bar in Westlands. Picked the biggest, ugliest group of Asian guys and started telling them to leave our girls alone. Told them otherwise, I'd start sleeping with their daughters. You can imagine what happened next.

Twenty-two.

—So what was all that about? Self-loathing? Self-punishment? I didn't know at the time. I just knew that they felt good, those cuts and bruises. I stayed home and nursed them a few days. Cherished them. Ran my hand over the lumps on my ribs and thought, I can still breathe. Counted the burst veins in my eye and thought, I can still see.

—I think for the first time in my life, I was glad to be living. I'd had a close call, a near miss. It was like, you have to nearly lose something to appreciate what it's worth. What I can't believe now is that I knew that much but still only thought about myself. I was a selfish bastard, Mollel. A shallow, selfish bastard.

Twenty-one.

—It took a long time for me to go and see her. At first it was because my ribs were too sore for me to leave the flat. Then I told myself I didn't want to upset her, my face all messed up like that. But my face healed. My ribs healed. And still I didn't go to see her.

—Work was a good excuse. You know I'm no slacker, Mollel. But I never worked so hard in my life. Extra shifts, double shifts. I was a one-man crime-fighting machine.

—I knew which hospital she'd checked into, and I always thought, Next time I go past, I'll go in and see her. But I never went past. Somehow I'd always end up taking a different route, even if it meant zigzagging through backstreets or circling through the suburbs.

Twenty.

—You know what made me go, in the end? It was Valentine's Day. Valentine's Day, Mollel. She always loved Valentine's Day. She never got anything romantic at home, and I played that game well. Knew what to buy her, where to take her, what to say to her.

—So there were all the office girls in town, wearing red. Red blouses, red belts, red dresses. Man, you know how they love to play the game, too. Slushy music on the radio. I was getting a hard-on just thinking about it. And then I thought, With her insurance, she's probably got a private room. Sure, she might not feel up to it, but who knows? Certainly a blow job wasn't out of the question.

Nineteen.

—I bought some chocolates and a bunch of Naivasha roses off a street vendor. Three hundred shillings' worth of red roses, cost me nine hundred bob. But what the hell, it was Valentine's Day.

—I was feeling pretty pleased with myself as I went into the hospital. That's part of the charade of Valentine's Day, isn't it—walking around, flowers in hand, the gracious lover. I could see that the nurse on reception was impressed. I gave the name, and she just stared at me. No such patient here, she said. There must be, I said.

Eighteen.

—The matron came over. Tight old *jike,* she was. Flowers meant nothing to her. In that job, she saw flowers every day, but I doubt she'd ever been given a bunch in her life.

—The patient you're asking for was discharged, she said.

—I'm like, discharged? I wonder why she never told me. But that's got to be good news, right? She's getting better?

—The matron told me they never even admitted her. She turned up, all right, letter of admission, all the paperwork in order, but these days, they always need pre-clearance from the insurance company. Just a formality. So they phoned, and the insurance had been canceled. Her husband had removed her from his policy. The company wouldn't pay.

Seventeen.

—It was all about appearances, you understand, Mollel. A young woman like that—when she dies, you can call it malaria, you can call it cancer, but everyone knows what it is. Her husband didn't want people knowing she'd got it from him. He didn't want people knowing he had it at all. So he made a big show of cutting her off. He played the betrayed husband really well. Even to me. The big joke was, he didn't know about his wife and me at all. As far as he knew, she'd always been faithful. And that was the thanks she got.

Sixteen.

—I found her, eventually, at her sister's house. Her sister didn't want to admit she was there, at first. She didn't want the neighbors knowing she had someone dying of AIDS on the premises.

—I didn't know the sister was caring for their grandmother as well. There, on the couch, was an old woman, all hunched up and bony. More like a skeleton than a living being. She could hardly move her head to look at me when I came in.

—She hasn't got long, the old woman, I thought. But I guess you know what I'm going to say. It wasn't the grandmother. It wasn't an old woman at all. That was my girlfriend, there. The woman I loved. My lover.

▲ ▲ ▲

Kiunga is silent for the final few steps to the next landing. When he reaches it, Mollel pauses.

—Fifteen, Mollel pants. Fifteenth floor. We're halfway up.

—Not quite, replies Kiunga. We started on the fourth floor, re-member?

Mollel leans on the rail. He looks down into the well. He turns and looks up.

—It's still a good place for a rest, he says.

They sit on the steps. The sound of a helicopter outside seems to stretch and reverberate throughout this windowless tube, traveling down to the ground and back up again until it fades into the walls, attenuates, and disappears.

Mollel wants to put his head in his hands, but they're too painful. He sits, instead, with the palms open before him like a book and feels the air on them.

—I let her down, says Kiunga. I didn't even have the courage to stick around and hold her hand at the end. And I think about it every day of my life. I'm not thinking about her *death*, Mollel. I'm thinking about her *dying*.

—Come on, says Mollel. We've got a job to do.

—Do you see what I'm getting at, Mollel? You've got a son. People around who care about you. It doesn't have to be like this. So you're going to die. We're all going to die. But you've got a chance to manage your con-dition, keep it under control. Make the best of your time.

—Sorry, Kiunga, says Mollel. You've got it wrong.

—I don't think so. I've seen you popping the pills. You've tried to hide it, but I know you've got HIV. It's not just this case that's eating you up. It's the virus.

Mollel stands.

—Let's go, he says. It's my turn to do the talking.

32 —Fifteen more floors, says Mollel, rising to his feet. He contemplates the staircase immediately before him.

He counts fifteen steps. Take each flight at a time. He gasps as his hand grasps the banister. One foot forward, he hauls himself up.

—Fifteen stories, he repeats. That's what my wife climbed every day. The secretarial college was on the fifteenth floor. She didn't like the elevator. It was always too full. She had to wait too long. The boys used to touch her. Pinch her.

Kiunga chuckles.

—Fifteen stories, up and down. No place to buy food up there, of course. She'd take a packed lunch, or buy a *mandazi* on the way in. But that morning she left her lunch on the table. I couldn't bear the thought of her getting hungry. I was on a late shift. So I thought, I'll take it to her.

Sixteenth floor.

—Ever think about what sixteen floors of reinforced concrete all around you is like, Kiunga? Ever think about the steel and pulverized stone that's holding us here?

—I try not to.

—Sure. That's what we all do. You think about anything too hard, it'll all just crumble to dust. You don't think about a landslide every time you climb a hill.

Mollel pauses a moment. Catches his breath. Catches his thoughts.

—The *matatus* were jammed that morning, he continues. I was hoping I'd catch her in the foyer, but it was past ten o'clock by the time I got through to Haile Selassie Avenue. I figured it would be quicker to get off the bus and walk. There was some kind of holdup ahead. There usually was. You know how the Americans were about security around their embassy. I remember hearing that squeal of tires and thinking, Kenyan driver. But then, gunshots.

Seventeenth floor.

—You know that street, Kiunga. It's like a concrete trench. Buildings on all sides. No one could tell where the gunshots were coming from. People tried to run, but they were all running in different directions. I wanted to go forward, but someone pushed me back. The last thing I remember thinking is, Oh God, I've dropped her lunch. Then it felt like the ground had dropped away beneath me. I slammed into a wall. And the wall kept pressing so hard against the side of my head, and I was thinking, What's this wall? But it wasn't a wall. It was the ground. I'd been thrown from my feet. And all the people who had been in front of me were on top of me. I managed to get up. I tried to look around, but I didn't even recognize where I was. There was a huge cloud of dust rolling down the street toward where I was standing. I just managed to turn my face away as it hit. Dust and grit and ashes. Mollel slaps the concrete wall beside him. —And whatever else goes into a building like this.

Eighteenth floor.

—I knew which way to walk because I could feel the way things were flying toward me. They felt like birds or bats at first, the things flying into my face. I swiped them. Clawed them. Pushed them down. But it was paper. So much paper floating everywhere. Then the cries started.

It was as though everyone had been too shocked at first but then found their voices. So many voices. But I knew I was going in the right direction. By that time I was having to climb. There was no road anymore, no pavement. Nothing was stable or solid beneath my feet. Everything rolled. Shifted. Rocked. Slid. I kicked off my shoes, was on my hands and knees, my fingers and toes. The first time I felt hair and skin beneath my hands, I tried to help the person up. But whatever I grabbed was far too light. Too limp. It just came away.

Nineteenth floor.

—But then someone was speaking to me. The voice was so faint, I bent down and could just make out the woman. Her skin was white, as white as chalk, and I thought, A *mzungu?* But it was the dust. Like white ash. We were all like that. She was so small. So slight. It wasn't my Chiku. *Where were you? I asked her. Are you from the secretarial college?* But she couldn't reply. I tried to push her aside, Kiunga. I tried to push her down, but her hand kept grabbing my ankle. I kicked it away. I kept looking. But they just kept getting in the way, those people, those bodies, one after the other. Anytime I found one I thought could be Chiku, I picked her up, carried her as far as I could out of the rubble. There was a sort of flat area there, where I could put them down. Someone had water, or sometimes I used spit to try to wipe their faces, but it was never Chiku. That's why I kept going back.

Twentieth floor.

—I didn't know it at the time. How could I? But the people I was pulling out weren't even from the same building the secretarial college was in. They weren't even from the U.S. embassy. They were people who'd been hit by debris on the street. The girls from the college on the fifteenth floor weren't going to be reached until days later, when they sent in the diggers. Of course it was a salvage operation by then, not a rescue. By that time I'd become a permanent fixture at the morgue. Because of who I was, they let me stay, cleaned me up. I washed next to the corpses in the sluice room. Someone gave me some clothes. Every time they brought a new one in, if she fitted the description, they'd let me have a look. But it was getting to the point where descriptions didn't even matter. I still felt the need to look.

Twenty-first floor.

—A reporter from one of the international papers had heard about me. Tracked me down. Apparently the rescuers at the scene had described this Maasai who, despite his own injuries, kept going back into the rubble to bring more and more people out. The writer wanted a hero. He said that not enough Americans had been killed to keep it on the front pages in his country anymore. He needed to personalize the story. He said the people in his country didn't know the difference between the Arabs who did this and the African victims. He wanted an African hero to put on his front page. We spoke. Someone took pictures. To be honest, I don't even remember what was said.

Twenty-second floor.

—You know, a lot of things didn't matter to me after that. Even my son. Faith took over a lot of the work. He was a baby. I didn't know what to do with him. She did.

   —And people wanted to talk to me. So I let them. The journalists came to speak to the hero of the embassy bombing. And I found they were interested in what I had to tell them. Not just about the bombing. About the police department, about how it worked. *Chai* money here, backhanders there. I suppose I must have told someone about how our division's new consignment of top-of-the-line patrol vehicles somehow turned into secondhand sedans with the chassis numbers ground off. Because it was the front page of *The East African* the following weekend.

Twenty-third floor.

—It would have been too obvious to sack me. So they sent me on sick leave. The psychiatrist was quite candid. He told me right at the start that he'd been instructed to find me unfit for duty. But after we spoke, he thanked me for not having to write a false report.

—I'd been having blackouts. Not thinking straight. He put me on the drugs. The drugs you've seen me take. That's what they're for, Kiunga. Not for HIV. But just like HIV, Kiunga, this illness can be managed. Never cured. But managed.

Twenty-fourth floor.

Mollel pauses to look back at Kiunga. He has a look on his face. A look of suspicion and distrust. A look Mollel has seen before. Many times.

—I knew I shouldn't have told you, says Mollel. I should have kept it hidden. Just like the people kept hidden in every village. The ones locked away by their families in case their madness infects others.

—I'm still the same person, Kiunga, says Mollel.

Twenty-fifth floor.

—But you're not, are you? says Kiunga. You're not the same person I thought you were. I've taken huge risks for you, Mollel. And you've hidden things from me. You never told me you were going into Orpheus House that night.

—I'm sorry, Kiunga.

—This whole investigation has been conducted your way. Cutting corners. Telling lies. I was prepared to go along with it when I thought there was a rational mind behind it. But now . . .

—We're nearly there. Let's put it to Kingori. He'll back my theory, I'm sure of it. I'm right about this. I can feel it.

Twenty-sixth floor.

Kiunga shakes his head. Mollel knows what he's thinking. What's the gut instinct of a madman worth?

—You can go back down now, says Mollel. Leave me to it. I didn't ask you to come along.

Kiunga stops on the stairs. Mollel continues.

Twenty-seventh floor.

—These blackouts, Mollel, Kiunga calls up from below. Do you still get them?

His voice echoes in the stairwell. Mollel heaves himself up a few more steps.

—Sometimes, he gasps. If I'm not taking my medication.

—And *are* you taking your medication, Mollel? *Are* you taking it?

Kiunga's voice becomes more distant as Mollel gets farther away. He can't bring himself to shout a reply, so he does not reply.

Kiunga's voice comes floating up again. —The night you broke into Orpheus House, Mollel. Did you black out then?

Twenty-eighth floor.

As he rounds the latest flight, Mollel leans over the banister and looks up. He's almost there. Just a few more steps to go. He turns and looks down. The staircases retreat below him in a foreshortened polygonal spiral, illuminated in sickly fluorescent light. Far, far beneath is a small patch of gray. If he were to topple now, to tumble over the railing . . .

—What did you do with my lighter, Mollel?

Kiunga's voice drifts up to him.

—The night Orpheus House burned down, Mollel. You had my lighter. You never gave it back to me. What did you do with it, Mollel? What did you do?

Mollel turns back to the staircase and begins to mount once more.

Twenty-ninth floor.

What did he do? He has no recollection. Only the blood, the operating table. Surely, *surely,* the scene of the crime.

He takes the last few steps wearily. Kingori will tell me, he thinks, repeating it in his head like a mantra. Kingori will tell me everything.

The final paces feel as if he is dragging through waist-high mud. He barely has the strength to take them. When, at last, he reaches the landing at the top, he sees a plain gray door with the word HELIPAD painted on it. A single keyhole—locked. Apart from that, there is no handle. No way of opening it. It's a fire escape. It can be accessed only from the other side.

He lies down. Feels the cool concrete beneath him. Closes his eyes.

There is a crash and a sudden blast of cold, crisp air. Revitalizing. He opens his eyes, blinded for a moment by the crisp blue daylight flooding in on him. Kiunga stands over him. The door flaps in the breeze, splintered lock hanging loose on its screws on the external side.

—I thought you'd left me, Mollel says.

—At least this way, says Kiunga, rubbing his shoulder, I've got a chance of taking the elevator back down.

33 The door gives out onto an enclosed set of metal stairs leading up to a gap in the overhang above. At this height the air is icy, despite the midday sun reflected from the buildings and the streets far below. The wide lip of the helipad that tops the building casts the gantry into complete shade. Mollel and Kiunga step out. Mollel tries not to look down and instead focuses on the small square of light up ahead.

The wind is powerful here. Not enough to disturb their climb, but enough to create the unsettling feeling that the next gust, or the one after that, might be the one that plucks you from the building and leaves you flying like a cinder in the air.

—Listen, calls Kiunga.

Mollel hadn't heard it at first, over the wind and the sounds of the city, but there it is—that curious, syncopated throb of a helicopter, the roar of its engines, the beat of its blades. Louder now, the gantry itself buzzes under Mollel's agonized hands and his weary feet. Up—and out. As his head rises above the small parapet, the city opens before him, dazzling, clear. The sensation is akin to flying.

A group of men, mostly wearing military fatigues and orange ear protectors, are clustered on the other side of the helipad. They've not seen Mollel or Kiunga approach. There is a raised section where the elevator ends. The doors are being held open, and a second group of men, dressed in business suits—carrying heavy, steel boxes—are coming out. Commanding them is David Kingori.

The army helicopter is now nearly upon them. As it finalizes its approach, the downdraft causes all those present, Mollel and Kiunga included, to crouch instinctively and grab onto whatever they can. The aircraft's belly is suspended above them. It wobbles, turns, lines itself up. Mollel relinquishes his grip on the handrail to cover his ears. For a moment, the noise is deafening. A change in pitch tells him that the helicopter has touched down. And mercifully, the scream becomes less intense and the blades slow from an invisible blur to a more leisurely pace, though they keep turning.

Mollel and Kiunga are on the far side of the landed helicopter now. A pilot, in sunglasses and civilian clothes, looks them over without curiosity. He casts Mollel a thumbs-up. Mollel returns it. He can see feet emerging on the other side, leaping out from the bowels of the machine. The men with boxes rush forward. Impossible, from where he is, to count how many boxes are exchanged. Fifteen? Twenty?

Above the engines, a shout. Words indistinguishable. Then the helicopter roars again, a puff of diesel fumes heralding its imminent takeoff. It rises, at first unsteadily, like a baby gazelle finding its legs. Then it pitches, teeters, hangs for a moment. Everyone is crouched once more. But as it departs, they right themselves, and the men near the elevator hurry to put the new steel boxes—exactly the same as the others—back inside.

The elevator doors close. Kingori is left alone on the helipad. He looks exhausted. He cups his hand to his eyes to watch the helicopter becoming a dot. Then he scans the horizon. He sees Mollel and Kiunga standing on the far side. He does not move. Mollel and Kiunga walk toward him.

He gestures to the skyline like a man welcoming guests to his home.

—Great view, isn't it? Have you seen Kirinyaga? Mount Kenya? The Kikuyus' holy mountain. It's visible only a few days a year from Nairobi. Auspicious, don't you think?

—If I were you, I'd be more worried about the smoke, says Kiunga. Kibera, Mathare, Donholme, Eastleigh. The city's on fire.

—And yet, from up here, it all looks so peaceful, says Kingori with a grin. Just breathe it in a moment, gentlemen.

—You're stealing the election! spits Kiunga.

—Come on, replies Kingori. You think those ballot boxes aren't already stuffed to the brim with opposition votes? All sides are playing the game, my friends. We just intend to play it better. Now, when that elevator returns in just a matter of seconds, my companions will take you into their custody. Whatever it is you came here for, you've seen things you shouldn't have seen, and I doubt very much we'll be seeing each other again.

—In that case, I'll get straight to the point, says Mollel. Lucy was carrying your baby.

There's a sudden grinding sound. The elevator doors open, and a group of men step out. They stop and look in surprise at Mollel and Kiunga. With them is an army officer who hastily unholsters his handgun and points it at them.

—It's *sawa*, says Kingori. They're okay, they're with us. He starts to walk to the edge of the helipad. Mollel and Kiunga follow. Kingori steps up to the railing. Looks down. There is a mesh net below. Through its wire grid Mollel can see the crimson pinpoints of GSU helmets pushing back a growing swarm of protesters at the gates.

—The autopsy came through, says Mollel. She was pregnant. We know the child was yours. You were the only person she was going with at that time.

Kingori shakes his head, not in denial, but in disbelief. —*Pregnant?*

—If you'd known it before you sent her away, you'd have forced her to have an abortion earlier. Still illegal, of course. But possible to do without risking the mother's health. She thought she was far gone enough to be safe. That's why she made contact again. She would have thought that no one could force her into a late-term abortion. It's practically murder. But she didn't count on how determined you were to keep your reputation. Or the fact that you had a hold over the one person in Nairobi desperate enough to conduct such an operation. Wanjiku Nalo.

—Boss, says Kiunga. His voice is low and urgent.

Mollel looks up, annoyed at his colleague's interruption. But Kiunga's glare is equally challenging. —I need a word with you, he says.

The two of them step away from the edge. Kingori remains there. He sinks his head into his hands.

When they're at a safe distance, Kiunga asks in low tones, —What are you doing?

—I'm trying to get the truth.

—By *lying?*

—I'm not lying. Honey told me about the baby, remember?

Kiunga stares at him in disbelief.

—*Honey?* He spits the name with contempt. —You know there's not been any postmortem, Mollel. You've just told him Lucy was carrying his baby. You've got no way of knowing whether that's true or not. You're staking the whole investigation on the word of a *prostitute?*

—Look at him, says Mollel.

Kingori is slumped. His swagger has evaporated.

—He looks broken, says Kiunga.

—Exactly. He's going to give us what we need to put the others away.

Kiunga shakes his head. —It's not right.

—Trust me, says Mollel.

—Trust your *judgment?* replies Kiunga grudgingly. How much are you keeping from me, Mollel? What reason have I got to trust your judgment at all?

Mollel looks up. Kiunga's raised voice has attracted the attention of the men in military fatigues. One of them approaches. —What's going on? he asks.

Mollel thumbs at Kingori. —He says you're to go back to the count, he calls out to them. Don't worry, there's plenty of time before the next consignment.

The man calls out to Kingori, —Is that right, boss?

Kingori nods and waves them away.

The men look at one another, shrug, and get into the elevator. The doors close.

—We need to stay calm, says Mollel. If we attract too much attention now, we'll end up going where those boxes are going. Dumped into a lake somewhere, probably. Our only link to safety is Kingori. And if he begins to suspect we're bluffing him . . .

—You're not bluffing him, hisses Kiunga. You're *torturing* him. Is this how you get results, Mollel?

Mollel does not answer.

—We'll do it your way, says Kiunga. Then we're through.

The two of them walk back to the railings.

—Was it a boy? Kingori asks them. I always wanted a boy.

—I'm afraid it was, says Mollel. By now the lies seem to hardly matter.

—What do you want to know? asks Kingori.

—Everything, says Mollel.

Kingori sighs. He motions his hand at the scene around him. —This?

—We don't care about the vote rigging. Who'd believe us, anyway? Just tell us about Lucy.

—James found her for me, he says. He was very good at that. He knew my tastes. She fitted the bill perfectly. I was very fond of her, really. She was shy. Damaged. She responded to tenderness the way most of those girls respond to diamond bracelets. I enjoyed her company. It was nice to be nice to someone for a change. But it wasn't going anywhere. A girl like that's all right for a little fun, but . . .

—When she started to get a little too needy, I told her, *It's over. We're calling it quits.* But I still felt sorry for her. So I put her in touch with some people I knew, some people who tried to get girls back on the straight and narrow.

—Orpheus House, says Mollel.

—My tenants, yes. I had no idea what it would lead to. It was quite some time later that George Nalo approached me with his plan. He said he could get funding from the Americans for a hospital. His wife would be director. But it had to be in a prominent location. The Americans like their generosity to be conspicuous. So, he said, he wanted me to sign over the land to him. I laughed in his face. *I could sell that land to developers and give you a donation that would run your hospital for five years,* I told him. *But you expect me to give it to you for free?*

—It wasn't about what the donors wanted, of course. It was all about him. Self-promotion. He needed to be more high profile, have everyone in Nairobi talking about what a great guy he is. Has he given you his talk yet about his lack of political ambitions? Don't believe a word of it. George Nalo is a politician through and through. I hadn't realized how much, until then.

—He told me about Lucy. She was a resident of Orpheus House now. Helped out with the other girls. A kind of outreach officer for them. She'd told him and Wanjiku all about our relationship. And he said Lucy was prepared to go public if I didn't agree to his demands.

—I sent James to track her down. It wasn't easy. The Nalos had frightened her off. Told her that I was dangerous. That I would try to silence her.

He gives a hollow laugh.

—Turns out it was the other way around. *They* were the ones she should have been afraid of.

—I didn't know that, though. I just saw it as convenient. I mean, girls like that. They only work for two things. Money, and fear.

So once we found her, we let her believe the myth the Nalos had created. That we were the big bad guys. She'd better do what we say. James played the part particularly well. He can be quite menacing when he puts his mind to it.

—And it worked. She became our girl on the inside. Feeding us information about the Nalos.

—They were the ones who had started playing with fire, but they were going to get burned. It didn't take Lucy long to realize what was really going on at Orpheus House. Sure, they were doing all the outreach, the health services. But they were also doing abortions. Turns out Wanjiku, she's a fanatic. Early term, late term, it doesn't matter to her. She reckons she is saving the children from a world of pain.

—I could have destroyed the Nalos if I'd wanted to. If I'd had any idea Lucy was carrying my son . . . but she was too afraid to tell me.

—And besides, it suited me, this situation. It was important to keep my name clean, with the election looming. State House made it very clear that there were going to be a lot of contracts handed out after the success of this campaign. I wasn't going to be the one to throw it away in a tabloid scandal.

—So I had James pay them a little visit. Let them know that if they kept quiet about me and Lucy, I would keep quiet about their little abortion racket. The stakes were much higher for them than they were for me.

Kingori shakes his head. —But I didn't know about my baby. I'm nearly seventy. I've got three daughters. I never thought I'd have a chance of a son. And they killed him!

—It looks like your man James was part of it too, says Mollel. Seems he takes protecting your reputation very seriously. To the extent of arranging an abortion behind your back.

—That stupid bastard, mutters Kingori.

—They killed your child. And they killed Lucy, too.

—You think it was deliberate? asks Kingori, raising his face to Mollel. His eyes are puffy, his jaw slack. For the first time, he looks his age. —You don't just think they botched the abortion? It was very late, after all. That sort of thing has to be risky.

—I don't think they botched anything, says Mollel. Wanjiku Nalo is the best in her field. From the sound of it, she was doing late abortions all the time. No, maybe that's how they got Lucy onto the operating table in the first place. Persuaded her it was the right thing to do. Wanjiku can be very persuasive. But Lucy's knowledge was a threat to them. They knew that after the election, their hold on you would be gone. So they needed to eliminate the threat. She let Lucy die, and together, she and Lethebridge got rid of the body.

—Jesus Christ! Kingori thumps the railing. A crow, somewhere on the metal staircase below, is startled, and it flaps away, cawing into the void.

—I'll do it, he says. I'll testify. I'll bring those murderers down.

34 —Here comes another helicopter.

Kiunga points to the pale horizon where a black dot is suspended, soundless. Kingori pulls out his phone. Its gold plate glints in the afternoon sun.

—I'll call James, he says. He'll back up everything I say.

—Where is he? asks Mollel.

—At his home.

—I knew it, mutters Kiunga.

—Have him come to Central. Kiunga can meet him there. I'll go and deal with the Nalos.

The throb of the approaching helicopter fights for dominance for a moment or two with the sound of the city, then surpasses it. The elevator doors open, and two men in fatigues come out. Between them, they are carrying a laden ballot box. They eye Mollel and Kiunga with suspicion as they pass, bound for Kingori, who is speaking on his phone.

—Let's go, says Mollel.

The two of them go to the elevator. Two more boxes are within, taped up with official seals.

—Help me shift these, says Mollel.

—I'm not touching them.

Mollel looks in surprise at Kiunga. —We've got other things to do.

—Those are real votes in there, Kiunga replies.

—They could be. Or, like Kingori says, they could be just as false as the ones they're switching them with. The opposition votes are just as likely to have been tampered with before they ever arrived here.

—We don't know that, mutters Kiunga. If I even touched one of those boxes, I'd feel—tainted.

—We don't have time for this, mutters Mollel as he grabs the handle of one of the steel boxes and drags it out of the elevator. With only one box remaining, there is enough space for them both to get in. Kiunga hits the button for the ground floor.

—That makes you part of it, he says as the doors creak shut.

Mollel reaches over and presses the button for the third floor.

—We'll be part of it, all right, if we walk straight into their operation. Let's give ourselves a bit of breathing space.

As the elevator judders into life, Mollel says, —You're a principled man, Kiunga. You don't want to be involved in something that's wrong. I understand that.

The small screen above the door illuminates the floor numbers as they descend. The two of them count the figures down in silence until they hit 3 and the doors grind open. The lobby beyond is empty.

—Sometimes, though, says Mollel, doing nothing is not enough.

He steps out of the elevator and pulls the remaining ballot box halfway through the door. Kiunga steps around and joins him just as the door begins to close. It hits the box, and the elevator alarm sounds.

—It'll take them a while to work out why the elevator's jammed, says Mollel. Might get a few more honest votes counted in that time.

They head for the stairs.

—Just like this case, continues Mollel. You may think I'm doing it wrong. But it's better than doing nothing.

—You know who you sound like? says Kiunga. Otieno.

Mollel laughs.

—No, really, says Kiunga. You both think you can throw out the rules if the end result's the right one. But where he does it out of caution, you do it out of recklessness. I used to admire you, Mollel. Until I realized that it's all just another symptom of your craziness.

Mollel walks over to the window. He can still hear the helicopter a hundred meters above them. But here, near the ground level, the sound of the crowd drifts over the gates, over the helmets of the GSU ranks, over the eerie calm of the empty grounds of the conference center outside.

—Did you ever beat out a confession, Mollel?

—Of course not!

—Otieno does it all the time. Did you see the stains in the interview room? That's not spilled coffee, you know. What you did up there was just the same. Sure, you didn't grab Kingori by the arms and hold him over the edge of the building. But you might as well have done. You lied to him.

—I forced a confession.

—By tearing him apart! You broke him, Mollel. I thought you were a different sort of policeman. One I could admire. But you're just the same as all the rest. That Red God you were talking about. He's got hold of you, too.

—Look at that city, Mollel says quietly. You want to see the Red God? He's out there. There will be plenty more Nairobians dead before this is over. But we've got the chance to get the people who killed one of them. Is that so mad?

Kiunga shakes his head. —What did you really see in Orpheus House, Mollel? An operating table, blood? Or was that all a lie, too, to persuade Otieno to keep on with the case? To persuade *me*? You've had it in for the Nalos since we met them. You *wanted* them to be guilty. If there was no evidence at Orpheus House, would you burn the place down to cover that up?

—I know what I saw, says Mollel.

—You might have *seen* it, replies Kiunga. But was it *there*?

Getting out of the KICC proves easier than getting in. As soon as they pass through the GSU ranks, Kiunga turns to Mollel.

—I'm in this up to my neck. The best I can hope for is that James Lethebridge backs up Kingori's story. If he does, I'll go bring him in. You're going to get the Nalos?

—Yes.

—Good luck, says Kiunga coldly. I'd like to say it's been nice working with you, Mollel. But . . . you know.

And he strikes off through the crowd of protesters in the direction of Central Police Post, where he left the car.

Mollel finds himself alone on the street just beyond the cordon, with no real idea of how he is going to get to Embakasi and the Nalos' campus.

He wanders onto the Uhuru Highway. It's almost deserted. The only movement comes from GSU trucks and one or two private cars. He flags a passing police car, but the driver ignores him. There are no *matatus* running. He wanders back toward the InterContinental Hotel in the hope of finding a taxi driver who might be willing or desperate enough to grab a fare on a day like this.

Outside the lobby he sees a khaki Land Rover, an elongated safari version, nine-seater, with enlarged windows for game viewing. Inside, like lobsters in a tank, are a group of elderly *wazungu* tourists. Their eyes are hollow with fatigue and fear. They all wear immaculate pressed khaki safari suits. Mollel guesses they've seen more of the wild than they anticipated on this trip. The Land Rover is idling, to keep the air-conditioning running for the passengers. The driver is having a conversation with the hotel security guard. Mollel interrupts him, flashing his ID.

—Where are you taking them? he asks.

—To the airport, the driver replies nervously. They're being evacuated. Check-in closes in forty minutes. Do you reckon we'll get through?

—The highway's clear, says Mollel. But it takes you directly past South B, and there are reports of trouble there. If I were you, I'd take the South C route via Embakasi. Could you do with an escort?

—Yes, please, says the driver, relief palpable in his voice.

—Let's go.

The tourists look up, startled, as Mollel jumps into the front passenger seat. They relax somewhat when their driver gets in.

—This is a policeman, he says. And the elderly *wazungu* smile and give Mollel a thumbs-up. The safari truck moves off, and Mollel starts to give directions. He feels a tap on his shoulder. One of the women in the group is pushing a small automatic camera at his face.

—Would you mind taking a photograph of us? she asks.

—Sure, says Mollel.

She explains how the camera works. The tourists pose. The fear and tension drain from their faces as they assume expressions of stoic good humor, already composing the caption in their minds: *This is us being evacuated from Kenya. Quite an adventure!*

Mollel takes the photograph and passes the camera back to the woman. She holds it up and looks at the screen with satisfaction. Outside the window, Mollel sees a kiosk overturned, people crawling in and running off with whatever pitiful supplies are within: sticks of laundry soap, razor blades, packets of flour. Now the other tourists are raising their cameras and snapping away.

The residential streets of South C flash by. The rows of houses run at right angles to the main road, guarded with high metal gates and barbed wire. Mollel catches the occasional glimpse of locals looking warily out from behind. There's no other traffic on the road, so the safari truck makes good progress, but Mollel is aware of how quickly the situation could change. In Swahili he says to the driver, —Anyone steps in front of the car or tries to stop us, just keep going. Understand?

—If you say so, says the driver with barely concealed delight, and he puts his foot down on the accelerator, as though having been granted official sanction to drive the way he's always dreamed of.

Mollel becomes aware of the drone of conversation behind him.

—Of course, one of the tourists drawls, you have to expect this sort of thing in Africa. However modern the place looks, tribal tensions are never very far from the surface.

The others murmur assent. —To think, chimes in a woman's voice, of all the money I've donated over the years. Well, I'll certainly be canceling that subscription when I get home.

—Very wise, Louise, very wise, says the first speaker, warming to his theme. If you ask me, all the aid we give them is part of the problem. If you treat people like children, you can't be surprised when they throw their rattle out of the stroller.

—They are children, really, aren't they? chips in another of the women brightly. I sometimes think they'd be better off if the modern world just left them alone in their mud huts. I mean, they always look so happy, don't they? It's only wanting what they can't have that gets them all upset.

—Africa's a basket case. We should just cut them loose. See how they fare.

The sentiment seems to represent a consensus among the tourists, and with nothing left to add, their gaze returns to the windows.

—Do they always talk like this? Mollel asks the driver in Swahili.

—Who?

—Tourists. Do they always talk as though you're not here?

—I don't know, the driver replies. I don't listen.

The sun is low, and it flashes from between the houses. In the red dust of dusk it's easy to imagine for a moment that the boys running away from a smashed-in car are simply playing with hoops; that the dogs pacing and jumping behind the chain-link fence are goats being herded for milking; that the woman sitting bleeding into her shawl on the curb is simply winnowing maize.

An African sunset.

The Land Rover slows. The road is no longer clear. Other vehicles have joined the traffic and are beginning to bunch up. Soon the safari truck comes to a halt.

Mollel leans forward to try to make out what's happening. The jam extends some distance up ahead. He realizes that they're close to the Nalos' campus, and the sight of a George Nalo Ministries bumper sticker confirms his suspicion. The cars are all headed for the church.

—I'll get out here, he says casually to the driver.

—Hey. What? calls one of the tourists. The others chime in with a chorus of, —What're we gonna do? We'll never make our flight! You can't just leave us like this! We need protection!

—What the *hell*, says one of the men in the authoritative, not-to-be-disobeyed voice of the white man abroad, do you think you're doing?

—I'm cutting you loose, says Mollel. Seeing how you fare.

And he gives them a jaunty wave as he hops out of the Land Rover and disappears into the throng of pedestrians streaming toward the dying red sun and the looming, glowering edifice of George Nalo Ministries.

35 Closer to the church, the cause of the jam becomes evident. Private cars are parked wherever they can—at the side of the road, tilted into the ditch. Some even seem to have been abandoned where they stood, leaving only the smallest gap through which to squeeze. Black-clad ushers at the gate, a panicky, frantic look on their faces, attempt to turn away the vehicles that have got that far: *no room, no room.* But still the people push in on foot.

Come nightfall, the Maasai men herd their cows into the *boma,* the area in the center of every Maasai village where livestock are guarded against predators overnight. The boys follow with their goats, which leap and trip to try to get inside, as though they know that once the *il-timito*—the thick thorn branches—are pulled into place, they will be safe from darkness and the lions who hide beyond.

So it is with George Nalo Ministries. The place has become a sanctuary for those who hope that divine providence—or, failing that, strength in numbers—will save them from the chaos that is engulfing their city.

Those people around Mollel now couldn't present a greater contrast to the first time he came here. No Sunday best: they have come dressed in whatever they happened to be wearing when they decided to abandon their homes. Many of the children are in pajamas; some, carried over their parents' shoulders, are still asleep.

Approaching the church building, Mollel feels he is being swept along by the crowd. In the gloom, it is even more impressive than in day-light. The interior, illuminated, silhouettes the bobbing heads in front of him. It feels as if the building is sucking them into the light.

The crowd streams around an elderly woman pushing a handcart. In it is a husk of a man, his hair grizzled, eyes closed, sunken.

—Can you help me, brother? the woman asks as Mollel passes. He raises his raw, peeling hands in excuse. She looks at them, her face full of pity, even in her own predicament. —God bless you, she says. Your suffering is almost at an end.

—Is it?

—Oh yes, she replies, and a smile breaks through her fatigue. The suffering of this world will soon be forgotten. These are the End Times.

He moves on and begins to become aware of a noise. It is loud and low. So low Mollel feels it in his teeth.

It is that of a swarm. When you first hear a swarm of bees, you can tell from the tone and the intensity how big it is and what mood the bees are in. But you can't place the sound. It's too low.

You can't tell what direction it's coming from, because it's coming from everywhere. All you know is, there are a lot of them, and they're dangerous.

Getting closer, the drone becomes more intense. The sound rever-berates in his head and his chest and begins to pound and split and frac-ture into thousands of human voices.

The hall opens up before him as he passes through the doors, and the space is filled with the crying and the laughing and the clamor and the jabber and the babble of tongues. The aisles are packed, overflowing even into the lobby, where Mollel encounters the first ecstatic figures, hands held aloft or clasped over their hearts, heads tipped back, eyes closed. They sway as they cry and speak; some have tears running down their cheeks.

The trance is transporting. Mollel is unnerved. His mind tries to tune in to each voice as he passes, but each one is successively drowned out by the next. He tries to grasp sounds, interpret meaning, but the sounds are elided and evade meaning, and it all collides and conflates into a primal, final cacophony.

But one voice begins to rise above the others. It is a gargle and gurgle louder than all the others. It stands out, amplified. Word-sounds resound. The rapt stand limply, heads lolling. They are oblivious, and Mollel finds he can no longer push himself forward. He has reached an impasse.

Craning, he can see the distant stage up ahead. It is bright. The lights pick it up and place it on an ethereal level. Floating in the middle of the luminous disk is Nalo. Microphone dangling from his fingers, other hand aloft, head thrown back. Slivers of white visible below his eyelids. Flecks of spit visible, even at this distance, at the corners of his mouth. His mouth opens and shuts, his tongue probes and gropes around sound. His voice fills the auditorium.

No Wanjiku. No Benjamin.

Mollel turns, but the crush is as thick behind him now as it is in front. He sees the woman with the cart. She has put it down, and she tenderly caresses the skeletal cheek of the prone man within.

The hubbub is ending.

—Praise the Lord, comes Nalo's voice.

The voice of another, unseen speaker comes over the PA. —Healing is about to commence, it says. Those seeking healing, please make yourself known to an usher.

The rapture over, it is slightly easier for Mollel to weave his way back to the woman with the cart.

—I'll take him, he says.

—But your hands!

He grasps the handles. Winces. But to his relief, the man barely possesses weight, and he lifts the cart on its axis.

—A miracle! the woman gasps.

Those around them look on, and as the word spreads, Mollel finds a way parting ahead of him. He pushes the cart forward, and black-clad ushers rush to meet him. They progress to the edge of the stage, where hands clamor to help him, and the old man is lifted and borne high and away. An usher takes Mollel's hands in his own, looks at them, and says, —This one too.

Mollel feels himself being impelled upward. The usher clips something to his shirt collar and slips a small, heavy box, about the size of a cigarette packet, into his pocket. —It's a microphone, he says into Mollel's ear. Don't speak until you're spoken to.

—Brothers and sisters, booms the unseen voice. The healing is about to commence.

The lights are blinding, and the heat of them brings a prickle of sweat to Mollel's skin. The usher who gave him the microphone moves away, and a stockier, more powerful figure takes his place at Mollel's side, grasping his shoulder forcefully.

—Just keep walking, a voice urges Mollel in his ear. Don't try anything.

It is Benjamin. He has taken Mollel's arm with his own good one— the other arm, injured in Kibera, hangs stiffly at his side. He holds him tightly. As they are brought up to Nalo, Mollel sees Wanjiku Nalo emerge from the shadows. She looks at him with a mixture of shock and anger.

The elderly man is the first brought up to the pastor. Nalo places both hands on the feeble shoulders. The sickly frame is being supported on all sides. His eyes are now open.

—What is your name, father? says Nalo.

The microphone on his collar picks up a voice crackling like dry leaves and spreads it throughout the auditorium. It sounds like Odolo.

—Well, *mzee* Odolo, Nalo says, what is your problem?

—I'm sick, says the old man. I cannot walk. I cannot move. I do not have long left.

Again, because his words are barely picked up by the microphone, Nalo repeats for the audience:

—He's sick, he cannot walk. He says his time has come. Well, your time may be near, old man, it is near for all of us, but it will not be today.

Then he takes one of his mighty hands and places it on the old man's forehead, across his eyes. —Lord Jesus, Nalo implores, this is your servant. This is your son. This good man is in need of your divine mercy. Please will you assist him, O Lord.

The hall begins to reverberate again with voices. This time they aren't speaking in tongues; they are raised in prayer. Looking down,

Mollel can see the figures nearest to the stage fervently reciting their prayers, fists clenched or fingers clasped, entwined. He looks back at the elderly man. Nalo finishes his prayer, and powerfully, shockingly, with a plosive *Bam!* he pushes the old man's head back.

It's obviously a practiced move. The ushers tip him simultaneously. The old man swoons backward in their arms while one usher places his feet underneath him. They then pivot him back to a standing position, and with a flourish, theatrically, they all step aside to reveal him there.

Standing.

The old man looks down at his legs in amazement. He looks up again, beaming. Tentatively, he lifts one foot, waves it, places it on the ground, does the same with the other leg. Then, in sheer joy, he shuffles a little jig. The audience cheers in throes of ecstasy. The old man raises a hand to acknowledge them, but wobbles, as though he might fall, and the ushers swiftly run forward to steady him. He is then assisted—to Mollel it looks as though he is carried—offstage.

Now it is Mollel's turn to be brought forward. Benjamin grasps him tightly on one side. On the other he feels a new hand clutch his arm. It is Wanjiku. She looks into his eyes.

—I need to talk to you . . . he begins. His own words boom out across the hall. Wanjiku glares at him. Her finger flies to her lips and then points down at the microphone on his collar. She shakes her head.
—*Not now,* she whispers. *After.*

She looks toward her husband. Nalo has come close. Mollel senses the ushers gathering behind him.

Nalo looks him in the eyes, and a flash of recognition passes across his face. He looks askance at Wanjiku. She nods. Nalo frowns, looks out at the darkness, where the massed audience now waits, filled with anticipation of the next miracle. He seems momentarily at a loss. Then he composes himself and says to Mollel, —What is your name, my son?

—Mollel, says Mollel.

Nalo repeats, —Your name is Mollel. We welcome you, Mollel. What ails you, my brother?

Benjamin and Wanjiku, each holding one of Mollel's arms, thrust his hands forward, turning them upright. The heat of the spotlights makes his palms throb agonizingly, and Mollel grimaces.

—Aah, booms Nalo. Your hands are badly burned.

A sympathetic groan goes up from the audience.

Nalo places his palm on Mollel's forehead. Mollel tries to pull his head back and away, but it is being thrust forward by one of the ushers behind him.

—But your hands are not your only ill, are they, my brother? continues Nalo. I sense . . . I sense a great disquiet in your mind. Allow us to help you, my brother. Allow the Lord Jesus Christ to assist you. Allow the Prince of Peace to bring you some respite from that which is torturing you.

The tumult in the hall is commencing again as the audience recognizes the prompt for them to break into spontaneous prayer. Mollel can hear it all around him, but he cannot move, cannot shift. He sees nothing but Nalo's hand over his eyes.

—Oh, Jesus, cries Nalo. Please, assist this poor, deluded brother. Please Jesus, bring an end to his suffering.

As before: *Bam!*

Mollel feels a sharp, jabbing pain in his arm.

Nalo's hand is removed from his eyes. Mollel looks down at his arm just in time to see Wanjiku Nalo pressing the plunger of a hypodermic syringe. He feels the pressure of the liquid entering his muscle, then feels the needle slide out as she removes it. He just has time to cast her a furious glance and open his mouth in protest before he is bundled forward.

And then Mollel is borne in a dozen pairs of arms and lifted upright: he is presented to the audience, spotlight shining in his face. He blinks and screws up his face like a newborn.

Absence of pain.

That's what he feels, and the deliverance is blissful.

He hadn't realized, until now, how much the pain had borne down upon him, constrained him. And now, held up by all these hands, he feels liberated.

—Are you healed? roars Nalo.

Mollel looks down at his hands. They are still raw. But now, instead of the heat from the spotlights searing him, his palms seem to merely glow and tingle as though warmed by the rising sun.

—Speak, Mollel. You have the microphone. Tell the audience. By the power of prayer, are you healed?

His eyes tell him his wounds are still livid. He knows that it is only the drug, whatever Wanjiku injected him with, that makes him feel this way. He looks at her, at Benjamin. They watch him anxiously. It would be the easiest thing in the world to denounce them now, to bring the whole edifice down around them.

The room is silent. Thousands of eyes are trained eagerly upon him. The fiction of the Nalos, their fraud, and their power is now wholly in his command.

George Nalo's eyes probe his own. They burn into him like the spotlights. Mollel's mouth is dry. He croaks, —*Your wife* . . .

He hears his own voice, like a stir of leaves, reverberate around the hall. This is not the way he wants it. He puts his hand up to cover the bud of the microphone on his collar. Nalo leans forward, his head inches from Mollel's mouth.

—Your wife, whispers Mollel. This time only he and Nalo hear his words. —Your wife is a murderer. She killed Lucy.

36 The girl stumbled through the night. Her face and arms were scratched. She had lost her calabash and the honey, and her mother would be angry that she had not even picked the berries she was sent for. She did not care. She just wanted to get home.

But she did not know the way home. The little bird had guided her with her eyes closed, and the country was unknown to her here.

She sat down and started to cry. But even as she cried, she felt a tiny vibration in the folds of her *shuka*. She sought it out and in the pale moonlight saw that it was a bee. A solitary bee.

It crawled out onto her arm, and she was too tired to even flick it away. She expected it to sting her. But it did not sting her. And she asked it, "Little bee, I destroyed your home. Why do you not sting me?"

"Why should I?" replied the bee. "My home is gone. My children are dead. Stinging you will not bring them back. But you have a mother, and she is missing you. I know this country well. I have gathered nectar from outside your door. Let me show you the way. Come."

And so the little bee flew off, and tired and hungry, the girl followed its buzz as she had followed the song of the bird.

She followed the buzzing. Just as the bird had done before, the bee stopped and waited every time she stumbled or had to rest. The girl marveled at the generosity and patience of this tiny insect who had lost everything.

After what seemed like an age, the bee said, "We are here."

The girl looked about her. She did not see her *boma* or her hut. She could not smell her mother's cooking or hear the bleats of the flock.

"This is not my home," she said.

"No," replied the bee. "It was mine."

And then the girl saw the remains of the fire and the bee's nest upon it, broken and burned.

And the bees that had survived, no longer stupid from the smoke, rose from where they had fallen upon the ground and, throbbing with rage, descended upon the girl.

"Wait!" she called out. "It was not my fault! It was the bird!"

But the bee that had brought her there replied, "Do you think it matters to us? The bird has flown. But you are here!"

And the girl's world went dark as the swarm clouded over the moon.

That was the point in the story when Mollel always pulled the coarse blankets over his head. Lendeva would laugh, and his mother would stroke him soothingly. He never understood, back then, why the story ended there.

But now, remembering the story for the first time in more than three decades, he realized why. It felt as if the cover were being lifted from his head. The story wasn't about the girl. It was about the bees.

His thoughts are interrupted by crashing cymbals and voices raised in song. How long he has lain there on the leather couch in the greenroom he does not know. But he is roused just in time to see George and Wanjiku Nalo enter, all smiles. He hastily lets his eyes fall shut—almost as rapidly as their smiles fall from their faces.

—Don't worry about him, says Benjamin. He's out cold.

Nalo says, —I thought your magic shot was supposed to perk them up, not knock them out.

—It's a mixture of adrenaline and opiates, replies Wanjiku. His file says he's on antipsychotics. No way of predicting what effect that sort of mixture would have.

So they had his police medical records. No surprise, really. Nairobi's not a city to hold secrets long, especially in the face of people as rich as the Nalos and as resourceful as Benjamin.

Still, if they believe him to be no threat, let them. He feels too weak for any confrontation. He's content to let them think he's unconscious and to see what he might learn.

—That was damn foolish, what you did onstage, Wanjiku says. Giving him the chance to speak like that. Whatever possessed you? He'd seen the syringe. He could have denounced us in front of the whole congregation.

—I knew he wouldn't, says Nalo.

—How could you possibly know that?

Nalo gives a sigh. Mollel hears a chair being dragged from under the table, creaking under Nalo's weight as he sits. —What a trial it is to have a wife of so little faith. You and your chemically enhanced miracles!

—Without my *enhancement* this church would still be in a tin shack in Kibera!

—And without me you'd still be performing backstreet abortions! growls Nalo. Do you think they come here to see Wanjiku Nalo? No. They come here to see George Nalo. And your assistance is not always required. I knew this Maasai would not denounce us, because I wasn't healing his hands. I was seeing his *soul*.

Wanjiku lets out a contemptuous snort, but Nalo continues: —I saw what was within him. A real, profound yearning for peace. But that was not all. I saw a fire.

Wanjiku scoffs. —That's hardly a revelation, with two burned hands.

—I saw a fire, and someone lost within it.

—Benjamin told you about the blind man. The one who died in Kibera.

—No, says Benjamin. I didn't.

—It wasn't a man, anyway, says Nalo thoughtfully. It wasn't him. The sense of loss was much greater. It was a woman.

—That just proves you read the papers, retorts Wanjiku. His wife was lost in the bombing, remember? That's why he's crazy.

Nalo, quietly, says, —Maybe that's it. Maybe that's why I saw it. But I had the feeling I was seeing something else. Something not in the past. Something yet to come.

—Your trouble, says Wanjiku bitterly, is that you believe your own hype. You're just a loudmouth with a knack for reeling off scripture. Without me you'd be nothing.

—Well, says Nalo, it looks like we're going to find out, aren't we?

—What do you mean?

—Why do you suppose he's here?

—He's still investigating Lucy's death, says Wanjiku.

—No, says Nalo. He's finished his investigations. He's come to make an arrest.

Eyes closed, Mollel can nevertheless feel the impact of Nalo's words. Beside him, Benjamin shifts uneasily. And Wanjiku spits, —What do you mean?

Softly, Nalo says, —I know where I was last Friday night, Wanjiku. I was in front of two thousand people at a group baptism ceremony, right here. But where were you?

Mollel hears movement and a sharp intake of breath. He raises his eyelids just enough to make out Nalo holding his wife's wrists. She must have tried to slap him.

—How dare you, she gasps. How could you?

Benjamin has sprung to his feet, and he pushes Nalo aside.

—Hurt her and I'll kill you.

—Relax, Mungiki man. Nalo laughs. —She's the one trying to hit me.

He withdraws his hands, and Benjamin tries to put his arms around Wanjiku, but she brushes him away.

—You'd like her out of the way, wouldn't you? says Benjamin. No more Orpheus House to get between you and the collection plate?

—I must admit, Orpheus House has been a burden to me, sighs Nalo. Not financially, I don't care about that. But what you do there . . .

—You see? cries Benjamin to Wanjiku. He's trying to set you up. He'll turn against you, just like I always said he would.

—He won't do it, Benjamin. We've been married thirty years. He won't betray me.

—He betrays you every day, with his hookers and his hangers-on! How can you stand by him, after all you know? After he refused to stand by you?

—Because he will stand by me, replies Wanjiku. You can't understand it, Benjamin, and I don't expect you to. But that's the way it is.

—Will he still stand by you when I tell him where you were on Friday night? Mollel's going to wake up any minute, and he's convinced you murdered Lucy. Will your husband stand by you when I tell Mollel you were with me—all night?

The silence in the room is broken by a strange panting sound. For a moment Mollel is at a loss to identify where it is coming from. Then he realizes it is George Nalo. He is laughing.

—Dear Benjamin, he wheezes. Did you think I didn't know about you two? It's part of our arrangement, you know. She turns a blind eye to my indiscretions, and I tolerate hers. It's not like you're the first.

—I'm so sorry, Benjamin, says Wanjiku quietly.

There is the sudden clatter of a chair falling over, and Mollel instinctively opens his eyes. He is afraid that Benjamin might attack Nalo, or Wanjiku—or both. But he sees the young man coming directly toward him.

—You're awake, says Benjamin. Good.

He bends over Mollel and roughly pulls him into an upright position. He looks deeply into Mollel's eyes. As he does so, Mollel feels Benjamin's hand go into his pocket as though he's being frisked. It's just for a moment, though, before Mollel is released once more.

—Now you're back with us, you can do what you came here to do. You can talk to these two about the death of Lucy. Make sure they tell you everything. I can't say you'll get the whole story. But it will make interesting listening.

With that, he casts a final, contemptuous glare at George and Wanjiku Nalo and storms out of the room.

Wanjiku looks solicitously into Mollel's eyes. —How are you feeling?

He's met the eyes of all three of them now. He arrived convinced that they'd conspired to murder Lucy. He no longer believes it. But he senses that he is close to the truth.

—I feel fine, he says. A bit weak.

—The drugs, she explains. You'll recover soon. How much of that did you hear?

—All of it.

—Then there's no point lying to you. Benjamin was right. He and I were together the night Lucy died. You can check at the hotel we were at. They—she casts her eyes down—they know us there.

Mollel puts his hands on the edge of the sofa to pull himself forward. He winces. The pain, so blissfully absent since the injection onstage, is starting to return.

—So much for your miracles, he says.

Wanjiku sighs. —Define *miracle*, Mollel, she says. In a city like Nairobi, it's a miracle that there's an organization here that can get people to dig into their pockets to help others. You know how many people partake of our services in one way or another? Education, health, welfare? The government's not looking after them, so someone has to. We've got children here who wouldn't be alive today if it wasn't for George Nalo Ministries. And the money doesn't come out of the air. A few miracles here and there are what keep the tithes rolling in. And besides, nobody's really tricking anyone. The people we perform this on always feel better, even if it's only temporary.

—But it's a fraud, says Mollel.

—Is it? The Lord moves in mysterious ways.

There is a loud knock on the door and the sound of some kind of scuffle. Mollel hears Benjamin's voice on the other side, and then the noise recedes.

—Tell me what happened at Orpheus House, Mollel says.

—It wasn't the night of Lucy's death, says George Nalo, breaking his silence. There was going to be a baby. We didn't want it to be born in the hospital. Too public. We set up the delivery room in the abandoned house.

—Whose baby was it? asks Mollel.

Wanjiku looks up at him. Her eyes are clouded with tears.

—It was *our* baby, she says. Our miracle baby.

Mollel looks from her to her husband. Nalo has his head in his hands. Wanjiku must be well past childbearing age. But he senses that she does not mean that kind of miracle. Some words come back to him, something Honey had said. *Some of these places take babies away from mothers in the delivery room.*

—Where is the baby now? he asks.

—Dead.

—If, maybe, we'd been able to have our own children, sobs Wanjiku, neither of us would have turned to other people.

George Nalo has extended a hand to his wife. He gently caresses her shoulder. The love between these two is not straightforward, but it is profound.

—I always took it as a sign from God, she continues. A punishment. For what we do. For the babies that never made it. But I thought I was doing the right thing at the time.

—And then Lucy came to us, says Nalo. She told me there was going to be a baby. Unplanned. Unwanted. *My* baby.

—George's baby, repeats Wanjiku. She was giving him the baby I never could. But she could never be a fit mother. A creature like that! Well, *I* could. We would deliver it secretly, at Orpheus House, then process the adoption through the agency. No one would have known any better. There'd be no scandal. George's secret would be safe. And finally, we'd have our baby.

But the minute I saw it crown, I knew what the problem was. It's called cyclopia. Sometimes they're born with one eye, sometimes none. In cases like this, there isn't even a brain to speak of. I did the merciful thing. Even if it had the synapses, the nerve endings in place, it wouldn't have felt a thing. I did not clamp the umbilical cord before I cut it. The little body drained of blood in a matter of seconds. We told the mother the baby was stillborn. But we never showed her the body. It would have been too distressing.

—So you didn't kill Lucy, says Mollel quietly. But you did deliver her child.

—You still don't understand, do you, Mollel? says Nalo. *It wasn't Lucy.*

▲ ▲ ▲

The door bursts open, and a group of black-clad figures rush in: ushers. They're all wearing the headsets used to coordinate the show. One of them pushes Wanjiku aside and makes straight for Nalo's throat.

—You liar! he shouts. Another, a woman, slaps Wanjiku full in the face.

Mollel feels himself being hauled to his feet. Benjamin, who has come in behind the ushers, hisses in his ear, —We'd better get out of here.

He pulls Mollel past more oncoming figures. Behind them, Mollel can make out Nalo's defensive protestations being shouted down by an increasingly angry mob.

And the swarm clouded over the moon.

Mollel stumbles through the darkness of the cold night
air led by the ex-Mungiki man. Above them, the stars
swirl lustrously. An infinity of points of light.

Mollel's head reels with the last comment of Nalo's:
It wasn't Lucy.

Benjamin leads him through the shadows of the church buildings around
him. They pick their way through groups of people sitting on the lawns
and against the walls, huddled against the chill—refugees, overflowing
from the main church.

They approach a door. He recognizes the building. It is the old
schoolroom, the temporary home of Orpheus House.

—What's going on? Mollel asks Benjamin, but the young man puts a
finger to his lips. Then he reaches into Mollel's jacket pocket and pulls
out the transmitter. He yanks the wire, stripping the bud microphone
from Mollel's collar, and throws the device to the ground. It shatters,
and batteries scatter.

Now Mollel understands the presence of the mob in the greenroom.
When Benjamin had checked whether he was conscious, he had reached
into Mollel's jacket to turn on the radio microphone.

—I know why you didn't denounce Nalo onstage, says Benjamin.
There would have been a riot. And there's enough of that going on

beyond these walls. But you gave me the idea. When I realized that Wanjiku was using me—well, why shouldn't everyone know?

—But there was no riot, says Mollel.

—The service was over. It didn't go out over the PA. Just the internal system. I kept guard at the door long enough for plenty of the technical staff to hear just exactly the sort of people they're working for. We don't have long. I'm sure Nalo will be able to talk himself out of it eventually. And I don't want to be here when he does.

Benjamin unlocks the door to the schoolroom and steps in. Mollel follows. Even though he knows it is there, it is a shock to see the gynecological table in the half-light. It brings back a chill memory of that blood-soaked night in the other Orpheus House. At least he knows now that he really saw what he saw, and it was not, as Kiunga had suggested, the product of his fractured mind.

Benjamin heads away from the table to the storage cupboard. He opens it, its keys jangling on their hooks on the inside of the door. —If you'd been less concerned with stealing our keys, he says, you might have seen this. It was right on the top of the pile.

He tosses him a slim cardboard folder. Mollel's damaged hands rise to meet it midair, but he is unable to grasp it, and the folder flaps to the floor, the contents sliding out.

He stoops to pick up a photograph.

—Take a good look, says Benjamin. Whatever you think of Wanjiku, she does not do what she does lightly. The law of this country says it would be more merciful to bring that child to full term, let it gasp for the few pitiful hours it can manage to survive in an incubator somewhere. Let me ask you, is that mercy? Is that God's love?

The photograph is of a baby. Its tiny body is wrinkled, pigmentless, covered with white residue. The umbilical cord is still attached, but it's been cut at the placenta end. There is no clip or knot on the cut. The baby—fetus—would have bled to death in a matter of seconds. And above the baby's body, the head. Or what should be a head. There is a chin. An ear is visible. But moving up, there is a sucking, lipless cavity where the mouth should be. No nose, no eyes. It is a stump. A smooth, rounded, unfinished, unmolded lump.

—God made a mistake, says Benjamin. Wanjiku was just trying to put it right.

—And that was what you were trying to do when you burned down Orpheus House? Trying to put things right?

—Trying to protect her, says Benjamin.

A wave of relief floods through Mollel. More than the drug that took away his pain, the confirmation that he did not start the fire fills him with gratitude. Now only one uncertainty remains. If Lucy was not the mother of the baby . . .

He picks up the cardboard folder. In the gloom, Mollel cannot make out for a moment the characters written on the front of the file. Then they form into words.

Mother's name: En'cecoroi e-intoi Kipuri.

The first name, in Maa, means *honeyguide.*

Honey.

The baby was Honey's.

And the blood all over the floor was the baby's. Wanjiku had probably lost control as she cut the cord. Its final few heartbeats would have sprayed its life fluids everywhere. No wonder it was a scene of horror. No wonder Benjamin returned to torch it.

The photograph of the faceless, headless creature remains in his hand. No wonder, too, that they chose to keep this from Honey.

Some of these places take babies away from their mothers in the delivery room. They lie to them. Tell them they had a stillborn. Honey's words come back to him. First in disjointed bursts, then a torrent.

Everyone wants a newborn. Do you know what a fresh, healthy baby can fetch on the open market?

Lucy's baby's alive out there, somewhere. We've got to find it.

It takes a murder to get anyone's interest around here, and even then, it's only you who seems to care, Mollel.

—Lucy brought her to us, says Benjamin. It was weeks before. Wanjiku knew the child was her husband's. She wanted it for herself. If there was no record of the birth, the adoption could be organized easily through the agency. So we set up the delivery room in Orpheus House. It was basic, but Wanjiku's an expert. If it had been a straightforward birth . . . But she couldn't do any prenatal scans. If she had, she would have known . . .

—What were you going to tell Honey? demands Mollel. You'd have taken the baby from her.

—We'd have told her what we did tell her. That it was stillborn. Only we didn't have to lie.

She knew it. No wonder she did not believe them.

—I wanted to bury it, says Benjamin. At least a little human dignity. But then we remembered that the whole site was going to be dug up for the new development. The body would have been found, questions would have been asked.

—That was when I remembered the storm drain. I'd heard it ring hollow under my foot a day or two before. We had to act quickly, in case Githaka, the caretaker, saw us. I scraped away the leaves, lifted the lid, dropped the bundle in. It had just started to rain. The flow was already quite heavy from farther up the pipe. The bundle just disappeared, like that. I didn't know where it would end up. I didn't care, so long as it was far away from us. It would just be another unidentified body found in Nairobi's ditches or sewers. No one would bother to find out any more.

The room falls silent. They can hear a distant helicopter, wailing voices, and the floating strains of a multitude of voices singing a hymn.

—You know she didn't believe you, says Mollel. She never believed you. She couldn't have. For nine months she'd carried that body inside her own. Felt its heartbeat; even if it only twitched in reflex, it would have moved for her. She would never have accepted that it could have just died. You should have shown her.

So this was her plan, thinks Mollel. She used the death of her friend to guide him toward the Nalos. Toward the nonexistent baby. Toward the adoption scam and the baby she believed had been stolen from her. She hoped that in investigating the murder, he would reunite her with her baby. Perhaps she did believe that the Nalos killed her friend. More likely she didn't have a clue at all. He feels an overwhelming wave of pity for her.

And then he remembers Lucy. If she wasn't killed at Orpheus House, it must have been in the park after all. Killed where she was found. Where the GSU witness had seen a woman that night with an elderly white man.

He reaches for his phone and turns it on. A message from Kiunga.

JL never showed.

So Lethebridge did not turn up at Central as Kingori had promised he would. Hardly surprising.

—James Lethebridge was supposed to assist us with our inquiries. But he didn't.

—Lethebridge, says Benjamin quietly. He's the killer?

Mollel does not answer. Instead he asks, —What was he doing here at church, the day I first met you? I saw him.

Benjamin says, —He's the point of contact between us and Kingori. When it looked like Kingori was going to throw out Wanjiku's plans for Orpheus House, turn it into a residential development, we let James Lethebridge know that we had some information on his employer.

—His relationship with Lucy, says Mollel.

—Yes. But he had something on us too.

—The abortions.

Benjamin gives a faint smile. —Yes. Even with the evidence destroyed, he had Lucy to testify to that.

—So it was a stalemate, says Mollel. Until he got rid of Lucy.

He remembers Sammy's words: he heard *two* women's voices. That's how he would have ensured Honey's cooperation and got Lucy out of the way. By killing her friend in front of her in the most ghastly way possible.

—We've got to find Lethebridge, says Mollel.

—We? asks Benjamin.

—You can't stay here, can you? Besides, I'm going to need you.

38 From up here, the city looks like a million points of light. But the power is off all over Nairobi, and apart from some security lights run from generators in the business district, most of the points are red, and flickering.

The city is ablaze.

Benjamin pulls the car into a side street. The reflectors of the silver Toyota glint in their headlight beam as they pull up. The Toyota is parked tight against a hedge, its front wheels twisted at an angle. A hurried, panicked park. It does not have the air of a car that someone intends to return to.

Benjamin parks next to it and turns off the engine. He and Mollel step out.

—Kiunga? calls Mollel.

One of the red points of light rises up, glows, and descends. The movement is followed by a cough.

—Here.

Kiunga steps out of the shadow of a nearby tree, exhaling smoke.

—How long have you been waiting? asks Mollel.

—Two cigarettes. Maybe three. Who's your friend?

—This is Benjamin, says Mollel.

—Sorry for hiding in the bushes. But I wasn't expecting you in a car.

And when I saw the dreadlocks . . . You know, the Mungiki are out in force tonight.

—That's why I brought him, says Mollel. Security in case we run into one of their roadblocks.

—And he was mine, adds Benjamin, in case we were stopped by the police. I stole plenty of vehicles in my bad old days, but I never had a serving officer ride shotgun with me before.

—It's a stolen car? Kiunga asks Mollel with surprise.

—George Nalo's, says Mollel with a shrug. Paid for by his congregation. How did you track Lethebridge's car down to here?

—After I tried to get him at home and he wouldn't answer the door, I had a watch put on the place.

—A watch? But this is an unofficial investigation. How did you manage it?

—Strictly unofficially, Kiunga answers. Seems like the guy I chose has done a good job, though.

—No one gave me a second glance, says a boy's voice. A ragged, barefooted figure appears from the darkness.

—Panya!

Mollel pats the boy on the back. It was a good idea of Kiunga's. A *chokora* is as good as invisible in Nairobi, even on the genteel streets of Lavington.

—He left his house about an hour ago, Panya says. The only problem I had was persuading anyone to take me from the house. None of the taxi drivers wanted to pick me up or believed I could pay them. The roads are all blocked, one way or another, anyway. Eventually I got a *boda-boda* who let me sit on the back. We had to do a lot of talking to get through. And a lot of riding around before we found this.

—Good work, says Mollel.

He goes to inspect the Toyota. He notes once more the scrape on the front fender. He opens the door, looks inside. Nothing in the rear. Nothing on the seats. He climbs into the driver's seat, leans across, and opens the glove compartment. The car's instruction manual, nothing else. Typical company car. He folds down the sun visors, feels inside the seat pockets, opens the ashtrays. Nothing. Nothing. Nothing.

He slaps the steering wheel in frustration. It rattles. He looks closer. The central boss consists of a plastic shell, which is loose. He prizes it off. Underneath, the car's air bag is loosely wedged in, crammed ineptly into its space. It's been deployed at some point and stuffed back into place.

Otherwise, there's nothing more to be learned from the car.

—He must have gone on from here on foot, says Mollel to Kiunga. What's nearby?

—There's lots of office buildings, says Kiunga. Company headquarters, that type of thing. But none of them would be open now. More likely he's gone to one of the posh hotels. There's the Fairmont, the Panafric. It's easy enough to check those out. They're not your sleazy downtown flea pits. You have to show ID when you sign in. We'll just ask if they've had any British passport holders arrive in the last couple of hours.

British passport holders.

Mollel slaps the side of the Toyota.

—The British High Commission, he says. He's gone to the British High Commission.

—Of course, says Kiunga. That's why he's left his car. They won't allow anyone to leave a civilian vehicle *close* to that place. Not since— well, you know what.

Mollel knows what.

—I heard on the radio that they're evacuating British citizens, says Kiunga. Once he goes through those doors, he'll be on British soil. We've lost him.

—We'll have to hope he's not got in yet. We'll get there quicker if we do what he did and leave the car here. Benjamin, can you look after Panya? And the Toyota. We may need it for evidence. Cars like these won't stay unnoticed long.

—Don't worry, says Benjamin with a grin. Chances are, anyone we meet from now on is going to be Mungiki. And I still hold some sway with my former brothers.

▲ ▲ ▲

The two policemen take off on foot down a side street. There's an alley at the end that leads out onto the road where the British High Commission is situated.

It's a wide, low, fortress of a building, built with the attack on the U.S. embassy very much in mind. Concrete blast barriers divide the road. Signs at regular intervals exhort NO STOPPING, NO DROPPING. A phalanx of guards—a mixture of Kenyan police and private security—lines the area in front of the commission, but they're not preventing people from going through. A small crowd has gathered at a tiny reinforced-glass window in the bare black slate wall. A sign above it reads ENQUIRIES.

—My sister lives in Manchester, one woman is sobbing. You've got to let me in. The woman behind the bulletproof glass is diligently avoiding eye contact with everyone on the outside. Instead, she points to a hastily handwritten notice that has been taped to the inside: "British Nationals Only Will Be Admitted."

—Have you had—Mollel pushes himself to the front—have you had a James Lethebridge come here?

—Wait your turn, please, sir, she replies with barely disguised contempt.

—I'm police, he says, showing his ID card.

—You'll still have to wait your turn. She studiously turns away. An Indian-looking man grabs Mollel's shirt.

—You're police, he says. Can't you do something? I can't get back to my home. I can't get my passport to prove that I'm British. And these racists . . . I'm from Wembley. I'm only here visiting my cousins.

Other people seem to be latching on to the idea that Mollel is some kind of official. In their desperation they paw at him, implore him.

Kiunga comes to his assistance. —Stand back, stand back!

—I'm sorry, I'm sorry, says Mollel. There's nothing I can do. He and Kiunga walk away from the enquiries window.

—We'll never be able to raise an arrest warrant before he leaves the country, says Kiunga, downcast. It'll be an extradition job now, and what chance do you think we have of that?

—None, says Mollel.

They pass another entrance that's darkened and locked. The sign says VISA OFFICE and lists weekday opening hours. In front of it is a hard metal bench. A private security guard is rousing a huddled figure.

—Come on, you can't stay here, he is saying.

—Please! implores the man on the bench. I'm British! Can't you just let me stay here, even if you won't let me in?

—You've been told, sir. No passport, no entry.

The man stands. —Just look at me! he says. He has a white face, white hair. He pulls up his sleeve to reveal pallid white skin. —Do I look Kenyan? Of course I'm British!

Mollel walks over and shows his ID to the security guard. —I'll take care of this, he says.

—Just get him out of here, says the security guard. He says he's British, but his passport is Kenyan. That means he must have wanted to be Kenyan, once. I guess he reckons it's not such a privilege anymore.

The security guard walks away.

—Hello, Mr. Lethebridge, says Mollel.

James Lethebridge looks at him, takes him in. A slow, creeping realization spreads over his face.

—You must be Mollel, Lethebridge says. David told me you were waiting for me, Sergeant. But I didn't expect to see you here.

Kiunga nods. —You need to come with us. There's no point trying to resist.

—Thank God.

A rueful smile plays across Lethebridge's lips. —I can assure you, officers, I won't resist, he continues. I'd rather go with the sheepdogs than be cast to the wolves.

39 On their way back to the cars, the sound of gunfire makes them pick up their pace.

—That's pretty close, says Mollel.

—The opposition has called for a mass rally in Uhuru Park tomorrow, says Kiunga. I heard a rumor that some of them were planning to attack the GSU base there tonight. If they do, they'll have to come right through here.

—We'd better not stick around, then.

Panya and Benjamin are waiting for them beside Lethebridge's Toyota. George Nalo's car is gone.

—You guys took your time, Benjamin says. There was a gang of guys here a few minutes ago. Not Mungiki, but regular looters, out for what they could get. Some of them had *pangas*. They wanted to take both cars, but they were happy enough when I handed them the keys to Nalo's. I guess the Lord giveth and the Lord taketh away.

A casual observer might consider the occupants of the silver Toyota Land Cruiser a strange assembly: two smart young men in front, the passenger dreadlocked; a gaunt, ashen Maasai and an elderly white man in the backseat; and, hunched on the jump seat in the rear, looking out through the glass, a ragged street boy taking his first ride in a car.

But there are no casual observers on the streets on this night, no disinterested parties, no innocent bystanders.

The car passes groups of men—and some boys—headed, it seems, for Uhuru Park. They walk purposefully, lithe limbs swinging, and something—sticks, or clubs, or *pangas*—bouncing at their sides.

As if to break the tension, Lethebridge chuckles.

—You know, he says, you really managed to wind up Kingori after you interviewed him that first time. He told me to hide up at home, to say nothing to you. But he was genuine when he phoned me from the KICC and instructed me to cooperate. How did you get him to change his mind?

—More to the point, says Mollel, turning to face him, why did you decide to flee? I had the impression that you always obeyed his instructions to the letter.

Lethebridge casts his eyes out the window into the darkness beyond. —I've never pretended to be a very brave man, he says quietly. I had the feeling that whatever happened next, David wouldn't be able to protect me anymore.

Kiunga drives them on a zigzag route through Upper Hill. He wants to avoid the main roads and ill-frequented ones alike, choosing a fine middle passage of routes that are unlikely to attract attention but wide enough to avoid an ambush.

—Let me tell you a bit about David Kingori, continues Lethebridge. He seems to be in the mood to chat, as a reaction to tension, or relief. —Do you know we were at school together? In England. He was the first black African in the school. How the other boys used to mock him! They would steal his jumper, ask him how he liked the cold. But he just smiled and told them he was fine.

—I was the one who was homesick. I'd been told all my life that England was my home, yet when I turned up there, I pined for the African air. No wonder I clung to David. He was all I had.

—We were a strange pair. We'd been raised together. My father and his were in business together. It didn't start that way. Before I was born, my father owned a six-hundred-acre tea estate near Kericho. David's father was the farm manager. But when independence came, my father decided it would be politic to appoint a local partner. Somehow, every year, there were reasons that more and more of the business had to be signed over to Kingori. Eventually my father became the employee.

Lethebridge gives a hoarse laugh. —He thought it was so unfair. He never really stopped to question the policy of the old colonial adminis-tration that had given him the land in the first place.

They seem to have outstripped most of the gangs, and the sidewalks are mostly clear as they start to descend the hill that runs down to the park. There, in the darkness, is Orpheus House—or what is left of it. Mollel looks over his shoulder as they pass, but makes out nothing more than a glimpse of the COMING SOON sign. Behind him, in the jump seat, Panya is asleep.

—David took over the business after we finished school. He gave me a job. I think he enjoyed having a white man work for him. Gave him cer-tain kudos. But more important than that, he knew he could trust me.

—Part of my job, even from early on, was to find him girls. I didn't mind. I just enjoyed the fact that I was bringing him pleasure. I knew they never meant anything to him. I gave him the unquestioning devo-tion he needed. They gave him everything else.

—Lucy was different. She had something else that he needed. Infor-mation.

—The Nalos were pressing David for the lease of Orpheus House. David wanted the land for development, but with George Nalo's follow-ing and political clout, he did not dare evict them. Lucy had been part of their operation. For a while, when she wanted to get out of the game, she had gone there, been taken in. She knew what went on. She told me about the abortions. How Wanjiku was a fanatic. She thought she was saving the babies from a life of suffering, Lucy told us. Better off dead than on the street.

Mollel looks at Benjamin. The back of his head betrays no emotion, no indication that he's even listening. He's too astute to interrupt Lethe-bridge's flow now. The old man had shown no sign of recognizing him from the church. Probably thought he was another police officer. Mollel can't help thinking he would have made a fine one.

—I didn't want to trouble David with the details, continues Lethebridge. I knew that this was what we needed to get the Nalos off our back. Their empire would have been ruined if it was revealed. Once they were gone, it would also rid him of this troublesome girl, too. Get things back to how they were. But I needed more than one woman's hearsay. I needed evidence.

—Then Lucy told me she had something on the Nalos that was dynamite. A friend of hers had got pregnant by George Nalo and had been given an abortion by Wanjiku. Late-term, too. Testimony like that would ruin them. They'd have to do what we wanted.

—Lucy was offering her friend up on a plate. I'd give her enough money to disappear, once I had the girl. But Lucy didn't trust me, any more than I trusted her. She wouldn't give me her friend's name. Wouldn't tell me where to find her. We had to meet her together.

—She had a plan. I would pose as a john. Her friend wasn't working at that time. It was still too soon after the operation. But she had agreed to help Lucy. She could do with some money.

Descending Upper Hill, Kiunga drives through the red light at the junction with Haile Selassie Avenue. As they sweep around a curve, the shadowy fringe of the gardens appears, lined with the imposing presence of GSU. Over their helmets and beyond their shields Mollel can make out the tented field hospital and the command trucks. The car continues parallel to the picket, skimming the edge of the scene of the crime, somewhere behind that cordon. Even at speed, the scraped concrete post is visible as the car that damaged it glides past.

—That's where you did it, says Mollel.

—That's where it happened, confirms Lethebridge. That's where they got me. They got me with the old twofer.

—Twofer?

—It's a classic hooker's trick. A good way of earning money if you don't want to go through with the act.

—I cruised down K Street at a prearranged time. Lucy came to the window. I acted like we'd never met before. She played it by the book.

—We spoke. She looked over at her friend nervously. She was playing it great. *Look,* she said, *there have been some strange characters around here lately. Do you mind if my friend comes along?*

—I acted reluctant. *Oh, I don't know,* I said. Then she winked and said, *We'll give you a twofer. Two for one.* Well, I mean, who could have resisted? I played along. Lucy got in beside me, and her friend smiled as she got into the back.

She was lovely. Tall, slender. My tastes don't run in that direction, Sergeant, as you might have guessed. But this girl. I might have made an exception if I'd been a few years younger. She had a way about her. Her smile was seductive. It made you want to forget about everything, all the troubles of the world, and just give yourself up to her. Do you know what I mean?

Mollel knows what he means. —What happened next? he says. Honey got into the car, then what?

—Honey? says Lethebridge with surprise. Is that her name?

—That's her name.

—Honey, repeats Lethebridge softly. Well, Lucy got into the front, next to me, and Honey slipped in behind. The plan was that I'd take them to the park. It was nearby, it was private. Once there, Honey would not be able to run away. And hopefully, we'd be able to persuade her to speak.

—But as we went in through the park gate, I felt a sudden pain. I didn't know what it was. I thought it was a heart attack. My time was up at last. I could not breathe.

Lethebridge fingers his neck thoughtfully.

—You see, the thing about the twofer was that it was all a ruse. The girls would get into the john's car, get him to drive them somewhere secluded, then mug him. But Honey had obviously decided not to wait for the car to stop. She'd grabbed the seat belt and was pulling it as hard as she could. I was just aware of her knee in my back, pressing through the seat, the stabbing pain. Trying to reach for the buckle . . . Then we hit something. And I don't know what happened next.

—When I came to, my face was in the air bag and the girls were gone. I thought at first they'd double-crossed me, but my wallet was still in my pocket. I got out. As my eyes grew used to the dark, I could just see them some distance away, up ahead. I could hear them too. It sounded like they were arguing.

—Honey was screaming. I could not make it out. Something about losing her baby. Lucy was saying *no, no.* I was groggy. I could hardly walk. By the time I got to them, I couldn't see Lucy anymore. Just Honey, standing over the ditch.

—Then she jumped in. I looked down. Lucy was in there, sprawled. And Honey was on top. I couldn't see what she was doing. I thought that Lucy had fallen, that Honey was trying to revive her. I was dizzy. So dizzy.

—I must have collapsed, because the next thing I knew, Honey was leading me back to the car. Her hands were wet on my arm. When I opened the car door and the light came on, I saw that she was covered in blood.

—*You say anything about this,* she told me, *and I'll do to you what I did to her. You understand?*

—I had no doubt she meant it, Sergeant. Her eyes were wild. When David phoned me and told me to cooperate with the police, I panicked. I knew she would come and get me. Do to me what she did to her friend. I just wanted to get away from here, get out of this country. As far away as possible.

—She told me to drop her somewhere. I can't remember where. All the way she was muttering, *They took my baby away, they took my baby away.*

They took her baby away, Mollel remembers Honey saying. *Can you even imagine what that's like, Mollel? Now Faith's trying to do the same to you. But don't worry. I'll never let that happen, Mollel. I'll never let that happen to you.*

▲ ▲ ▲

He thinks of Kawangware, of Faith's house. Where Honey is. With Adam. And with Faith.

—Stop the car!

They're past the park now, on the deserted roundabout at the head of University Way. Barely half a kilometer from Central Police Post. But Mollel's tone of urgency compels Kiunga to come to a screeching halt halfway around the traffic circle.

Mollel opens the door and leaps out.

—Where are you going? cries Kiunga.

—Take him to Central, orders Mollel.

—You're going after Honey? Let me drive you!

—You heard what Panya said. The streets in that part of town are blocked off. No car's going to get through. I just about might.

—Leave her until morning, protests Kiunga, making to turn off the engine. But Benjamin steadies his hand.

—I've seen this man jump into fire, he says. You're not going to stop him.

And he turns to wish him well, but Mollel is already gone.

40 He runs.

Sometimes he passes a group headed in the opposite direction, toward the city center. The boys—sometimes there are boys with them—cheer him as he passes, as though he is running a race. They wave their *pangas* aloft in support. But the men hardly cast him a glance. They pace on, determinedly. To them he is a night runner, and he might as well be invisible. They have no concern with the otherworldly this night.

He runs through deserted suburban streets. Walls blank and windows barred. Hurlingham, Dagoretti, Lavington—church placards and business signs mark off the names of the neighborhoods, but there is nothing neighborly about them.

I won't let her take your child from you, Mollel.

He feels no pain, no fatigue. The urgency of his mission impels him: the act of running, too, recalls his youthful days of trotting for hours behind the herd. Perhaps it's also the Nalos' miracle cure that gives him the heightened perception now, to see it all so clearly.

Honey wouldn't know, yet, that he had discovered she was the killer. She still needed him. She needed him because she believed her baby was alive and had been farmed out for adoption by the Nalos. That was why she had led him to them, Mollel understands now. She thought that if she exposed their racket by blaming them for Lucy's death, the adoption agency would be investigated. She'd be able to track down her baby. Get it back.

So it is essential that he does not alert her. When he gets to them, he must maintain the pretense. At least until Faith and Adam are safe.

As he nears Faith's house, where middle-class Lavington merges into Kawangware, he begins to hear the sound that's become so familiar in the last few days. It's the sound of breaking glass, of cries, of screams. Of women and children bawling in fear and men boiling with rage.

He hadn't expected the trouble to spread this far. Kibera and Mathare, sure. They were tinder just waiting for a match. It didn't take much to set those districts up in flames. But sleepy little Kawangware, with its up-and-coming pretensions?

Then he remembers the good-for-nothings who had been hanging around outside Faith's house on Christmas Day. They'd skulked off soon enough once Kiunga had sent them on their way, but he had no doubt that on a night like this, they'd be looking for scores to settle.

His heart pounds violently as he realizes it's not just Faith and Adam in danger—but Honey, too, for that matter. Anyone inside that property would be a Kikuyu, as far as an angry, drunken mob was concerned. And the Kikuyus have just stolen the election—haven't they?

People are heading past him in the other direction. Not the male gangs of before—these are nearly all women and children. He stops one woman—bent nearly double under the weight of a sleeping child strapped in a *khanga* on her back—and asks her, —What's going on?

—The GSU, she answers breathlessly. They've bottled up Kawangware.

Mollel picks up his pace. He hopes that somehow the GSU might agree with Faith's silly snobbery and decide that her house is in Lavington. Place their blockade a couple of streets to the west, with her on the safe side. But he knows they won't. It would make no sense. The broad strip of James Gichuru Road is the natural defensive position to take. Rounding a corner, he sees with dread that he is right. A heavy line of riot officers, with trucks and armored vehicles, is stationed at the junction of James Gichuru and Gitanga roads, completely cutting off Kawangware.

The residents of Lavington might feel grateful for the barrier, but it means that inside Kawangware, anything could happen.

And it probably is happening right now, to judge by the constant arc of missiles that rain down on the GSU troops. Mollel runs, zigzag, seeing a flash of flame whoosh past his eyes just an instant before a glass bottle explodes on the ground next to him. His legs are splashed with cold liquid, and the oily stench of fuel oil fills his nostrils. He wipes his leg with his hand and rubs the viscous fluid between his fingers. The sting on his burned flesh makes him catch his breath. Then he steps on and extinguishes the already-dying flame of the rag tied around the neck of the bottle. He counts himself lucky that whoever filled it didn't know the difference between diesel and petrol. But he might not be so lucky next time. He can already see blue flame spreading over the roof of one of the GSU trucks, the men nearby scrambling to douse it with an extinguisher.

Mollel pushes himself toward the front but can't get through the line: the GSU men have interlocked their arms, shields forward. They are so intent on the mob facing them that they don't even appear to notice him trying to weave his way in.

He gives up, exasperated. He starts to look for an alternative way around, but the troops have blocked off the only way in and out. He can even see the green corrugated iron roof of Faith's house, just a few dozen meters away. At least it looks intact. He hopes Faith would have had the common sense to snatch up Adam and make a dash for it while she still had the chance. But knowing Faith, he feels sure she would not have left her home. Which means that she, Honey, and Adam are still in there.

—Hey! What the hell do you think you're doing? Grab him!

Mollel feels himself grasped on both sides and spun around. He is face-to-face with the pugnacious features of a GSU sergeant.

—Take him away, boys. Give him a good going-over. I don't want to see his ugly face again.

Then his eyes screw up. He scrutinizes Mollel more closely. —Hang on a moment, he says. Haven't I seen your ugly face before?

—You're Mwathi, says Mollel. I'm one of the police officers investigating the murder down in Uhuru Park. You said your daughter was the same age as the victim.

Mwathi's face breaks into a broad smile. —Let him go, boys, he says. He's one of us.

Mollel is roughly released. —That's the first time I've been called *one of us* by a GSU man, he says.

—We're all in this together now, says Mwathi. Unless, of course, you'd rather be in there, with *them*.

He nods his head toward the crowd beyond the line.

—Actually, says Mollel, I would.

Mwathi laughs incredulously. —Are you insane? They'd rip you apart.

—I don't think so. I'm not in uniform. And no one's going to think I'm a Kikuyu, with these ears. As far as I'm aware, no one's turned on the Maasai, yet.

—Give it time, says Mwathi. Give it time. So why do you want to throw yourself into that lion's den? Feeling suicidal?

—My family's in there.

Mwathi's eyes flicker with pity. —Where are they?

—In a house near the edge. If you could just push the cordon forward a block . . .

Mwathi shakes his head. —We can't do it. We're having enough difficulty holding the line as it is. Look, if they're inside a house, they'll probably be all right, if they just keep their heads down. Then, when it gets calmer . . .

Mollel squeezes the sergeant's arms tighter. Feels the agony in his hands. —I can't wait, he implores. They're in danger. The killer. The killer of the girl in the park. The killer's in there too. With my family.

He feels his knees begin to buckle. Mwathi looks down at him, skeptical at first. But his face changes as he realizes that Mollel is telling the truth.

—The murderer's with your family? he asks.

—I didn't know. Mollel is gasping. —I didn't know. I thought they would be safe.

—This is what we'll do, says Mwathi, pulling Mollel to his feet. I'll let you through. But you'll have to take your chances. If you make it to the house, you got to stay there. You understand? Don't try to get out. Not until all this is over.

—Okay, says Mollel.

—And as for that murderer, says Mwathi, you do what you've got to do. Kill him if you need to. No one's going to ask any questions about another body around here, come morning. Give me your ID.

—What? Why?

—You won't want it in there.

He's right: if Mollel gets robbed or searched, his police ID would be as good as a death sentence. But he feels denuded handing it over. First his uniform, now this. It's as though he's been stripped of everything that marked him as a policeman. Now he's just a man.

Mwathi rattles his billy stick against the helmets of two GSU men on the front line. —When I give the order, let this one through, he bellows. Close ranks immediately afterward. Now!

The two men unlock their arms, and Mwathi pushes Mollel through the gap. He immediately stumbles on a brick. Mwathi shouts, —Good luck. And sorry!

—For what?

—For this, cries Mwathi as he brings his billy stick down on Mollel's shoulder. The pain courses through him. But he understands: Mwathi is giving him a chance with the mob. He takes his cue and runs, head down, toward the opposing line.

41 The blow from the stick did the trick: welcoming arms greet him and pull him in. His disheveled state is the perfect alibi. No one questions that he is anything other than a fellow rioter unlucky enough to have tasted summary GSU justice.

—Come, brother, says a voice with a thick Luo accent. You can't stay here.

He is helped, hobbling, through the throng of angry voices to rest on a concrete curb. His rescuer kneels beside him and glares into Mollel's face with angry eyes.

—What did they do to you, those bastards? he hisses.

—I was just trying to get home, mumbles Mollel weakly.

The young man in front of him shakes his head. —They've been waiting a long time for this, he says. Those Kikuyu thieves shared out the country when the English left. They were happy to share with the Kalenjins when Moi was in power. But now it's time for the Luos! The Luos and the Luhyas, together we outnumber them. It's our turn! And yet, what do we get? This! Here, let me see your hands. You're injured, my brother.

Mollel is struck by the simple concern the stranger shows him—in stark counterpoint to the visceral hatred in his words. Mwathi, too, on the other side, had shown him humanity. Was this always to be the way, that Kenyans would be capable of individual kindness and group animosity?

He thinks about David Kingori on the roof of the KICC, supervising the ballot rigging. For all his vainglorious words about the Kikuyu homeland, Mollel never had the feeling that he was motivated by tribalism. Rather, that he was part of a deeply entrenched elite and was desperate to dig himself in deeper.

But Mollel feels the point would be lost on his newfound savior. Instead, he asks, —What's happening farther inside?

The young man shrugs. —Some of the shops have been looted. The Kikuyu-owned ones, mainly. Your family should be all right, if they're Maasai. You lot aren't part of this.

—I seem to recall an old Kikuyu woman who lives near here, says Mollel. Do you know what's happened to her?

—Her time will come, says the young man bitterly. Her house is well protected. We've not had a chance to clear out all the cockroaches yet. But if the GSU keep us shut up here all night, there'll be plenty of opportunity.

—Thanks for your assistance, says Mollel, rising. As he does so, there is a flash of light, and a cheer goes up. A petrol bomb has obviously hit an enemy target. The young man bends to lift the stone Mollel had been sitting on. He prizes it up, and the last Mollel sees of him, he is carrying it toward the chaos.

Mollel looks around him. The streetlights are out, but in the glare of the fires he can see the familiar junction of the side street running to Faith's house. He walks past the point where Kiunga caught Adam on his bike. As he approaches, he sees, with relief, that the house seems to be unscathed, apart from some graffiti scrawled on the high metal gate.

He stretches and looks over, between the spiked barbs that run along the top. The power is out in the whole neighborhood, but the diffuse glow of a candle or kerosene lamp flickers somewhere from behind the kitchen window. He bangs on the gate—nervously at first, afraid of attracting unwanted attention—then louder. A shadow falls across the window, but there is no other sign of movement from within. Why should there be? They're probably terrified.

He contemplates his options. Shouting would not be heard above the general racket outside. Throw a stone—but that would only send them scurrying for refuge deeper inside the house. Scale the gate—but the spikes on top are cruel, expressly designed to keep people out. Crueler still is the sparkling razor wire Faith had recently installed, but her prescience had at least kept the family safe so far. The place was impenetrable.

—So you decided to join us after all?

It is his friend with the stone. It's gone now, and in its place he carries a length of metal pipe. He's not alone. There's a mob of them, a breakaway group from the front line. Mollel thinks he recognizes some of the lads Kiunga had warned off the place a few days previously. They're drunk: some of them are carrying what looks like *chang'aa* in plastic bottles. But they also carry *pangas* and other makeshift weapons. He does not doubt their ability to use them. He steps back slightly, casting his face into the shadows.

—There's no getting out of Kawangware tonight, the young man says. We might as well settle some scores while we're stuck here.

They're not drinking from their bottles, Mollel realizes. That's not *chang'aa*. It's petrol.

—I've just been checking this place out, he blusters. It's not worth it. The security's pretty tight. Even if we did get in, one GSU push forward would see us trapped in there like rats.

This brings a laugh from the men. —They're not going to push forward, says one. Not if they know what's good for them.

—I heard that one of the old woman's relatives is a policeman, chimes in another.

—Exactly! says Mollel. That's the sort of trouble we don't need.

—All the more reason to torch the place, says one lad, pushing forward. He is in Mollel's face, and Mollel's suspicions are confirmed: he was one of those hanging around on Christmas Day.

—I know the policeman, too. I think he's the father of the little boy who lives here.

Mollel tries to quell the anger that is consuming him. A fight with these men now would leave him dead, and useless to those inside. Measuredly, quietly, he says, —Oh, yeah?

—Yeah, slurs the lad. I seen him teaching the kid how to ride his bike. Even spoke to him once. Cocky Kikuyu bastard. Thinks he knows how to speak Jaluo.

He means Kiunga, Mollel realizes. Still, the lad looks him up and down, as though trying to place the face. But he's too drunk to make the connection.

—I'll have that bike when we're done with the people inside, shouts another one of the men. I bet she's got lots of other nice things in there, too.

Mollel wants to fight them. He wants to grab a *panga* out of one of their hands and kill them all, slash them to pieces. This is what it takes, he thinks, even as his heart is pounding. This is what it takes to make the Red God rise up inside of you. To give you the rage you need to make you a killer. To cut people up. When someone threatens your family, your child. Threatens to take away everything you have and destroy everything you love. And there's no recourse to law, no appeal to order. No one will protect you and no one will stand up for you and fight on your behalf. All you can do is kill.

This is what Honey felt.

This is what is destroying Kenya.

—Wait a minute, wait a minute, he says hurriedly. You've got something there. The old woman, she's pretty well-off, yeah? I bet she's even got money stuffed under her mattress. All Kikuyus do. Right. So the last thing we want to do is burn the place down. She's got stuff in there that we need.

He can sense the others taking in his argument. Greed and envy beginning to overcome even hatred. —So look, he continues. Let me get in there. Help me over the wall. I'll open up the gate, get access to the house. Then we can help ourselves. What do you say, boys?

The proposal is met with a cheer. But Mollel's sense of relief is short-lived. He's bought himself some time. But even if he manages to get Adam, Faith, and Honey out of there, he's still got to get them past the mob. And they won't be satisfied with looting the property. They're out for blood.

—You, says Mollel. The way I saw you pick up that stone, you can definitely lift a skinny guy like me. Come on, give me a boost.

Now the decision's been made, he doesn't want to give anyone time to think about it. Hands are cupped, and Mollel steps into them. — Now, on three, I need you all to push me over. Okay?

He counts. On his count of three, he is impelled upward, higher than he had expected, so he fails to grasp the smooth metal at the base of the spikes, but places his hands, raw flesh down, on the top of them. His impetus has given him just enough thrust to avoid bringing his hands down with force; instead, he pitches his palms down against the rear of the spikes and pushes himself forward. His trouser leg gets caught and rips, and he is thrown onto the gravel on the other side of the gate, head-first. But at least, he thinks as he staggers to his feet, he was not impaled.

There is a cheer from the other side. He makes a show of examining the inside of the gate. —It's padlocked, he calls. Wait here. I'll try to get into the house. Don't try to follow me. They may be armed.

—Get a move on, one of them urges him.

He runs to the kitchen window. Like all the windows of the house, it is barred. He can see a kerosene lamp burning on the table inside. But no one there. He bangs on the glass. —Faith? Honey? It's me, Mollel!

It's no good. He dare not shout too loud for fear of the men outside the gate hearing him. And he can only imagine the fear that Adam, Faith, and Honey must be feeling now, listening to someone banging on the window and shouting.

Strange, he thinks, how he's still concerned about Honey. He knows that she killed Lucy, and he's convinced that she has the capacity to be a real threat to Faith. But somehow, thinking of the old woman and the young boy huddled in fear inside the house, he's glad that Honey is there with them.

Then he thinks, *She's not Chiku.*

It comes as a shock to him, the realization that he'd been carving out that role for her. But it had felt good at the time, the comfort she had provided him, the protection he felt he was providing for her. He feels angry, foolish: she's suckered him. She is a professional. It is what she does.

All his assumptions about Honey have been wrong. He can't assume that Faith is safe now. He hopes that Honey will be rational enough not to harm her while she still thinks he is on her side. But after what she's done to her friend . . .

He can't even assume Adam is safe.

He picks up a flowerpot and smashes the kitchen window. —Faith! He hisses through the gap. Damn these bars. —Honey? Adam?

—What are you doing? comes a voice from over the gate. He looks back, sees a row of eyes watching him.

He knows where they will be. There's a storage cupboard off the main hallway that has no windows, no external wall. It's the safest place in the house. If they haven't already taken shelter there, they will now that they've heard the breaking glass. They're unreachable.

He goes around to the other windows, looking in, hoping for a glimpse of someone, a point of contact. But there is none.

—Come on, Maasai, booms a voice once more. Get a move on, or we'll storm the place.

The last time he prowled around a house like this, it was Orpheus House. Getting in there had been simple once he had the key. He remembers the standing ruins, the roof caved in. It must have burned to the ground in minutes. Just like this house, the roof was a flimsy corrugated metal construction, with only wooden joists and a thin layer of ceiling board below, fine for keeping the rain off, but deadly in a fire, when the whole structure would come crashing down. He desperately hopes none of the thugs outside are getting impatient to use their petrol.

The roof—of course. He runs back to the kitchen, where a rain barrel stands by the door, and hefts himself up on it. From there it is a fairly easy scramble up the drainpipe, using the guttering as a handhold to get onto the metal roof. He edges along—luckily the pitch is relatively shallow—until he feels a row of galvanized nails under his throbbing hands.

His theory is simple: rather than attempt to breach the seam between two sheets of metal, he'll start at the bottom edge and pull. If he's lucky, once the first set of nails gives way, he'll be able to use leverage to pull out enough to peel the sheet back.

He stands at the edge. Even this single-story height gives him a dizzy feeling, with the fires and confusion just beyond the compound fence. The mob of men waiting at the gate holler and hoot at him. He casts them a wave of acknowledgment, then crouches and grasps the edge.

His hands flash with pain. But he defies it: feet spread, he heaves, the metal edge cutting into his raw, damaged flesh.

Nothing happens.

It's going to be harder than he imagined. Looking down, he sees that the sheets lap each other, so that one side is pinned down by the next. With a crowbar it would be easy enough, but . . .

—Hey! he shouts to the men outside. I need a bar or something.

The man who had picked up the stone waves his metal pipe in the air.
—How about this?

—Perfect, yells Mollel. The man raises the pipe and pitches it, spinning, over the wall. It sails in an arc toward Mollel, who ducks, and it crashes with a clatter onto the roof and immediately begins to roll downward. Mollel dives and grasps it just as it teeters over the edge.

With the pipe in hand, he sets to work prizing the edge of the metal sheet free. Raising one corner, he is now able to get a purchase on the sheet he wants to lift.

He strains again. It's slippery this time. His blood runs along the edge. The sheet is still not moving. A jeer rises from the watching mob.

—Come on, Maasai, one of them yells. If you get in, you can have first go on the old woman!

He pulls again, gasping. Every muscle in his body is part of this effort. Pain burns through him. When he feels something give, the minutest of shifts, he thinks at first it is his own body giving way. But it is not. It is the metal. Another heave, and it comes again, more definitely this time. He scrambles to realign his hands on the greasy sheet. And heaves.

With a creak, the sheet begins to come free. He pulls, and nails pop from their positions. One final effort, and he folds the sheet back, revealing a gap just wide enough for him to squeeze through. The mob cheers him, and he can't help casting them a grin and a triumphant wave as he edges around, and down, and in.

42 He thinks of the mice, or rats, that had scuttled in Orpheus House. Now he is the one padding carefully across the rafters. He tries to recall where the hatch is, but he can't even picture the layout of the rooms below.

—Faith? Honey? It's me. Mollel.

No sound. And nothing to see, either. The faintest glimmer of light leaks in from the hole he forced in the roof. He feels his way along the rafters with his feet, picking his path under crossbeams and over water pipes.

He pauses. Against the sound of the clamor from outside, he thinks he hears a noise. He listens, trying to separate the strands of sound—that which is outside from that which is below.

It is prayer.

Unmistakably, directly beneath his feet he hears prayer. Faith's voice: the Lord's Prayer. He bends his head down to be sure. Moves around so that he can bring his ear to lie flat against the board of the ceiling of the room below.

A blade thrusts up right in front of his eyes. It pulls down, leaving a hole, a sliver of streaming light. He cries out.

—No, no! It's me!

The blade appears again, between his legs. It's a *panga*, probably the one that Faith uses to cut plants in her garden. He recoils, feels himself toppling backward from his perch on the rafter. He feels his back hitting the ceiling board, feels it giving below him, and with a sickening, split-second splintering, it breaks and he free-falls, landing with a crash and a cloud of dust on the floor of the hallway of Faith's house.

He blinks. Dazed. Looks up. Honey is standing over him, the small, curved blade of Lucy's knife in her hand. Beyond her, through the doorway of the storage cupboard, he can see Faith standing on a box, the *panga* raised. Adam is at her feet.

—Dad!

—Thank God it's you, cries Faith. We thought it was those *wamera* trying to get in. What have you done to my home, Mollel?

—Any closer with that *panga*, he says, and I'd have been circumcised a second time.

As he rises to his feet, he is almost knocked over once more by a sudden oncoming rush. He feels warm limbs around his neck, and skin against his cheek. Adam is squeezing him with violent affection. Mollel puts his own arms around his son and lifts him up as he stands.

For the first time, he realizes what he could have lost. And he never wants to let the boy go.

Honey touches his shoulder and plants a gentle kiss on his cheek.

—I knew you wouldn't let us down, she says.

Reminded of her presence, Mollel reluctantly lowers Adam and detaches himself once more.

—Where were you when we needed you, Mollel? demands Faith. We've been here all night with those yobs shouting threats and throwing stones. We thought . . . we thought they were going to kill us.

Faith sits down on the box and buries her face in her hands. Honey goes over to her and places her arm around the old woman's shoulders. The small, cruel knife is palmed in her hand.

—Shh, Faith, she says comfortingly. Mollel got here as soon as he could. He was on his case. He had work to do. Did you find anything out, Mollel?

She raises her eyes to his. There is the faintest glimmer of challenge in her gaze.

—Not much, he says. The shape this city's in, I doubt one little murder's even going to count anymore. I think I've hit a dead end. Have either of you got your phone? I can try to call for help.

—Don't you think we've tried? wails Faith. The network's down. Probably everyone in Nairobi's trying to call for help right now.

—What do you mean, a dead end? demands Honey. You're still going to investigate the Nalos, aren't you? Forget about the murder. What about finding Lucy's child?

She strokes Faith's neck while she turns the knife in her hand.

—The priority right now, says Mollel, moving Adam behind him and edging forward, is to get out of here. Faith, what have you got in the house that we could defend ourselves with?

—I've got this *panga*, she says, looking up at him fearfully. There are some knives in the kitchen. And there's Ngugi's old walking stick around somewhere.

—Okay, says Mollel, that's a start. Honey, that little knife's not going to be any good to you. Better give it to me.

Honey looks up at him. —Why don't I hang on to it, just in case?

—It's evidence, remember? says Mollel. He is close now. He holds his hand out, palm up. Burns and lacerations: a crippled hand. But a hand that's going to take the knife.

Honey gives a quiet laugh and hugs Faith to her. The blade dances beside Faith's ear, her cheek, her neck.

—She's shaking, Mollel, sobs Faith. Can't you see she's terrified? We all are. Let her keep the knife if it makes her feel better.

Mollel's palm remains open, insistent.

—Give it to me, Honey.

She looks him in the eye. Her dark eyes shine with tears.

—You know, don't you? she says.

—Give me the knife, he repeats softly.

—I'm sorry for lying to you, Mollel. I never thought anyone would take a *poko* like me seriously. Most people would agree with Wanjiku, that the baby's better off elsewhere. But they don't know me, Mollel. I'd be a good mother. No one's got the right to take a baby away from its mother. No one had the right to take my baby away from me.

—From *you*? says Faith, jerking her head up. She gives a cry of pain.

—Careful, Honey! shouts Mollel.

—You're hurting me!

Honey tightens her arm around Faith's neck. The tip of the knife is pressed against her jugular.

—Mollel was the only person who ever listened to me, Honey cries into Faith's ear. The only one who really wanted to help me. And she told me, Mollel—she looks up—she told me how she was going to take Adam away from you. You were right. She thinks you're not a fit parent. Well, they did it to me. I'm not going to let her do it to you.

—Gran! shouts Adam.

Faith stares wildly in fear and astonishment. At that moment, there is a crashing sound. Metal collapsing. The gate to the compound has been forced.

—Take Adam and go, Mollel! shouts Honey. He doesn't need to see this! The two of you should be able to get out of here if you go, now!

Adam's arms grasp his waist. —Don't let her do it, Dad! Don't let her hurt Gran!

—What anyone else says or thinks means nothing to me anymore, Mollel. But I want you to understand. I need you to understand.

—We can talk about it later, says Mollel. Please, Honey.

But even as he says it, he knows she won't leave this place.

She has a far-off look in her eyes. Her words begin to pour out quietly, softly. As though she is speaking to herself as much as to them.

—I woke up in my apartment. I was on the mattress. Lucy had curled up next to me. That was what we did whenever we both needed to sleep at the same time. We were both used to it. Every Maasai is. I never really got used to sleeping alone, without the smell of hide and smoke and brothers and sisters all around.

—Her skin had the sweet, milky smell of a baby. And then I remembered: my baby!

A rattle overhead signals another shower of missiles hitting the roof.

—Honey, whatever it is you've done . . . begins Faith. But Honey tightens her grip.

—You don't speak, she hisses. You're just the same as them.

—She's not, insists Mollel. She's not the same.

He advances toward Honey, but she casts him a look full of warning and danger.

—Hear me out, Mollel. You're going to hear me out.

He raises his hand, backs off a few steps.

—When I started to feel the pangs of labor, two months ahead of time, Lucy had been the one who insisted I go to Orpheus House. She said I would get free treatment there, that it was the safest way to deliver my baby. I was nervous. The baby was *his*, after all. George Nalo's. How could I trust his wife to deliver it? But Lucy told me Wanjiku had no idea. She thought her husband practiced what he preached. Lucy said I had nothing to worry about. That she'd be there with me.

—And yet—when I awoke, they told me that my baby had died. Just like that. No apology, no explanation. And no body. They told me that it was deformed, unhealthy. It couldn't have lived. But hadn't I felt it, every twist and turn and kick, inside of me?

—I knew that child. I knew it was healthy. I knew it was still alive. And it had been taken from me.

—*I'm sorry, Honey,* Lucy said. *But what sort of a life would the child have had, anyway?*

—She told me she had to leave. She'd taken a risk bringing me there. But she wanted to check that I was all right before she left Nairobi for good.

—She explained that she needed to get away from her boyfriend. She was going to go back to her village, back into Maasai life. She'd shave her head, put on the *shuka*, extend the holes in her ears. Someone would take her, even as a second wife. She would disappear.

—But she needed money. She had no family anymore. No one to give cattle as a dowry. That was why, she said, she'd be in contact in a few days' time. She needed my help to do one last job before she left Nairobi forever.

—The job, she told me, was to rob a rich old *mzungu*. He was one of her clients. He always picked her up on Friday nights. It was a regular thing, apparently.

—Recently she'd been persuading him to go for a twofer. He'd been reluctant at first—imagine, she'd said to me. A K Street regular, too conservative for a twofer. But she'd been working on him. My friend's really beautiful, she told him. She's young, but experienced. And if you don't want to join in—well, you can always watch.

—And then she said, *You know, Honey—if it's nice, I might be open to persuasion myself.* And she smiled.

—She really wanted me along. She *needed* me along. She said she'd call me to confirm the meeting place, in a few days time, when I was feeling better.

—She put a bottle of pills on the window ledge. A few hundred shillings underneath it, for food.

—It wasn't until after she'd gone that I realized I didn't even know if my baby had been a boy or a girl.

A horn blares outside. Mollel looks back nervously.

—I had a lot of time to think, those next few days, Honey says. Her eyes are glazed, trancelike. ——For the first time ever, I began to feel as though I could not trust Lucy. It was that smile that did it—that seductive smile. As though I were another client to be played with on the street.

—She needed money, she told me. Money for a dowry. Yet how much money would we get from robbing a john? Neither of us could drive, so it wasn't like we could take the car. Even a *mzungu* wouldn't carry enough cash to make it worthwhile. I should know—I've been through thousands of wallets in my time, when they're sleeping it off or have gone for a piss. A few thousand shillings, maximum. And that's without splitting it.

—No, if she really intended to return to Maasai life—and this, at least, sounded true—she would need a pretty impressive dowry to find any decent husband. He'd know, from her lack of family connections, that she'd run away. Anyone could see just from looking at her that she'd been in the city. And now she wanted to disappear into a village somewhere? It could only mean one thing. And to overlook that, her dowry would have to be large. Say—a hundred thousand shillings.

—A hundred thousand shillings, Mollel.

—The price of a child.

—It all began to come together for me.

—Lucy had told Wanjiku Nalo that my baby was her husband's. And knowing that the couple would not want any evidence of the pastor's infidelity, Lucy had suggested a solution. Sell the child into adoption. Get some desperate foreign couple to take it on. Take it away. As far away as possible.

—And all Lucy would have asked for this little task—for offering up such a troublesome child to be simply spirited away—all she would have asked was the going rate. The payment from the prospective parents. The facilitation fee. A modest sum, all things considered.

—A hundred thousand shillings.

—I still didn't know what Lucy's true plan was with the robbery. I didn't trust her anymore. But I knew that it was my last chance to see her before she disappeared forever. And my only chance to try to find out the truth while there was a possibility that my baby was still in the country. So when she called me, I went to meet her, as arranged, on K Street.

—It took some effort to get there. It took even more effort to look convincing. Being successful on K Street is not just about the way you look, you know. It's about the way you walk, you hold yourself. That poise. The allure, the sexual promise must be evident in every footstep, every sway of the waist. The way you crook one knee when standing, to emphasize your hip. The way you dip your belly to heighten your buttocks when you lean in a car window. It's a performance, a dance. And just a few days before, I'd been in labor.

—It was painful. Painful physically, and even harder mentally. I hadn't been on the streets for months, and my body felt ravaged. The glances from the men told me I looked fine, though. I was fooling them. I just kept telling myself that whatever happened, this was not going to be a normal job. I wasn't going to have to go through with *that*—not for a long time.

—She met me, and we kissed. This time she lingered a second longer than she needed to. Caught my bottom lip between hers as she pulled away, and then looked at me and smiled. It was calculated. She played every trick on me that I played for the johns—her hand on my forearm, her eyes cast down, then flashing up, then looking away—every trick I had taught her.

—She thought she could seduce me. Foolish girl. She didn't realize that with every flutter of her eyelashes, she was confirming her treachery.

—The *mzungu* wasn't far behind. He came along in his four-by-four, pulled over so that we could get in. As we'd arranged, Lucy got into the front passenger seat. I slipped in behind.

—*You're right,* was the first thing he said to Lucy. *She is beautiful.* And he gave me a look in the rearview mirror. There was no lust in that look. Not one hint of lust. Just pity.

—I knew for sure, then, that it was a setup. This man was no john. He wasn't even *straight*.

—The plan, as Lucy had explained it to me, was for him to drive us to a quiet place. No one around. Uhuru Park, she reckoned, would be safe enough that time of night. Once we got there and he'd stopped the car, she was going to pull a knife. She always carried one when she was working the street, tucked into her dress beside the curve of her back. We'd take the old man's wallet, phone, throw his keys into the bushes, and run off into the park.

—I could tell, though—from the look that passed between them— that it was *me* they wanted to get alone. Well, I wasn't going to give them the chance. We headed up K Street, back onto Kenyatta Avenue. All the time I was thinking, What do they want from me? What are they going to do to me?

—By the time we reached the Uhuru Highway roundabout, I had it figured out. Whoever this guy was, Lucy had some hold over him. She's managed to persuade him to assist her with her final task. When she left Nairobi, she didn't want any loose ends. I was the only one who knew where she'd come from. We'd talked so often about her home. I knew exactly where she could be found. And anyone who wanted to find her could find her through me.

—And she would have known that if I ever found out about the adoption—or even suspected that I'd lost my baby because of her—I would have every reason to turn her in.

—I wasn't ready to let them do it. I wasn't going to give up that easily.

—As the car slowed for the roundabout, I thought about jumping out. I could've done it. But I remembered the baby. It would be a few weeks yet before any international adoption could be finalized. If she told me the truth now, I might be able to stop it. To get my baby back. If I didn't get the truth that night, I might still be able to track her to her village. But it would be too late.

—So as the old man turned the car into the park, I leaned forward and grabbed his seat belt. I pulled it. As hard as I could.

—He swerved, and we bounced over the curb. But I didn't let go. We hit something, flew forward. His air bag went off, but I still didn't let go. I didn't let go until I heard him gurgle. And he went limp.

—Lucy's nose was bleeding. She hadn't been wearing a seat belt, either. But she'd had time to brace herself. She was a bit beaten up, nothing too bad. She opened the door and stumbled out.

—I watched her stagger off. And then she was gone from the headlight beam. The old man was not moving. I got out, went after her. Caught up with her at the drainage ditch.

—I suppose her injuries must have been worse than I thought. She was there, kneeling. She was acting vague, concussed. Her head was rolling on her shoulders like a weight. I took her face in my hands. They came away wet. Blood.

—*What did you do with my baby?* I asked. *Where is it? Where has it gone?*

—But she just laughed. And started to cough. The blood bubbled up in her throat.

—I shook her. She was slipping away. She pitched forward, started sliding into the ditch. She was so heavy, I couldn't stop her. She took me with her, but I kept shouting, *Where is my baby?*

—I couldn't believe she had cheated me at that final moment. She had stolen my baby, sold it.

—I kept shouting long after she was dead. I was still shouting when I found the knife in my hand, the knife she kept ready in the small of her back. It was such a tiny thing. When I held it, it felt like I was punching her. Punching her dead body. Punching her where she had wounded me. Had cut the life out of me.

—I heard the white man's voice. He was standing over us. Horrified. *What have you done?*

—I got up. I didn't bother explaining to him. Lights swept across his face, and in his eyes I could see terror. Even then I could see that it might be useful for him to think I could have killed her.

—The lights were getting brighter. There were vehicles coming in, crackling across the gravel. I held the knife to the old man's ribs, and together we walked back to the car as if nothing had happened. It was starting to rain when we left.

Mollel reaches into his pocket and pulls out a crumpled photograph. He holds it in his damaged hand, proffers it to Honey.

—Take a look.

It is a baby. A dead baby. An incomplete baby.

Her baby.

—It's a trick, she says weakly.

—No, Honey, it's not. It's your baby. Yours and George Nalo's. I've seen the records. It never could have survived.

—Oh, Honey, says Faith. What have you done?

There is a loud bang at the kitchen door. And another.

—It's not murder, says Mollel. If she died because of the car crash, you have nothing to feel guilty for. Come with me. Make a statement. There's nothing here we can't deal with.

There is a clatter as the knife drops to the floor. Honey's body is limp. She no longer holds Faith. Now it is Faith holding her.

She mutters a few quiet words in Maa.

Faith stands up tentatively and walks over to Adam. She scoops up the boy in her arms. —We've got to go now, she says.

Mollel extends his hand. —Honey? Are you coming?

The sound of splintering wood crashes through from the kitchen. Mollel turns toward it. Light streams in, powerful white light. From it, he sees a figure emerge.

—Sorry about the door, comes a shout. Mwathi is standing there. —We've forced the line but can only hold it a few minutes. Are you coming or not?

Faith runs forward, Adam in her arms. She runs toward the light, through the shattered kitchen door. In the compound, a GSU truck is parked on top of the fallen gate, its engine running, headlights blazing.

—Come on, Honey!

Mollel grabs her wrist and pulls her with him toward the doorway. He runs out, ducking, as a hail of missiles flies over his head, bouncing off the roof of the house. Faith and Adam have already taken shelter in the cab. Mollel turns to help Honey in—

—and she is gone.

Mwathi scrambles in the other side, behind the wheel. He releases the brake and starts to back out.

—Wait! shouts Mollel, standing in the door. There's someone still in there!

—Your killer, I suppose? says Mwathi. Leave him. He's going to get what's coming to him!

Mollel looks back at the house. The broken doorway stands black and empty in the beam of the headlights. —Honey! he shouts.

—She won't come, says Faith. Not now. She's made her choice.

Mwathi throws the truck into gear and starts to back out. A petrol bomb arcs overhead and bursts on the gravel in front of them in a curtain of blue flame.

Something crashes on the roof of the cab, and Mollel slams the door shut just as liquid fire begins to pour down the side. The cab is filled with the stench of burning, and the window at his side snaps with the sudden heat.

The truck lurches back and swings around the gatepost. Mwathi grinds it into first and puts his foot down. GSU men on either side of them scatter as the vehicle roars past; they lift their shields above their heads and run in its wake. As the flames pour away from the side window, Mollel has a fleeting glimpse of faces contorted in hate, baying at the truck as it passes. And then they bump and rumble toward the GSU line, which parts, and the truck is suddenly surrounded by silence and the blackness of night.

—Honey, breathes Mwathi, turning off the engine. Funny name for a murderer.

43 —You sure you want to do this? asks Kiunga.

—I'm sure, says Mollel.

The city mortuary is overflowing with bodies, but here at Central CID, a lone corpse occupies a cell all of its own.

Mollel bends over the bench. He takes a corner of the sheet and gently folds it back.

He flinches at the sight of the familiar face. Despite the round hole in the forehead, it looks peaceful. The dreadlocked skull behind it, however, is gaping and open.

—I'm sorry, says Kiunga. It's tough to lose someone you trust.

Mollel replaces the shroud.

—He saved our lives, continues Kiunga. It was just after you left us. If we'd kept going, we'd probably have been all right. But they were all around the car before I even noticed.

—We were only a few hundred meters from here. I couldn't raise the police station on the phone, so I blasted my horn, hoping to get their attention. The back window shattered. Panya scrambled forward, but they had him by the ankles. They dragged him out. Lethebridge was screaming at me to drive, to just plow down those in front of me. I would've done it, too, if it wasn't for Panya.

—Then Benjamin got out of the car. Someone swung a *panga*. It took off the wing mirror, but he didn't even flinch.

—He spoke to them, Mollel. I didn't catch it all. It was Kikuyu, but it was that strange dialect the Mungiki speak. He spoke to them, and he told them we were going. He picked up Panya despite his injured arm, and I helped Lethebridge out of the car. The old man's face was pretty cut up from the glass. We were walking toward Central. I could see that some of the other officers had come out. They were armed. They'd heard the horn. We were just steps away from safety.

—When I heard the explosion, at first I thought the gang had torched the car, that the petrol tank had gone up. I turned to look. The gang was scattered, but the car was intact. And then I saw Benjamin crumple to his knees. The last thing he did, you know, Mollel, was lay Panya down on the ground. So gently.

—The guys at the station house had shot him. They saw the dread-locks, you see. It was all about the dreadlocks.

In the CID office, Panya is playing with a baton. Someone has found him an old uniform, and he flounders about in the oversize shirt tucked into trousers belted with cord. He seems to be lecturing Mwangi about putting his feet on the desk.

—Where's Lethebridge now? Mollel asks Kiunga.

—Kingori's taken him. We've not got enough to bring charges at the moment. Maybe, when all this has settled, we'll persuade Otieno to look at an obstruction charge. But from what you've told me, we'd never make accessory to murder stick. Or blackmail. The Nalos aren't going to back that one up.

—He's going to walk, isn't he? says Mollel.

—Looks like it, boss. I guess I don't call you boss anymore now, though. You'll be back to traffic. I'll be back to Mwangi. Solving crimes. Catching thieves. Letting them go when they don't fit with Otieno's statistics. Dishing out beatings and taking bribes.

—That's not you, Kiunga.

—No, it's not, says Kiunga. It might have been. It would have been, a few years from now, if you hadn't come along. You showed me that police work doesn't have to be done that way.

He breaks into a grin.

—I'm not saying I'd do it *your* way, either, mind you. Jesus Christ!

Back at his flat, Mollel finds Faith and Adam in the sitting room, in front of the TV.

—Have you heard? asks Faith. Kibaki has had himself sworn in at State House. The electoral commission's declared him the winner. They've not even finished counting the votes yet!

If it weren't so serious, Mollel would find Faith's outrage amusing. Just a few days ago she had been lamenting what might happen if President Kibaki were not returned for a second term. But then, a lot had happened in the last few days.

She stands and walks toward the kitchen. There's a big pan of *chai* on the stove; she ladles Mollel a cup. He wraps his hands around it gingerly. He's grateful that during a lull in the chaos that morning he was able to get a few groceries—enough to last them for the next few days. This latest news is not going to do anything to calm tensions in the city.

—Any news on Honey? she asks.

He shakes his head.

—That poor girl's going to face a higher judgment than we can give her, says Faith sadly.

—She refused to believe that her baby was dead, Mollel says. She constructed a fantasy in which it survived and was adopted. Just to spare her the guilt.

—Guilt? asks Faith. It wasn't her fault.

—I've been thinking about what she said, replies Mollel. Those final words I heard her speak. She said something in Maa. She said: *I ate my baby.*

Faith looks at him with incredulity.

—It's an old Maasai expression, he says. When a woman has a miscarriage or a stillbirth, she's said to have eaten her child. It's usually blamed on having had sex when pregnant. When you consider that she probably didn't even know she was carrying the baby for a long time . . . and who she was . . .

—She wasn't a murderer, though, says Faith. If she had come with you, as you suggested, she might have had another life.

Mollel fingers the red silken tie hanging over the back of one of the kitchen chairs.

—No, he says. She was a murderer. All those things she said about Lucy. The manipulation, the seduction. When she was talking about Lucy, she was talking about herself. Those were the tricks she used on me. Lucy didn't die because of her injuries in the crash. Honey murdered her. Premeditated, cold-blooded murder. The reason she didn't come out of the house was because she knew I knew that. I'm just not as good a liar as she was.

Faith crosses herself. Then she looks at the tie in Mollel's hands.

—That's nice, she says. Why don't you wear it more often?

Adam comes in from the sitting room.

—The news is boring, Dad, he says. When will they start showing cartoons again?

—I don't know, Adam, says Mollel. Maybe in the New Year.

A Note About the Author

Richard Crompton, a former BBC journalist, lives in Nairobi, Kenya, with his wife and their three young children. This is his first novel.